Born in London in 1874,  ,
a scion of a family long f
the British Empire. The a
director of the Bank of E ;
Bros.) he was educated a ...., and joined
the diplomatic service in 1898. In 1904 he became a journalist
and reported the Russo–Japanese War in Manchuria; later he
was a correspondent in Russia and Constantinople. He is
credited with having discovered Chekhov's work in Moscow
and helping to introduce it to the West. Baring is remembered
as a versatile, prolific and highly successful writer, who
produced articles, plays, biographies, criticism, poetry,
translations, stories and novels. He is regarded as a
representative of the social culture that flourished in England
before World War I, his work highly regarded to this day for the
acute intimate portraits of the time.

Daphne Adeane

MAURICE BARING

HOUSE OF
STRATUS

This edition published in 2001 by House of Stratus, an imprint of Stratus Holdings plc, 24c Old Burlington Street, London, W1X 1RL, UK.

www.houseofstratus.com

Typeset, printed and bound by House of Stratus.

A catalogue record for this book is available from the British Library.

ISBN 0-7551-0094-8

To
R E

CHAPTER I

The drama of life, in contradistinction to the drama of the stage, is not only made up of little things, but the producer takes care that the minute thing which turns out afterwards to have been significant and important, perhaps a turning-point, is unobserved when it occurs, not only by the actors themselves, but by the onlooker, should there happen to be one.

This little thing was a Private View – a Private View at one of the smaller galleries in which continental and outlandish artists, and the bolder and more advanced among home-grown painters, exhibited their wares.

To Basil Wake, barrister, in his house in Barton Street, Westminster, one spring morning, came a card which stated that Messrs R & C Jessal had the honour to invite him (and friend) to an exhibition of paintings by Walter Bell, and (in smaller type), Don José Henriquez, from 15th March to 6th April inclusive: Private View – Thursday, 14th March, at 340 New Bond Street, London, W.

He received these cards because his wife, Hyacinth, had artistic tastes. She had been painted by more than one well-known painter, and was a recognised personage in the artistic and literary world. Basil Wake cared little for pictures, and not at all for Private Views.

As he walked up to the opposite side of the breakfast table to ask for a second cup of tea, he took the card with him and gave it to his wife.

"Would you like to go with me?" she asked, looking up at him.

"I can't today. I shan't get away in time."

"No, of course not."

"But I suppose you will go?"

"I think…well, as a matter of fact, no. *I* have got a busy morning, too." She put the card aside with her letters. "By the way, don't forget dinner's at half-past seven tonight."

"Half-past seven."

He went to the door, taking *The Times* with him.

"You don't mind going?"

"I'm looking forward to it. I've heard Caruso. I like that kind of music. You don't want this?" He pointed to *The Times*.

"No, thank you. I've seen all I want to see, and I've got *The Daily Mirror*. Half-past seven."

He paused at the door.

"Who's going with us?"

"Sybil and Michael."

"Oh!"

He left the room abruptly, and Hyacinth wondered whether she was being fanciful or not in thinking that he seemed pained. She waited till she heard the front door bang, and then she went to her sitting-room and rang up a number on the telephone.

"Can I speak to Mr Choyce?… Is that you?… Are you busy?… No, not at all… Nothing… Nothing… Would you like to go to a Private View?…any time between twelve and one… No, not too early… Very well, I'll meet you there… I've got a ticket… No, he can't… Don't forget you're dining here. Half-past seven… A box. Mrs Lyons gave it to me… Only Sybil and Basil… He likes *this*… All right, half-past twelve… It's quite tiny, we shan't want to stay there long... I believe they are... Goodbye, half-past twelve."

Hyacinth Wake had a busy morning before going to the Private View. She had many things to get through. First of all she had to order dinner. As her sister-in-law, Sybil Ripley, was coming, she ordered it more carefully than usual. Her sister-in-law was observant and critical, and Basil listened to what she said. Her opinion carried weight with him.

Then she had things to buy for dinner...dessert, flowers. She went upstairs to put on her hat, and settled that she was not dressed for a Private View, not even for a small one. She must put on something else...something that would look as careless and as everyday as what she had on already, but which in reality...it was all a question, nobody knew better, of detail. She had a talent for the picturesque, not the dowdy kind. She had, when she first came out, been thought pretty. Then she married Basil – a marriage which his parents thought a disaster and her parents a pity, although she was better off than he. His parents believed in his career, but what can one do with the young nowadays? – the result: she was merged in the ranks of the unnoticed, till she was suddenly "discovered". Walter Bell painted her and exhibited the picture at the Academy. It was one of the pictures of the year. Everyone said it was clever. Some people disliked it. Sybil Ripley said it was like, but cruel. Basil hated it. But it was the fashion to say that Hyacinth Wake, although not a beauty, was *arresting* and attractive, and always looked different from anyone else.

She accentuated the difference. By degrees she dressed up to it, introducing a bolder, more fantastic touch. In the evenings she nearly always wore something unusual, and her hats were "amusing" in the sense in which French artists use the word. She attracted many. She was an addition as well as an ornament to any company. Her looks, her clothes, her bronzed hair, with its satin-like lights, were effective. She talked well, she listened still better, she never said a spiteful thing. She was good-humoured, gay, assimilative, and many-sided. Most people found her society exhilarating, a few (and among them Michael) thought it intoxicating; some women said she was affected and others that she was shallow, that there was really "nothing there" – nothing "to" her.

Men were comfortable in her society. She bored no one. It was about six years after her marriage that she met Michael Choyce. He was twenty-five, about a year younger than she was; the only son of a retired Foreign Office official. He was a Member of Parliament, and Parliamentary private secretary to a Cabinet Minister. He was good-looking, well-mannered and full of ambition, with the glamour of a University career that had been athletically brilliant and academically respectable. He had excelled on the river and (with difficulty) taken a Second in History. He had great natural facility but he refused to develop it, and serious reading bored him. She swept him off his feet, and their intimacy had gone on steadily and continued for eight years.

So pleasantly indeed, with no more quarrels and reconciliations than are necessary for comfort, that the eight years seemed to have gone by in a flash. They saw each other every day. They wrote to each other if one or the other were absent every day, and they were always asked out together. Wherever and whenever the Wakes were asked anywhere, Michael Choyce would be sure to be asked as well. Basil accepted this. He liked Michael. He trusted his wife. He was absorbed in his work. He had several friends and one or two engrossing hobbies. Hyacinth was always nice to him, always amiable. She had ceased to love him before she met Michael – as soon as they were married. Marriage had been somewhat of a shock and entirely a disillusion to her, and the reaction she felt was terrific – especially when it became clear she was to have no children. She concealed this and determined to make the best of things, and not to moan over what was irremediable.

4

And so she did. She had managed to jog along comfortably, till she had met Michael. Their intimacy had outwardly been slow in forming, but Hyacinth had known the end of it from the first moment she had set eyes on him. The crisis came about a year after she had made his acquaintance. She accepted the new situation. She determined that whatever might happen, Basil should never be unhappy, and she managed well. She made the relationship seem natural. She made Basil look upon Michael as a piece of the furniture that was there, something that was *always* there, and that he, as well as she, could not possibly do without. So things had gone on for eight years. Basil's life, on the other hand, had been unadorned or unmarred, as you will, by any romance. Most of his friends were men. He had one woman friend; she was ten years older than he was, unmarried, not ill-looking; she wrote successful novels with melodramatic plots and caustic observations. Basil was devoted to her, and she was a comfort to him. Hyacinth encouraged this friendship; she managed to steer with skill along a course which was not without dangers, difficulties, and pitfalls. There were her sisters-in-law to begin with – Basil's sister, Sybil, who had married a banker, and who was jealous of Hyacinth's looks and success; and there was the wife of Basil's younger brother, who was in the Navy. There were also aunts of Basil's and of her own (her parents were both dead), but they lived in the country and gave no trouble, so everything up to now had gone smoothly.

But Hyacinth was now for the first time in her life beginning to feel uneasy. It had seemed to her that lately, just lately, there was a shade, oh! only a shade, of difference in Basil's attitude and in his manner.

She said to herself again and again that it was her imagination, as Basil had not said nor done a thing which led her to suppose that anything was different from what it had been during the last eight years… And yet…this morning, for instance, when he had given her that ticket for the Private

View, and she had asked him whether he would go with her, when he had said, "No," and she had said, "Of course," was it her imagination? She distinctly thought that he had looked at her more sadly than usual. He always looked puzzled; but there was an adumbration of a shadow on his fine forehead. Hyacinth always said Basil, with his fair, curly hair and overhanging brow, and sunken eyes, had a Greek head…but this morning she had thought his frown had for a moment deepened – had she shown a sign of relief?

She had felt relief. She was afraid Basil might have said yes. He had, often, when his work was over early, looked in at a Private View for a moment on his way back to luncheon. She had not wanted Basil to come with her. She wanted to go with Michael. She had one or two things she wanted to say to him. It was absurd, as she had seen him no longer ago than tea-time yesterday, and yet so it was.

No, she came to the conclusion. It was absurd. Again, when she had mentioned the opera and Michael coming there, hadn't he looked annoyed? But when she had suggested Michael's coming some days before, he had leapt at the suggestion. And then, why had she lied about the Private View? What had made her say she was not going, when she had determined to go? It was a useless lie. Nothing, she knew, was more foolish.

She made a point of telling Basil the truth whenever it was possible. It gave her a sense of safety – of providing for future emergencies, like putting money in the bank.

If her suspicions were well founded, it was the time above all others to tell the truth. Supposing Basil were to change his mind and go to the Private View? What would he think? It would have been easy to say she was going. Until lately she *would* have said she was going with Michael. This proved to her that there *was* something different in the situation.

Well, she could put Michael off? It would make everything safe. She rang him up again; but he had gone out. She need not go herself? She could go in the afternoon?… By the time she had dressed, she had settled that she would not go – but she dressed carefully all the same, and put on a new hat. It was not worth risking. It was unlikely, most unlikely, that Basil would change his mind…but if…

She walked across St James's Park, up St James's Street to Piccadilly. It was an encouraging morning…the first fine day in March. The daffodils in the park chased away her gloomy forebodings. By the time she had reached St James's Street, she was convinced that she had been making a mountain of a molehill. If Basil were by some chance to get away earlier than he had expected, and come to the Private View, it would be easy for her to say she had changed her mind. That Michael should be there was not unnatural. Walter Bell was a well-known painter…and a friend…

She had been foolish.

She shopped conscientiously till twelve, and had her hair waved. She bought flowers and fruit for her dinner, and some early asparagus; she was greedy, and ministered to greed in others.

It was half-past twelve by the time she reached the exhibition. She went in without hesitation. Michael was waiting in a room downstairs in which there were pictures for sale which had nothing to do with the exhibition.

"I thought you were *never* coming."

"*I am* late… I…well, I had to buy some fruit."

They walked in; the gallery was not crowded.

The pictures in the larger front room were in oil. There were some landscapes done in France, Spain, and on the Norfolk Broads. Bold pictures, with strong effects of light and shadow. There were portraits, too, the head of a professor, a study of Réjane, and an Italian singer, "sketch portraits," some that seemed unfinished – swift, vivid impressions – others almost over-elaborate, detailed architectural scenes. In a further smaller room there were one or two pictures by the other artist. These also formed part of the exhibition, but as the author was dead, and a foreigner, and scantily represented, his name, though mentioned on the card, and his pictures, although included in the catalogue, were given less prominence. He was Henriquez – a Spaniard – he had died young. There were not many pictures in the room, but it was about his life-work. There were some gipsy scenes, an impression of a bull-fight, a sketch of boys practising bull-fighting in a village, the head of a *Flamenco* singer; and on the line, right in the middle of the wall, as you went in, a more important picture, the "Portrait of a Lady." She was painted full face, the head, the shoulders and arms, with only one hand showing.

She was looking up; the eyes seemed to be appealing to someone or something. The hair was waved back as if it were in the way. The eyebrows were arched. The mouth was in tune with the eyes. There was something appealing about the face. Something a little exotic… It was a picture that you could look at as you look into still water, and then feel that you had not yet seen anything.

And there was another peculiarity about this picture. It was *intimate.* You were not sure you ought to be looking at it. Just as someone said that Eleonora Duse's acting made one feel like a cad, as if one were looking through a keyhole at what was too private for alien eyes, so this picture made you feel that you had trespassed upon a privacy unawares, as Hamlet stumbled on his uncle at his orisons. You felt you were looking at this woman when she was by herself, alone, with her intimate thoughts, unaware of the possibility of an intrusion. So natural, so revealing, was the call in the eyes and the smile.

It affected both Hyacinth and Michael in this manner.

They were both startled.

"Oh!" said Hyacinth.

They stood before it in silence.

"I like that one the best of all," Hyacinth said.

Michael said nothing for a moment, and then: "Yes, so do I. What a charming woman! I wonder who it is. I think she must be foreign… Italian, perhaps."

"I don't think so. I think she is a Créole."

"Like Joséphine?"

"Yes. Like Joséphine."

As they were looking at the picture at some distance away from it, two men walked into the gallery and walked straight up to it. One of them was tall, he wore a frock coat. The other was shorter and dressed in untidy tweeds. They stood in front of the picture for a time in silence.

"I'm glad he didn't finish it," said the shorter of the two men. "He would have spoilt it."

His voice was strained.

"Isn't it finished?" said the other. "It seems to me more finished than most of his pictures."

"He wanted one more sitting for the hand; you see, it is hardly indicated, and you remember her hands – her hands – like flowers?"

"Yes – how could one forget them? I think the eyes are good."

"Yes – almost *quite* good. He has caught her look – but she was not paintable."

"No, she was not paintable," said the tall man. "By the way, what have you done with the sketches Bell did?"

"I have destroyed nearly all of them. They were failures. They made me *sick*. I can't bear photographs or even pictures of people I have known – they always seem to me to immobilise the person at the wrong moment."

Some other people walked up to the picture, and the two men went away.

Hyacinth and Michael stood in the same place a little farther back. They could hear what the people said. They were fascinated by this picture and the effect that it seemed to have on the spectators. The newcomers were a smartly dressed man with an oldish lady. She talked in a loud, hoarse voice. Hyacinth touched Michael's sleeve and said in a whisper, looking at the newcomers: "Lady Jarvis and Guy Cunninghame."

Michael nodded.

"Yes, that is Daphne," the lady whom Hyacinth had identified as Lady Jarvis was saying. "Poor child, done just before she died – in Spain. Bell told me Henriquez didn't even have time to finish it. He was to have had several more sittings. It's his best picture, and so promising, and like her."

Hyacinth, who did not want to be drawn into conversation with the newcomers – not at once, at any rate – had, as she had seen them come into the room with the corner of her eye, in a swift evolution dextrously steered Michael to the wall on the left, so that he and she turned their backs on them. But while they appeared to be absorbed in the picture of a church at Seville, and exchanged remarks, they were listening to what was being said about the portrait.

"Isn't it clever?" Cunninghame was saying. "What an artist! What a tragedy his dying! I think it's *wonderful*! And exactly like her – at her best. *I* always admired her. She wasn't everybody's fancy. It was a beauty that grew on one; I saw her very seldom."

"She lived a lonely life…" said Lady Jarvis.

They turned to the right. They had not yet noticed Hyacinth, or, if they had, they pretended not to.

Two more people came in – a foreign-looking man with a black beard, and an opulent art-patroness in an enormous hat and a cloud of chiffon. She made staccato comments.

"Ah, yes, that's Daphne Adeane – poor thing. Very like her, isn't it? *I* don't care for it; almost a caricature. I call it *cruel*. I never admired her, but I think she was better-looking than *that*. I always thought her affected."

"Yes?" said the man, and changed the subject. There was now a small crowd before the picture.

"I must go," said Hyacinth. "Basil is coming back to luncheon."

"So must I," said Michael.

They moved towards the door, and as they were going out, Lady Jarvis caught sight of them.

"My dear Hyacinth," she said, "have you been here long?"

There was an exchange of how-do-you-do's between the four. They discussed the pictures.

"The Walter Bells are clever, but rather *mannered*. He is beginning to imitate himself," Cunninghame said in a loud voice. The lady in chiffon made a mental note of the saying. "I admire Henriquez much more. The picture of Daphne Adeane is much the most interesting thing in the whole exhibition."

"Yes," said Hyacinth. "Who was she?"

"Didn't you know her? Well, I suppose you wouldn't have; she was never in London, or at least hardly ever, during the last years. She came from the Tropics. I think she was born in Jamaica, or the Seychelle Islands, or somewhere like that – something outlandish – and she married a man, Adeane – you know, in the City – and she was very delicate and had to live either abroad or at Bournemouth because of the climate. She was interesting to look at, but that was all. There was simply nothing 'to' her, as the Americans say, beyond her looks, of course."

The two men who had been the first two people to look at the picture after Hyacinth and Michael arrived, brushed past them and left the gallery.

"Nothing *to* her," he went on. "She *looked* mysterious, but that was all. She was like a bird. She was, in fact, like all subtropical people, she twittered and looked nice. She died about a year ago. I knew her through Elsie Caryl, when she had a house at Bournemouth. Are you going to the opera tonight? *Bohème* – Melba."

"Oh, there's your husband looking for you," said Lady Jarvis.

11

Hyacinth turned round, and there was Basil. He walked up to them with a quiet smile.

"I got away earlier than I expected, so I thought I would find you here," he said to Hyacinth.

He said how-do-you-do to the others, talked about the pictures, slowly and deliberately. He admired the picture of Mrs Adeane; he knew her husband.

"He employs me sometimes," he said. "A good chap – very fond of burgundy and beer and music. He smokes long pipes."

More people arrived – a faded lady with greyish hair, and her daughter, who had been out two years. It was Lady Weston. She knew Lady Jarvis and Cunninghame well, Basil and Hyacinth slightly, and Michael not at all. She was introduced to Michael, and introduced her daughter to him. Michael was struck by the daughter's appearance: by the grace of her figure, by a certain harmony of line and charm of texture; an unusual radiance, which he did not define at the moment, and was perhaps only half aware of, but the line of the song came into his head:

"…the melodie
That's sweetly played in tune…"

He made a few remarks, and then, all at once, he was disappointed. He found nothing to say. Then there was a silence. The group was shuffled. Basil and Michael exchanged words; Lady Jarvis, Lady Weston, Hyacinth, and the girl, whose name was Fanny, impressions. They all talked fast and loud, except the girl, who said nothing.

Basil came back to them.

"We must go, Hyacinth," he said. "I've got a taxi."

"A taxi! I wondered at your getting here so quickly." They said goodbye, and as they went away, Hyacinth heard the lady in chiffon saying to a newcomer:

"Clever, of course, but rather *mannered*. He is beginning to imitate himself. I admire *Henriquez* more. The picture of Mrs Adeane…" etc.

Basil seemed to have considered Hyacinth's presence as a matter of course. He seemed to be behaving as if he knew she would be at the exhibition. It was all natural; so much so that Lady Jarvis and Guy Cunninghame thought he had come to meet her by appointment. As Hyacinth and Basil drove home, Basil said:

"By the way, I have put off Michael for the opera tonight."

"Oh! Why?"

Hyacinth all of a sudden felt unaccountably embarrassed.

"Because I quite forgot that I had asked Sir James Lumsden the other day, and there won't be room. I told him, and he quite understood."

"Sir James Lumsden! You never said…"

But she was too much embarrassed to argue. She felt she was losing her head.

"Surely we all five could squeeze in?"

"No," said Basil quietly, but with determination. "No, my dear, there is no room for Michael."

CHAPTER II

Michael had not been sorry to give up the opera. Although not what is called "musical," he liked certain music and liked the opera, but he did not like hearing an opera with Hyacinth in a box, as during the *entr'actes* you always had to leave it. People took your place, and there was no one whom he wished to see in particular. He had dined at the Club and had spent a pleasant evening.

The next morning he received an unexpected telegram. His Uncle Joseph was seriously ill. Michael's parents were both dead. He could not remember his mother, and his father had died when he was still at Cambridge. His uncle had up till now given him an allowance and paid for his Parliamentary expenses, as his father had little, and Michael's own capital brought him in no more than four hundred a year.

His uncle was a squire who lived in Norfolk, and enjoyed racing, shooting, and reading biographies. He was a violent Whig, and was so delighted at Michael standing on the Liberal side, and regarded it as so extraordinary that his nephew should agree with him, that he was ready to do anything.

He had lived all his life in the country, at Hockley Hall, East Anglia, an old Tudor house, built of red brick and panelled throughout, and full of interesting things. But Joseph Choyce had always resolutely refused to have it done up. It was

14

draughty, damp, and in need of repair. There were no bathrooms and no improvements. The house was lit with oil lamps and candles.

The telegram was from the housekeeper. She asked Michael to come to Hockley at once. His uncle was asking for him.

The first thing he did was to telephone to Hyacinth. He had been going to stay from Saturday to Monday with some friends of hers. He told her the news, and that he was obliged to put off the visit.

There was a pause on the telephone, and Michael thought, although on second thoughts he dismissed the idea, that Hyacinth, instead of being annoyed, seemed, if anything, relieved.

"Can I see you before I go?" he asked.

"What train will you go by?"

"I'm afraid I shall have to catch the 11.30."

"Then I'm afraid it's impossible. I've got Sybil coming here."

He promised to let her know directly he would be back. He made arrangements for going away.

When he arrived at Hockley he found no one there but the doctor, the housekeeper, and an old friend of his uncle's, a Colonel Doyle (now retired), who had been staying in the house.

He was allowed to see his uncle, who appeared to recognise him, but was too weak to speak. Uncle Joseph died peacefully that evening. The funeral was held on the following Tuesday. It was largely attended by the neighbours, and Uncle Joseph's solicitor, Mr Brasted, came down from London.

He greeted Michael, after he had got through the preliminary ritual of gloom and condolence, with an expression of good-humoured pity, which seemed to say, so Michael thought: "I'm very sorry for you indeed, but it can't be helped, and we must make the best of it."

The will was read out after the funeral, and Mr Brasted put on his spectacles – he was a rubicund man, fond of claret and roses, and wore a luxuriant beard – and peered at Michael over them across the writing-table. After reading the will he expounded it. He imparted the information drop by drop. Uncle Joseph, he explained, was far less well off than the world had supposed.

"He was too," said Brasted, coughing, "unprofessional in his business habits. Would" – another cough – "have his own way."

The result of the will was that Uncle Joseph had left his nephew, with the exception of legacies to his old friend Doyle and to the servants, the main bulk of his money, but his house and the estate as well. This would entail death duties, and thus, so far from Michael actually benefiting from the will, it would be doubtful if the legacy would not prove to be a burden. It was doubtful whether he would be able to remain in Parliament. Michael listened absent-mindedly while Brasted poured forth a slow stream of comment. He appeared to be taking in what was being said, but in reality his mind was far away, wandering from possibility to possibility, reviewing the future from every possible angle at an immense distance from the present.

He left Hockley the next morning. When he arrived at his rooms in Curzon Street, he found a letter from his only surviving aunt. This was Lady Robarts, the widow of Sir Philip Robarts, who was his mother's brother. She asked him to luncheon. She evidently wanted to know all about the will. Michael was not exactly afraid of her, but he knew she was more than a match for him. With her white hair and her little head, she was still pretty as well as dignified. She was superficially gentle, but fundamentally rigid and conventional. Her manner was soft as honey, as soft as her cooing voice, but every now and then you felt a tiny, steely stab emerging from the velvet, and you felt that in any conflict, she, not you, would be victorious. Her own two children were dead. She lived in Chesham Place, and she regarded Michael as a part of her personal property. She had one other nephew and two nieces, the children of a sister-in-law who was dead. These two nieces were both of them prosperously married, so Lady Robarts felt that her duty towards them had been fulfilled. Michael was now her chief preoccupation, and she was bent on finding him a wife. She was not well off herself, for at her husband's death the baronetcy and the estate went to a nephew, and she was left with an annuity.

Michael found her alone in the sitting-room, which opened out of the dining-room, on the ground floor. She was, as usual, dressed with expensive simplicity – in black, sent from Paris – and she wore a bunch of violets. There was an air of past romance about her: something that suggested du Maurier's pictures, Owen Meredith, Whyte-Melville, "the White Rose."

"Let us go into luncheon, dear. We will talk over things," she said, lowering her voice almost to a whisper, "afterwards."

They discussed the topics of the day during the meal. After luncheon they went upstairs to the drawing-room on the first floor, and Michael was allowed by his Aunt Esther to smoke. Philip (her husband) always smoked, she said, as an excuse. She cross-examined him about the will, and, when she was in possession of the facts, "What about Parliament, dear?" she said. "You won't be able quite to afford it any longer, will you?" And she hinted at the figures of his possible budget in a gentle, deprecating manner, which, nevertheless, hit the sore points with an unerring accuracy.

"I know," said Michael. "Brasted seemed to think…"

"Oh, he's a lawyer, isn't he? They're so tiresome, ain't they? and so slow – so many words and it all means nothing. I'm sure he would be wrong. I really think, dear, there is only one thing to be done."

"What?" Michael had no idea what she was driving at.

"Well, dear, for you to marry – some day."

"Marry! Me?"

"Well, some day, dear – it would make us all happy." Who "all" meant was not specified.

"But who would marry me?" said Michael, wishing to gain time. He did not want to say no, as he could not give his real reason for thinking marriage out of the question, which was Hyacinth.

"I know some nice girls, dear. You have never looked at girls – at least, not lately, but there are several who have come out last year and this, who, besides being everything one likes, and who would be able to marry, are so pretty – really pretty. You see, dear, you never looked – and it's such a pity, you see, you're all the same, dear. You don't notice girls till they are married, and then you rave about them and it's all too late – so sad. Philip used to say the same – and then you say, 'Why was I not told of these charmers before?' "

"But do you know any one in particular, Aunt Esther?"

"Well, I know one. She has been out for two years, but she's only just come to London, because her father was a diplomat, and he died at Copenhagen last year, as you know." (Michael didn't know.) "After the break-up they stayed in Italy for a year. Now she is coming out in London. She has something – I mean something to marry on – such a nice girl, nice in every way, well brought up and clever – and such good manners – and that's getting so rare – and she's so pretty, dear."

"Who is this paragon?"

"Well, dear, she is the daughter of an old friend and contemporary, Cecilia Weston, and her name is Fanny Weston. Her father, you know, was Sir David, the Minister at Copenhagen, and doing so well when he died suddenly. Cecilia brought the girl to tea the other day. I thought her charming and so different from the usual rather vulgar girl one sees."

"Lady Weston? But I know the girl – at least I've met her. I found her rather difficult to get on with."

"Where did you see her?"

"Only at a Private View, for a few minutes."

"Oh, at a Private View – full of people and pictures – poor girl, how cruel for her! Nobody is at their best at a Private View, and then you know, dear, you are so frightening for girls – you've got such a reputation."

"What sort of reputation?"

"Well, for not liking girls, and for being so particular – you frighten them."

"Who told you that?"

"Nobody told me, dear – but everybody knows it, because it's true."

"What do you want me to do?"

"I think if you could meet her. Supposing you both came to luncheon; would you come if I ask her?"

"Yes, Aunt Esther – of course – but you won't expect me to marry someone I'm not…someone I don't like?"

"Of course not, dear. I only want you to see people, sometimes; you see, you never, never go out; one never sees you anywhere."

"I thought I spent my time going out."

"Well, you don't go where girls are to be met," she said in a honeyed voice. "You go to those Bohemian parties – in Chelsea, and on the Thames."

Lady Robarts meant Hyacinth, but she was wise enough to go no nearer to that dangerous topic.

"Well, I must go to my office. I will meet anyone you like, Aunt Esther."

Michael was not only ready to promise this, but he was ready to fulfil the promise, and to see as many girls as his aunt pleased, so inwardly sure of himself did he feel, and so convinced was he that nothing, nothing on earth, would persuade him to marry – at present, at least.

That evening he went to tea with Hyacinth, by appointment. She was alone, sitting in her little drawing-room, which was full of flowers and drawings and water-colours by her painter friends. There was a caricature by Max Beerbohm, a crayon by Rothenstein, and some water-colours by Brabazon on the walls.

Michael sat down in his accustomed chair, and lit his accustomed cigarette, and went on, rather than began, to talk. It was as if he was going on with a conversation that had been interrupted. He told her all about his uncle, the funeral, Colonel Doyle's deafness and general absent-mindedness, Mr Brasted's exposition of the will, the neighbours – various small incidents. Hyacinth listened attentively, breaking in every now and then with a slight laugh.

"The net result is, I am saddled with heavy death duties, an estate that is of no use to me, as I haven't enough money to keep it up, and a house that is too large for me, which needs, I don't know how many thousands spending on it, difficult to live in, and impossible to let – the irony is that it's near my constituency! And now there is no one to pay my Parliamentary expenses, and I can't afford to do so, myself. What do you think Aunt Esther's solution of the matter is?"

"What?"

"That I should marry."

There was a pause.

"Isn't it absurd?"

"I don't know," said Hyacinth; "we all of us marry some day, I suppose; and, after all, it's natural she should want it. She looks upon you as her son."

"She's a born matchmaker."

There was another pause, and then Hyacinth said: "I'm not sure it wouldn't be the best plan."

Michael felt something strange coming to him, as if he were playing a part in a dream, and looking on at himself, as one sometimes does in a dream.

"But that would mean that everything would be over. You can't mean that?"

Hyacinth said nothing. She was looking down. There was a long pause.

"You mean it is all over?"

There was another pause. Michael suddenly felt almost uncannily absent-minded, detached, unmoored, adrift, and at the same time abnormally conscious of his surroundings. His body was there in the room, the familiar room, painfully conscious of every small detail around him. He counted the ornaments on the chimney-piece and read the invitation cards. There was the card for the Private View, printed in black and red. There was an invitation to dinner from Lady Agincourt, who lived outside London, which he had accepted because Hyacinth had said she was going.

There was that foolish little French eighteenth-century clock which struck the quarter when it was the half, and which was always out of order. It was striking now; he counted 1, 2, 3, 4, and three-quarters – wrong as usual! And there above the chimney-piece was the picture by an unknown painter, an oil-painting, a park at twilight, all black and pale green; that picture seemed to be a part of the fibres of his being.

And then he became aware of a barrel-organ in the street; it was playing a song called 'Thora'.

Then he seemed to come to. He leapt from his chair.

"You mean you're tired of me! It's *you...you!* You want to get rid of me... Oh, *do* tell me the truth, please!"

She shook her head weakly – and then...there was a break in her voice which she was determined to conquer, and did conquer.

"My dear, it's not my doing, not my fault."

"Basil?"

She said nothing; but it was an affirmative silence.

"What has happened?"

"Nothing, everything. I don't know. It *has* happened. That's all I know. He has said nothing...practically nothing...but one knows...it's unmistakable. I can't explain. Don't ask me to. It's the end. I knew it must come."

Michael snatched a cigarette from the table and lit it. "I do believe the whole thing's *nonsense.* It's your imagination. I'm perfectly certain Basil has never thought of anything, never dreamt – if he has said nothing, it means he thinks nothing. You can't expect me to accept such an idea. It's all rot, unless, as I say, *you* want to put an end to it."

He was wavering, and no longer quite so confident, and he walked up and down the room smoking feverishly.

Hyacinth went on wearily. There was no fight, no note of persuasive argument in her voice, no desire to convince. It was as if she knew the case, the bare facts were overwhelming.

"I put off going Saturday to the Walsleys…so even if your uncle hadn't died…he has been so generous… But the opera, you remember…surely you understand me now!"

"You can't expect me to give up…you can't expect us…" He was becoming incoherent.

"There has been no scene," she went on, "no row, nothing…just nothing…it's far worse…he has been wonderful. I'm so, so sorry for him. I have behaved so badly."

Michael caught fire again – the final flare-up.

"That's nonsense," he said, "nonsense; and I believe the *whole thing is nonsense*. I won't, I can't believe it; at any rate, I *won't* give you up, I *can't*, unless it's you…unless you are tired of me, tired of the whole thing, and want to get rid of me. I suppose there's someone else. Who is it?"

"Don't, Michael…please, please, please, there is so little time." She looked up at him piteously. "It was silly of me to say that, as it's no use thinking of that *now*, but I promise you it's as I say, you must believe me…and you *do* believe me. He knows you're here now. He practically arranged that; he will be back presently. He meant me to say goodbye, I suppose, and after today… Oh!" She buried her face in her hands. "I'm all right…it had to happen sooner or later – I always knew that. I had always faced that from the very first. Oh dear! But don't let's talk of it any more; let's talk of the future, like two sensible beings. Basil is going to take me abroad for Easter, and almost directly – next week. He thinks" – she smiled – "I want a change of air – a change. I do. But you? You have got all your career, all your life before you, which I was only spoiling, because a woman in my position is always a dead weight on a man's life. She spoils his life, and the better she loves him the more she spoils it. Now you will be free of that dead weight – the chain."

"Don't say that," he said gently. All his show of resistance was at an end; he had known in his inmost self from the beginning it was true. The resistance had been automatic, an irrepressible expression of revolt which he knew was unreasonable, unfounded, indefensible, and bound to fail.

"You must marry."

"People talk as if one could marry anyone, and if anyone would be ready to be married. The idea to me is quite horrible. You see it would be a *mariage de convenance*. It couldn't be anything else."

"I believe that in the long run they are the best and the happiest marriages – perhaps the *only* happy marriages – but either way it's a lottery."

"Who will arrange it for me?" he said bitterly.

"Your Aunt Esther. You see, you have got your career."

"My career! You don't think I have any illusions about that? I did at first. When I started; when I came down from Cambridge I was naively ambitious. I wanted to play a part in the world. I believed in politics," he laughed. "But now, well, I don't say I haven't some kind of ambition left; I have. I want to make the best of it; but – it's different. I would willingly chuck the whole thing, but what else could I do? One must have an occupation. One must work. I can't do anything else. It's too late now. I would rather be anything else in the world, at times, but what's the use of saying that *now*?" There was a pause. "Supposing you are right, and I've got to marry – who in the world will marry me?"

"Has your aunt got anyone on her mind?"

"I believe she has. She talked of a girl we saw the other day, at the Private View. What a long time ago that seems *now!*"

"Oh! Cecilia Weston's girl! Yes, yes…that is the girl you will marry; oddly enough, it flashed across my mind the other morning at the Private View. I said to myself: 'That is the girl Michael will marry.' How funny! I had forgotten that for the moment."

"How can you say such things?"

"She's beautiful," Hyacinth went on, taking no notice of what Michael said.

"But she varies. Her beauty will *depend* – on all sorts of things. It is an *inside* beauty, like a living thing, a flame, or a flower that droops and expands according to the weather and the atmosphere and the temperature…not a wax bust or marble statue that never changes. I think there is a great deal in her. You must be kind to her. She's very beautiful, I think – that silvery look about her and those wide-apart eyes."

"How can you talk like that? You expect me to marry someone I've got to be 'kind to'!"

"You might fall in love. So much the better for you, and I was going to say, so much the worse for me – at least that's what I would have said last week; but it's different now."

Again the dream sensation came to Michael.

"Hyacinth, is this all true? – really true?"

"Yes, it is true – quite, quite true."

"But, Hyacinth…"

"Hush! That's the front door. It's Basil; he said he would be in by half-past five; it's a quarter to six. He's let us have an extra quarter of an hour. Goodbye, my dear darling. Goodbye, goodbye," she whispered.

Basil came into the room.

"Hullo, Michael!" he said, in as friendly and natural a way as he had always done. He took a cigarette and asked for a cup of tea.

"I've got to rush off," said Michael. "My lawyer is coming to see me at six. Goodbye, Hyacinth; goodbye, Basil."

"I suppose you're having all the usual bother," said Basil, following him to the door. "Do you want a cab?"

"No, I'll find one."

"Goodbye," said Hyacinth.

CHAPTER III

Michael rang up Hyacinth the next morning from force of habit, but he was told the telephone was out of order.

Hyacinth and her husband, he learnt from a common acquaintance, were leaving for the Continent. A few weeks later Michael was asked to stay at Langbourne Park, in Hampshire, which belonged to Mrs Branksome, a friend of his Aunt Esther.

He accepted the invitation. He had lived during those first weeks as if stunned. It seemed to him so unreal, so impossible to be alive without the daily companionship of Hyacinth; he was numb rather than miserable; he could not believe that the new situation was real. He had not that feeling of torture that he had experienced in the early days of their intimacy when he had been prevented from seeing her for a day, or even for a few hours, or when she had been ill. It was different now, and yet life seemed to be as different as if he had suddenly lost a limb. That was it – something had been cut away, irremediably and irrevocably, like a branch from a tree; the rest of his being went on sprouting automatically. He felt he did not care what he did, nor where he went. He had no doubt that his life with Hyacinth had come to an end. He knew that she had meant it. He knew it was ended for ever. He must make the best of it, but the future seemed an infinity of dreariness. He had made up his mind to take no decision for the present.

At Langbourne he found a young party. His aunt and Lady Weston were the only representatives of the older generation. There were two undergraduates from Oxford, a clerk from the Foreign Office, and Mr Geoffrey Charles, a public-school master, who was coaching Mrs Branksome's youngest boy, George, a candidate for Eton. Mrs Branksome had three daughters, two of whom were just out. And there was Fanny Weston.

It was a hot Whitsuntide, almost too hot for the time of year. They spent the whole time out of doors, riding on ponies. The two elder Branksome girls were receiving attentions from the young men. The eldest – Margaret – exquisitely English in health and freshness, was being courted by Clive of the Foreign Office, who seemed to have every attribute except money. Alice, the second daughter, a miniature roguish replica of her elder sister, was being pursued by one of the undergraduates, Hedworth Lynne, who, being the heir to an old title and an impoverished estate, had just declared his intention of becoming a Tolstoist and leading the simple life. At present he had not yet finished with Oxford. His younger brother, Tommy, who was a huge athlete over six feet, and who had only just left Winchester, spent all his time with Mabel, the third daughter, a dark elf, who took after her father. Mrs Branksome, who looked too young to have grown-up daughters, and whose complexion was as fair and clear as theirs, looked on approvingly. Michael was thrown together with Fanny. He admired her. There was no doubt about that; but she was distractingly changeable, absent-minded, and altogether puzzling. At moments she would seem lifeless, listless, not entirely there. At other times, after a ride, or in the evening, she radiated light. She seemed detached and indifferent, as if nothing could ever make her strive or compete, as if nothing were worth her strife or her competition – and yet this gave no

27

impression of conceit or vanity, but merely of a calm facing of
fact:

"I strove with none, for none was worth my strife."

Her eyes were magical, mischievous. They were like dark
diamonds, and there was something aloof about her. At
moments he thought her beautiful. He found, after sitting next
to her at dinner, that she was not so difficult to get on with as
he had thought. In fact, she was *different*. He had always made
up his mind that girls were impossible to talk to, and he had
heard rumours that this girl was supposed to be "clever."

He met with no trace of anything fringing on the
bluestocking, but he thought her perplexing. She was quiet, but
every now and then she said something that amused him,
something which seemed to have a touch of malice, and her
eyes would suddenly flash and then immediately after seem far
away, as if she had not meant what she had said, or did not
know what it meant – a blend of innocence and mischief. She
was unexpected. She did not seem to pay any attention to him,
not really to notice his presence. The first night at dinner she
talked to Mr Charles, the schoolmaster, with the result that he
fell in love with her at once, and proposed for the next morning
a private reading of Browning's poems in the garden. This
incident was not unnoticed by Hedworth and Tommy, who
encouraged the romance and mischievously did everything
they could to throw Fanny and the lovesick Mr Charles
together.

The first two days Michael saw little of Fanny, and he spent
most of the time talking to Mrs Branksome, Lady Weston, and
his aunt, when he was not riding or fishing. There was a trout
stream not far off, and Colonel Branksome, who was grey-
haired, absent-minded, and scholarly, had a passion for fishing,
and divided his time between trout and books.

It was not until the third day of his stay that Michael really broke the ice with Fanny. They had all gone for a ride in the afternoon, to the New Forest, which was not far from Langbourne, and Michael and Fanny had been thrown together. Mr Charles had not come with them: he was looking after his young charge. Fanny was slightly flushed after a gallop. She looked her best. She seemed to lose her shyness; she talked to Michael easily, but she seemed to misunderstand him wilfully, and he did not know whether she was laughing at him or not. He felt she was leading him on – she was; that she was a hussy – she was; she meant to be so – as much as possible.

They talked of first impressions, and how far people corresponded to the idea you had of them beforehand. How mistaken one was, as a rule. "For instance," said Michael, "I was quite wrong about you. I thought you were *serious*."

"And do you think I'm not?" she asked quietly.

The answer was almost violent.

"I think you are…"

"What?"

"Well – unscrupulous…"

"What makes you think that?" and her eyes shone with enjoyment.

"The way you behave to that poor Mr Charles."

"Mr Charles? Why?"

"He's desperately in love with you, and you lead him on."

"Oh no!" she laughed. "He's always like that. It's good for him. He's always in love with everyone. I am not the only one, I assure you." She laughed, and her laugh was extraordinarily captivating. It had a clear ring, but it was not at all loud. She suddenly changed the subject: "I imagined you different."

"What did you think I was like?"

"I thought nothing really. I went by what I heard of you from other people. One can't help hearing opinions."

"Awful things, I suppose?"

"On the contrary, you were held up as a paragon…"

"That's worse."

"What's worse?"

"To be held up as a paragon."

"But it wasn't as a paragon of all the *virtues.*"

"Of what then?"

"Of all the vices by some – but, there were two schools; they agreed on certain points."

"Which?"

"That you were spoilt, particular, easily bored, and hated girls."

"And do you think they were right?"

"I'm not sure."

"Then you don't believe in first impressions?"

"Oh no!" (vehemently); "not at all."

"I" (pensively) "am not sure I do, either."

"No? I thought so."

"Why?"

"This conversation *'must cease,'* as they say in the newspapers…here are the others."

That was the first approach to intimacy.

The older women watched the progress of this situation with excited interest. Mrs Branksome sympathised with Lady Robarts. They both agreed after the first few days that Fanny was in love with Michael, and that she was hiding it. There was to them no doubt of it. They were right: Fanny had fallen in love with him at first sight. The moment she had set eyes on him at the Private View, she had said to herself, "That is the man I should like to marry." Everything about him appealed to her – his well-poised head, his straight eyes, his rather careless ways, his large hands, his untidy clothes, his puzzled frown and sudden smile, his low, hesitating voice, and his laugh, which did not often break out, but when it did, was infectious.

But the question which was exercising everyone in different ways, including Michael himself, was: "Is Michael in love with Fanny?"

The older women thought the situation hopeful. The wish was, of course, to a certain extent father to the thought. Mrs Branksome was frankly and cheerfully optimistic. She wished the thing to happen, she prayed for it to happen, and she had no doubt that it would happen. At the same time, she shook her head about her two daughters. She did not wish either Margaret to marry a penniless clerk in the Foreign Office, who was known to have extravagant tastes and no expectations, or Alice to wed an heir to nothing but death duties, who was already threatening to be a socialist.

Lady Weston was not so confident. She was sceptical rather than pessimistic by nature. She herself had in her youth been the centre of many romances: a poet had wished to run away with her; an attractive adventurer, who had rapidly made millions and finally ended in gaol, had proposed to her; and she had been painted by Millais at the height of his early fame; and then she had married a diplomat, and had spent her whole life abroad – in Paris, Constantinople, Buenos Aires, Athens, Rome, Tokio, and finally Copenhagen. Her husband was on the eve of being made an ambassador when he died of double pneumonia. He was a sound rather than a brilliant diplomatist, but he had humour as well as sense. He was an admirable husband. When he had died, a year after Fanny had come out, Lady Weston mourned him with sincerity and missed him with lasting regret.

He had inherited money and land from relations, and left her more than comfortably off, and Fanny was considered an heiress. She was the only child. Lady Weston was determined to find her a suitable husband, and Michael, she thought, would be the very thing. She knew, of course, all about the past affair with Hyacinth Wake, but she considered that an asset rather than a drawback – an asset, as it was in a sense an education and a guarantee for the future; it was so much better, she thought, for that to happen before than after marriage. Besides which it was, she felt sure, definitely ended. She felt that in her bones. That Michael was here at this party, instead of in Surrey, where she knew Hyacinth and her husband were spending their Whitsuntide holiday, and the demeanour of Michael himself, seemed to mean only one thing. But she was not certain about the situation. She felt that Michael was attracted by her daughter. He had been astonished by her, astonished to find there was so much in a girl, that she stood up to him; that so far from running after him she seemed to be indifferent, although her mother knew better… Still, he was deceived, and he was attracted by her looks…he wanted to marry…he wanted to have children…he had told his aunt so, and he could only marry someone who was reasonably well off. So what was the obstacle? The obstacle, in her eyes, was Fanny herself.

She knew that her daughter was proud, and she felt that if she suspected that Michael was marrying her just for the sake of marrying, she would certainly refuse him. She prayed that Michael might be endowed with sense and sensibility and not commit a fatal error.

Lady Robarts saw the matter in a more practical light. She was convinced that the marriage was necessary, the only solution; that nowhere would Michael find a wife who would suit him better. All depended on him. He must go in and win; she did not believe the girl would refuse him if he showed any determination.

She knew that the girl was fond of him; if so, the rest was easy. It depended on him.

As for Fanny, she was wildly in love with Michael, and it seemed to her too good to be true that he should love her. She dared not think of it. She thought that she was hiding her feelings. She was being no more successful in strategy than the ostrich.

She could not believe that the unbelievable might happen.

Michael was torn by doubt, but he still felt like a somnambulist. All this was not real to him. He was happy in Fanny's company; he admired her. She attracted him. He thought her delightful and incomprehensible; he did not attempt to understand her; she was a fascinating teasing enigma. Was she perhaps a "sphinx without a secret"?

But he felt sure of one thing: that were he to leave Langbourne the next day and never see her again, he would not be heartbroken. Again, he did not feel that he would ever get to know her. He felt he could never be intimate with her as he used to be with Hyacinth. He felt she was too different, that they were made of a too sharply different substance. She was too detached.

But then, if he was to marry, and it seemed to be indicated – he did want to marry, to settle down, to have children; he wanted to be able to go on with his Parliamentary life and his career, to have a definite occupation in his life – a home; if all this was so, whom else could he marry?

He was not in love with Fanny, although she attracted him. That was the sad fact at the root of it all. Did that matter? Would it come later? Could he make her happy? He felt he could. He was confident.

She would be a help. She was clever – clever in dealing with people and situations, one could see that. Her father had been a practical diplomat, of wide culture and experience, and her mother was shrewd and full of insight.

The days went on; a radiant Whitsun week, and the Whitsuntide holiday began to draw to its close. In a day or two he would have to go back to London.

The night before his last day he went into his aunt's sitting-room before dinner and said he wanted to have a talk with her. She was sitting in an armchair in front of a small wood fire doing needlework. She was delighted. She thought the critical moment had come.

He decided to plunge.

"Aunt Esther, do you think I can marry Fanny Weston?"

"Well, dear, why not?" She didn't look up from her work.

"Well, do you think she would marry me?"

"Not if you don't ask her, dear; that is quite impossible. You haven't said a word yet, have you?"

"No, not a word…you know, I seem to know her less well now than I did the first day. She's an odd girl. I don't understand her a bit."

"She's so fond of you that perhaps it makes her shy, and she tries to hide it because she thinks you don't care for her."

"I like her very much, and I think she is beautiful – sometimes…clever too…sensible… I mean there is no nonsense about her. But do you think I could make her happy?"

"Yes, dear; of course you could. The poor girl is desperately, head over ears in love with you – a child could see that."

"Do you *really* think so?"

"I am quite sure of it; we are all sure of it."

"Who's all?"

"Her mother, Edith Branksome…everyone."

"It's all very well for you to say that, but she doesn't seem to notice if I am there or not…and it's frightfully difficult to get a word with her alone now."

"Of course it is…that proves I'm right…men never understand these things. It's not their fault, poor dears!"

"All the same, Aunt Esther, I'm *not* what's called *in love* with her. I mean if she were to tell me tomorrow that she was going to marry someone else, or if I knew I was going to Australia tomorrow and knew I should never see her again, I don't believe I should really care. It wouldn't be…well, I shouldn't be broken-hearted. Well, if that's so, do you think I have the right to ask her to marry me? Do you think I could make her happy? I should try to, of course. I do really want to marry, I want to have children, to settle down…and if I am to marry, I would rather marry Fanny than any other girl I have ever seen – and I suppose one must marry a girl. I could not marry a girl like Margaret or Alice, charming as they are. I mean it's great fun riding with them or playing billiard fives with them; but they seem to belong to a different world. I am too old, I suppose. I seem to them an awful old crock, I expect; but with Fanny it's different. I feel I might get on with her if only I understood her…"

"That's the ideal situation, dear. I can imagine nothing better. It's the very best thing in the world that could happen – I mean your feeling just like that. That holds out the very best possible chance of a happy marriage. Philip used always to say, ' Don't start too well.' If you felt you understood her thoroughly now, there would be nothing left for later, and you would probably be unhappy. As it is, it leaves something for the future, and just the right amount. You needn't hesitate, dear; you mustn't let the opportunity slip through your fingers. It may never happen again, and that would be such a pity. I think she is the very nicest kind of girl – and then, dear, there are other things; one must look at the practical side, too."

"I couldn't marry someone just for their money."

"Nobody wants you to, dear; but you can't marry someone who has no money at all."

"Then it comes to the same thing."

"No, dear; don't be foolish. The point is, you are fond of Fanny. You are attracted by her. And she is in love with you, and you know you can make her so happy – what more can one expect? And then, she would be the very wife for you. David Weston's daughter, brought up abroad – with none of the English awkwardness – and speaking French, and knowing the world, and pretty manners."

"I would try to make her happy."

"I am sure you will find that you will be wildly in love with her. So much better it should be like *that* than the other way. I've seen so many marriages begin too well, and then all get troublesome. One can't ever be twenty-one twice. You mustn't expect that, dear. You are now on the verge of being middle-aged; in a year or two you will find you are forty, and it's such a break to be forty. Not thirty-five even, but forty." She sighed. "And then you will want a companion to share the rest of the journey with you – someone who is attractive, kind, and sensible, and well brought up, and will make a good wife and a real mother; and here is the very thing here – asking to be asked. I think she is one in a thousand."

"But supposing she refuses?"

"Then you will wait a little and propose again – not too soon; but I don't think she will."

"But do you want me to propose at once? Wouldn't it be better to think it over for a few months?"

"Oh no, dear. There's nothing like the present. Her mother was telling me only yesterday that she's already refused two very nice and quite possible young chaps." Aunt Esther used a sudden slang expression or word at unexpected moments. "You can't expect that to go on for ever."

"How old is she?"

"Just twenty; she has been out two years."

"Well, then, you want me to try my chance before I go away?"

"Yes, dear, I do so want it."

"And you will take the responsibility if it's a failure?"

"Of course, dear, I will; but it won't be a failure. There is the dressing bell. You must leave me. Do it as soon as possible, and if she says 'no,' don't believe it. Remember a woman's 'no' nearly always means ' yes.' In Fanny's case I am sure it would mean 'yes.' "

"All right, I will think about it."

"No, promise."

"Very well, I promise."

Lady Robarts' maid came into the room and Michael went to dress for dinner.

He sat next to Fanny at dinner that night. They had the same kind of conversation as usual, only it seemed to Michael that she was perhaps less elusive than usual; she did not try to put him off so much or to change the conversation, or to tease him just at the crucial point, as her habit had been; and then she looked entrancingly well, all in white, attractive, like a classic priestess with a twinkle. She was happy – she reminded him of something. Those eyes…what was it? Who was it she reminded him of? Where had he seen someone like her? The question teased him; he seemed again and again on the verge of being able to catch the thistledown thread of memory, but again and again it eluded him. At last, in a flash, it seemed to come to him. It was a picture; but no sooner than he seemed about to open the door, when the key slipped from his fingers and vanished – a picture…yes, but where had he seen it and who was it? He could not remember. Something seemed to shut in his mind with a click like a photographic shutter. He gave up the vain effort.

"You remind me," he said, as these thoughts went through his mind, "so much of a picture. Only I can't remember what picture, nor where I saw it."

"Really? That's very odd, because Colonel Branksome told me yesterday I reminded him of a picture."

"What picture?"

"Oh, I forget. A portrait of someone I had never heard of – *not* Mona Lisa," she added, with a swift gleam of mockery.

"No," he said, smiling; "someone more beautiful than that."

Fanny blushed, and the effect of her confusion was distracting. Michael thought she must be more beautiful than any picture in the world, and he felt he was losing his head.

After dinner Mrs Branksome arranged that she and her husband, Lady Weston, and Aunt Esther should play bridge, and the young folk should play at billiard fives in the billiard-room. This left Michael and Fanny alone in the drawing-room, as the bridge was played in the Colonel's study. They had the whole evening before them, and before they were rejoined by the others, Michael had proposed to Fanny and had been accepted. When the bridge-players came into the room, Lady Robarts, Lady Weston, and Mrs Branksome saw at a glance from the expression on Fanny's face what had happened, and they exchanged glances of silent and mutual congratulation.

Michael told his aunt, and Fanny told her mother, before they went to bed. Many tears were shed upstairs, and there was a great deal of conversation before the three old ladies and the three girls went to bed. Mrs Branksome said she must tell her husband. He had sat up late downstairs over a book, and when he did come up and she told him the news, he was so absent-minded and engrossed in the book he had been reading on fishing, that all he said was: "Oh! he's going to marry Daphne Adeane, is he? I suppose they'll spend their honeymoon in Norway?"

CHAPTER IV

The engagement was announced almost at once. The wedding was to come off towards the end of August (as soon as Parliament rose), at St Margaret's, Westminster, with the Branksome girls and two tiny cousins of Michael's as bridesmaids. The summer months passed quickly. Michael was busy. There was an air of bustle and excitement about everything that summer. The weather was hot and steadily fine. Presents and congratulations kept pouring in.

Michael saw Fanny every day, and he repeated to himself every day how wise his choice had been, what a fortunate man he was; and everybody told him the same thing. Hockley was being done up, just enough – for the present – to make it habitable for Fanny. They were both opposed to any alterations that would alter the character of the house; and Michael refused to hear of electric light. He liked bathrooms with geysers, because they entailed less alteration. He liked the house to be shabby and dignified. He detested change.

On the Friday to Monday before the wedding, which Fanny was spending with her mother, he gave a final bachelor party at Hockley to his four best friends: George Ayton, who was in the House of Lords and a keen politician, an Under Secretary in a Government office; Stephen Lacy, married and in the City – refined and talkative and tanned by the Tropics; Jack Canning, formerly in the Army, and now ADC to the Governor of South Africa, but home for a few weeks on leave – absent-minded, soft-voiced, and neat; and Walter Troumestre, who was married, a traveller and a writer – exuberant and untidy. George Ayton and Jack Canning were Michael's contemporaries. Walter Troumestre was eleven years older, and Stephen Lacy two years younger. The workmen were still in the house, cleaning, mending, repairing. Michael enjoyed picnic life in general, and none of his guests minded it. Walter Troumestre and Jack Canning were used to camping out in wild countries, and George Ayton spent much time in a sailing boat.

They spent all their time out of doors, on the marshes and in the woods. Troumestre and Lacy, who were Catholics, bicycled to a neighbouring village for Mass. In the evenings they drank Uncle Joseph's excellent port and claret, and it was hot enough for them to sit out of doors till late and smoke in the garden.

They had a great deal to say. They were all of them old friends and had not met for a long time. They talked shop: school and university shop – Michael and Canning had been to the same private and public schools; George Ayton and Michael had been together at Cambridge; war and travel shop – Michael had met Walter Troumestre in South Africa, and George Ayton had met Lacy in Ceylon.

On Sunday afternoon Michael and Canning went out for a walk. Jack Canning was Michael's oldest friend, but he had not seen him for some time. They never wrote to each other when they were absent, and when they saw each other they would rarely exchange confidences, and sometimes not even trouble to talk. Between them there was complete intimacy; and yet there were in each one of them whole continents which were unknown to the other, which shows how relative a thing the completest intimacy is. Canning was a man with whom you could be comfortable whether you talked or not.

They were walking through the large woodland; on one side of them was a long sheet of water. They were both of them nature lovers, and both of them observers of the habits of birds and beasts.

"Water-rail, wasn't it?" said Canning, pointing to a bird in the rushes by the margin of the water.

"Yes," said Michael absent-mindedly. "I wonder if you will ever marry?"

"I couldn't afford it now."

"But you've got 'expectations'?"

"My uncle…yes…possibly he might…one never knows."

"Has he got other relations?"

"I don't think so. I don't know."

"I would bet on your marrying."

"You would be right. I shall if I can… I mean you know all talk about marriage *in general* is absurd. The whole point is marrying *one* particular person. You probably realise that for the first time!"

"Yes, of course." A rumour flashed through Michael's mind that Jack Canning was in love with a beautiful Italian in South Africa; on the other hand, he knew that he had for years wanted to marry a girl.

"I believe the younger one is when one marries, the better. I am too old."

"Then it's a bad lookout for me. I shall certainly marry if I can, but it can't be yet, and I am no younger than you."

"The Italian episode is untrue – or nothing," thought Michael. "Oh, but then for you it's different!"

"Why different? – I don't understand."

"I mean you are essentially a marrying man, that is obvious; but I'm not sure I am – I'm not sure whether I am right to marry – whether I really have the *right* to marry."

"As long as you *want* to marry – that is to say, to marry one particular person – you certainly have the right to. And you *do* want to? You have found the right person?"

"Oh yes – Fanny is one in a thousand. I'm tremendously lucky. You will like her when you know her, really – "

"I like her already," Canning interrupted.

"You will have to come and stay with us. My mother-in-law has lent us her house in North Devon for the honeymoon. It's on the coast. After that we shall settle down here."

"You will have to live in London?"

"Oh yes; I suppose so. But Fanny hates London, she says, as much as I do – she wants English country life after having lived so long abroad. However, there's no help for it. Perhaps we shall take a small flat. By the way, my last bachelor dinner is at the Savoy on Tuesday; will that be all right for you? The wedding's on Thursday."

"Of course."

"I'm rather dreading the wedding. I think all that's so unnecessary – the crowd, the flowers, the hymns, the wedding march, the rice. It's like a farce."

"Other people enjoy it."

"I suppose the women do."

They walked on in silence for a time.

"I wonder if George Ayton will ever marry?" Canning said.

"Not at present. Mrs Shamier – he's devoted to her. It's been going on for years. But I suppose even that won't go on for ever."

"I don't think an affair ever lasts for ever."

"And people get over everything, I suppose?"

"It depends."

"I suppose that change is the law of life – change of age – change of air – change of people – "

42

"I don't think I agree. I think – don't you agree with me? – that sometimes one comes across people who are faithful for ever? Don't you agree?" Canning asked wistfully.

"What do you mean by 'for ever'?"

"Well, I mean practically for ever – faithful to what was the most important thing in their lives."

They were nearing a small belt of fir trees.

"I don't know," said Michael. "Crossbills?" There was a sadness in his expression as he looked up.

"Yes," said Canning, "they are common this year…but I *do* envy you with all my heart."

"Yes, I know how lucky I am," said Michael, feeling ashamed of himself. He knew now that Canning still wanted to marry the girl he had been longing to marry for years. He had been faithful. He would always be faithful. Jack Canning was his superior in every way. But how different from himself! What an odious part he in comparison was playing. He was marrying a girl when in reality he still loved someone else. A marriage of convenience – *mariage de raison.* What would Jack Canning think of him if he knew the truth? How disloyal of him it had been to think for one moment that there could have been any truth in that rumour about the Italian! It was obviously a lie. He thought of the girl Jack Canning wanted to marry – Jean Brandon, a pale creature with sea-blue eyes, who lived with a tiresome aunt. If Jack knew the truth, how he would despise him!

"I think," Canning went on, looking at Michael with his slow eyes, in his gentle, rather hesitating voice, "that you are the luckiest man in the world. To be engaged to marry the girl you love and who loves you – a girl who is beautiful and charming. It's impossible not to envy you, old chap, but you *know* I don't grudge you your happiness and luck – your great good luck. I am awfully glad. I can't tell you how glad I am."

"I know you are," said Michael, more ashamed of himself than ever.

"When I first heard of it, I thought it was too good to be true."

"I hope," said Michael, "I shall deserve my luck." He abruptly changed the subject. "Walter Troumestre's marriage is a happy one."

"Yes, that *is* a successful marriage."

"Do you know his wife?"

"No, and I don't know him very well. I met him during the war first. What is his wife like?"

"Very pretty – uncommon looking; her mother was a foreigner. They live in the country most of the time."

"I suppose they are not well off?"

"No; they live in the dower house of a big house that belongs to Stephen's brother, Bernard."

"I haven't seen him since Africa. Married, isn't he?"

"Yes…too much. Isn't it awful to think that if a marriage is a failure there is no remedy for it? It goes on for ever."

"But then I suppose that's just what's wonderful about it when it's a success?"

"I hope I shall make Fanny happy," he said.

"Of course you will."

"I shall have a damned good try. After all, one is meant to marry. One can't call life life if one doesn't. Dr Johnson was right. One is meant to marry and to have children. Only, of course, one can't help feeling rather anxious at moments, can one, when one knows that one is marrying a girl who is *one in a thousand*…and that you are responsible for her happiness?"

"As long as you love her, everything will be all right. I shouldn't bother about anything else."

"No, it's no good bothering, is it? What must be, must be. But when one sees so many marriages around one fail, one can't help feeling rather nervous."

"There's nothing to be nervous about. I suppose you think it's too good to be true?"

"I suppose that's about it."

They were reaching home, and while Canning was envying Michael for his marvellous luck, he felt like a man with a weight upon him, or like someone caught in a trap from which there was no escape.

Dinner, their last dinner, went off with forced gaiety, stimulated by claret and old brandy. Stephen Lacy drank deeply and became uproarious, quarrelsome, and gloomy. George Ayton smoked cigars in silence. Walter Troumestre strummed on the pianoforte. He played by ear. Michael and Jack sat in silence on garden chairs in the garden just outside the door. It was a still autumn night. There was a full moon.

Walter played tunes from *The Merry Widow*, which was going on in London.

Michael felt that this was his last farewell to life as he had known it. Next week he would have to start afresh. The wedding was so soon. Only three more days. This was the last time he would ever spend a few days in a country house with friends as a bachelor without responsibilities – free. But was one ever free? After next week life would be different.

Was it a mistake? Was he about to commit an act of folly – a crime? Would he ruin Fanny's life as well as his own? It was too late to go back now.

"You ought to play the Wedding March," said Stephen Lacy sardonically. "It's a lovely tune. At my wedding, thank Heaven, we had no music. It was a mixed marriage."

"Play that again," said Ayton, taking no notice of Stephen. "That dance – I like that tune."

Walter played the valse from *The Merry Widow* again.

"Somebody," said Lacy, "ought to write an opera called *The Merry Widower*. A widower *has* got something to be merry about."

"You're rather truculent tonight, Stephen," said Walter.

"Sorry," said Stephen, hiccoughing. "Play something soothing – something which will remind me of the Tropics and the spicy garlic smells, and all that I have said goodbye to for ever."

Walter played the "Love Song of Har Dyal."

"My wife used to sing that," said Stephen, "used to sing it when we were engaged, and I used to think it lovely." His voice was harsh, and it grated. He walked out of the room into the garden.

Walter got up from the pianoforte and went to help himself to a whisky and soda. Michael overheard him saying to Ayton, as he walked past the open doorway, "Poor Stephen!"

"In a year or two," he reflected, "they will be saying, 'Poor Michael,' or perhaps, 'Poor Fanny.'" He wondered which would be worse.

"I believe," he thought to himself, "that the honest thing would be to chuck the whole thing; but perhaps everybody feels like this just before they are married, and at any rate I will have a good try to make her happy – a damned good try. My marriage has just as much chance of being a success as any other – in fact, a better chance. After all, I'm fond of Fanny. And I believe she's fond of me. *She's one in a thousand.*"

George Ayton went up to Michael, and suggested bridge.

"Very well," said Michael, "but you must find Stephen, as Walter either can't or won't play."

Stephen was fetched from the end of the garden and consented to play, and they went on playing till half-past twelve, while Walter strummed in the next room.

When they went to bed, and Michael was undressing, Stephen walked into his room.

"Sorry I was such a beast after dinner," he said.

Michael laughed.

"I thought it was the old brandy," he said. "It's rather potent. It used to make Uncle Joseph peevish."

Stephen sat down and lit a cigarette.

"The fact is," Stephen went on, "weddings depress me. I suppose it is because my own has been such a failure."

Michael did not know what to say.

"I suppose you feel happy in your mind about it," Stephen went on; "but if you're not, then *don't* do it. Break it off, *at all costs*, at the last moment rather than do it. Don't mind what's called 'behaving badly.' Anything is better than making the fatal mistake. No one knows that better than I do because I have done it, and I tell you, Michael, it's Hell! You *can* break it off if you want to. I *couldn't* – that's the difference! I was *obliged* to marry, but you can get out of it easily."

"But, my dear Stephen, I'm not dreaming of breaking off my engagement."

Stephen laughed. He was still feeling the effects of the brandy, and he had had more than one whisky and soda while playing bridge.

"You can't gammon me" – his utterance was thick, slow, and deliberate. "You don't want to marry, and you know it. You are 'kidding yourself' you like that girl. You are marrying for conventional reasons – because you want to settle down and have a family, and a career, and be a blooming member of the Cabinet, and all that. But don't tell me you are in love with the girl, or that you are counting the minutes till the wedding-day, because I shan't believe you. You can't kid someone who has been through the same thing. One recognises the symptoms all too well. You can kid the others. You *do*. Poor old Jack is envying you, and so is George, I believe; but you can't kid me…and I tell you straight, old chap, chuck it now while you can, while there is still time, because it is *Hell* – Hell to be married to someone you don't really care for, however 'nice' she is. Hell, I tell you. There is no Hell like it. And once in it, one can't get out. I suppose you could divorce – but you wouldn't; who would?"

"You are talking rot," said Michael. "Nothing in the world would make me break off my engagement now."

"I dare say not. I don't expect it would, but you would give your eyes to all the same, and you will be making an almighty mistake if you don't! You ought to do it, if only for the girl's sake. It will be nice for her when she finds you out."

"Don't talk such damned rot, Stephen; go to bed." He was getting annoyed. "You're still blind, that's what is the matter with you. Go and sleep it off."

"You may be right, but, as the sailor said, 'I'm drunk and I shall get over that,' but you're a bloody fool," he hiccoughed half in imitation of the sailor and half in earnest, "and you'll never get over that – if you marry that girl. Goodnight, old boy. Sleep over it, as they say, and think better of it tomorrow morning, and forget it if you can. Goodnight."

"He is drunk," thought Michael, but he felt disturbed none the less. He knew it would be impossible for him to attempt to sleep at present. He never felt more wide awake.

He lit a cigarette and walked down the passage to Walter's bedroom.

He called him, and Walter shouted to him to come in. Walter was in bed, smoking a cigarette and reading the *Adventures of Sherlock Holmes*.

Michael sat down by his bedside.

"Do you think I am right to marry?" he said.

"How do you mean *right?*"

"Well, it's like this – I'm awfully fond of Fanny, and I believe I can make her happy, but I'm not really what's called 'in love' with her."

"Are you in love with someone else?"

"Oh no… I have been, I…was for a long time – but that's all over. You see, I shall never feel like that again. I'm too old, some bits of me are dead – quite dead. But I think I could make a good husband, and I want to marry. And Fanny is everything one could wish – good, good-looking, sensible, clever; and I am sure I can make her happy. Do you think there is any reason why I shouldn't marry? I ask you because I know how happy your marriage has been. You have never regretted it, have you – not for one moment?"

"Not for one moment."

"But then you were always in love with your wife long before you married her?"

"Directly I saw her – the first moment."

"But I feel you are a good judge, all the same. Do you think I am doing something criminal – criminal towards *her*, and making a mistake as regards myself? You see, the awful thing is that the mistake goes on for ever. Tell me frankly what you think."

"I think you are probably right. I think it would be wrong to break it off now, I think you are almost sure to be happy. Only, you see, one never can tell how a marriage will turn out."

"But yours turned out so wonderfully. Who should know better than you?"

"Yes; but then perhaps my marriage was exceptional…there is no reason why you shouldn't be just as happy as I have been." There was a curious break in his voice. "No reason, because you are certain, aren't you, that she is fond of you?"

"Yes; I think she really is fond of me."

"That is all that matters," said Walter. Again his voice seemed sad, and Michael thought there was a shade of melancholy in his eyes; his voice was certainly not natural. He was surprised.

"Then you advise me to go on with it?"

"Of course, it would be rather difficult to break it off now, wouldn't it?" No, his voice was not natural.

"It would, but even that would be better than doing something which would turn out afterwards to be…"

"A mistake?"

"Well, I meant more than a mistake. A crime."

"I don't think you will be doing that," said Walter. He seemed to be controlling himself. "I don't think the mistakes one foresees come off. The troubles that happen come, I think, from some unexpected quarter, and one can't avoid these. I think all that you are afraid of is nothing. You are suffering from what priests call *scruples.*"

"Do you *really* think so?"

"Yes," he said, laughing lightly, but there was something hollow in the laugh.

"And you think it's really all right?"

"Perfectly."

"Well, goodnight, Walter."

"Goodnight, Michael."

Michael went to bed, but not to sleep. He lay awake and counted the hours as they struck from the neighbouring church clock.

The two conversations that he had just taken part in raced through his brain. It was Walter's words, not Stephen's, that were affecting him. Stephen's argument against the marriage had persuaded him to a certain extent that he was right to marry. Walter's arguments in favour of the marriage had almost made him wish to break off his engagement. Walter's words had upset him. It was not what he had said, but the way he had said it. He had always thought of Walter and his wife as *the* ideal married couple. Now, not by what Walter had said, but by what he had left unsaid – by his look, by the tone of his voice and his whole attitude – he felt that, in spite of all outward appearances, Walter was not, or was no longer, happily married.

He recalled the occasions on which he had seen Walter and his wife, Rose Mary, and all that he had heard about them. He remembered at one time hearing someone say that Rose Mary was in love with Bernard Windleston, Stephen's brother…but that was a long time ago. It was probably untrue. People said that because they were close neighbours, and bound to see a great deal of one another. And then in the country neighbours invented anything, and the rumours percolated to London.

In spite of this, Michael felt that there was something wrong in Walter's *ménage*. He was not happy…and if even a marriage so seemingly successful, that started under such favourable auspices, went wrong, what chance would he have?

He went through all that had been said between himself and Stephen, and between himself and Walter, and, as happens to the sleepless, his mind seemed to be exasperatingly clear; but the more he thought about it, the clearer it became to him that it was Walter who had used the more powerful arguments against his marriage. It was broad daylight, and he heard the housemaid "doing" the passage before he fell into a troubled sleep.

CHAPTER V

When Michael got up and went out into the open air the next morning, he felt that he had been foolish, or rather that he had been through a nightmare. The friends parted; he went back to London, and then came the wedding. Jack Canning was his best man. It was said to be a pretty wedding, and the bride, like all brides, was "a vision."

Lady Robarts, so the newspapers said, looked handsome in mauve. She always ordered a gown from Worth in Paris once a year, whatever her circumstances. He was, she said, the only dressmaker who knew how to make one look nice.

Then came the honeymoon in North Devon, at a very small house at Westercombe, full of old-fashioned books and water-colours, which had been left to David Weston by his mother. It stood high up on the cliffs facing the sea. On the other side to the south was the moor. There was a small garden, with hedges of escallonia and some dahlias. The weather was hot, steamy, and soft. There were showers of warm rain, and the sun would hide for a morning behind the sea mist, fringing it with silver. The warm west wind was blowing, and there were purple streaks in the pale green sea. Fanny and Michael basked in the aromatic warmth, sat for hours on the cliffs, and picnicked on the rocks. Sometimes they would drive to a farmhouse, through the high lanes, and have tea, with strawberry jam and clotted cream. Or they would ride over the moor. They had two ponies and a pony-cart. It was still hot enough to bathe.

The honeymoon passed swiftly. Fanny was happy. And Michael was as happy as people are in a dream – where there is no work – but he felt the hour of awakening must come. It came for him when they went back to Hockley, when their everyday life began again. It was then he realised that he knew his wife no better – no better now than he had done before they were married.

It was then that he began to ask himself when would complete companionship, the new revelation of mutual understanding, begin? It was surely time it should begin now.

They were having breakfast in the hall. The sun was streaming through the mullioned windows. Michael had finished breakfast; he had finished reading *The Times* – finished reading, that is to say, all that interested him – and Fanny was reading an illustrated newspaper. He said something about an incident in the day's news.

"Yes," said Fanny; "so I see."

The conversation came to an end.

Michael felt he ought to go on talking, and could think of nothing to say.

There was a pause.

"What would you like to do today?" Michael asked at last.

"Oh, anything."

"I shall be busy all the morning, but in the afternoon we can do anything you like. What would you like to do?"

"Anything *you* like."

There was another long pause.

"Shall we go over to Knaystone? I thought perhaps you would like to see the garden."

Knaystone was a house about five miles off, where an old friend of Michael's uncle lived, a naturalist and a lover of birds; his name was Cuthbert Lyley. He was a cousin of Hyacinth Wake's, and she used sometimes to talk of him.

"Yes," said Fanny, but without enthusiasm. "I think that would be perfect."

"His sister, Mrs Tracy, is there. She lives with him, you know," Michael said apologetically. "He wrote to me two days ago and asked us to come over one day when we could. She wants to meet you so much, and you will love her – she's a dear."

"Yes; do let's go, then."

"You are sure it won't bore you?" said Michael. "You know his sister is really a jolly woman, knowledgeable and practical about all sorts of things. She is a good gardener, and you will be able to get ideas from her for the garden here."

Fanny blushed. She had looked forward to perhaps having ideas of her own about the garden.

"I believe she is charming," she said.

It was settled that they should go to Knaystone. The visit went off well.

They drove there in a dogcart. The old house at Knaystone had been burnt down in the 'eighties and rebuilt by Cuthbert's father. It had been thought a triumph of modern artistic architecture at the time – modern Elizabethan, with the stamp of the 'eighties on it. It had gables, tall red-brick chimneys, black woodwork, and small plate-glass windows. The rooms were low, the ceilings heavy with white stucco. There was a large conservatory. The hall was paved with Morgan tiles. There was an oak staircase, highly polished. The drawing-room had a Morris wallpaper; there were some water-colours by Edwin Lear and by Mrs Lyley (who had been an exquisite artist), some photographs of Watts' pictures, and a few studies by Mrs Cameron; and on an easel, draped with a piece of green brocade, a picture of the late Mrs Lyley by Millais. He had painted her dressed in black stamped velvet, with a fichu round her neck and a red rose in her hand. In the corner of the room there was a panelled grand pianoforte, inlaid with gold and silver metal-work.

Michael and Fanny found Cuthbert and his sister in the garden, when they arrived. Cuthbert Lyley was about fifteen years older than Michael. His face was refined and scholarly, his eyes trustful and melancholy, his voice gentle. His wife, who had been beautiful and gifted, had died shortly after their marriage, leaving no children behind her. Cuthbert had worshipped her, and he never got over her death. When she died, he sold his London house, where they had been the centre of a charming group of friends in Kensington Square, and retired to the country for ever. His hobby was ornithology and (had been) gardening. He was comfortably off. Occasionally he published articles in the reviews – meditative essays on nature and books – and he was once reluctantly persuaded to publish a volume of these anonymously. The book was called *From a Botanist's Notebook.*

It made little stir, but it is still collected by the fastidious. He had one sister, who married a stockbroker. When her husband died and her two daughters were married – this happened two years after the death of Cuthbert's wife – she went to live with her brother for good. But she still kept on a flat in London, as she said that a touch of London every now and then was necessary to her.

No two people could have been more different than Cuthbert and his sister. For that reason, perhaps, they got on well. She was ten years older than Cuthbert, rooted in reality, sensible, direct, and unconventional. She took nothing for granted. Everything about her was first-hand. She was fond of the young, and at heart romantic, warm-hearted, impulsive, greedy, and passionately inquisitive.

Directly they arrived, Mrs Tracy took the situation in hand.

"Dear Michael, this is kind of you," she said, "to bring your lovely wife so soon. I've been longing to see her. Cuthbert shall take you for a walk in the woods and give you all the bird news, and I will have a talk with your dear wife in the garden. Go along, Cuthbert; it will do you good."

Cuthbert smiled a melancholy smile, and assented. He and Michael wandered off into the woods, while Mrs Tracy did the honours of the garden. She managed the garden – that is to say, most of it. She thoroughly disagreed with her brother's ideas of gardening, which were old-fashioned. He gave in to her and let her do what she liked, reserving for himself a small rock-garden to play with. He had ceased to take interest in the garden when his wife died, and he no longer cared what happened to it. He let his sister do whatever she pleased.

Mrs Tracy was welcoming and friendly, but Fanny soon felt that she was being submitted to a kindly but penetrating scrutiny, and also that certain remarks she made were being used to check information that had been received from others. Every now and then, too, Mrs Tracy in her flow of cheerful egotistic talk would ask a searching question.

For instance, she said, talking of Scotland: "My cousin – Hyacinth Wake – she has gone to Scotland this autumn, and asked me to stay; but Cuthbert didn't want to go, and I didn't like to leave him."

"I don't know her," said Fanny, feeling that Mrs Wake had been mentioned with some, to her unguessed, purpose. "I only saw her once for a moment at a Private View."

Fanny suddenly wondered whether she was being compared mentally with Hyacinth, and whether Mrs Tracy was making up her mind on some definite point; she did not know why this should be, except that the Wakes were, she knew, old friends of Michael's.

"I thought her so pretty," she added.

"She *is* pretty," said Mrs Tracy; "picturesque, that is to say, if one admires that type of beauty. Personally, I prefer something more…well, something more natural. She's *too* picturesque for me; or perhaps too modern. I'm old-fashioned, dear."

"You think her affected?"

"Well, not exactly affected, but artificial."

56

"Yes." Fanny was sincerely indifferent and detached. But she felt that her indifference and all that she had said on the subject was being noted – with satisfaction. Mrs Tracy asked her how long they were staying, whether they were going to take a house in London, where they were going to spend Christmas, whether she had made the acquaintance of the other neighbours, how the improvements at Hockley were progressing, whether they had a new gardener, whether they were going to put in electric light, and what Michael thought about the political situation.

Fanny felt relieved and exhausted when Michael and Cuthbert came back, and they were told it was time for tea. As they were driving home, Michael said to Fanny:

"Mrs Tracy is a jolly woman, isn't she?"

"Yes."

"And capable. She manages everything for Cuthbert. She does the garden...everything...he is unpractical and absent-minded, as you noticed."

"I thought the garden beautiful."

"Yes; I should like to have a border like that."

"We might – in time," said Fanny.

Michael wanted to ask her if she was fond of gardening. It seemed to him so strange that he did not know. And yet he could not, because he felt that it seemed silly. He felt he ought to know. It was inconceivable that he shouldn't know...and yet, he didn't. He knew she liked flowers – that was not difficult. It flashed through his mind how he and Hyacinth would discuss such things...they would talk over everything; it didn't matter if he knew anything about it or not. Hyacinth would have told him every detail about the garden – what was right, and what was wrong. It didn't matter if he knew, if he were interested in the subject, or knew anything about it. The point was, that directly she told him something, or talked to him about something, he became interested. She would tell him the plots of books he knew he never could or would read, the plots of plays and operas he didn't want to see, and he then felt as if he had seen them; the histories of people he had never known, of some he never would know, who were dead or impossibly out of reach – and all this was as thrilling to him as if such things had intimately concerned him. But now…it was different. It would come right in time, of course. But how silent she was! What was she thinking about? What was that behind that serene mask?

If he had only known, she was thinking about all the things that she longed to say, and which she felt she couldn't say. She made up in her head a hundred things to say to Michael when he wasn't there. She said to herself: "He will understand this and that; I shall be able to tell him this and that," but directly it came to the point, and she was there face to face with him, she could say nothing, the ideas had all gone. Her lips were sealed. It had been like this ever since the honeymoon. During the honeymoon all had seemed well, because time had seemed to rush by them, and they moved in a swift dream. But that was over. It was life now – daily, realistic, prosaic life.

Every day she seemed to drift farther away from him, and every day the barrier, that barrier of unaccountable silence, seemed to grow higher and broader. It was not that he was not nice to her…he was perfect.

"I believe he loves me," she thought; "but what is it that makes this reserve? Is it my fault? It must be. I can't laugh with him or at him lately. I used to before we were engaged. Is he comparing me the whole time with someone else?" The idea was intolerable.

Michael had resolutely put the thought of Hyacinth from him. At least once every day his thoughts seemed to wander round the castle in which, in mute exile, the forbidden subject was imprisoned, but directly he found himself getting near it he gave his mind a wrench and refused to approach it. "It was not as if," he said to himself, "not as if I were comparing her with Hyacinth. I am *not*; I should never dream of doing that."

But today, driving back from Knaystone – it was the first time he had been to visit strangers with her, and it reminded him of the times when he used to visit people with Hyacinth, and how afterwards Hyacinth would retail for him every detail of the visit, whether he had been present at the incidents or not; for instance today, if he had been to Knaystone with Hyacinth, and she had been left alone with Mrs Tracy, Hyacinth would have told him in detail what they had talked about, would have summed up her character, would have criticised what she did. The garden, for instance; she would have said, "This was good because of this...that was perhaps a pity; but no doubt she was right all the same." She would have seen everything. Nothing would have escaped her.

She would have made him laugh, not only at what she had seen, but he would have laughed at her and with her: at her, for seeing so much that he had not seen; with her, for having seen the few things he had seen himself. Would the day never come when he would be able to talk to Fanny like that? Of course she was different from...but, no, he was not comparing them. He never had and never would compare them. They were poles apart, and as for Fanny, she was a treasure; he realised that more strongly every day.

"The garden is lovely, isn't it?" he repeated aloud.

"Yes, *lovely*," said Fanny, but she reflected that she didn't really like it. It was professional and competent. Mrs Tracy's aim was to make certain things grow that other people failed with. She liked to triumph over obstacles. She aimed at the difficult; she didn't care much about colour; she had no eye for design. She took a practical view of gardening and despised all sentiment connected with it. She had an unerring memory for botanical names, and determination and perseverance, so that she triumphed where many failed; but the result was more interesting to the expert than pleasing to the visitor.

"We must really do something to the garden at Hockley."

He remembered how clever Hyacinth used to be about such things. She had a genius for arranging and suggesting. Fanny, he was afraid, did not take interest in outdoor life. That came from living abroad. All the while Fanny was thinking that the garden at Hockley could be made beautiful, but that if Mrs Tracy interfered with it, it would be ruined. She was so afraid of this idea maturing in Michael's head that she abruptly changed the subject.

"I forgot to tell you," she said, "that I had a letter from Mrs Branksome by the second post. She says that they are at Langbourne, with Dick and Tommy, and Mr Charles, and that they are having great fun."

"Oh, really," said Michael.

"She is not," he thought, "interested in gardens. What a pity. I wonder what does interest her? I'm afraid just those things that I don't understand."

But these were Fanny's thoughts: "Michael thinks I am a *fool*. He thinks I couldn't understand the things he is thinking of. Why can't I tell him this isn't true? Why can't I break through the wall? What *is* the wall that is growing up between us? It seems as light as a feather, and yet as strong as steel, as transparent as crystal, and yet impenetrable. I feel it's my fault."

They drove on in silence.

"The country is looking jolly, isn't it?" said Michael.

"Yes, lovely," she said, looking at the turnip fields, which were shining like emeralds under the yellow foliage of the trees.

"Does she really care for the country, or would she rather live in London?" he wondered.

"It will be a wrench to go back to London," he said.

"Yes, won't it?"

She was dreading the thought of London life. She loved Hockley with all her heart. She had fallen in love with the place, and it was just the country she had always longed for, especially when she had been in places like Tokio or Athens.

"I believe," thought Michael to himself, "that's it. It's lonely here for her, of course, and a change does everyone good. She wants to go to London."

"We shall have to go, all the same," he said. "Will you enjoy house-hunting? I shall leave all that to you."

He remembered how eagerly and cleverly Hyacinth had once found him rooms.

"Mother is clever at it," said Fanny.

"So is Aunt Esther."

"I feel," thought Fanny, "she will choose us the house," and she shivered.

"What part of London would you like best?"

"Oh, anywhere. Westminster would be convenient for you, wouldn't it, so as to be near the House?"

"Yes; but it's too low down and too damp. I would rather live somewhere higher up. I don't think it matters where one lives in London, as long as one's not too far off."

He said this nervously and hurriedly, because Westminster reminded him of the house to which, until his marriage, he used to go every day, and all at once the sight of it rose vividly in his mind. He saw the little staircase, the courtyard at the back, the caricature – of a modern novelist – by Max Beerbohm on the wall, and he read the legend underneath it; – the water-colours, the crayon drawing, the coloured cushions, the foolish clock on the chimney-piece striking the wrong time at random, and every now and then breaking into a frivolous chime; and there near the tea-table, Hyacinth... Hyacinth dressed in something new and quaint, Hyacinth arranging the flowers, Hyacinth pouring out the tea, Hyacinth lighting a cigarette, Hyacinth sitting on that sofa – telling him the news, going on with the conversation that they had the evening before – that conversation that never began nor ended – Hyacinth smiling, Hyacinth laughing, Hyacinth looking anxious, and then Basil...

making the usual joke; Hyacinth looking up at him – Michael. He wondered where she was now, and what she was doing. No, he was not comparing her with Fanny; he would never do that, but of course it was impossible to forget certain things; for instance…

"Where would you like to live?" she asked him.

Michael returned to the present with a start, like someone who has been abruptly awakened:

"Oh, I don't know… I think all London houses are alike. I wouldn't mind where we live; but not Westminster – that's too damp and slummy."

CHAPTER VI

Michael and Fanny came back to London in the middle of October. As Fanny had suspected, it was Michael's Aunt Esther who chose their house.

She chose it gently but firmly in Grosvenor Place. It was furnished, and they took it for a year, till they could look round.

There was a sitting-room for Michael on the ground floor, and a dining-room; a front and back drawing-room on the first floor, and bedrooms upstairs. Fanny hoped to have a house of her own some time. She and her mother knew far more about houses than Lady Robarts, as they were used all their lives to leaving houses and taking new ones and making the best of things, and dealing with decorators, upholsterers, painters, and second-hand furniture shops.

Michael was ready to let them do whatever they liked. As long as he had a leather armchair in his sitting-room in which he could sit and smoke, he cared little what happened to or in the rest of the house. But Fanny and her mother thought it wise to give in to Lady Robarts' suggestion about the furnished house, and then to look round and choose a house that would really suit them.

Grosvenor Place, as Lady Robarts explained, was so convenient. It was "near the House, but not too near"; by this she meant sufficiently distant from Barton Street, Westminster.

Fanny arrived in London in good spirits. She was looking forward to the new life that she felt was beginning. In London she felt it would really begin.

Michael was anxious to give a house-warming dinner. They discussed at length who the guests were to be. Fanny's mother was to come, of course, and Lady Robarts and George Ayton, Jack Canning, Michael's chief, Sir Henry Leith (the Cabinet Minister), and his wife; that made eight, and they had room at their table for ten; and, as Michael said, if they were eight they might just as well be ten, and they wanted another couple to liven things up, so Michael said.

"Who is in London?" said Fanny. "I know so few people. The Branksomes are in the country. Mr Lacy?" They were having breakfast.

"We can't ask him without his wife, and I can't stand Bessie."

Fanny reviewed in her mind all the friends she had heard Michael talk of, or other people talk of in connection with him, and her mind flew back to the occasion on which they had first met at Walter Bell's Private View. He had been there with a Mrs Wake, and her husband had arrived later, and they had all gone away together; and on the way home she had asked her mother who that Mrs Wake was…she was striking-looking and unlike other people, and her clothes were *different*. Her mother had told her that she was the wife of Basil Wake, a rising barrister, but somewhat briefless, who had been overshadowed by a brilliant father, and that Mrs Wake – Hyacinth, as her mother called her – was a delightful woman, although some people thought her a fraud. She was really, Lady Weston said, kind and clever, in spite of a certain intermittent silliness, which entirely disappeared when you knew her well and when she was with people whom she knew well.

And then later, at Langbourne, she had heard Hyacinth Wake mentioned. The Branksomes knew her – her name, she had noticed, recurred in the visitors' book several times with a photograph – different photographs – and in each there was something unusual in the clothes worn. They never seemed to match the epoch. She had stayed there, so Fanny had noticed, always at the same time as Michael. The Branksomes, too, talked of Basil with familiarity. They evidently knew him well. She remembered that when she had said something about Mrs Wake to Margaret Branksome, Margaret had not pursued the subject. She had said, "Oh yes, Hyacinth," and then had gone straight on to some other topic; but then Margaret Branksome was disconnected in her ways and in her talk, and it was impossible to get her to concentrate. Mrs Tracy had asked her about Hyacinth Wake – they were cousins, it was true. But she remembered, nevertheless, the impression when Mrs Tracy had mentioned her.

The Wakes had not been at her wedding, but they had been asked, and they refused because they were in Scotland.

"Why don't you ask Mr Wake and his wife?" she suggested.

"Oh no," said Michael rather hurriedly; "they are in Scotland."

"I don't think they are," said Fanny, "because I saw him in the street the day before yesterday, and surely he would have to be in London by now?"

"He hates dining out, and I don't expect…she is here."

"Do let's try. I should like to know her. I think she looks so nice."

"I don't think they'd do for this dinner…not with the Leiths and Aunt Esther… I think we want something rather different. You know what I mean. I think we might ask someone from the Foreign Office for your mother – Eddy Wister, for instance, and his wife."

Edward Wister was Private Secretary to the Secretary of State.

"Very well," said Fanny. She acted upon this, and they accepted.

This conversation had a singular effect on Michael. It inspired him with a longing to see Hyacinth. He felt he could not live another day without seeing her. After all, he argued with himself, they would have to meet; the world, let alone London, was so small; and the world they both lived in was tiny. They would be bound to meet almost at once. There was surely no harm in his seeing her. Now that everything was over...they would, of course, meet on quite a different footing. It would really be more sensible and more convenient for all of them if he were friends with Hyacinth – just as everyone else. Fanny must get to know her too. They would like each other, and Basil would like Fanny.

Nothing was worse than an artificial, strained situation.

He would write to her that day from the office. That he should want to do this, that he felt he could, proved to him how impossible it was that he should be disloyal to Fanny...

"I must go," he said, and he hurried off. He walked all the way to Whitehall, and during the whole walk he was composing a reasonable letter to Hyacinth. At the office he hurried through his official correspondence, and after he had seen his chief for a moment, he lit a cigarette, and sat down to write:

I see in *The Morning Post* that you have come back to London. I knew this before, as last night I walked home from the office through Barton Street (it is on the way, as we live in Grosvenor Place) and saw your blinds up. I have been thinking things over, and have come to the conclusion that as we are bound to meet soon, and can't possibly pretend to be strangers, there is no reason we should pretend *not* to be friends. No reason why I shouldn't see you every now and then, just as I see anyone else. It would seem odd, in fact, and everyone will be bound to think it odd. I was wondering what would be best – whether I could just come to tea one evening? It seems to me that would be the easiest and most natural thing to do. I think it would be best for all concerned, best for you, for this to happen. If we suddenly met – as we are sure to do *soon,* as the world we live in is the same one, and very small – we can't possibly pretend suddenly to be strangers; and if we don't meet at all, *except by accident*, we should be on the same footing as if we were strangers. People would be bound to notice it. Let us, at any rate, meet *once*, and talk this over. If you disagree, it need never happen again. I will do exactly what you think best. I do so want to consult you about this and a few other things. One cannot cut life in two... Of course I quite understand that everything must be different, and I know you would understand exactly what I mean and what I am feeling if I could have just five minutes' talk with you. It is impossible to say anything in a letter... I do beg of you to believe that I do not wish to annoy you or to be disloyal to anyone in any way, but I do think it would help matters, and be the best thing for everyone, if we could just meet quite naturally in an ordinary way like old friends, which everybody knows we have been; just because one is married it will seem *odd* to cut one's old friendships out quite suddenly, and apparently for no reason. We have taken the house in Grosvenor Place for a year. In the meantime we will look about for something permanent. Aunt Esther chose the house. It is all right, but not up to your standard. Luckily, Fanny doesn't mind those things. She doesn't *care*. Please let me know what you think.

M.

That evening he again walked home through Barton Street. It was, he said, practically the shortest way.

An answer came to his letter the next evening. It ran thus:

DEAR MICHAEL, – I quite agree that we are sure to meet soon, and that is only natural. I don't see that we should gain anything by discussing this, or anything else. *Please* don't ask me to do this. It is not possible, and please don't write any more, or be hurt with me if you do and I don't answer. Because I *can't*. I have thought this all out, and I do beg you to believe that there is nothing else to be done except what we have been doing ever since your marriage. – Yours, etc.,

H. W.

The act of writing this letter, of posting it, and receiving an answer to it – even the uncompromising negative that he did receive – made Michael dimly feel a change in the atmosphere of his life, of his married life. It disturbed the moral atoms, or the spiritual microbes, or the mental overtones, and all those invisible and intangible *imponderabilia* that go to make up the waves of communication between one soul and another.

He felt, although he did not admit to it himself, that he had done something irrevocable, something that had changed things. And Fanny, although she knew nothing, and had as yet no idea that Hyacinth Wake had ever played any part in Michael's life, felt dimly that something had happened too. She did not know what, but she was conscious of the moral disturbance in the atmosphere. Michael was attentive to her, considerate in every way, charming – nothing could be nicer. He went out of his way to please her, to do what she wished. He brought her back little presents in the evening – flowers; and sometimes something good to eat – chocolates, or a Camembert cheese for dinner. That was it. He was just too attentive, for with all this she felt that his real self was miles away, that he was not there, but definitely somewhere else. That is what she thought at times. At other times she found fault with herself, and blamed herself for talking and thinking nonsense.

The house-warming party went off well, and about ten days later they were asked to their first dinner-party, as a married couple, by Edward Wister and his wife. Edward Wister was a man of wide culture, his wife was artistic and half foreign. They had a newly decorated house in Kensington with some interesting modern French pictures. They were well off, entertained largely, and had musical evenings, and sometimes

even a short play should some available foreign star be in
London. When the invitation came, and Fanny handed Michael
Mrs Wister's note across the breakfast-table, asking them to a
"tiny" dinner, and ending with, "I have to warn you that there
may be a little singing after dinner, as Raphael Luc is dining
with us; but there will be a bridge table downstairs for the non-
musical" – "Shall we go?" Fanny asked; "will you risk the
music?" This second question irritated Michael. He felt he was
being put in a lower category.

"Oh! we can't possibly refuse," he said. "You see, he is the
chief's greatest friend."

Fanny did not grasp the logic of this reason, but she
accepted the invitation. It was, they found when they arrived, a
large dinner-party of over fourteen people.

The first person Michael, and indeed Fanny, noticed as they
entered the drawing-room, which was on the first floor and
reached by an oak staircase, was Hyacinth Wake.

She was dressed in Venetian red, and silver, with a silver
Russian band in her hair. Michael's heart beat so hard that he
felt the whole room must be aware of it. He was unconscious
of the others present – of Lady Jarvis' voluble and rather hoarse
welcome; of Lady Mellor's somewhat critical scrutiny; of Sir
Arthur Mellor's questions and answers, to which deafness gave
a double point of irrelevance; of his chief, with his wife with
her jingling jet; Raphael Luc, the singer; Ella Dasent, the
striking actress, and many others. His main preoccupation was:
how should he, and when should he, be able to talk to
Hyacinth?

He said "How do you do?" to his host and hostess, was
introduced to some strangers, greeted some friends, as one in
a trance, and then the moment came for going down to dinner.
Hyacinth was standing at the other end of the room talking to
someone he had never seen. She had nodded to him and
smiled, and had then taken no further notice. He was asked by
his hostess to take in Lady Jarvis, and when the time came for

doing it he had forgotten what he had been told, and he had to guess by a process of elimination. Lady Jarvis helped him out. She thought that he seemed absent-minded, but she did not go so far as to wonder why, nor as to put two and two together, although she was aware of his past romance and knew the Wakes well. She took for granted it was over. They went down to dinner into a gold dining-room with a picture by Sargent at the end of it.

Michael was between Lady Jarvis and Ella Dasent, who gave him no trouble, as she told him all about the play she was about to try first in the provinces before bringing it to London. It was adapted from the French, and was about a morphomaniac, "very psychological and subtle, with a strong 'Ella Dasent' part for me," she said, carefully enunciating her words.

Hyacinth was sitting at the end of the table, out of sight, as there was a large barrier of flowers all down the table. Fanny was sitting on the other side of the table between two men who were unknown to Michael, and hitherto to her.

It was lucky for Michael that he was between two talkative guests; they divided their time with equity between him and their neighbours, and while they did so neither of them drew breath.

Every now and then Lady Jarvis gave Fanny a searching glance. She had been surprised at the marriage, and she wondered how it was shaping. Fanny was not looking well, she thought, but perhaps there were excellent reasons.

"We are going to have some music after dinner, Raphael Luc; – that will be a real treat," Lady Jarvis said to Michael.

"Unfortunately I'm not very musical" – but then, remembering that he might want to stay upstairs and not be relegated to the card-room, he added quickly, "I mean I don't understand classical, difficult music; but I do enjoy tunes and songs, sometimes – and the opera – and I believe he sings beautifully."

"Oh, better than anyone," she said; "and charming light songs."

"Fanny will enjoy it. She is *really* musical."

After dinner, when the men were left to themselves, Michael found himself next to Sir Arthur Mellor, who congratulated him on his speech in the House of Lords. Michael was after a time aware that he was being taken for George Ayton. They did not stay long downstairs, and when they reached the drawing-room Michael perceived that Hyacinth was sitting next to the fireplace, talking to Lady Jarvis and someone else; between him and her there was a barrier formed by another group. He rushed through this barrier, seeming almost to be climbing over the furniture, to reach Hyacinth; and just as he was reaching her, and was in earshot, Mrs Wister came up to him and said: "We are going to have just a *little* music. M. Luc has promised to sing just one or two songs. But perhaps you would rather play bridge."

"Well, if I might, I would rather listen to the music," said Michael. "I have never heard Luc, and I have heard so much about him, and I shouldn't like to miss it."

Mrs Wister was delighted.

"Of course," she said, "there are plenty of bridge players. Jack (her husband) is going to play; he has no ear, poor dear!" (and then, making a rapid calculation, she said to herself, "That will make one table; and then there is Sir Arthur and, and let me see, I can get two more with ease; but who will be the fourth? There are a few others coming, I hope, but they will all of them want to hear the music").

"Your wife doesn't play, I think?" said Mrs Wister to Michael.

"I'm afraid not. But she is very musical."

"I will willingly make a fourth," said Hyacinth.

"You, Hyacinth! but you adore Raphael's singing. I won't hear of it."

"Well, do you know, I really would like to play bridge tonight – just one rubber at least. I will come up later." And getting up from her chair she put her arm round Mrs Wister, and drew her slowly away from the group, talking to her in an undertone, and leaving Michael disconsolate behind.

As she went out, Mrs Wister said to her: "You are too unselfish, darling."

Under a pretence of fetching a cigarette for Lady Jarvis, Michael went to see whether there was a possibility of joining the bridge tables, but it was too late. They were made up. Raphael Luc went to the piano; a few of the after-dinner guests had arrived, and they were all drawing little gilt chairs around the Steinway, when Fanny said to Michael in a whisper: "Aren't you really going to play bridge, Michael?"

"No," he said. "I particularly want to hear the fellow sing. I'm told he's wonderful. He sings the songs *I* like."

"I don't think you *will* like it," she whispered. "I think it will bore you to tears."

"Yes, I shall like it," he said. "He sings light, funny songs."

Mrs Wister came up to them. She smiled at Fanny.

"Your husband wouldn't play bridge tonight," she said. "He's quite right. There's no one like Raphael. Even unmusical people enjoy it."

"Don't you really want to play?" asked Fanny.

"No, I don't really," he said almost savagely.

Raphael Luc sat down at the pianoforte, and everyone else took their places. Raphael looked round as if searching for someone, and then he said to his hostess: "Where is Madame Wake?"

"She's playing bridge now, but she's coming up presently."

Luc shrugged his shoulders. He sang a French song from *La Grande Duchesse*, and the audience was enthusiastic, but he seemed to be sulky and in no mood for singing. He was annoyed at Hyacinth's absence. She was his favourite audience, he always said he sang better when she was there. Fanny drank in every note, and enjoyed the exquisite phrasing and the appropriateness of accent. He sang a melancholy Venetian song. Fanny looked at Michael. "He is not listening to a note of the music," she said to herself. "What is happening to him? What is the matter?" Michael would have enjoyed it if only Hyacinth had been in the room. Her absence at this moment was torture to him.

There was a pause. Raphael Luc began another song, and then broke off abruptly in the middle of it. He lit a cigarette and said something in French to Mrs Wister in an undertone.

Mrs Wister went out of the room, saying, "Don't move; the music is going on presently." Luc went on smoking and the guests began to talk.

Almost immediately Mrs Wister came back again with Hyacinth.

"Mrs Wake wonders whether you would mind taking her place at the card-table for a few moments?" Mrs Wister said to Michael. "M. Luc especially wants her to hear this song, which he has composed for her. There's no one else here who knows how to play."

"Of course I will," said Michael, and Fanny was not startled, but she noticed that the tone of his voice was recalcitrant. She watched him as he went out of the room. He looked miserable. He was looking at Hyacinth Wake; Hyacinth was not looking at him. Fanny had the horrible sensation that someone was about to tear away a secret veil and reveal forbidden sights and secrets, and that in a dreadful gleam she was about to be face to face with what she dreaded, with what she had thought too terrible, too unbearable to be true.

She made a supreme effort of will, and turned her thoughts away from all sinister possibilities and all possible shadows of disaster; with a wrench she forced herself to listen to the music.

It was a sentimental tune, purposely sentimental, with an accent of the 'forties or 'fifties about it. It suggested crinolines, chignons, and camellias.

N'écris pas! Je suis triste, et je voudrais m'éteindre;
Les beaux étés sans toi c'est l'amour sans flambeau.
J'ai refermé mes bras qui ne peuvent t'atteindre;
Et, frapper à mon cœur, c'est frapper au tombeau.
N'écris pas.

N'écris pas! N'apprenons que mourir à nous-mêmes.
Ne demande qu'à Dieu…qu'à toi si je t'aimais.
Au fond de ton silence écouter que tu m'aimes,
C'est entendre le ciel sans y monter jamais.
N'écris pas.

N'écris pas! Je te crains; j'ai peur de ma mémoire;
Elle a gardé ta voix qui m'appelle souvent.
Ne montre pas l'eau vive à qui ne peut la boire.
Une chère écriture est un portrait vivant.
N'écris pas.

Fanny looked at Hyacinth. She was sitting next to the
pianoforte. Raphael Luc seemed to be singing for her, and for
her only.

"Is she then so very musical?" Fanny asked herself.

She was looking down, and Fanny wondered whether she
was really appreciating it. She seemed rapt with attention, as if
she was absorbed, living in the music, but that, thought Fanny,
can be easily simulated; and she was deathly pale, but that
again could hardly be the music.

Luc sang the last verse of his song with matchless grace and
complete understanding of the given substance, epoch, and
values.

N'écris pas! ces deux mots que je n'ose plus lire:
Il semble que ta voix les répand sur mon cœur,
Que je les vois briller à travers ton sourire;

Il semble q'un baiser les empreint sur mon cœur.
N'écris pas.

Michael had not gone downstairs. He had found another and
more willing bridge-player on the way. He had listened to this
song, standing in the doorway, watching Hyacinth all the while,
not knowing that Fanny was watching her too; he understood
the words, and the song pierced him like an arrow.

"Yes, that's beautiful, Raphael," said Hyacinth, when he had
finished. "One of the best songs you have written. And now sing
'Maid of Athens.'"

Fanny asked Michael to take her home after that song, as
she had a headache. They were silent as they drove home in a
hansom.

"That fellow does sing most awfully well," Michael said.

"Yes," said Fanny. "You enjoyed it, didn't you?"

"Yes," said Michael, "I did – what I heard. I only heard a
little."

Two or three nights later they went to a play – Fanny,
Michael, Jack Canning – it was the night before he was sailing
for South Africa – and Margaret Branksome. The Branksomes
had arrived in London.

They all went to *The Merry Widow*. During the first *entr'acte*
Michael went up to a box to talk to a friend. Fanny, Margaret,
and Canning stayed in their places. Margaret and Jack Canning
were absorbed in a discussion of the play. Fanny was not
listening, and thinking idle thoughts. In the midst of her
daydream she heard a female voice behind her saying:

"*I* think she's so like Hyacinth Wake."

Another voice answered – a man's voice:

"And do you think *he's* like Michael?"

Then the female voice said, "H'sh!" and Fanny could almost
feel the man being kicked on the shin or nudged.

That little fragment of conversation did what Raphael Luc's song had almost done, or perhaps it finished the work. It gave the *coup de grâce*.

It was now that she understood;…it was as if someone had taken the curtain of the past and torn it in two. She saw what she had thought impossible. She realised the whole of Michael's life now. Of course;…why had she not noticed it before? She lived once more through the whole evening at the Wisters. Everything was plain now. The arrival, his effort to reach Hyacinth; all the manoeuvres, his staying upstairs to listen to the music, he who so rarely liked music and loved bridge…and Hyacinth evidently not wanting the interview and evading it, and Luc's sulkiness changing the situation; and then, since she was obliged to come, she arranged for Michael to go down; and in spite of all, he came back!

So that is what it had been! It was Hyacinth that she was being constantly compared with… She remembered a thousand things, from the day they first met in the picture gallery. The scene came back to her. How clear the relationship between Hyacinth and Michael seemed to her now!… "It must have come to an end just before he came to Langbourne," she thought. She remembered Basil's face… Had he…?

"He never loved me…his Aunt Esther arranged it…a good match for him, a *mariage de raison*…" And at that moment she felt the whole fabric of her life and of her future, which the architects, builders, and workmen of Hope and Illusion and Youth had been so busily and so gaily building, singing as they worked under her orders and personal supervision, and which had arisen and shone, shot with all the colours of the morning, like Tristram's faery castle, or some ethereal Parthenon on the top of a fabulous Acropolis, now in one second come crashing down about her. The pillars were laid low, the marbles had crumbled, the colours had faded and vanished, the altar was a smoking ruin. Henceforth the temple could only be a home for

76

bats, lizards, reptiles, and rats, and weeds and mould and dust. It was ruined, done with for ever.

Michael strolled back into the seat.

"Well, she is lovely, isn't she?" he said, referring to the principal actress. "She reminds me of someone, and I can't quite think who."

"Mrs Wake?" said Fanny, with perfect unconcern.

"Yes. She is a little like her," said Michael cheerfully, "now I come to think of it."

CHAPTER VII

The next day when Fanny awoke she wondered whether all that had happened had been a dream.

She felt dreadfully ill, and she told Michael the reason that morning before he went to the office. The situation seemed to her to be full of irony. The telling of this joyful news ought, she felt, to have been the happiest moment of her life. Michael appeared to be overjoyed. He little knew what was going on in her mind. He had no idea that she had noticed anything or that anything had happened to disturb her.

He made plans for their future. They would go down to Hockley for Christmas. It would be ready by then, for at the present moment it was full of workmen. Perhaps, later, it would be good for her to go to a warm place. Perhaps her mother could lend them the cottage at Westercombe, where they had spent their honeymoon, for a week or two in the spring.

"I couldn't possibly go there," said Fanny. "It's too relaxing."

"Very well, just as you like; we will try and find something else."

Their life went on as before. Michael went to his office every day. Every now and then they were asked out to dinner. Sometimes they went to a play. Michael made no more attempts to see Hyacinth. She convinced him that she had once and for all made up her mind not to see him by her behaviour when they met on another occasion. He realised that Hyacinth meant what she said. They were not even to be friends, henceforward mere acquaintances. All that was over – more so than ever. Michael thought it was absurd as well as intolerable, but he realised that her decision was final, and that there was nothing to be done.

As for Fanny, it would be difficult to describe her loneliness. She felt that Michael was separated from her, that he did not and never had belonged to her. She had few friends. She had lived abroad all her life, and so knew hardly anyone in London, – a stray diplomat and his wife on leave, one of the clerks at the Foreign Office, and some foreigners. She had few friends and no great friend. The Branksomes were in London, but they were too young for her; she felt centuries older than any of them. The prospect that loomed before her was one of unrelieved gloom. She magnified everything. Her state of health made her make the worst instead of the best of things.

Fanny was a gifted woman. She spoke French, German, and Italian fluently and easily, she was a fine pianist, with a delicate touch and a faultless sense of rhythm, and she had a definite talent for modelling. As a girl she had always been full of resources. She knew how to rely on herself. She had never felt lonely or bored. When her father had been Minister at Athens she had learnt modern Greek, and she had many hobbies. She learnt how to bind books in Rome, and how to paint flowers in Japan. But now all this seemed like dust and ashes to her. She felt that London was becoming unbearable to her, and at the beginning of December she told Michael that she could not stand the fogs, the wet, and the cold, and that she must go to Hockley. Michael agreed that she wanted country air, and so did the doctor. She was looking pulled down, and she felt wretched. As Hockley was too far off for him to come up every day to London, he settled to stay in London and to go down to Hockley every Friday till Monday. There were still workmen in the house, but the greater part of the work was done. The work still going on in the bathrooms did not trouble her. Her mother offered to stay with her at once, but Fanny said the house was not ready, and would not be ready till Christmas; at least, there would not be room for more people than Michael and herself. Michael had asked George Ayton for Christmas and Lady Weston.

When Fanny was first left by herself in the country she felt a sense of relief. She could be herself, let herself go, give reins to her feelings, and take off the mask that she felt that she was now wearing daily, and which she knew was eating into her flesh – in other words, give herself up to her misery and abandon herself to it utterly. She gave herself up to her sorrow; to her sense of irretrievable loss, disappointment, and failure. She felt that she had made the supreme mistake; that nothing could mend or remedy the disaster; that Fate or Providence had played her false, and there was nothing to be said or done. She must accept the situation.

Her neighbours made attempts to see her. She did the minimum that was required of her. She shrank from the society of Cuthbert Lyley. She felt that if she were to see more of him he would be capable of not only guessing that she was wearing a mask, but of reading what was behind it.

Then there was the Rector, the Honourable and Reverend Thomas Rowley. He was an oldish man, with kind grey eyes, grey hair, and distinguished hands. He was diffident, shy, and cultivated. He held High Church principles, but without extravagance. He was perhaps slightly awed by his square and level-headed wife, whose suave manner seemed to lend increased authority to her decided opinions.

Fanny felt happy in the society of this clergyman, but she did not encourage his visits, for here again she feared an excess of sympathy. She was frightened of giving herself away.

For the first three weeks till Christmas she did nothing at all. She felt she couldn't read a book, or open the pianoforte, or think of any of her old hobbies. She gave herself up to her misery, and she let it have full play. She did not attempt to be sensible or reasonable. She knew she was being foolish, hysterical, almost mad, like the most foolish heroine in the most foolish book. But at the same time she felt that if she did not behave like this, if she tried to put the slightest brake or check on herself, she would lose her reason; that madness, in fact, lay in any other course. She saw Mrs Tracy once or twice, and so as to avoid any examination or scrutiny which she was unable to face or to bear, she surrendered the garden to her once and for all. She let Mrs Tracy interview her gardener and tell him what was to be done for next year. She made no objections, not even a suggestion, and she stood by while Mrs Tracy ordered and countermanded and arranged all the things she particularly disliked, and vetoed what was near to her heart. She looked on almost with satisfaction. What did it matter? What did she care? What did anything matter?

Michael came down every Friday fairly cheerful from London. The framework of this life suited him. He was engrossed in his work. He went to his club both before and after dinner. He had a few friends in London, and he sometimes brought down a fellow-member of Parliament or a club friend to stay for the Sunday. There was a little shooting, and he and his friends would shoot on the Saturday. He would say to himself that everything was going on as well as could be expected; but he knew this was not true. He longed (now frankly and openly) for a glimpse of Hyacinth, and thought it was foolish of her not to let him see her; but he still hoped that in time perhaps, if he left things alone for a little, all might still be well. But the thought of Fanny was more cruel than that of Hyacinth. "I shall never get to know her," he thought. He was delighted at the thoughts of having a child – but even this joy was marred. Fanny was not looking well and seemed tired and silent, but that, considering the circumstances, could hardly be wondered at. Before Christmas the house was finished, and ready for visitors. Three bathrooms had been put in. All the bedrooms had been either repainted, repapered, or repanelled. The work had been done by Michael, under his Aunt Esther's direction. Fanny had not said a word. She just let things happen. She did not much mind the result. Michael's aunt was sensible and practical, and her taste, although old-fashioned, had nothing obnoxious about it.

The old rooms downstairs had been left as they were. The bedrooms had been "improved," and given a late Victorian air. They had cheerful striped wallpapers with friezes of ivy leaves. Fanny herself had not lifted a finger and had scarcely made a suggestion, excepting for her own sitting-room and bedroom. Michael had consulted her about these, and insisted on her choosing what she wanted in detail. This she had done to please him more than to please herself, for at this moment she felt that nothing could please her.

At Christmas the house was ready. Michael was delighted with the result, and Fanny kept on thinking how excited she might have been...would have been...if everything had been different. At Christmas, Lady Weston, Aunt Esther, George Ayton, and Mr and Mrs Shamier, who were friends of Michael's and of George Ayton's, arrived.

The rooms were decorated with holly, a large yew log burnt in the open fireplace in the panelled hall. There were crackers, plum-pudding, turkey, and milk punch. A Christmas tree was arranged by Mr Rowley for the school-children, and Cuthbert Lyley and Mrs Lacy came to dinner on Christmas Day. They all went to church in the morning. It was a cold, traditional Christmas and the country looked like a Christmas card. Christmas cards and picture postcards came to Fanny from abroad, from friends all over the world. Michael gave her a bracelet, chosen by Aunt Esther – what was called "a handsome ornament."

The guests stayed till over the New Year; then they went back to London. Michael suggested to Fanny that she should come too, but she said that the country was better for her, and that London did not agree with her. She played her part admirably, although she felt it a strain. But it was good for her, she felt, to have something to do that was a strain. It kept her going. Aunt Esther was satisfied and cooed approvingly to her and to Michael: "Dear Fanny is looking so well, *considering;* of course she can't help feeling a little tired. It's so good for her to be in the country and to go for nice long walks."

Her mother thought the marriage was a success. She thought Fanny was tired and sometimes felt wretched, but was that to be wondered at?

The two people who were less decided or less optimistic in their views were Cuthbert Lyley and his sister. Mrs Tracy on several occasions asked her brother if he thought the newly married couple were happy. He refused to be drawn, and said that such matters were beyond his ken. But in reality he, being the more sensitive nature and having certainly as much insight as his sister, was wondering too. He would never have admitted it. He was reserved and disliked gossip.

Life went on in the same groove till Easter. Then Michael suggested that Fanny might like a change. But she refused to leave Hockley for the present, and the doctor backed her up. He said the air was good for her and the life she was leading was healthy. But soon after Easter she went back to London, to the house in Grosvenor Place, and in the first days of May her baby was born. It was a boy, and it was called Peter, after Michael's father. Fanny was ill during and after her confinement, and at one time her life was feared for. She got through it, and when she was convalescent she went down to Devonshire to stay with her mother for a few weeks.

She felt no desire for a London season, but she came back to London in July so as to be with Michael and help him.

She had, for the time being, lost her looks. She looked pinched, dull, and faded, as if her beauty had been washed out by oceans of salt tears – which was indeed true. But you could see, in spite of this, that all the elements of youth and beauty were there, ready to be evoked should they be touched by an enchanter's wand.

Her spirits were low. She loved her child, but she did not seem to have the strength to realise it. The colours of life had gone for her. Michael seemed to be enchanted at having a son. He was busy; Parliament was going on. He came down on every Friday to Devonshire, just as he had done to Hockley. He made his life as full as possible. But however firmly and frequently he told himself that his marriage was, after all, a success, at the back of this the thought of Hyacinth lingered still, like a thorn; he could not forget – he now did not even try to forget – although up to now he had never seen her to talk to, even when they met in a crowd in a stranger's house.

He was astonished at the change in Fanny, although he noticed it perhaps less than other people, he thought it was temporary, the result of everything; she would get looks and her spirits back. Her spirits? – had she got any? Had he mistaken her character? When he had met her for the first time at Langbourne he had thought she had hidden reserves of fun, humour, malice. Had he been mistaken? Had this been his imagination? Had he married someone, and then found he had married someone else? He remembered Mrs Tracy saying it was the fate of all women. Was it now the fate of a man? Or was it his fault? Was Fanny now thinking the same? Had she imagined him to be something different? However it might be, there was nothing to be done now, and after all, things were satisfactory; they had got a boy – a strong, healthy baby. Fanny had been ill and had recovered; the doctor was pleased with her. His Parliamentary career was progressing. It was absurd to complain. So he said, but all the time disillusion and disappointment gnawed at his heart, and deep down within he was sad with an infinite sadness. He knew that he cared nothing, and never would care, for his career. It meant nothing to him. It was all dust and ashes. He knew now, although he would not admit it to himself, that he was not in love with his wife; never – so he secretly feared – would be; and that he had not forgotten Hyacinth. So far from having forgotten her, he thought of her every moment of every day; and the saddest thing of all was that he thought of her most when he was with Fanny. He knew now – although he never had put it into words – that he compared Fanny with her, and found Fanny wanting.

Fanny realised this. She felt, too, that she could make no effort. She could not and would not compete with the shadow of the vanished Hyacinth. What made her feel bitter about it was that she felt – no, she said to herself that she *knew* – that if Michael really got to know her as he had known Hyacinth, he would like her the better of the two.

Michael, she suspected, did not know the real Hyacinth. He had loved her, and in loving her had probably invested her with the qualities that she lacked. Not that she was unlovable. She was nice, amiable, gay, and no doubt in some ways a clever woman; but Michael admired her for the qualities that Hyacinth lacked, and that she, Fanny, felt sure she possessed. Michael would praise Hyacinth's originality, unconventionality, and independence (though she had never heard him do so), whereas she was, so Fanny thought – unjustly – a slave to fashion and to convention. She had heard him praise her taste in literature, art, painting, on one occasion, and music, and Fanny had known, had seen – so she thought – for herself after one dinner-party that Hyacinth consulted safe authorities on these subjects. It did not prevent her, she thought, from having a character, a personality and admirable qualities, both positive and negative, of her own. Fanny felt that, and tried to admit it to the full – but she could not help being biased; she could not help underrating Hyacinth. She felt sure that in these matters, all that Michael did not understand – music, for instance – Hyacinth would impose upon him. He would look upon her as an authority in musical matters, just because she knew what to say and not to say should a musical topic be mentioned. (Fanny had never heard her do this.) And Michael thought, she knew, that Fanny knew nothing, because she refused to play things which were beyond her reach, or to go to concerts where music that she did not understand was given. The truth was, that Michael was much more musical than Fanny gave him credit for, and was always longing for her to play; but he was ashamed to ask for the tunes he liked because he thought she despised them.

Michael had met Hyacinth once or twice since the fateful dinner-party, and they both met her again soon after Fanny came back to London, and Fanny had a good opportunity of watching her. It was at a dinner-party at Lady Jarvis'. Hyacinth had been unable to suppress an upward leap of the heart when she saw, as Fanny came into the room, that her looks were eclipsed. This affected her as the rainbow the poet. But she was sufficiently intelligent and pessimistic to know that such an eclipse might be temporary, because Fanny's looks were founded on permanent elements, but depended on mood, and it only needed health and happiness to bring them back. Hyacinth understood that. (The health might be forthcoming, but there seemed at present little chance of the happiness.) Fanny had been taken in to dinner by Guy Cunninghame, a young man with a large income and little occupation, who knew everybody and a little about most things.

She sat opposite Hyacinth, who was between an artist and a lawyer, and she had the opportunity of observing her, especially as one of her neighbours, Sir Arthur Mellor, was deaf and absent-minded, and Guy Cunninghame was monopolised by his neighbour, an American.

She watched Hyacinth, although she did not appear to be doing so, with care, minutely and thoroughly. Nothing escaped her. She knew what she was saying to the lawyer and what to the artist. She studied the theory and the practice, the art and the craft of Hyacinth's conversation and attitude, and her conclusion was that Hyacinth was either a clever woman or a supremely good imitation of one.

Her first impressions were confirmed as she listened to Hyacinth's talk with the artist about music and pictures. She talked about music to him. She did not mention pictures. She left that to him, and he did it. Fanny even recognised in the conversation things that Michael had said, that he probably had heard her saying, but which Fanny thought were not her original thoughts. They bore, she said to herself impatiently, the mark of some other, some alien mint. Then when she talked to the lawyer her attitude was different, simpler…nothing now paradoxical or unexpected…she became childish and listened to him as if she were a child sitting at the feet of a schoolmaster. The lawyer seemed happy, and not only told her several anecdotes but recited her a long poem by Wordsworth which he admired. She admired it too, she said; she always had admired it. It was one of her favourite poems by Wordsworth.

"Wordsworth and Hyacinth – what a contrast!" thought Fanny bitterly, as she looked at Hyacinth's satin-like hair and white face, and the rather startling arrangement in scarlet that she was wearing. "Surely she is artificial!" she thought.

"How beautiful Hyacinth is looking!" thought Michael.

"And all this time she is watching me," Fanny thought to herself, "and is wondering why on earth Michael can have married me…and she is probably pitying me, for it is obvious, as plain as daylight, that he still loves her, although she won't let him speak to her. I must say I admire her. I think she is a heroic woman – or is she really tired of him? Is she pretending? Is she a consummate actress?"

After dinner, before the men came up from the dining-room, she exchanged a few words with Hyacinth till they were absorbed in a group. They talked of the country, of North Devon, of her father, whom Hyacinth had known, and of the places abroad where Fanny had lived.

After dinner, as usual at Lady Jarvis', there was music – an English pianist called Solway, and a few songs by an amateur, a Mrs Housman, who came after dinner, late, after Solway had finished playing, and with whispered apologies to the hostess.

Fanny was introduced to a Mr Mellor (a nephew of Sir Arthur Mellor), a Government official. He was silent, but evidently, so Fanny thought, musical. Solway had played a Beethoven Sonata and Mellor had made no comment on it. Mrs Housman, who Fanny thought was beautiful and uncommon-looking, sang two old English songs, and then she went away, as she said she had to go home. Her husband was not well.

"What a wonderful singer!" Fanny said when it was over. "Who is that Mrs Housman?"

"Her husband is in the City," said Mellor. "She is a great friend of our hostess, and she received a musical education abroad."

"I could listen to her for ever... I believe even Michael," she thought to herself, "would have enjoyed it. But he, of course, is playing bridge with George Ayton and Guy Cunninghame downstairs." She was right, Michael would have enjoyed it; and not many months later George Ayton, who was less musical, learnt to enjoy it.

There was no more music after Mrs Housman left, but supper downstairs. Many of the guests were going on somewhere. Fanny asked Mellor if he was going to a dance, but he said he never went to dances, and liked getting to bed early.

When they had said goodnight, and Fanny had fetched her cloak from the ladies' cloakroom downstairs, just as she was walking into the narrow passage which led into the front hall, she heard her neighbour at dinner, Guy Cunninghame, talking to someone, some woman she didn't know. It was one of the guests who had arrived after dinner.

"And who was that you were saying goodnight to in the dining-room, after supper?" the female voice asked.

"Oh, that's Lady Weston's girl; she married Michael Choyce."

"Not Fanny Weston?"

"Yes."

"Good gracious! Poor child! I didn't recognise her. She's entirely lost her looks!"

"Yes, I suppose so," said Cunninghame in a bored voice. "Wasn't Hyacinth looking well? And Louise Shamier – By the way, George Ayton..." the sentence remained unfinished, the conversation was interrupted or stopped, and when Fanny came out into the passage they had gone.

CHAPTER VIII

Michael and Fanny went to Hockley at the beginning of August. They were asked to stay in Scotland for the grouse-shooting by an old friend of Michael's, who had a lodge in Caithness.

Fanny did not feel up to it, and she insisted on Michael's going by himself. It was only for a short time. She would be happy without him, and her mother could always come and stay with her.

After some discussion he consented to go. He was away during the month of August.

No sooner had he come back to Hockley than he was greeted by the news that his Aunt Esther was seriously ill. He went up to London at once, and she died before he arrived. She left him all she possessed, and her London house. She considered her nieces to be amply provided for. He stayed in London for the funeral, and until the business entailed was satisfactorily settled.

After consulting Fanny, he settled to sell the house in Chesham Place. He had no difficulty in finding a purchaser. They talked of the house they would ultimately choose to live in London, but no decision was taken for the moment. Fanny was indifferent, and Michael was lazy about taking steps, disliked moving, and was contented with his house in Grosvenor Place.

The autumn went by quickly. Michael was busy with the affairs of his constituency, and Fanny helped him. She went to meetings, fêtes, and garden parties, and entertained at Hockley. They gave a large garden party in September themselves. At the end of September Michael went back to London for good.

Fanny stayed at Hockley. She preferred the country, she said. Michael would come down as before, on Fridays, and stay till Monday. He acquiesced in the arrangement, and indeed it suited him. He was busy and engrossed in his work. He tried to fill his life, he tried not to have time to brood.

Hyacinth, he heard, had left London for good. She and her husband had taken a small house in Surrey, close to London, and Basil went up to his work every day. Michael would not even have the chance of meeting her now at strangers' houses.

Fanny made three friends: firstly, Cuthbert Lyley, who in spite of the scant encouragement she gave him, soon got to know her well; secondly, the Rector, Mr Rowley. Fanny liked him. He was refined, understanding, and an exquisite musician. He played the organ, and Fanny would listen to him playing in the church by the hour. The church and the rectory were a stone's throw from the house. She never discussed religious topics with him, although, strangely enough, she did with Cuthbert Lyley. Fanny had been brought up in a strange manner by her father. His teaching was a blend of scepticism and orthodox Protestant tradition. His mother had been half Italian – a pagan. He took a "sensible" view of such things, which included tolerance for all creeds, sects, and fads. Fanny's mother, on the other hand, had been brought up in the heyday of the materialistic revival. She had known George Eliot and George Lewes personally. She would sometimes say that she considered it, on the whole, one's duty to conform outwardly to the "mythology" of one's epoch, and certainly to bring up one's children in it. This negative attitude had had a curious effect on Fanny. It had sowed in her the seeds of a general disbelief in all creeds. She profoundly disbelieved in Christianity as professed and practised by the Anglican Church, which was the only Church she knew save by hearsay; but she paid no homage to her mother's idols – Auguste Comte and Huxley meant nothing to her, and she couldn't even read George Eliot's novels. She disliked the Victorian period, and she went back to the Greeks and the Latins. She had as a girl in the schoolroom enjoyed reading translations of Greek plays, and with the help of modern Greek, which she learned colloquially at Athens, and a Greek master and dictionaries, she had even tackled the original texts.

She was instinctively drawn to the Greek attitude on life; the austerity, the idea of sacrifice, everything which she found so different from what most people understand by "Pagan."

She had read a little German too, especially Goethe's *Faust* and Heine's songs; but she had put all that aside since her marriage – she was afraid that Michael would think her a blue-stocking. She read nothing but novels, and few of those. She kept all her tastes to herself – so much so that Michael thought she was not fond of reading. This saddened him, because he was himself a passionate if one-sided reader, and delighted in certain books – ballad poetry, Fielding, Dumas, Heine, Browning; but it never occurred to him to discuss such matters with Fanny. With Hyacinth, on the other hand, he had discussed these things for hours.

Fanny, in the course of her travels, had constantly come across Catholics, but she had rarely discussed even the fringe of their religion with them, because she looked upon Catholicism as *"le Christianisme au grand complet,"* and it was against that complete creed that she felt most rebellious.

Cuthbert Lyley divined that there was a world of thought and seething ideas, wild revolts, desperate reticences, possible and impossible loyalties, allegiances to strange causes, seething in her mind. But he was too discreet and too sensitive ever to approach a region which he felt was guarded, or to knock at doors which he felt might open upon secret rooms, or contain forbidden cupboards. When they met, they talked gardening, birds, flowers, or about the topics of the day – politics even – which interested neither of them greatly.

Fanny's third friend was the doctor's wife, Eleanor Saxby. Dr Saxby was a middle-aged, sensible, and busy man, much liked by the people. He was a clever doctor, and it was thought that his gifts were thrown away in this small village. It was the life he preferred. He had married young. It was almost a runaway match, as his wife was the daughter of a Bishop whose aristocratic and autocratic wife had strong views on what were and what were not possible marriages. Saxby in his youth had started life with little. Eleanor was a delightful woman. To see her was to like her. She was natural, and radiated fun. She loved Fanny at once, and understood her enough; she, too, under a superficial easiness and friendliness of manner, was reserved. Fanny knew at once that they would be friends, but intimate never. They would each wear a mask to each other always. Fanny also saw that the Rector's wife, Caroline Rowley, was a sphinx. If you had said that to any of the parishioners they would have laughed. To the outward view she was short, square, and sensible. She wore mittens and spectacles, her silver hair was parted in the middle. She belonged to Mudie's, and took in *The Saturday Review*. Her conversation was as clean-cut and as frank as her handwriting. She seemed to see not only through you, Fanny thought, but all round you, like Homer or Velasquez. Fanny felt that with her no mask would be of any use. Not that Mrs Rowley ever attempted to invade her privacy. She consulted Fanny on parish matters and discussed the latest novel. She was a great reader.

The society of Cuthbert Lyley, Eleanor Saxby, and the Rector and his wife was more than a pleasure to Fanny. It filled up her life, and enabled her to think that little by little, in the ruins of the shattered fabric of dreams that lay about her, she would one day be able to build something in which she could lead a decent life.

And then she had her child, an adorable baby, and Fanny loved children; and her happiest hour in the day was when he came down in the evening. But children, she knew from the first, however dearly you love them, do not make up for the other thing, and especially for the loss of the other thing. And Fanny felt that she had lost, or rather that she had never, never for one moment possessed, the love of Michael. The bitterest thought of all to her was that she felt it might have been, that it was not impossible. She believed that Michael could by nature have loved her more than he did Hyacinth. She saw Mrs Tracy often, and with her, to safeguard herself from too much shrewdness, too many questions, too much scrutiny, she adopted the attitude of a disciple seeking the advice and help of a wise teacher. She consulted her on domestic and social points, and let her manage things for her; she gave her so much to do and so much to manage and to think about, so many questions to answer, that Mrs Tracy had no time to think of anything else.

The remaining factor was her mother, and Fanny managed to hoodwink her – fairly well. Lady Weston was not as satisfied as she would have liked to be, but she would not admit even to herself that any mistake had been made.

She laid down the axiom that Fanny was happy, and that the marriage was a success. Michael, in any case, was behaving admirably. He was getting on, and was well spoken of everywhere – a rising man. He would be a Cabinet Minister one day. Fanny was making him an excellent wife; she did her duties in the county and in the constituency. It was a good thing too that she had plenty to do, and there was something to do all the year round.

The people liked her. They thought her sensible and amiable, but they were brutally frank in expressing their surprise that she could ever have been thought a beauty; or rather they noted and corroborated the loss of her looks; they said she had been admired, and not without reason, before her marriage.

Michael's popularity had been increased by his marriage, and especially by the birth of his son. There had been presentations, addresses, speeches, as after the marriage. Fanny did not mind this side of her life. She rather enjoyed it – it gave her a better chance of hiding what she did not wish to show, namely, how unhappy she was, what a great mistake she knew she had made; and it filled up her time. It prevented her from thinking and brooding. It also allowed her to think she was perhaps being of some use, perhaps doing something for others in the world.

People took advantage of her readiness to help, and scarcely a week passed without engagements – to open or hold a stall at a bazaar, to go to sports, a lantern-slide lecture, or to preside over this or that, so that sometimes Fanny felt that she was leading the same kind of life as a minor royalty.

There were other neighbours too. There were the Logan-Knaystons, into whose family Stephen Lacy had married. And about eight miles distant, a prosperous man, a Mr Carrington-Smith, who had taken the picturesque manor-house of Seyton and spent his holidays there, partly for the shooting, and partly to gratify the tastes of his æsthetic and advanced wife.

"We can't say that Fanny is lonely, or that she hasn't plenty of people to see," her mother would say. For Lady Weston had no patience with people who were bored, or with people who did not want to see their neighbours. One had to put one's share in the pool and to do one's best to be pleasant, "or else how could the world go round?" But when at the end of September, Lady Weston heard from Fanny that Michael had gone back to London, and that she was "staying on," she was alarmed. She suggested coming down to stay, and Fanny, who did not want her mother to come just at that moment, felt obliged to say "yes." There was no possible reason for saying "no."

Lady Weston arrived, and Fanny met her, armed to the teeth with plausibility. There was so much to do… Michael was coming down every Friday… The house in Grosvenor Place was being repainted – only Michael's sitting-room was immune… She was being more useful to Michael in the country than she could be in London… There was a bazaar to open next week, in the middle of the week, and she had promised to preside at a Mothers' Tea in the village, and then there was the big concert at Ilminster. She was a patron… Michael, of course, had to be in London; otherwise it would have been a good thing if he could have come too.

All this sounded plausible, more than plausible, reasonable; but nevertheless it did not convince Lady Weston. She felt that Fanny was keeping back something, or indeed many things. However she thought: "We must make the best of it, and the great thing is to keep her occupied."

She was dissatisfied with Fanny's looks. She was thin and white, and her face had a washed-out look. The radiance had gone from it. Lady Weston could not believe it was the same Fanny.

Fanny, on the other hand, was equally desirous of keeping her mother occupied. She begged Michael, if possible, to bring a friend to stay with him the next Friday to Monday, and someone who would be nice to her mother; and as Lady Weston was most agreeable and full of life and bubbling with interest, this was not difficult. In the meanwhile she took her mother to see the neighbours. Lady Weston was a passionate sightseer, and loved meeting new people. One afternoon Fanny suggested driving over to Seyton. Lady Weston was overjoyed at the idea. They drove over in the motor-car that Michael had just bought.

The manor-house of Seyton was not large. It was situated in open country, just beyond a wood. It was a low, two-storied stone house, built in 1736 or 1737 by a disciple of Inigo Jones. One wing had been destroyed by fire, so it had left an L-shape; the walls were covered with creepers – a blazing red at this moment.

The rooms were low, but beautifully proportioned. There was a subtle elegance about the whole house. Everything in it seemed to be right. There was not much furniture, but what there was seemed to have grown there. Nothing seemed to have come from a dealer's shop, or to be there to obey the eccentricities of a collector or of a millionaire.

This was odd, because her mother explained to her that the house had been sold by the Rippleworth family, to whom it had belonged for years, and had been bought by a financier called Ralph Adeane, who was not a man of taste, and yet he had not spoiled it; on the contrary, one had only to look round to see that.

"Adeane?" said Fanny. "Was it anything to do with that Mrs Adeane whose portrait we saw at the Walter Bell Exhibition?"

"Yes. Her husband."

"Oh, then I expect she was a woman of great taste."

"I really don't know. I never met her. But she was said to be charming. Rather reckless, I imagine. But she must have been *very* attractive. She did a lot of harm."

"Colonel Branksome said I was rather like her – or her picture."

"Did he? He has odd ideas. I'm not sure she was a sensible woman."

"You think I am sensible, Mother? I'm glad of that." She laughed.

"You certainly have some sense. You inherited it from your father."

They were waiting in the small square panelled room for their hostess while this conversation was going on. Over the chimney-piece there was a portrait of a youth in Charles the First sea-green clothes with buff-coloured boots and a plumed hat; and on the chimney-piece were some lovely little Dresden china harlequins with patchwork tailcoats of pale green and black, and some pink-and-white shepherdesses and columbines.

In the corner of the room there was a spinet. There was not much furniture; only a few chairs, a round satinwood table with a few books on it, and a small table with a glass top which contained a collection of delicate miniatures. There was a tall clock in a corner of the room, that told the quarters with silvery chimes. They had not to wait long for their hostess.

She had perhaps been arranging herself, as her costume was rather startling. It was an arrangement in black and white stripes, made in the style of the latest Munich pictures. She looked like an illustration from *Jugend*. Mr Carrington-Smith was in London. He only came down, she said, for Sundays.

The conversation halted a little. It was not quite time for tea.

"Shall I show you the house?" said Mrs Carrington-Smith. "It is rather *amusing.*"

"We should love to see it," said Lady Weston, with great decision. "Who does it belong to now?"

"Still to Mr Adeane. He bought it from the Rippleworths years ago. And he always lived here till his wife died."

"When did she die? I forget."

"About two or three years ago, I think. He has never lived here since. He always lets it."

"But where does he live himself?"

"In London…and he goes abroad a great deal in the winter. I believe he is delicate."

"There were some children, weren't there?"

"Yes; two boys, I think; they are at school."

"Did you know Mrs Adeane?" asked Fanny.

"I saw her once at a concert or a Private View. She was admired. She had a kind of success in some sets. But it is not a type of beauty that appealed greatly to me."

"What type was it?"

"Well, I don't know how to describe it. It was not *interesting*. It was rather old-fashioned. There was something which reminded me of the Empire epoch about her – Empire and Miss Austen – a period I detest. And then there was something – well, almost South American – about her, something *Cuban*, which I never care for. I believe she was a Créole – so uninteresting. I don't think Créoles have any souls; they are like *birds*...poor things," said Mrs Carrington-Smith, reflecting to herself that a Créole couldn't possibly enjoy George Meredith or Henry James or Bergson.

She led Fanny and Lady Weston into the dining-room first. A small square panelled room, with one or two pictures let in to the panels, Fragonard-like scenes, and some beautiful glass on the sideboard.

"Is all the furniture Mr Adeane's?"

"Everything; and he makes a very odd condition when the house is let, that nothing is to be *altered* or *moved*. Two rooms we are not even allowed to use at all. He keeps the key of them, and we don't know what is inside them. As, however, the furniture is quite nice...good of its kind, although it's not my period...we don't mind that."

From the dining-room they went into the drawing- room.

"This is the drawing-room," said Mrs Carrington-Smith. "*She* must have used this. That is her harp in the corner, and that is her harpsichord. She liked collecting those funny old instruments evidently, and that funny little escritoire with the small drawers and the little green cloth flap was her only writing-table. She couldn't have written many letters. And those are her books in that little bookcase; with her bookplate – such a sentimental one. Such funny books! Just look at them – *The Necklace of Princess Fiorimonde*, with pictures by Walter Crane; *The Last Days of Pompeii*; *The Daisy Chain*, by Charlotte Yonge. And then the French and foreign books are still funnier: *Manon Lescaut; La Morte*, by Octave Feuillet; *Léila*, by Georges Sand; Sully Prudhomme's poems... Alfred de Musset. Some Spanish books – oh! and *Friendship*, by Ouida! Just fancy – Ouida!"

There were two large sashed windows in the drawing-room, and in the middle of the wall a glass door that opened on steps which led down into the garden. The walls were white and gilded, and there were portraits of cavaliers and ladies of the Stuart and Queen Anne period, and men and women in powder. Over the chimney-piece there was a portrait of Anne Lady Rippleworth, by Lawrence, in claret-coloured velvet and wearing an emerald pendant. The furniture was covered with a faded shiny chintz. There was a smell of potpourri in the room.

"What is that?" asked Fanny, pointing to what looked like a large writing-table, which was inlaid with coloured tiles.

"Oh, that was her drawing-table. You see there is a glass of water on it? It is put there every day by the housekeeper. That is one of the things we are not allowed to touch. And the drawers are full of painting brushes and colours."

"Mrs Adeane used to paint?"

"Oh yes, there are 'albums' full of her water-colours. Such funny water-colours! Everything is painted quite small and minute, like the landscapes on Dresden china. And there are 'views' of the Campagna; ruins, and Paestum, Amalfi, Pompeii, Corfu, and that sort of thing. But what is so odd is that she didn't belong to that epoch at all. She was not much older than I am, but her mind seems to have belonged to Byron's period, or earlier – to the time when people admired Salvator Rosa, Caravaggio, and *ruins* – and read 'Lara' and Thomas Moore, and all that; with a touch of the sentimentality of the Second Empire thrown in – Ouida and Musset, for instance. All her music is there, and it is nearly all Offenbach and Audran – *La Fille de Madame Angot, Le Petit Duc, Giroflé-Girofla*, Strauss' valses, and Goddard and Tosti's songs. I mean *Johann* Strauss, not Richard, or even the delightful Oskar! And just look at that. How absurd!" And she pointed at an early Victorian walnut work-table which stood in one of the windows with skeins of silk and a piece of canvas all ready for a needlewoman.

"Yes, fancy," said Lady Weston. She was not interested. She was noting the furniture and appraising it, and came to the conclusion that in this room, at any rate, there was nothing "good."

"Well, that is almost all," said Mrs Carrington-Smith, "except the staircase, which you must see, and the library. There are two more rooms downstairs, but they, as I told you, are shut up." She opened the door.

"We will look at the library first." They walked through a door, up some steps, along a passage, and came into a small square room furnished with filled bookcases, except for a small window and a large fireplace. The books were all old. Folios, herbals, in their dark calf contemporary bindings, and a quantity of smaller books in faded white vellum with gilt lettering.

"The books are valuable and interesting, but they evidently neither of them ever used this room, as one could see the books had never been touched. *He* used this as his sitting-room."

They went back through the drawing-room, and as Mrs Carrington-Smith opened the door, Fanny had the sharp sensation that someone had just left the room. It was as if she had caught sight of the whisk and heard the rustle of a vanishing petticoat or train, or as if a speaking voice had ceased to speak or a sounding instrument had just been shut, and the strings were still vibrating. There was more than atmosphere in the room. There was the trace, the sense, of an actual presence, a presence which had just gone. Fanny was sharply, painfully conscious of this. They walked through the drawing-room into the hall. The staircase was a fine example of wood-carving. Here more pictures of ancestors hung on the panelled walls.

"That's all I can show you," said Mrs Carrington-Smith. "The bedrooms are not interesting."

She had no intention of showing the bedrooms, which were beautiful.

"There are some fireplaces – the usual thing, you know; and then there are the rooms we can't open. We have to be very careful, you know. Mr Adeane left his housekeeper here, who looks after everything like a lynx. I will show you the garden."

The garden was small but exquisite. There was a terrace with beds shaped like fleurs-de-lis and in other patterns, with box hedges round them, full now of snapdragons which had not yet been damaged by a frost. There was a wall with a border of cherry pie and verbena and lavender, roses and pansies. You walked down to a bowling-green. Beyond it there was an enclosed flower and kitchen garden, mixed with fruit trees, rose trees, grass paths, and red brick walls with espaliers.

Fanny thought it the most beautiful garden she had ever seen, but her mother sniffed at it.

"I call that rather a *silly* garden," she said. "It is neither one thing nor the other."

"Nowadays," said Mrs Carrington-Smith, "we should plan it differently. I would give the world to be able to do what I liked with the house and the garden. One could make it so beautiful; but then, as I told you, we are not allowed to touch a thing. However, we've only taken it for a year, with option to renew."

"Is the picture that Spaniard did of Mrs Adeane here?" Fanny asked.

"No, not that I know of; unless it is in the room which is locked up."

"Is that room a bedroom?" asked Fanny.

"There are two rooms locked up…a bedroom and a sitting-room – both of them hideous, I dare say."

They went in and had tea.

CHAPTER IX

Fanny stayed for the rest of the autumn at Hockley, until Christmas. Michael went to London in November, and came down on Fridays. Fanny became more and more attached to the country, and to Hockley. She tried to occupy herself as much as possible. She did her duty as a Member's wife, and besides this she gave time to her hobbies. She practised the pianoforte once more, and played duets with the Rector, and she took to modelling again. She made herself a studio in one of the attics, and there she would spend perhaps the happiest hours of her life, modelling small figures. Cuthbert Lyley admired her work. She had real talent, he said, and he sighed, thinking of what a waste of talent there seemed to be in the world. In other times, and other circumstances, Fanny might, he thought, have been an artist. As it was, she had an amusing hobby. Michael admired her work too, but Fanny was ashamed of it before him, ashamed of everything she did before him, and never let him see anything if she could help it; never even let him hear her play. This was, he thought, because she thought he knew nothing of such things and cared for nothing artistic. She was far from thinking this, but she did not know how much Michael cared for certain things – for poetry, fine pictures, for instance, Greek and Roman sculpture even, and how much and how often he used to discuss such things with Hyacinth.

"Fanny," he used to say to himself, "thinks I'm an uneducated clodhopper. So I am, but not so uneducated as she thinks." He longed for some outlet of expression, for some source of sympathy, and found none anywhere. He threw himself into his work and into outdoor life, and all that he could share with his men friends. George Ayton went to East Africa in the autumn of that year, big-game shooting, and he was anxious for Michael to go with him; but it was impossible for Michael to get away for so long. Christmas was spent as before, at Hockley. Lady Weston was there, and there were the usual festivities. Directly after Christmas Michael went back to London, and his life slipped back into the old groove.

Lady Weston tried to persuade Fanny to spend more time in London. Fanny appeared to agree and promised to do so in future, but when the time came she stayed in the country. Lady Weston was alarmed. "If she is not careful," she said to herself, "she will lose him." But Fanny complained of nothing. She was happy, she said, in the country; she had so much to do.

She did make visits to London from time to time. But as time went on these became rarer and shorter. She was making for herself – as she had intended – she had made for herself a hut among the ruins of the temple of her lost illusions.

Michael was attempting, but less successfully, to do the same thing. His hut was his work, and outdoor amusements – riding, fishing, and ornithology. It was not, he found, enough. Try as he would, he could not get rid of the toothache at heart which nothing seemed to allay.

Once he wrote to Hyacinth, telling her he could bear it no longer; he must see her, if only for a moment. But this time she only sent a note with "Please don't" written on it.

The next turning-point in his life came in the middle of the summer. He had been at Hockley from Friday till Monday, and was going up early on Monday morning in the train.

He had with him an attaché-case full of letters, which he had not had time to open, and *The Times*. Fanny was with him. He read his letters and then he glanced through *The Times*, which Fanny had been reading. He asked her if there was any news.

"No," she said, "really nothing."

He felt, he could not say why, that she was not telling him the truth. He opened the first page; there was nothing interesting. He scanned the Parliamentary reports, the Foreign news, the correspondence, the theatrical notes, the racing news, an article on old buildings.

"No, there isn't anything," he said, and he threw down the newspaper. At that moment he felt that Fanny was relieved. She began talking of other things. They were going to the opera that night. Michael liked certain operas, and he felt that in going he was giving Fanny a treat that she enjoyed. They sometimes seemed to like the same music, but perhaps they liked it in a different way.

"Don't forget the opera tonight," he said. "Melba *is* singing."

"Yes," said Fanny, but did not pursue the subject. Michael thought this odd.

"We will dine early. Half-past seven. I don't want to miss the beginning. George can come. I heard from him this morning. We should have room for a fourth in the box – but I think three is enough."

Fanny nodded, and made no comment.

Michael went back to his letters. When he had done with these, he began reading an article in a magazine which he had bought at the station, but his mind wandered. Fanny was reading a novel.

Michael threw down the magazine, and for a time looked out of the carriage-window while he smoked his pipe.

Fanny handed him a letter. "This may amuse you," she said. "It's from mother." It was a long letter describing the entertainment of some Indian princes at a garden party near London. He read the letter, paid it its due meed of laughter (a forced chuckle) and appreciation, and gave it her back. Fanny took up *The Times* once more. The time passed, and they were not far from London when Michael said: "Can I have *The Times* for a moment? There is something I want to see."

Fanny handed it to him. He looked through it, but apparently did not find what he wanted. He was throwing down the newspaper onto the seat next to him, when a name caught his eye among the "Deaths" – *Wake*. He paused a moment. He looked out of the window. They were nearing London, the houses were becoming plentiful. The country had come to an end. He noticed a tall chimney and an advertisement recommending Bovril. He read it slowly. Then he turned his eyes back to the newspaper. He forced himself to read the announcement. Fanny was engrossed in her novel. He read:

"WAKE. – On the 26th of June, in London, Hyacinth, the wife of Basil Wake…"

He put down the newspaper and looked out of the window until they arrived at Liverpool Street Station. He saw Fanny into a cab and drove in another to the office.

"Fanny read it," he said to himself – "she was afraid I was going to read it – she knew when I did read it."

Fanny had seen it the moment she took up *The Times*. She had tried with all her might not to do anything that might make matters worse. She prayed that Michael would not see it, would not receive the news in that manner. She hoped she might not give herself away. She tried to behave as naturally as possible, not to betray her fear lest he should read more. When the journey was nearly at an end, she felt that all would be well, although, of course, it was no solution. He would have to hear, but she could not help feeling that any other way would be better…or less terrible… And then the opera that night. Something must be done, but what?… And then…she knew…knew without looking at him…without seeing anything…while she was deep in her novel…that he had read it. After she had left him at the station, hardly daring to look at him, she waited at home for Michael to take some step. She knew he would. He did, the moment he arrived at his office.

He told his clerk to telephone to Fanny that he would have after all to go to the House that night, and if he looked in at the opera he would be late. She was not to expect him to dinner, but to get someone else. *Bohème* was one of the last operas he had ever seen with Hyacinth. It was the opera he was to have gone to with her on the day of shipwreck. All that day went by like a dream. He wondered how he could possibly get news. He knew no one whom he could ask, although he had many friends who knew Hyacinth. He was thirsting for a little scrap of news.

Although he had not seen Hyacinth since his marriage except in the distance, at dinners and parties, the knowledge that she was alive had made the whole difference. Now she was gone – gone away for ever. There was not the chance of either seeing her, or of saying goodbye, or hearing from her. He tried to say to himself that this made no difference. She had been dead to him ever since his marriage. But he knew this was not true.

The world seemed to him to be swathed in a grey blanket, and now for the first time he felt that he had really buried his youth and all that went with it...dreams, hopes, joy, love, expectation...he had nothing to look forward to. There was Fanny, of course, and Peter. Fanny was an admirable woman, but she did not love him, and he, to tell the truth, could not get on with her. He could not understand her. He had misunderstood her from the first. Their marriage had been a mistake – a failure. Marriages, like plays, were either a success or a failure. His was a failure.

The funeral, he found out later in the day, was the next day. There was to be a Requiem for her at St Peter's and St Edward's, Palace Street, Westminster, at 11.30 (she was a Catholic). Fanny knew what he must be going through, and she was profoundly sorry for him. She longed to help. She longed with her whole being to say a word, to make some sign of sympathy. But she knew it was impossible. She had always tried to be fair about Hyacinth, and she had almost succeeded. She recognised how well, how heroically (sometimes) Hyacinth had behaved, for Fanny never really believed that Hyacinth had been tired of Michael. On the contrary, she thought her heroic behaviour had probably killed her. But she never could be *quite* fair. Try as she would, she never could understand what Michael saw in Hyacinth. She could not help thinking that he had been taken in, and saw in her qualities that were not there. As for her death, she thought this the crowning tragedy for herself as well as for Michael; it would make things worse instead of better for both of them. It would seal an everlasting image of Hyacinth in his mind. He would not see her change and grow old and grow different. He would always see her now as he had last seen her, brilliant and striking and gay and young-looking, for Hyacinth looked young. Her death would make the barrier between them greater than ever. How she longed to talk to someone about this. How she longed to open doors! She longed to shout her story on the housetops. But instead of this she ordered dinner, and knowing that Michael would not go to the opera, she telephoned – before she received his message – and tried to get another woman and another man. They had a small box, and she did not want to spend the whole evening alone with George Ayton. She tried all the friends she could think of, and failed. They were engaged. Just as she was despairing, Lady Jarvis rang her up about something else, some charity entertainment she was getting up later. Fanny asked her whether she could possibly come to the opera, saying she was in a fix, and could she bring or suggest a man? She explained the situation.

"Well, as a matter of fact, I have got someone dining with me," said Lady Jarvis; "but I think he would greatly prefer going to the opera to a *tête-à-tête* with an old woman."

"Oh, do please come. Who is it?"

"Well, as a matter of fact, it is Leo Dettrick."

"Not the writer?"

"Yes, the writer."

"Well, that does frighten me a little. Will he get on with George Ayton?"

"Oh, perfectly; and I expect," she laughed, "he will be at your feet."

"Very well, do please bring him if it doesn't bore him, but ring him up first and ask him if he doesn't mind. I would far rather you did that...and we are dining rather early – at half-past seven."

Lady Jarvis promised she would, and she did. She informed Fanny later on in the morning that Mr Dettrick would be delighted to come to the opera and was looking forward to it.

Leo Dettrick was well known as a writer, but little known as a man. He spent his time either travelling or living abroad. He was unmarried. He liked the Tropics, and sometimes wrote about them. His books were short and various; and he had written many, but they were uncommon, and their flavour was peculiar, strange, strong, and unmistakable – you loved or hated it; it was caviare to some. They were not widely popular; but they appealed to readers beyond England; his reputation was already European. He had few friends in England, and he had always avoided being lionised; when he was in England he usually lived in Cornwall, by the sea. He was fond of sailing.

Lady Jarvis he had known for some time. There was a special link between them, but more of that later.

Lady Jarvis arrived punctually at Michael's house in Grosvenor Place, and with her was Mr Leo Dettrick. He was just reaching middle age, the moment when you look back and realise that youth is over; but he still looked young. He was not good-looking, but his eyes were extraordinary. They seemed to burn their way through you, and he had gleaming white teeth like a wolf. Altogether, he looked like an untamed animal. That night, as she was dressing for dinner, Fanny had felt mortally tired, as if she could hardly get through the evening. She received her guests with mechanical grace, and her subconscious self did the welcoming admirably.

She felt unaware of the presence of either George Ayton or of Mr Dettrick. She forgot for the moment that Dettrick was a writer, although she had read all his books, and some of them several times. He did nothing to cause her to connect him with his writings, and afterwards when she thought it over, she realised that she had felt no link between him and his books, nothing in him that faintly reminded her of the violent and intuitive writer upon whose understanding she had so often rested.

When Lady Jarvis and he walked into Michael's sitting-room downstairs, where Fanny received them, Dettrick seemed startled into an extraordinary degree of shyness.

Lady Jarvis had told Fanny he was shy, but she had expected nothing like this. It was only afterwards when she went to bed that night that she thought of it. At the time, everything happened to her as in a dream. She worked purely mechanically, like a musical box. Leo Dettrick sat next to her, and she talked to him feverishly on every topic under the sun throughout dinner, and he answered in monosyllables. Fanny noticed this, in subsequent reflection, but not at the time. Had she thought of it at the time, it would have made her uncomfortable.

When dinner was over, Lady Jarvis explained to Fanny that Mr Dettrick would only be able to stay for one act of the opera, as he had to catch a train. He was not living in London, but he was staying with some friends in the suburbs; he was so fond of music that he did not want to miss the first act. It was, after all, the best act.

The house was full that night. Fanny's box was in the upper tier. They were not bothered with visitors. George disappeared in the interval. Dettrick said "Goodbye" with stammered thanks. He had a slight impediment – not a stammer, but a slight guttural burr in his speech, which made him sometimes hesitate, and often difficult to understand. Fanny noticed this for the first time as he said "Goodbye."

When Fanny was left alone with Lady Jarvis, Lady Jarvis said to her:

"Well, what did you think of him?"

"Who?"

"Leo Dettrick."

"Oh, of course – yes, Mr Dettrick. He's very nice, isn't he? – charming; so good-looking," she said absently.

"Good-looking?"

"Well, I mean striking-looking."

"I think he looks rather like an orang-outang, or a were-wolf."

"Yes, a were-wolf," said Fanny absently. She realised that she had hardly looked at him.

"Does he remind you of his books?"

"His books?… Do you know… I had really forgotten for the moment that he had ever written books," she laughed. "He is not like an author, is he? Not that I have met any English authors, and very few foreign ones."

"Of course he's shy with strangers, but you must have made an impression on him."

"I! Why?"

"Well, to have made him as shy as that…didn't you notice it?"

"Yes, I suppose he was shy." But even now Fanny had not come back to life. She was still in another world. She had not yet realised the evening. She was not yet awake.

"Where is George?" she asked.

"I don't know. His magnet has left London."

"Louise Shamier?" Fanny inquired absently.

"No. That's all over… It's someone else…"

"Someone I don't know, I suppose."

111

"As a matter of fact, it's my friend, Clare Housmann... You heard her sing at my house. Poor George, there's no hope for him."

They were silent for a while. They were both thinking of Hyacinth.

Lady Jarvis thought it best to say: "It's very sad about Hyacinth Wake, isn't it?"

"Yes; and how sudden! What did she die of?"

"They say she had been ill for some time, only nobody knew it. She had an operation, not a dangerous one. In fact, they said it would be nothing – and she died."

Fanny liked Lady Jarvis, and felt she understood. She also longed to say:

"It will make poor Michael so unhappy."

Instead of which, she said, "It will make him very unhappy," meaning Basil.

"Oh yes," said Lady Jarvis seriously. "He was so fond of her."

George came back into the box. He looked disconsolate, as if someone whom he wished to see and whom he had been used to seeing in this place was not there. They sat through the rest of the opera, and when they came home, Michael had not yet come back from the House.

Fanny went to bed, and as soon as she got to bed she seemed to wake; never had she felt more wide awake; the sort of somnambulist trance she had been in hitherto seemed to leave her. Every detail of the evening came back to her with startling vividness. She saw Leo Dettrick now distinctly. She remembered what they had talked about, or rather what she had talked about, as his conversation had been limited to "Yes" or "No." He was, she thought, a curious man and singularly unlike his books. Then she thought of George Ayton. He had loved Louise Shamier for so long, and now all that was over. He loved someone else, someone he could only just have got to know. Everything came to an end in the world. So Michael had loved Hyacinth. That had come to an end...for her, that is to say. He had married; he had made a *mariage de raison*, and all that must have been Hyacinth's life had suddenly come to an end for her. And yet it had not come to an end: Michael had never ceased to love her. He had loved her more since his marriage, Fanny felt certain of this. She felt certain, too, that Hyacinth had never ceased to love Michael. Now she was dead. What would happen? Michael would hate her, Fanny, she felt. "He won't be able to endure the sight of me. I must go back to the country tomorrow." And yet, what did he see, what did anyone, or rather all of them, see – all men, that is to say – in Hyacinth? What was the mystery? The charm? She was nice-looking, striking, picturesque, but not nearly so pretty as hundreds of other women Michael knew. She was intelligent, but not really clever or amusing – not witty nor funny, as others. Perhaps it was this, she thought. She was a nice woman. She was never spiteful. She was gay, and good-humoured, and good-natured, and took trouble, and had equable spirits, and was always nice to everybody.

"Why can't I be like that?" thought Fanny. "There are some people I can't talk to…try as I will. It's not because I don't want to – I should love to. But I can't. Michael sees all this, and compares me with her, and he sees me not being able to do what she did so well. Oh dear! and so it will always be till the end."

She heard Michael let himself in late, at two in the morning. She herself did not get to sleep till it was daylight.

While Fanny, Lady Jarvis, and George had been having dinner, Michael had walked from the House of Commons into St James's Park, and from St James's Park to Green Park. He walked up the broad path past Spencer House and Bridgwater House. It was a fine, hot evening, and the park was crowded with people lying on the grass, and walking about. One of the Guards' Bands was playing in a kiosk. He sat down on a green chair, paid his fee, and listened to the music.

He intended to have a little food somewhere, and then to go back to the House.

He had heard what had happened to Hyacinth in the course of the day: the operation, which had been thought to be nothing, how she had been taken to a nursing-home, and then the sudden death...and the bitterness of grief came over him like a wave. The band was playing the Wedding March from *Lohengrin*; this was followed by a selection from *The Gondoliers*. How gay the tunes sounded! The melodies seemed to spring up from a well of joy. The "Regular royal Queen," the "King who lived, as I've been told, in the wonder-working days of old," the "Highly respectable gondolier," the lovely ditty, "Take a pair of sparkling eyes," the Gavotte, the Cachucha... He and Hyacinth had often been together to the Savoy to hear Gilbert and Sullivan...whenever, in fact, they had a chance. He never mentioned Gilbert and Sullivan to Fanny. He felt she would despise it. He was wrong. She often played through the operas when she was alone at Hockley. She had no idea Michael liked them. He had never told her. She thought all music bored him *really*, and that he pretended to like it for her sake, lest she should think her playing annoyed him.

Children were playing in the grass. Lovers were walking hand in hand, or with an arm round a waist, saying nothing. A few soldiers in red tunics swaggered by. It was the end of a really hot day, at the end of June. There was hum of talk and laughter. The clatter of the traffic, the jingle of hansoms and the hooting of motor horns, came from Piccadilly. People were going out to dinner. It was what *Punch* called "The Festive Hour." The end of one of the gayest days of what was called a brilliant season.

Michael stayed on this chair till the selection from *The Gondoliers* came to an end. Then he strolled back again down the broad walk. He thought he would go to his club and eat a sandwich. He walked through the passage towards Ambassadors' Court. Here he changed his mind. He could not

face the club. He walked past Clarence House into the Mall…
London seemed that evening like a picture in a picture-book.
The air was so clear, the houses clear-cut, clean, and sober, as
they are in fresh coloured prints.

The sun was setting in a cloudless sky; a tepid warmth
seemed to rise from the pavement. There was an awning
outside Stafford House and a red cloth on the steps; the guests
would soon be arriving. Michael walked past the sentry at
Clarence House; he looked at the calm, radiant evening.

He remembered a little poem of Heine's that Hyacinth had
read to him. It began:

> "Mein Herz, mein Herz ist traurig
> Doch lustig leuchtet der Mai."[1]

In it the poet describes himself leaning against a lime tree
high on an ancient rampart. Beneath him is the still blue moat,
a little boy is rowing a boat, and angling and whistling; beyond
the moat there are pleasure-houses, gardens, and people; oxen,
and meadows, and a wood.

The maids are washing the linen and romping in the grass.
The grumbling mill-wheel is scattering its dewy diamonds.
There is a sentry-box at the grey tower, and a red-coated
soldier is pacing to and fro. The sun shines on his musket; he
presents and shoulders arms.

"I wish he would shoot me dead," said the poet Heine.

"I wish he would shoot me dead," said Michael.

---

[1] "My heart, my heart is mournful
But glad is the sunshine of May."

CHAPTER X

A year after what was told in the last chapter – a year which for Michael and Fanny had been not unlike the preceding year – Leo Dettrick settled that, as he had tried and failed to write both in London and abroad, he would try the country. He consulted his old friend, Lady Jarvis, who in her turn consulted her friend, Cuthbert Lyley. A vacant farmhouse, not far from Knaystone, which belonged to an elderly spinster, was to let from June till the end of September. He went to see it and took it, but it was not until he had lived a whole month there that he sat down to write his impressions to his old friend, Francis Greene.

He wrote as follows:

THORNDYKE FARM,
ELSTON, EAST ANGLIA,
June 1910

"Dear Francis, – So far – I will tell you at once to put you out of your misery – the Norfolk farm that Lady Jarvis found me is a success. The house is – well, it suits me. Arrangements work fairly well. It is cool now, which is a blessing, and the garden is the nice old-fashioned kind I like. It is enclosed by a wall. There are rose trees…the old-fashioned kind that smell good…stocks, nasturtiums in great profusion – petunias which are gay, and sweet geranium and Sweet William – fruit trees and vegetables.

"It is, of course, small. The spare room is ready, so you can come when you like, but it is rather a long way to come just for Sunday, and I don't suppose you would be able to stay longer? The house is low, two-storied, faded red brick, covered with honeysuckle – slate roof...two sort of wings...a large dining-room, very low, with a beam across the ceiling... It was the kitchen, and the kitchen fireplace is as it was – a sitting-room next door – a long deal table, where I work.

"One bedroom on the other side of the hall on the ground floor; a large bedroom upstairs and two smaller ones. Giovanni seems happy, and has made friends with the inhabitants... As to inhabitants, no one immediate for me, but in the neighbourhood not many miles off there are, or there is, a man called Cuthbert Lyley, whom I have known a long time...retiring and reserved, and will be no bother – a resource; and then there are some people called Choyce at the manor-house, Hockley.

"I met Mrs Choyce once in London last year at the opera. Do you remember my telling you I had met some-one who had reminded me of *her*? By the way, *her* house is to let again... One could go over it...but I shall not go near it. They say that Adeane will not let anything be touched, and that the house is exactly as she left it. So Cuthbert Lyley told me. I am going to stay with him next Friday for a day or two. The new book is getting on, but it is still only in the stage of a charcoal sketch, and I am doing a great deal of rubbing out. Let me know if the whim seizes you to come, and when, how, etc. – Yrs.,

"L.D."

A fortnight later:

117

"THORNDYKE FARM,

June 1910

"I am just back from Knaystone, where I have been staying with Lyley since last Friday. It's no good thinking of work today, so I shall write my Diary – only I shall write it to you; if it's too long and tedious you needn't read it. I enjoyed my visit. The house is late Victorian and uninteresting, but comfortable, and there is a nice atmosphere about it.

"The inmates were Lyley, his sister Mrs Tracy, who is older than he is and a great deal more human; Mr and Mrs Choyce and Mrs Choyce's mother, Lady Weston, who is the widow of rather a distinguished diplomat, and what people call 'handsome.'

"Choyce is a Member of Parliament and Private Secretary to one of the important politicians... He spent most of his time with Lyley; they are both ornithologists. This left the two older ladies together, and threw me in the company from time to time of Mrs Choyce.

"She *is* like her. I can't tell you how or why. She has not the same colouring. She is a good deal fairer, for one thing. She hasn't got that Southern look...nor those eyebrows...nor the same coloured eyes – but there is something; it is like hearing a tune which reminds you of another and quite different one... Do you remember that phrase in the Schubert C Major Symphony which I told you was like Schumann's song about the nightingale at the window... 'aus meinen Thränen'?... Well, it's like that – but not more... It is in her line – and she has the most beautiful graceful line – and a little in her expression, there is the same sort of feeling of a *tune* about her... Is she pretty? you will ask. Yes, I think she might be, *very*...her figure is entrancing, and she has got wonderful eyes, but she looks tired, and apathetic, and sad, when she is not talking... She has got two children, but they are neither of them here; a boy and baby – only a few months old – a girl...

"It is only when she is not talking that she looks sad. When she talks, her face lights up. I think I know what it is in her that reminds me of *her.* It is the complete naturalness…that way of looking at everybody, everything, and every idea straight in the face, that first-handedness; that habit, gift, or whatever you call it, of taking nothing for granted… I sat next to her at dinner the first night…she was different from what she had been like when I saw her before in London. I had thought her then preoccupied and absent-minded. Here she was quite different… Alive, alert, on the spot, gay. We talked about getting into new houses, my house, what different surroundings meant, possessions, pictures, books, whether one was happier with them or without them. She said she could never read the books she possessed, only other people's, and she supposed she had favourite authors, but she never read them, or hardly ever. I asked her what her favourite book was. She said, 'Do you mean the book I would rather have written, or the book I would take with me to a desert island?'

"I said, 'The book you would most mind the destruction and annihilation of.'

" 'I have hardly read a book for ages,' she said, 'except a novel every now and then from the library, well, not since I was a girl. But the book I think about with most fondness is, I think, a book of fairy tales called *The Necklace of Princess Fiorimonde.*'

"I was startled by that, by her knowing that book…the only place I have ever seen it was in *her* house.

" 'Fancy you knowing that,' she said.

" 'Fancy *you* knowing it,' I repeated.

" 'We had it in our schoolroom…my first schoolroom in Vienna,' she said. 'I haven't read it for years.'

" 'Oh,' she added, 'German fairy-tales are the best of all. They never become soppy.'

" 'You hate soppiness?' I asked.

" 'I don't care about it,' she said. ' It sounds silly, but I prefer what are called "pessimistic" books to optimistic books.'

" 'The Russians?'

" 'I used to read them – I have not read many.'

" 'Used to – but don't you read now?'

" 'Hardly ever… I haven't time.'

" 'But what do you do?'

" 'There is the constituency, letters to write – people to see.'

" 'That's your work. But what is your recreation? You must have a hobby?'

" 'I used to practise the piano, and I'm fond of modelling – silly things in clay. I give in to hobbies as easily as a dram-drinker to drink. There is no hobby I can't understand. I could quite easily collect beetles or do fretsaw work.'

" 'And yet you don't read?'

" 'Reading isn't a hobby.'

" 'And do you like music?'

" 'Very much.'

" 'You go to concerts?'

" 'Local ones, and even perform at them.' She laughed. 'You know the kind. But I play duets with Mr Rowley, the clergyman. He is a musician, and sometimes we play trios; Mr Lyley plays the violoncello beautifully.'

" 'Can't we have some music here?'

" 'Mother doesn't much care for it, nor does Mrs Tracy.'

" 'And your husband?'

" 'He is fond of the opera.'

" 'You aren't?'

" 'I like some operas.'

" 'Wagner?'

" 'No, not much…really only one…but I used to enjoy the opera abroad; and the opera I liked best of all those I ever heard was Gluck's *Orpheus*… I used to hear it at Copenhagen.'

" 'You were there a long time?'

" 'Two or three years; it was Father's last post. He had just been appointed to Vienna when he died.'

" 'Did you like diplomacy?'

" 'Don't give me away to Mother, but I *hated* it…and yet in a way I suppose I ought to be thankful, for owing to it I saw certain things and met certain people I should never have met otherwise.'

" 'Did your father like it?'

" 'He liked it and hated it, and liked it all the same. He had a great sense of humour. He observed all the little things, and it amused him to put down in a diary that the hereditary Duke of Ruritania, when he received him, was not shaved, or that his collar stud was missing. He kept a diary…it is very funny.'

" 'Will it ever be published?'

" 'Not, I suppose, till we are all dead. My mother would certainly not allow it.'

" 'And would you?'

" 'I am afraid I'm *un*moral. I've no conscience. I'm what's called a moral idiot – as well as the other kinds,' she laughed.

"And then the conversation was interrupted, or I had to talk to Mrs Tracy. I find I have been writing now for nearly three-quarters of an hour, and Giovanni says that my dinner is ready, so I must stop; but what I wanted to say is this – you have probably guessed it already – I felt at the end of this first conversation that I had known Mrs Choyce for years. I will write again tomorrow, or perhaps tonight after dinner. I want to get all I have to tell you off my chest before I go on with my work, otherwise I shall not be able to do any work at all."

Later:

"I am going on with my letter now this evening, in the hopes that I may finish what I want to say, and have a clear head to write, to begin my work again, tomorrow.

"Saturday was a lovely day. We sat in the garden in the morning. I talked to Lady Weston. She is an amiable and intelligent woman, who has seen and known thousands of people. She is cultivated and well read, but I don't believe she cares two straws about anything of that kind. I believe she takes the last novel from Mudie's, but she can talk about anything, and she mentioned Meredith and Tolstoi and Gorki. She is energetic, vital, interested in life and people and things. I can see that she thinks her daughter isn't interested *enough*. Her daughter's profound indifference irritates her. I believe it even irritates her that her daughter should do her duty or her duties as well as she does. Everybody, so Mrs Tracy and Lyley told me, is agreed on this point, that Mrs Choyce is an admirable Member's wife – works hard, does all the boring things, entertains, is civil to everyone. Never shirks, sits through the most dreary meetings, attends Committees and jumble sales, and opens bazaars. She is, in fact, very popular; but her mother sees – I think – that she does it all mechanically, as though she were saying, 'What does it matter after all what I do? This is no worse than anything else.' That is what irritates her mother. Mrs Choyce is not happy. Not happily married. That is what annoys her mother, who probably not only would never admit it, but is, I dare say, responsible for the marriage. What makes me think so? I don't know. Choyce is more than just a 'good fellow.' He is attractive, full of life, good-looking, nice manners, nice ways, full of fun, well read, interested; but somehow they don't meet on the same plane; there is something wrong somewhere. He with regard to her behaves like a man who is in perpetual exile, and she with regard to him behaves like someone who had made a mistake. At least this is what I feel. I may be wrong. I think Lyley sees this and understands them both *and* the misunderstanding. Lady Weston doesn't, nor does Mrs Tracy, who is sentimental and romantic and rather crude, in spite of a great dose of shrewdness and worldly wisdom.

"The second day, especially in the evening, Mrs Choyce was looking better. She is changeable… In the afternoon we went for a walk in the woods – Lyley, Choyce, Mrs Choyce, and myself.

"Mrs Tracy took Lady Weston to Ilminster. They wanted to see the antiquity shops. Lyley and Choyce said a few words out of civility to us, and then plunged into bird lore and observation. The number of obscure birds there seem to be in these woods is extraordinary. Had I been alone I would have listened to them with pleasure, for, as you know, technical talk on any subject is agreeable to me; the less I understand it the more I enjoy it – but why don't I care for literary shop? I dislike it more than words can say, although I can talk literature with you and others by the hour. I could with Mrs Choyce, although she pretends or says she has never read a book since she was grown up… Her education must have been odd. She swears to me that as the result of her life abroad, of their continually roving from place to place – she says there were continual changes of governesses and of programmes of work – she swears to me that she never learnt history further than Caractacus, and that she knows practically no English history at all, except Alfred and the cakes…and what she gathered from a few of Walter Scott's novels.

"And you know, every now and then, I'm not sure she is not pulling my leg, because in spite of this fundamental ignorance, as she called it, she spoke of the *Agamemnon* of Æschylus. I pulled her up.

" 'You forget,' she said, 'that we were *en poste* in Athens, and besides my governess I had a Greek master, and I used to gabble modern Greek, and he dinned the Classics into my ears.'

" 'You enjoyed them?'

" 'I like that kind of thing…the absence of sentiment… looking things in the face…accepting. It is all so clean and straight, *business-like*, and there is no nonsense about it.'

" 'Yes, I suppose so,' I said… 'I don't know Greek, and I have only read those things in translations; but I don't get much pleasure from it, I confess… It is all – well, *Greek* to me. Now when I read a modern novel like *Anna Karenina* I feel what people say they feel when they read or see a Greek play, the sense of being moved by an inevitable sense of things going on, heedlessly, inexorably, to some tragic catastrophe…'

" ' Well, I feel…' and she laughed, 'or I used to feel – but after all I was only a schoolgirl – in Greek plays, just what people say they feel when they read *Anna Karenina*.'

" 'You don't like Tolstoi?'

" 'Not much…not his personality nor his characters – I don't even like Anna herself. And although women don't often like women in books, or like them differently than men, I believe most people – men and women – like *Anna Karenina*. I don't.'

" 'What women do you like in books?'

" 'I like the heroine of *Pride and Prejudice* – Elizabeth.'

" 'I believe you have read everything.'

" 'I promise you not,' she said. ' I have read an enormous amount of Tauchnitz' novels, as those used to be easy to get. So it makes a funny mixture. Ouida. A lot of Ouida.' (That again was like *her.)* 'Whyte-Melville – I used to love his books…Jane Austen, Emily Brontë, and a lot of modern people nobody has ever heard of…that is my education, or my mis-education.'

" ' And French books?' I asked.

" 'Oh yes, I used to read French books. Papa used to let me read what I liked. He thought it was a good thing for girls to read French novels. Perhaps that is why I read so few. They were not forbidden. But I discovered one or two I liked. I enjoyed them. They don't bowdlerise. And then I have read books by modern English authors,' she said, looking into the distance, and there was a spark of mischief in her eyes. She was teasing me, but I wouldn't take the bait. I changed the subject, and we talked of travel, of the places she had seen, of the places I had seen…just as the conversation became interesting, Lyley and Choyce met us, and I resigned Mrs Choyce to Lyley, and walked home with Choyce. And so we walked home.

"I found him a pleasant companion. Curiously enough, he talked about foreign travel. He told me he was, or would be, immensely fond of travelling, but never could get away.

" 'Can't you get abroad in the recess?'

" 'I could *now*,' he said, 'but I don't think Fanny would care for it. You see, she has had enough travel to last her a lifetime – and her only wish and pleasure now is to live in England.'

" 'You have been in England for some time?'

" 'Yes, ever since we married.'

" 'He talked of his life, of his work, of politics – foreign politics. He seems to me to have an interesting mind. And *to have had* ambition, but no longer to have it now. I should say he was '*un grand désabusé*'. They tell me he is likely to be a Cabinet Minister some day, but I don't think he much cares, although he makes a pretence of taking these things seriously, and he is genuinely interested in his work in so far as it is an occupation; but it is that and no more, I think. I don't believe he has any real ambition, and I don't believe he will be one of the Ministers who leave a mark or make a stir in Parliamentary history. Perhaps it is just as well for him. He has no illusions about party politics – none whatever. He likes one or two of the politicians personally…respects few. I believe if he had his way, he would be off tomorrow big-game shooting or climbing Mount Everest, or looking for wild flowers in Tibet. I think he is still under the shock of some past mental, moral, or sentimental experience – I don't know what – and I am certain that his marriage is based on or marred by some fundamental misunderstanding. Poor chap! And poor Mrs Choyce! How oddly these things are arranged! I have been writing now for nearly an hour, and I have only reached Saturday afternoon. I am really too sleepy to go on any further. I am going to bed and I will go on with my letter tomorrow. Shall I? That is the question. Not if the story flows well; in that case you will have to wait...till the next week, or the next check – till the next time I run dry. Goodnight."

The next morning:

"I got up early – very early. I woke up at five o'clock and couldn't go to sleep again. It's a lovely day; everything was ready, favourable, and propitious for writing. I sat down at my table, having planned, mind you, more or less vaguely what was to come in my mind, and lo and behold! the words, ideas, wouldn't come! Not the first time? Yes, I know... Writing, I have always told you, is planchette, only before you can get the planchette to work mechanically, some sharp-pointed instrument must wound and stab you – that is to say, some experience or impression...when the wound is healed, the writing begins.

"That is, I suppose, what Wordsworth meant by saying that poetry was emotion remembered in tranquillity. Well, I thought I had at least reached that stage. I thought the planchette was working famously. So it was, till this morning. I was pleased with the story and I didn't think I had come to a check; but this morning nothing will happen. I have been sitting for an hour and a half in front of a blank piece of paper, biting my pen. So I have given it up as a bad job... It is no good forcing oneself. I will try again this evening. In the meantime I will write to you. But I had so many things to say last night, and now I have forgotten most of them, the thread has gone. Sunday was a delightful day, more beautiful and hotter than ever, and we spent it lazily, no one went to church except Mrs Tracy.

"The Choyces felt they need not go. I expect they get all the church they want at home. We sat in the garden most of the time, played croquet a little; some people came to tea, the people who have got *her* house – a City man with an absurd *red*-stocking wife; they are leaving it for good at the end of the month.

"But I talked to both of them as much as I could. They asked me to go over. I don't think I could face it, but I accepted...

"You know Mrs Choyce *is* like her; she has the same way of looking at you straight in the face... I know what the real likeness is: it is that – that in both of them *everything is motionless except the eyes*...apart from that dancing light, *a great stillness.* – Yrs., L. D."

CHAPTER XI

The London season was over. The recess had begun. Michael, in the middle of August, went to Canada with some fellow-Members of Parliament to attend an agricultural conference. He was to be away until the end of September. Fanny stayed at Hockley. Later they were perhaps going to Italy.

Fanny's little boy, Peter, was just over two years old and her baby girl, Hester, just six months. The children had made a difference to her life. The little boy was a strong, dark-eyed imp, always getting into mischief, with a grave face. He seldom laughed. He sometimes smiled. His nurse said he was an old-fashioned child and he picked up odd words.

Fanny had a series of visitors in the house: her mother; Margaret Branksome, who had married Dick Clive of the Foreign Office; and Cuthbert Lyley and Mrs Tracy. Fanny seemed, so her mother thought, to have improved in health and spirits during the last two months. She had not been to London at all during the summer, as she had not been well after the baby was born, and the doctor had recommended her not to face the fatigue of the London season. Michael agreed.

Leo Dettrick, whom she had met at the Lyley's, often bicycled over to see her. He had, so he said, begun a new book, but his work was progressing slowly, and he was discontented with it. He had not published anything for three years.

He made a habit of bicycling over in the evenings. There was a large reference library at Hockley and a great many maps. Dettrick made this the excuse. He would come over to consult the map, and stay for tea or for dinner as the case might be. His farmhouse was only five miles from Hockley.

Fanny became used to his visits and looked forward to them, but she hardly gave them a thought. She looked upon Dettrick as a busy man and as an artist who was engrossed in his work. She did not treat him as a human being. Nor did she connect him with his books, which seemed to her different from him, as if they had been written by someone else. It was not that he did not speak about them. He did. He told Fanny about the new book he was writing, and discussed the plot with her and asked her advice. "He asks," thought Fanny, "but he does not listen. Perhaps it helps him to make up his own mind. If I gave advice he would not take it." It amused her. She liked him. His society exhilarated her – and yet he was a strange, uncouth person who expressed himself in conversation with difficulty, not only because of the slight burr in his speech. At times he seemed to have difficulty in pumping the words up from some deep cistern. At other times they would come pouring out helter-skelter, the end of the sentence before the beginning. He thought quicker than he spoke, and his sentences often began at the end, as the words of an amateur typist are often spelt backwards because the writer thinks faster than he can type, or types slower than he can think. He was argumentative, and as soon as she began to know him she found they disagreed on most subjects. Fanny enjoyed teasing him and stirring up his spirit of contradiction and kindling his disagreement.

One Saturday towards the end of August she asked him to stay from Friday till Monday. He accepted with alacrity. Her mother was there, and Cuthbert Lyley, without Mrs Tracy, who was staying with some friends. Seyton had been evacuated by the Carrington-Smiths. They had often asked Dettrick to go over and see them, but he had always made an excuse as he meant not to go.

But this was not to be. They were sitting in the veranda after luncheon on the Saturday afternoon. It was a hot August afternoon, full of the noise of an over-ripe summer, at the time when you think warm days will never cease. The garden borders, planted this year by Fanny herself, without the advice or rather in spite of the advice of Mrs Tracy, were a blaze of colour – salvias, dahlias, bergamot, phlox, gladioli, aconite, love-in-a-mist.

"What shall we do this afternoon?" asked Lady Weston. She was one of those people who are not happy unless they are doing something. Dettrick would have been happy to stay in the garden.

"Shall we go to Seyton? You never have seen Seyton," she said to Dettrick. Dettrick made no answer as Lady Weston had made an affirmation and not put a question. "Mr Dettrick ought to see it, oughtn't he? And now they're gone (meaning the Carrington-Smiths) it will be so much easier."

Fanny felt that Dettrick was perturbed by this proposal. She saw that he hesitated; she did not know the reason. Lady Weston did not notice his hesitation.

"Don't you think that would be a good plan, Fanny? Could we have the motor? If we started about three we could be back for tea."

"Would you like to go?" Fanny said to Dettrick. She felt sure, not exactly that he did not want to go, but that there was something, not an obstacle, but some reason that was making him hesitate.

"Yes, of course, I should be delighted to do anything you like."

"Very well," said Lady Weston; "let us settle on that."

Coffee was brought at that moment and Fanny made the necessary arrangements.

"It's not far," said Fanny.

"I ought really to do some writing," Dettrick said.

"On this lovely afternoon?" said Lady Weston.

"You must see the garden there! It's lovely!"

At three o'clock they started. They were welcomed by the housekeeper, Mrs Holloway, with deference. She looked at Dettrick kindly, but he did nothing to show or express recognition. As they were on the threshold of the door, Dettrick said – and there was a note of hoarseness in his voice:

"You have both of you seen this house a thousand times before. The housekeeper will take me round, and I will meet you in the garden."

Fanny felt that this was final, that for some reason he wished to go over the house by himself, without them, so she said to her mother, "Yes, I don't think I do want to see the rooms today. They are probably all covered up and stuffy, and the garden is so lovely. Come on, Mother."

Lady Weston was taken reluctantly, but forcibly, to the garden.

"I should rather like to have seen the bedrooms," said Lady Weston. "I have never seen them."

"Not today, Mother, darling. It's too hot and stuffy indoors."

"But isn't it rather rude of us to leave Mr Dettrick all alone?"

"Oh no. He wants to be alone. He wants to describe a room in his new book," Fanny improvised, "and I am sure he hopes this will give him an idea. If we go with him we shall only bother him."

"Very well, dear, I suppose you know best," Lady Weston said plaintively. She thought that it was absurd to think one could ever do what one liked if one's daughter were there.

They strolled down to the garden, and to the kitchen garden.

"How will he find his way?" Lady Weston asked.

"The housekeeper will show him the way."

"But he hasn't been here before?"

"Not that I know of. He is fond of old houses, and he makes a point of describing them accurately – you can tell that from his books, can't you?"

"Yes, certainly." Lady Weston had never read one of his books through, but she didn't find it necessary to commit herself one way or the other. She disliked Dettrick's form of literature. She knew it was "good" and disliked it all the more. It bored her.

Dettrick was away a long time. He met Lady Weston and Fanny in the kitchen garden.

"I'm so sorry to have been away such a long time," said Dettrick. "The housekeeper and I found that we had acquaintances in common, and that made her rather garrulous."

"She seemed to take to you," Lady Weston said. "She didn't like us at all. She looked at us severely. That is probably because she knows that we are friends of the Carrington-Smiths."

Fanny hoped that her mother would now stop talking about the house. She could not have explained why, but she felt that Dettrick was suffering.

"What an amusing, quaint, old sundial that is," she said, going up to it. "I wonder what the inscription means?"

"It's the usual inscription," said Lady Weston, "about only telling the sunny hours, which I always think rather silly. Let's sit down on the seat. It is really too hot to walk about any more."

"Oughtn't we to be going home?" said Fanny.

"There's no violent hurry, just let us sit and enjoy ourselves a moment. I am fond of this garden, and this house. I think it has a great charm. If I hadn't the house in Devonshire I should like to take it and be near you. It would just do, not too big and not too small. Of course it would be a bore not to be able to touch anything, but I can't help feeling that that rule was made especially for Mrs Carrington-Smith. I could imagine her making dreadful havoc in a house like this, but I don't believe for one moment that the owner would mind my slightly rearranging the things."

"Do you know the owner?" asked Dettrick.

"No; I have never met him nor her. You see we were so much abroad. I heard of her…she – "

"Oh, look!" said Fanny.

"What?" said her mother.

"It's a very odd thing; I thought I saw a white cat on the wall opposite, but I see now it isn't…it was the light."

"I never met Mr Adeane nor Mrs Adeane," Lady Weston went on, taking no notice of her daughter's fancies, "but my husband, I think, knew her, and I think I recollect his telling me that she…"

"Oh!" said Fanny, with a note of despair in her voice.

"What is the matter, Fanny?" asked Lady Weston impatiently.

"I quite forgot that I asked Mrs Saxby to come to tea this afternoon, and it's already past half-past four. We shan't get back in time unless we start at once."

"You really are too forgetful, Fanny dear," Lady Weston said peevishly. She disliked being interrupted when she was about to launch upon a comfortable sea of reminiscence. She enjoyed telling reminiscences of her husband and his friends more than anything in the world to an appreciative listener. But she got up, nevertheless. They walked back, not through, but round the house, to the front door, and Lady Weston gave the housekeeper five shillings.

"The house is still to let?" she asked as they were getting into the motor.

"Yes, my lady," the housekeeper said, and volunteered no further information.

"Mr Adeane won't come back this summer?"

"He's abroad, my lady."

"Oh, Mother, please let us start, I am so late," said Fanny. And they drove home. Dettrick sat in front next to the chauffeur. When they got home, Fanny said to her butler:

"Has Mrs Saxby arrived?"

She had not arrived.

"We will have tea in the veranda, and I am expecting Mrs Saxby." But Mrs Saxby had evidently forgotten the appointment, as she did not visit Hockley that afternoon.

Directly after tea, Dettrick went up to his room. He had some letters to write. This is what he wrote to his friend, Francis Greene:

"HOCKLEY, *August* 1910.

"DEAR F., – I went to Seyton this afternoon. Lady Weston proposed to go after luncheon. I couldn't very well say *no*, and although I hated and feared the ordeal, and thought it would be positive torture, yet in a way I wanted to go. But I was determined at all costs I would not go over the house with them –

"I have been interrupted, and begin again.

"We drove over in a motor. It's only about ten miles off. It is to let and nobody has taken it yet. The Carrington-Smiths who had it went away at the end of July or before. A. is still abroad. Mrs Holloway met us. She recognised me, but made no sign of having done so till we were alone. I proposed that, as Lady Weston and Mrs Choyce had seen it so often, I should go over the house by myself, and meet them in the garden; and Mrs Choyce seemed to catch on to this, and she dragged her mother, who is never really tired of sight-seeing, and, I think, wanted to see something she had not seen before, to the garden. Mrs Holloway took me to the drawing-room. The chairs have got brown holland covers over them, but otherwise it is exactly as it used to be. The drawing-table was there, with the glass of water on the green tiles, and that china pallet with a little piece of green oxide of chromium (transparent) on it, the green she could never get matched, do you remember?

"The harp is there, and the harpsichord, and I asked Mrs Holloway if the harpsichord was ever tuned, and she said – 'Yes, regularly, by a man who comes down specially from London.' I looked at the bookshelf. They were all there: the fairy tales: *Monsieur le Vent et Madame la Pluie*, etc., the little Tauchnitz Ouida bound in blue, the book bound in vellum in which she meant to write extracts. There was only one extract in it. Do you remember what that was? She copied it from a picture, not from a book. From a picture that she picked up in Perugia that last time they went to Italy. She showed it me when she came back – and then I never saw it again. It was worked in silk and represents the sea. There are some cliffs on the left-hand side, worked in silver, with a little white church and a steeple on them. There are two boats on the sea, a cloud and a triangular sun in the sky, and a large cross floats on the waves, and on it a flaming heart with a scroll worked in blue silk and gold thread, and on this scroll is written, *'Velut mare contritio mea.'* She copied that out in her book. That, and nothing else. There was nothing more to say. I don't know where it is now. We went upstairs. First to a small square room with beautiful panelling and a high white carved chimney-piece. That, Mrs Holloway said, was his room. The next door had been her bedroom. Everything has been left. The walls had no panelling, just an old-fashioned Victorian wallpaper. On the inside the bed, a small four-poster, Chippendale, there was a crucifix, and over the chimney-piece a picture of Harry when he was two years old. There are no other pictures. Next to her bed, on the right, just over the *prie-Dieu*, there was a small ivory statue with *'Stella Maris'* engraved under it. Mrs Holloway opened the shutters. On the dressing-table there were a bottle of rose water in an old-fashioned black bottle and a bottle of lavender water with an enamel label on it.

"The windows look out south on to the lawn. We opened one of them, and the sun and the noise of summer poured into the room. I missed the noise of the mowing machine which I associated with the house, but it was Saturday afternoon.

"I asked Mrs Holloway no questions, except about the house, and she said nothing. She went to fetch something while I was looking at the bedroom. She asked me if I would like to see the guests' rooms. I said yes. We went into what was called the Blue Room. It was beautifully arranged. A four-poster bedstead and blue-grey silk curtains, the walls panelled and painted a faint faded yellow which was once perhaps canary colour. Then we went to the Oak Room, which had no oak in it at all that I could see – but a Morris wallpaper with a dark background with flowers, and dark blue curtains. All the rooms were carefully arranged, and there were writing paper and quill pens on every writing-table. A guest might have gone into one of the rooms at any moment and found everything ready. There was another guest room called the Priest's Room which was panelled, and that was all I saw. I went downstairs then, and looked in at the dining-room, which was just as it used to be, with the glass on the sideboard, and the little room near the hall. Then I went to the library. That, too, is the same, and there is the smell of his tobacco in it. We passed the room that's locked up. A. keeps that locked. 'That's the sitting-room?' I said. 'Yes,' said Mrs Holloway; 'and the bedroom next door is locked as well. It was used directly Mrs Adeane was taken ill, being more convenient for the nurse, who slept in next door in the sitting-room. It is there that Mrs Adeane died. I could not open it for anyone, but everything has been left as it was. Those are her books by her bedside – her travelling clock, watch, rosary, and her Missal. Everything in the sitting-room has been left, down to the letter on the writing-table which she had begun when she was taken ill, and had not had time to finish. Not a thing has been moved. Even the flowers were left to fade in the bowls.'

"I asked whether A. ever came here now. She said he had only been once in the last two years, and that he had not come into the house. He had talked to Mrs Holloway out of doors. He lived more and more abroad, and she felt sure he would never come back. He had still got his little house in London. The house had been let twice; once before the Carrington-Smiths had taken it, but it was too far from London for a City gentleman.

"We were back again in the drawing-room, and it was difficult to believe that she would not suddenly walk in, and yet I felt as if she were farther away than the farthest star. People talk of feeling the presence of those who are dead. I don't know what they mean. I felt everything about her and of her and by her and from her and to her was here, except herself. That was gone – and oh! so far! It seemed impossible that it could be the same place, or I the same person, when one remembers... I remember coming here once when I expected to find her, and she was not here. There was only A. and the children. She had had to go to London suddenly, and I remember the strange deadness and desolation about the place, and I remember wondering then what one would feel if one knew that she was away for good – could never come back; and I felt sick at the thought – dizzy – so much so that even A. noticed it, and thought I was ill, and suggested a whisky and soda, and I had to pretend that I had rheumatic pains...and now you know it was different. I felt as if the whole place had ceased to exist, and as if I were dead with it, a ghost walking about in a land of ghosts, or in a dream-world, and as if Lady Weston and Mrs Choyce were unreal, like people in a dream.

"And then Mrs Holloway brought me back to reality by saying, 'There is one more room you might like to see.'

" 'What's that?' I asked.

" 'The Chapel,' she said. ' The room that was used as a chapel. It was left just as it used to be, by Mr Adeane's orders.'

"We went down the passage where Harry and Jack used to romp in the mornings, past the housekeeper's room, to that room at the end of the corridor which you remember. We walked in. It was just the same, except the little lamp was not lit. There were flowers round the two statues – roses and tiger lilies.

" 'Mr Adeane left orders that there were always to be fresh flowers in the vases,' Mrs Holloway said, in a whisper; 'but I should have put them there in any case.'

" 'Yes, of course,' I said. ' I suppose there are no services here now?'

" 'Oh yes, sir,' said Mrs Holloway, 'on Sundays, that is to say. Mr Adeane left strict orders, and made all arrangements that all was to go on just as usual. Father Jackson bicycles over every Sunday from Ilminster, just as in old days, even when the last tenants, and those before, were here.'

" 'But who comes?'

" 'Oh, sir, just the same as before, a few from the village and the neighbourhood. There's always enough, and Miss Elstree from The Towers plays the harmonium.'

"Curiously enough, this was the only room in the house that did not feel empty. Here I could imagine that she might really walk in and kneel down, as I so often saw her do, at that little rail, or sit in that chair and open one of those books, or tell her beads. The chapel was the work of her hands, and nothing about it was changed.

"I think it is wonderful of A. to have had all that carried on, considering he disliked it. I wondered if the children ever came here, but I did not like to ask. On her chair there was a book and a small pocket-handkerchief. I looked at it, and Mrs Holloway saw me looking at it, and said, 'Yes, sir, everything was left exactly as it was that morning.' We left the chapel, walked back down the corridor, and I looked for one moment into the schoolroom. That was the same, and it seemed the emptiest room of all. The schoolroom books were there in the shelves – *Noël et Chapsal*, the Grammar, Smith's Latin Primer, *les Fables de la Fontaine*, a few religious books, the *Child's Catechism*, and *Stories from Homer*.

"I felt in this room that the anguish was almost intolerable, so much did one need to hear a laugh. That room was always full of laughter.

" 'Where are Master Harry and Master Jack spending their holidays?' I asked.

" 'With their aunt, Mrs Ralston, in Hampshire,' she said, and made no comment.

"I remember seeing Mrs Ralston once. She was A.'s sister, a forbidding widow, with a large family and decided theories. It made my heart ache for Harry and Jack.

" 'But they are happy at school, aren't they?' I asked.

" 'Happier at school than in the holidays, poor lambs,' said Mrs Holloway. The dressing-bell is ringing – I must stop – I will try and go on tomorrow – "

The letter was never finished.

CHAPTER XII

Leo Dettrick had only taken his farmhouse till the end of September. The day before Michael was expected back from Canada, and he himself was leaving his cottage, he bicycled over to say goodbye to Fanny. He found her in the garden, which was full of Michaelmas daisies and chrysanthemums, picking the heads from the dead pansies which grew among the rose-beds in front of the house. She was by herself. The children had gone out with their nurse.

Lady Weston had left her some days ago.

"I've come to say goodbye," he said. "This is my last day."

Fanny went on weeding abstractedly.

"You are being turned out?"

"Yes, the owner of the farm comes back tomorrow. It is a 'she' and not a 'he' – a Miss Frip. She has been spending the summer abroad in Switzerland."

"Will you take the house next year if she lets it?"

"Most decidedly. It suits me exactly. It is just the right size, and quiet. One ought to be able to work there."

"Didn't you?"

"I haven't done much this summer, less than I expected to; but still I've made a beginning. I'm not sure the book isn't wrong and that I shan't have to start all again."

"I shouldn't do that. What you told me of it sounded excellent."

There was a pause.

"And what are your plans?" he asked.

"I can't tell till Michael comes back. He will be here tomorrow. Before he left he wanted to take me abroad. He talked of going to Florence for October, or perhaps Venice first, and then Florence. But I'm not sure that I shall go."

"You don't like going abroad? You've had too much of it?"

"It's not that. I don't think he wants to go. I think he is doing it for me. He thinks I have been lonely all this time."

"I hope you will go, for if you do we may meet. I am going to be in Italy for October and November."

"Really? – at Florence?"

"Florence, and then Rome."

"And after that?"

"I shall go back to London. I suppose you will too?"

"I suppose so…for a time. We shall be here at Christmas. You must come and stay with us."

"I should like to, very much. Will there be many people?"

"No; just ourselves, and my mother, and Michael asks someone as a rule. You see the house doesn't hold many."

"I hope I shall be able to get the farmhouse next year. This is the country I like best, and it's not too near London."

"Does Miss Frip let it every year?"

"I'm afraid not. She let it one year in the winter, but that's no good to me."

"Thorndyke is not the only house near here that you could get. There are others. There's Seyton, for instance; but I suppose that would be too big?"

"Much too big, and apart from that I could never live there."

Fanny said nothing.

"I used to know the Adeanes. I don't know why I have never told you this before, especially after that day we went there with your mother. It was silly, but I couldn't. It was *silly.*"

"I understand. I felt you had been there before."

"I used to know them very well. I used to go to Seyton, and I saw them in London often."

"Mr Adeane was in the City, wasn't he?"

"Yes, and he had interests in Buenos Aires. That is where he met her."

"She wasn't foreign?"

"No, English, but her mother was Spanish. *Spanish*, not South American. She was born in the Argentine. It was a curious story. Adeane went out there on business, and he met her when she was a young girl, and he fell in love with her at first sight. You know what he was like. A man of business, but a good sort; honest, matter-of-fact, business-like – but kind. He thought of nothing but his business. I think she was eighteen when he met her. Her mother was dead, but her father was alive; there was some opposition to her marriage. Religious differences too. She was a Roman Catholic and he was not. He *said* he didn't mind. The children had to be Catholics. That he accepted too (although I think he minded *that)* and her relations minded. They asked her to wait. She wouldn't wait. She was determined to marry Adeane. Her father and her relations forbade the marriage for a year. Then she pined away and fell ill. She was delicate to begin with; they were frightened and gave in – and so they were married. They went to England. Adeane was well off. They saw Seyton by chance one day; she set her heart on it, and he bought it for her. They lived there and in London. This climate, especially the climate of this county, was too cold for her. Adeane knew it and tried to make her live abroad, but she refused to live abroad, although they went to Italy and later to Spain. They had two children – two boys; they are both at school now at Birmingham. She fell seriously ill quite suddenly when she was twenty-five years old. You see they had been married seven years. She was always delicate, always ill. They lived at Bournemouth for a time, and spent the last winter or a part of it abroad, before she died, in Madeira;

but she didn't like living abroad, although she had been brought up in the Tropics."

"I suppose he was devoted to her?"

"Oh, quite. He never got over her death. He has never been to Seyton since, and he spends the whole winter abroad now in Madeira."

"Aren't the children any comfort to him?"

"I don't think they are. He doesn't understand children, still less boys. He is shy of them. His sister looks after them. She is a nice woman, but – I believe they are happy at school."

"Poor things! Did you know them first abroad?"

"No, I met them in London at Lady Jarvis', and they were friends too of a friend of mine, my greatest friend – I have talked to you about him – Francis Greene, the doctor. He met them abroad somewhere."

"And did he know them well?"

"Yes, he was a friend both of his and of hers. Nothing romantic or sentimental, I don't mean. He is not that kind of man. I mean he is a man for whom romance and love do not exist. He might marry for practical reasons."

"A Sherlock Holmes?"

"Yes, a Sherlock Holmes. But a fine character."

"So was Sherlock Holmes."

"Yes, but Francis has wonderful insight and an extraordinary intuition."

"So had Sherlock Holmes."

"Yes; but he is different. He is just as energetic, but he has no craving for excitement."

"He doesn't have to take cocaine?"

"No, he doesn't have to take cocaine."

"Did she like him?"

"She only cared for her husband and her children; and if you knew how unlike she and Adeane were, you would be surprised."

"I don't know what he was like, but I once saw a picture of her."

"By Henriquez, at Walter Bell's exhibition?"

"Yes. Was it like her?"

"Yes, in a way and not at all. People say 'So-and-so is not paintable.' It is true. I suppose in a way nobody *is* paintable. At least not those people who depend on their beauty *for the fourth dimension.* Time or tune or whatever it is…she was like that. Her features were nothing extraordinary. They were irregular. But it was the other thing, the thing you can't even define. Expression, I suppose, or rhythm – or fascination. She was like a summer's day, like the scent of verbena or syringa. She had soft, speaking, unforgettable eyes, and a shimmer about her – a softness – that no picture could give…and lovely hands. And she was like a piece of music – what is called suspended, I think – I mean something that is asking for an answer, or one of those Spanish or Russian tunes that never seem to end…that end on a question…is it called on the dominant? Anyhow, on something which makes another beginning imperative, something which leaves you always unsatisfied."

"Did the painter Henriquez know her well?"

"Not very, but he was madly in love with her. He died of it."

"Did she love him?"

"No, and he knew it."

"She never repented her early marriage?"

"I don't think so, never."

"I call that *wonderful…*wonderful to know one's mind at that age, so young."

"If she had repented, she would never have shown it. Nobody would ever have known."

"How curious, with all her upbringing, she should have liked England."

"Yes; she never wanted to go back to South America. She did not mind going abroad to France or Italy, but she would not hear of going to the Argentine. She used to say it would be bad for the children."

"But what about her relations? Did she never see them again?"

"Never. At least not there. Her father came over to see her in London twice, and then he died. Her other relations – uncles and aunts – didn't count; they gave her up as a bad job when she married. She was fond of her father."

"Was she religious? – I don't mean bigoted, but strict?"

"Not bigoted. But very... I don't know what you call it. I think she cared. She never talked about it, at least not to me. She knew that I – "

"I suppose she thought it all meant nothing to you."

"That's it... 'invincible ignorance.' "

"And didn't she mind?"

"I don't know...oddly enough, in my case I think not. I think she minded Francis Greene's unbelief, because his was based on Science, and more violent – it was dogmatic. I think she thought mine simply silly – founded on nothing. She knew I couldn't help it – that I would give worlds to share her Faith."

"Did she talk about it?"

"Never. She wasn't, you see, a person who talked much. She was shy – till you knew her well."

"And then?"

"Then she did talk... It was not that she said much, but she said just enough to make you understand everything."

"Do you think she was happy?"

"No, but then who is happy in this world?"

"But if she loved her husband as you said she did, why wasn't she happy?"

"She loved him...certainly. She never stopped loving him. But I think she probably expected a great deal when she was young, and then found out suddenly that everything was going to be different. I expect that when she was a girl, when she married, she built all sorts of castles in the air – lovely castles…and then probably I expect they came crashing down to the ground. It wasn't Adeane's fault…it was just life. She thought life was going to be different – we all think that, don't we? And then I expect that on the ruins of that beautiful fairy castle she built herself a small wooden refuge in which it was possible to live and be more or less comfortable, but I am not sure that the effort of building it and pretending it was a success didn't kill her."

"Yes, I see. Did Mr Adeane always think she was happy, and was he nice to her?"

"He behaved beautifully to her always, but I am not sure he thought she was happy. I don't know what he thought. We shall never know. Nobody will ever know. He wasn't a 'strong silent man,' but he was one of those inarticulate people; it is impossible to guess what they are thinking about."

"Did she like being at Seyton?"

"Yes; better than anywhere else. It was as if she had lived in another life in that place and belonged to its period. I mean any period between the seventeenth century and Waterloo. She was like a foreigner – not a person from a foreign country, but from a foreign *time*. She spoke another mental language and thought different thoughts than the people around her. She used to play the harp and the harpsichord and sing a little. She had not much voice, but it was wonderfully delicious to hear her. She sang French and Spanish. I used to like watching her in the chapel."

"Is there a chapel at Seyton?"

"Yes; on the ground floor, built out onto the garden at the end of the corridor, only one storey – nothing above it. Didn't you see it?"

"No; we were not shown that."

"I used to like watching her in the evening kneeling alone in the chapel in front of one of those images, quite straight…you know, with her arms outstretched as still as a statue and a veil of black Spanish lace on her head. It was a wonderful sight, and

I told Henriquez that he ought to have painted her like that, but he said he couldn't."

"You saw her often?"

"Yes, constantly…nearly every day, but hardly ever alone; there were always people there, and yet I knew her better than anyone I have ever known or ever shall know. I don't mind telling you that I loved her and I lived for her, and for her *only*, and thought of nothing else, and think of nothing else now, and that ever since she died I haven't lived at all. You see, I haven't been able to write a book since then. I am trying to write one now, but you know how little I have done. So far – you see how difficult it is for me. I have tried travelling. I have tried everything, but I can't forget. I'm made like that. She was my life, my whole life. It was enough to see her, to know she was alive and breathing. Her sheer existence proved to me the existence of God. I knew she didn't love me and could never love me – I don't think she was happy, but it wasn't that, it wasn't any reason of that kind. It was something much bigger and much deeper, something profound, that you could not express – that she did not express…and then there were whole regions in her that I had no idea of."

" 'Silver lights and darks undreamed of.' "

"Yes. Her religion, for instance – all that meant and means nothing to me, was and is to me unintelligible. She might just as well have believed in Olympus. She knew that. I told her I didn't understand how she could have married Adeane. I didn't understand how she could be friends with Francis Greene, although he was, and is, my best friend. I mean I didn't understand it being that – and nothing more. If they were friends I would have thought she cared for him altogether, and she didn't. He is very good-looking and attractive. It was just like that; she was a puzzle. There was no one like her – but oddly enough you are like her in an odd way – you remind me of her although you are not in the least alike."

147

"It's funny you saying that; someone else, a friend of ours, Colonel Branksome, once said the same thing. He said I was like Mrs Adeane. But you think she cared for no one except her husband – not for the Spanish artist and not for Mr Greene – I mean Dr Greene?"

"No; she never gave them a thought. She liked them as friends. She was Southern in that. She liked a little court of friends round her all day, smoking cigarettes, and for an endless conversation to be going on all the time and every evening if possible – Robert Adeane didn't; it bored him. Francis rather liked it. I hated it; it got on my nerves. You see, there used to be other people. There were always people wherever she was; she changed even East Anglia into a Spanish, South American *patio*. She attracted everybody. If it was here, it would be the priest, the doctor, the clergyman, the squire – your husband's old uncle loved her. The women used to say she was a dangerous woman, but even when they got to know her, they were charmed. She charmed everyone by doing nothing – she spoke so little. She just moved and smiled and looked at you, appealed to you in a way – and everybody found it irresistible."

"And what used she to do in London?"

"Oh, just the same thing. She used to be at home after dinner in the evening and sit in front of a tea-urn giving people tea and cigarettes. She always went to bed late. Three or four people would be there every evening."

"You and Dr Greene?"

"Yes, and others – Henriquez – all sorts of people."

"Was she fond of things? I mean, had she got hobbies – was she fond of reading? You say she was musical?"

"She read very little, I think. She was fond of one or two books, and liked picture-books and certain poetry, especially foreign poetry. She read Spanish and French, of course, and then she used to paint water-colours, all sorts of things, little tiny Watteau-like scenes, as on china, or just ordinary views.

She had a delicate touch. You could tell at once whether she was playing the harp or the harpsichord, or the piano; it was the same when she painted or planted flowers. I can't describe her. You will think I am talking foolishly, and that I am exaggerating. I am a writer and an artist and a man of imagination, and it is my *métier* to *imagine*, and to see *what is not*. But Adeane, the business man, felt it too, and married her because of it. And Greene, who is a fanatical scientist, a man with one idea, who thinks of nothing but his work, who has no distractions and no recreations, no hobbies and no sentiment, whose only relaxation and recreation is to work out of hours and to *talk shop*, he *felt* exactly the same thing, and always said so, and says so *still*. So it is not only *my* imagination."

"Poor man, he must miss her too."

"Yes, he did at first, but of course he has his work, and, as I say, there is nothing romantic or sentimental in his nature. *He is a realist through and through.*"

"People like that are, I think, often sentimental at heart."

"I agree, but Greene isn't. He is a man with one idea. I have never seen anyone else in the world like him. One hears of people who are single-minded. I have never seen them. He *is* single-minded."

"What exactly do you mean by single-minded?"

"Well, I mean people who are devoted to some thing, to some cause or to some idea, outside of themselves, to that and nothing else."

"Like an artist?"

"Oh dear no! Artists are the most ruthless egotists in the world. They only think of the thing they are doing for themselves, and in relation to themselves. They may be passionately devoted to it – to their work – and if they are artists, they *are* devoted to it. But woe betide the poor human people who come in their way! They use them like so much cannon fodder; so many meat bones to make stock with!"

149

"Is that true?"

"Of course it is. Look at Goethe. Have you read his life?"

"Yes, I have."

"Well, look at all those poor people – Lili, Lotte, Frau von Stein, whatever their names are. Why, he used human beings for copy for his poems till he was eighty. He was right. We are the gainers, but they, poor people, were sacrificed, and all other great artists did the same – Shelley, Victor Hugo; and, I dare say, if you knew the truth, Shakespeare and Homer. We haven't got Shakespeare's autobiography, but we have got his sonnets, which are more intimate than any autobiography. I read a thing in a poem the other day which said:

> 'Even to one I dare not tell
> Where lies my Heaven, where lies my Hell,
> But to the world I can confide
> What's hid from all the world beside.'

That is the motto, the creed, the confession, the *sine qua non* of *all* real artists. That is the secret of art. That, I think, was Shakespeare's case, Homer's, if we only knew, any artist's case, what all artists do – every one of them – unconsciously no doubt. But Francis Greene is not an artist, and he would never dream of doing such a thing. He would think it *abominable*. Not that he doesn't take as much interest in his work as we artists do in ours. He does. He takes more interest in it, because we don't – or I don't, at any rate – like talking of our work out of hours, but he is never happy unless he is talking of his work, in season and out of season, every day and all day to everyone or anyone. But he would never dream of making copy out of anyone or anything that had touched him personally. He is like a priest in these ways."

"But no more would you, would you?"

"Oh yes, I would – unconsciously, perhaps, but I would do it."

"Do you mean to say that you would use things that you had seen, which had affected you personally, for your books as copy?"

"Well, it depends what you mean by 'copy.' I don't mean copy in the same way as news. I don't mean that I would say, 'That's a good thing; I will put it in my next book,' making a note of it for the purpose. But I do mean that everything I see and do, every emotion I feel, every impression I receive, every relation I have to anyone else, every experience I go through, every pain I suffer, every joy I share in, every enthusiasm that catches me, every affection, every passion which falls to my lot, are ultimately destined to be transmuted and made use of, directly or indirectly; they are turned into something else. All the experiences of any artist – however sordid, however sublime, however holy, however passionate or intimate – go through, you can call it the crucible, or the furnace, if you like, as in Huntley & Palmer's biscuit factory, and ultimately come out at the other end as diamonds (or as biscuits) – works of art good or bad, as good as Shakespeare, or as bad as – well, as any of mine, if you like. But that is the process; so it is, and so it has always been, and so it will always be. The moral is, don't love an artist; and the moral is the same for a man or a woman. I mean it is just as fatal for a man to love a female artist as it is for a woman to love a male artist."

"But do you mean to tell me that you looked on Mrs Adeane, for instance, as so much copy, and that one day, under some guise or other, she will appear in a book?"

"No, I don't mean that. But I can tell you this, that although in my books there never has been, and never will be, any direct or indirect allusion to anyone or anything that might possibly be construed into being Daphne Adeane, I have never written since I knew her, and I never shall write till I die, a single sentence that is not impregnated with her, just as a wine-skin is impregnated by having held wine, or a muslin bag by having been filled with lavender. The flavour, the scent, is there for ever – 'You may shatter and break the vase as you will' – you know the rhyme."

"Do you think these things – that feeling, I mean – lasts for ever?" asked Fanny.

"Not often; but when it does, it is really for ever – there is no end till death – and perhaps beyond."

At that moment the butler announced Mrs Saxby. She had arrived for a long and comfortable visit; she had a great many things to say, to settle, and to arrange. Dettrick saw that it would be difficult to outstay her, so he said goodbye. The next day he left for London.

CHAPTER XIII

When Michael came back from Canada he gradually realised that there was a change in his home.

Dettrick had gone to Italy. He was to be away some time. The change that Michael noticed was in Fanny. She was the same person, and yet different. She seemed to have come to life, not that it made things easier for him. He did not feel nearer to her than before, but he looked on at her from the outside, and wondered.

The journey to Italy was abandoned. There was too much to do at home. Fanny seemed relieved. She said she had no wish to go to Italy.

She heard about Italy from Leo Dettrick, who wrote to her about once a week, sometimes more often. She answered his letters, but his letters were generally longer than hers.

She was busy, more busy than she had been for a long time. In December there was a General Election; that meant hard and exciting work. Fanny had never done so well as a Member's wife before, and it was the talk in local centres that although Michael was a good Member, and no doubt a rising man, he owed a great deal to his wife. Michael admitted this to the full and was grateful. Unfortunately, he expressed his gratitude to everybody except to Fanny herself.

To sum up, the result of the slight change in the relations of Michael and Fanny was wholly pleasurable to Michael, but he looked on at the change from the outside. He did not share it. He wished to share it, but he did not know how.

As for Fanny herself, she too was beginning to feel different. She said to herself that her life was full, that the children were becoming daily more enchanting, that her life was interesting, that Michael's career was important, that Leo Dettrick was an amusing new element. All this was true, but it was not the whole truth. To get at something like the whole truth we must consider the case of Leo Dettrick.

He went to Florence and Rome, and no sooner had he settled abroad than he finished his book with a rush. He had told Fanny that this was impossible. The impossible nevertheless occurred. He had been working at it slowly and intermittently ever since June, and although during the time that he had spent at his farmhouse he had not got through much work on paper, he had planned the book in his mind, and had discussed it so fully with Fanny that the book was really created. "*Il ne restait plus que de l'écrire.*"

He wrote to Fanny about this as well as other things, and reported progress, asked for advice, agreed, disagreed. She was often stung into argument and she enjoyed it. Her letters amused him. She teased him in these, and the *malice* that he suspected in her conversation here became apparent. They became more intimate by letter than they had been before. This did not in reality change the nature of relation between them, but rather it set a seal on their peculiar intimacy and defined it once for all.

Fanny wrote to Dettrick as to a great friend, but as impersonally as if she were writing to a solicitor. Dettrick wrote to Fanny with freedom, but there was no personal note in his letters. There was no hint in either of their letters of anything approaching an *amitié amoureuse*. At the critical moment of his friendship with Fanny he had formulated and established the principle that with the death of Daphne Adeane, his life – that is to say, his sentimental life – had come to an end. Fanny had accepted this principle and this theory, and it had made everything easier.

Fanny had felt the same thing with regard to herself, although she did not say so. She made no confidences. She felt that her sentimental life was over. So they had met like two fellow-exiles or two prisoners in the same prison, communicating with each other by taps on the wall. Dettrick stayed abroad till Whitsuntide, and when he came back his book was published. It was called *Exile*. It was dedicated to "F. C." Michael enjoyed it even more than Fanny, who was more critical. It expressed much that he had himself experienced, and that he had never seen expressed before.

When Dettrick came to Hockley at Whitsuntide, Fanny realised that she knew him better than before he went away. Their correspondence had made, she understood, a difference. At the same time she felt that she had reached the limit of their relation. It would never be different, she would never know him any better, or more intimately than she did at present; nor did she want to.

Dettrick did not think about it. He did not think about the future. He was engrossed in the present, in his ideas; and without his knowing it, Fanny had become a necessity to him. She was a part of his life.

He admired Fanny. He had begun by admiring a hidden likeness to Daphne Adeane he had detected in her; he had felt her to be sympathetic, understanding and receptive, and then helpful. He admired her, so he had told himself, and it was for her character and her mind. But now there was no doubt that he admired her looks as well. They had changed. She seemed to be coming to life, like some plant that has endured an overlong winter, and suddenly breaks into a surprising and unexpected spring. The truth was, she was beginning to taste life. Fun had come back into her life. She had learnt or rather remembered how to laugh, because she had someone to laugh with. And when Michael came back from Scotland he found the Fanny, or hints of the Fanny, he had known before they were married – when they were engaged – a mischievous Fanny, laughing at you quietly from the corner of her eye and saying unexpected things, sometimes of a startling directness.

If fun had come back into Fanny's life, work at the same time had come back into Dettrick's life, and something had come back into Michael's life, at least, he felt there was something there which should come back, but he had the uneasy feeling that perhaps he would not be able to capture and retain it.

His life and Fanny's resumed its normal course with this small but all-important difference. Besides the new solid fact that Dettrick was now a permanent part of their lives, Michael enjoyed his society and constantly asked him to spend Sundays with them. It became a habit, and it ended by his spending every Sunday at Hockley, if he was not otherwise engaged. Fanny did not go to London at all. She was laid up in the spring, and in August Michael took a small shooting lodge in Scotland and asked Dettrick and George Ayton to stay with him. This year Fanny went with them, and she enjoyed herself thoroughly. Michael was overjoyed at the change in her spirits, but he sadly recognised that he could not, as it were, share this new phase.

Early the next year he went to Russia with a British Mission. Fanny did not feel up to the journey. She was expecting another baby. She was looking forward to the birth of this child as never before. She wanted another boy. The baby was born. It was a boy. Dettrick was godfather – he had taken Thorndyke this summer – and it was called Leo after him. Fanny was radiantly happy. She felt that a new life was beginning for her; but an unexpected blow was awaiting her. The baby died about a month after it was born. Fanny was inconsolable. She refused to go to Scotland. Michael went by himself with George Ayton. He was sent abroad in the autumn to Egypt, and he wanted to take Fanny with him. She was disinclined to leave the children, but Michael, at the doctor's advice – he said that change was imperative – persuaded her to go. They stayed there till Parliament met, and then they came back to England.

Dettrick was settled in London and he had published another book. This book was called *The Raft*, and was, just as much as its predecessor, the fruit of conversations and discussions with Fanny. When Michael and Fanny were on their way back to London, Fanny said she would like to live in London this year. She felt that she had sorrowed and brooded long enough, that she had been selfish, that she was being a wet blanket on Michael's life, and she resolved to turn over an entirely new leaf. She felt she had the health and strength to do this, for the climate of Egypt had done wonders to her. She came back looking a changed being, and never since her marriage had she been in better health or spirits.

Michael was pleased when she told him she wanted to come to London. He, too, had been severely stricken by the death of the baby, and he had been sadder still for Fanny. He thought it cruel that this should happen just as he hoped Fanny was going to take a new lease of life. Then, beyond all hope and expectation, the stay at Cairo worked miracles. They had made a number of new friends at Cairo, and Fanny had been admired, courted, petted, sought after, made up to by the foreigners as well as the English people there. She understood foreigners and foreign life, and dealt with them in an easy way. This, too, was a revelation to Michael. He saw a new unsuspected Fanny developing under his eyes. He heard and saw people admiring her beauty, and praising her charm and intelligence, her culture. Why had she kept all this from him? Why had he left it to others to discover? He had been a fool. He had been living for the last years in the past, when near him, with him, next to him, there was an adorable presence. But surely it was not too late? Surely their married life had not lasted too long to make mistakes irreparable? Well, he must try, he would try and he would succeed.

"The fact is," he thought, "I am for the first time falling in love with my wife."

He was struck at every turn now with some new facet in her character.

She certainly was different from other people. She arrived at true conclusions with unerring swiftness, and she startled you by revealing in a word that she knew what you were thinking about.

"I have been a fool," thought Michael, when Fanny made the remark to him about living in London as they were travelling up from Dover to London after staying a few days in Paris, where Fanny had bought clothes and been greatly admired by the French people. "But it is not too late."

Dettrick met them at the station, and he too was startled by the change in Fanny's appearance, which he noticed at once. Michael asked him to dinner that night, and when he came into the room and was greeted by Fanny, who wore one of her new Paris frocks, he was more startled still. He could hardly speak.

"You are looking wonderful," he said. "Cairo has done you good."

"Yes," she said, laughing; "I think it suited me, and I feel as well as if I had had a good bracing."

Michael had to go to see his chief after dinner. Dettrick and Fanny sat by the fire in the drawing-room upstairs. They were both smoking.

"You really enjoyed it?" said Dettrick. They had exhausted the conventional travellers' tales and experiences at dinner.

"Yes. I enjoyed every moment of it, especially Luxor."

"I thought you were enjoying it, your letters were so short."

"I never had time to write, and I had too much to say."

"What did you enjoy most?"

"The people were such fun – you see, I haven't been abroad for a long time."

"You always used to say you hated it."

"Yes, but there is all the difference in being abroad as a tourist or abroad because you are obliged to be. As a tourist I think it *is* great fun."

"They must have made up to you tremendously."

Fanny laughed. "Yes, they were kind. There was a Russian I liked, and we became great friends; and then there was a French savant who taught me hieroglyphics, and a charming Austrian."

"Not to mention English people, I suppose."

"Well, there were some nice English people. Very nice people at the Agency; and then I met Andrew Wallace."

"The writer? Did you like him?"

"He liked me," Fanny laughed again. "He thought I was *wonderful*. Well-read even! He didn't notice the gaps. The only person who had ever understood his stories! And yet I never thought them difficult, did you?"

"No, I should think not. I can't bear him. I know he's clever and writes well, and all that – but I can't bear him. You couldn't really like him, not if you knew him well."

"I did get to know him well. He was in the boat when we went up the Nile."

"You are only saying all this to tease me."

"No. I am quite serious. It was most interesting."

"Yes. But did you *like* him?"

"I think he's got genius – "

"But I mean as a man. You will talk of him as a writer. I admit he's plausible, but he's a fraud, really. He's an actor. He was acting to you."

"Possibly, but if the acting is good enough to take me in, that is all I ask."

"But did you really like him?"

"Like is such a silly word – "

"Is he going to be a real friend of yours?"

Fanny said nothing at first, and looked pensive – "I don't know."

"Well, you had better give me up altogether if he is." He got up and began pacing up and down the room. "You won't have room for both of us in your life."

"I think there might be," she said calmly. "You are so different. He is not coming back till May. He is writing a long book."

"All about the desert, I suppose, with a lot of local colour and…"

"Yes, all about the desert, but no local colour – he read me some of it."

"And you admired it?"

"Yes, I did. After all, you admire his books."

"I admire his early work, but I think he has been spoilt by success, and I think what he writes now is hardly worth reading."

"You will admire this new book."

"You have inspired him."

"I hope I did," she laughed.

"You are a devil, Fanny," said Leo, sitting down again. "Everybody thinks of you as a sort of shy, calm, retiring creature, and really – you are a hussy."

"A failure in hussies. I think I was born one, and then I forgot and played a part. I mean, I had to be a decent Member's wife for Michael's sake, but now I feel different. Now I mean to enjoy myself – I think I have been silly. It was partly ill-health and various things, but I think I have been spoiling Michael's life. Making things dull for him. I mean to do better. I think that if I amuse myself I may amuse him. I'm not going to live at Hockley this winter at all. I am going to stay here until Easter, and then at Easter I am going to take Michael to Paris. We are going to stay with some French friends we met at Cairo, a Madame de Luce. She is half-English and well off and pretty, and Michael is rather in love with her, and he will enjoy it, and I don't mind."

"You are not jealous?"

"Yes, fearfully, but not of her. I would be jealous of the right person if he met her."

"What sort of person?"

"I can't think of anyone *now*, but I know the type – exactly. It's a type that takes all men in. A nice type, which makes it worse. I mean, they are really, as a rule, *nice* women. That makes it more irritating; they are just not what men think they are. I am even jealous of the past."

"Of Michael's past?"

"Yes, very."

"Would you be jealous of the past in anyone you were fond of?"

"I think so, always."

There was a pause.

"And did Michael have any other affairs?"

"He flirted with a Mrs Logan, the wife of a Colonel, and with Madame de Luce, and with an Italian lady who I thought was a beauty; but do you know, Leo, that I believe a very odd thing happened?"

There was a long pause.

"Well?"

"Nothing; I don't know what I was going to say."

"Of course you do; tell me."

"I really forget what I was going to say – honour bright."

"Shall I tell you what it was?"

"You can tell me anything you like, but you don't know."

"You were going to tell me that you thought an odd thing had happened, and that odd thing is that Michael was falling in love with his wife. Aren't I right?"

"Oh no. You don't understand Michael or me, as to that."

"Oh, don't I! And I will tell you more. It's *too late.*"

"What nonsense you talk. Do you think I'm a bad wife?"

"Admirable! but that's different. I'm not talking of you. I mean, it's too late for him. You will always be an admirable wife – what's the good of talking, you know what I mean."

"I don't think I do."

"I mean simply this, that Michael is falling in love with you. That he wasn't in love with you before when you were in love with him. But now it is too late. Not too late for you to love, but too late for you to love *him*. You will probably love someone else."

"Have I ever told you anything that was not true?"

"No; I think you are truthful, the most truthful human being I have ever met."

"Well, you must believe me now when I tell you that I have never given anyone a thought but Michael."

"I dare say, I am talking about the future."

"Let's leave the future alone."

"Do you mean to tell me you are happy?"

"Yes. My life is full, and then the children – this may sound silly, but it isn't – the children are such a *new* joy, such a fresh joy since we came back. I shall never leave them again."

"How old is Peter?"

"Peter is five, and Hester is three, and a darling."

"Children are not enough."

"My life is full – "

"When you say your life is full, that you have never given a thought to anyone but Michael – that's true *now*, but you are absurdly young. Your life, that part of your life, has hardly begun. It is foolish to talk like that. One never knows, you may meet someone in the street tomorrow whom you will passionately love."

Fanny changed the subject.

"By the way, George Ayton was at Cairo."

"How was he?"

"Still very sad at times, but he will get over it."

"I forget what happened. The love of his life went into a convent?"

"Yes, and he thinks she may come out, but she won't; and if she did, she would never set eyes on him again."

"What makes you think that?"

"There are some things one knows. Lady Jarvis, who is or was a great friend of hers, told me what she was like."

"Was Lady Jarvis at Cairo?"

"Yes, for a short time. She is in London now. She came back before we did. By the way, Andrew Wallace told me he knew a friend of yours."

"Who?"

"The friend I am never allowed to see."

"Francis Greene?"

"Yes; he told me he is a wonderful man."

"Haven't I always said the same?"

"Always; that is just why I have wanted to see him."

"He's been so much away, and, as I have told you over and over again, he's shy, he dislikes seeing new people, he won't go out, and he hates women."

"All women?"

"Yes."

"I wonder."

"I should hate you to see him and not like him. He wouldn't be at his best, you would think him awful, and then I should mind. I shouldn't get over it."

"I don't think, from what I was told, I should think him awful."

"And then it's impossible to get him to go anywhere."

"Andrew Wallace told me he had many friends."

"Yes, friends. That's different."

"But Lady Jarvis knows him; she was there when Andrew Wallace talked about him."

"She's seen everybody once… I promise you, he never goes out."

"Won't you bring him to tea one day?"

"You've asked me that a million times before, and I've nothing new to say, but I do say it again. No, no, and no; certainly not, I would sooner die; I know it would be a failure, and I should never get over it."

"But why should it be a failure?"

"I couldn't bear you not to like Francis…and I don't think you would like him."

"You don't know, and you never will know the people I would like or not…you thought I would dislike Andrew Wallace."

"And so you do. You only said all that to annoy me."

"I promise you I didn't; but let's leave that. Why mayn't I know Francis Greene?"

"I couldn't risk it."

"Never?"

"No, never."

"But you wouldn't mind my getting to know him through someone else."

"Oh no."

"Does he know I exist?"

"I have talked of nothing else to him for the last three years."

"Very well, we'll leave it to chance. I won't insist."

"Yes, that's right. Leave it to chance."

Michael came back, and they talked of other things. This conversation was on one point prophetic. The next morning Fanny went out shopping. She took a taxi in Piccadilly from the rank. She got into it and told the driver to go to Shaftesbury Avenue. As the taxi was turning, another ran into it. There was a sharp, short collision. Fanny was flung forward and received a severe blow on the head, and she was cut and bruised.

She was taken out of the cab, and although conscious, she was dazed and did not know what had happened. There was the usual crowd and a policeman taking notes. A man came up and said he was a doctor. He asked Fanny where she lived, and he took her first to a chemist and bandaged her, and then he took her home and made her go to bed, and telephoned for Michael. Michael arrived almost at once from the office. The doctor told him what had happened, that Fanny was suffering from concussion and must be kept in a dark room for a few days. It would not be serious. She would, he thought, be all right in about six weeks, only she must take things quietly. "I suppose you have got a doctor?" he said.

"Yes," said Michael, "Dr Alston, but at this moment he's away attending some conference." Michael liked the looks of this man, whose face, as he thought, was familiar to him. He thought it sympathetic.

"I wish you would come again; I don't know of anyone else."

"Very well. I know Alston well. He's expected back in a few days. I could look after Mrs Choyce till he comes back."

"Let me see, where do you live?" asked Michael.

The doctor gave him his card. On it was written:

FRANCIS GREENE, M.D.,
200 CAVENDISH STREET.

CHAPTER XIV

Fanny made a quick and satisfactory recovery. She only saw Dr Greene once more, because her own doctor came back to London, and Greene at once told him what had happened. Francis Greene was not a general practitioner. He was a specialist engaged in the study of nerves. His name was a household word in the scientific world. But he had practised, and his powers of diagnosis and his psychological insight were said to be as remarkable as his knowledge. Fanny had been delighted to make his acquaintance for the fun she anticipated of teasing Leo Dettrick.

But the acquaintanceship was cut short, because Dr Greene left England shortly after Fanny's accident, for Australia, where he meant to stay a year.

Fanny was well by Easter, and Michael took her to Paris, where they stayed with their new French friend; but before they left London, Michael asked Fanny whether she would not like to have a new house, and Fanny accepted the idea with delight. She chose a small house in Queen Anne's Gate. It did not need much doing to it, only painting and cleaning. They were living in it by the middle of May.

A new phase began in the lives of Fanny and Michael, and Fanny when she looked back upon this period in after years could hardly realise it. It was like a blur: a golden dream. Was she happy? She did not know, but it was as if she had taken opium and were taking part in an unsubstantial pageant, a fantastic Decameron. She had regained her health, her spirits, and, above all, her beauty.

Fanny was surrounded with friends. First of all, there was Leo Dettrick, who came to see her every day; and there was Andrew Wallace, who had come back from Egypt. Although he did not go out much, he had a host of friends in London, and he made loud and ubiquitous propaganda for Fanny. He said she was the most beautiful and the most interesting of the younger women in London.

And so Fanny (as once before Hyacinth) was in a sense discovered; she woke up one morning and found herself, if not famous, in italics. There were no pictures of her or paragraphs in the newspapers, but there was a subtle aroma of interest and rumour about her. If you said "*Fanny Choyce,*" every one knew who you meant. No explanation was necessary. And if you mentioned her, this would almost certainly lead to her looks being mentioned.

She was known in the political world, but she only went to large entertainments when it was necessary; Andrew Wallace had introduced her to the Bohemian world. She went out little, although many hostesses tried in vain to pin her down to engagements and visits. She refused to stay at country houses. It bored Michael, and they spent every Friday to Monday at Hockley and filled the house with young people. Yet she attracted people like a magnet. She was occupied; she always seemed to have plenty to do, and she was supremely indifferent. She and Michael entertained a group of friends to little dinners and suppers. They went to the opera and the Russian ballet.

Michael liked sitting up late, and people would drop into the house late after dinner. Their house was a comfortable refuge for their foreign friends.

Leo Dettrick resented this. He regarded Fanny as his property, and he could not bear to hear her talked about by people like Guy Cunninghame, nor to see her friends with Lady Jarvis, although, perhaps because, it was Lady Jarvis who had introduced him to her. Michael liked it. He was proud of Fanny, and moreover she arranged the kind of things that amused him. Michael asked his friends to Hockley and Fanny asked hers. They did not clash. George Ayton was often with them. Jack Canning was still in Africa, and was not expected home till the end of the summer. Stephen Lacy came when he could. (Walter Troumestre had died in the autumn just before they went to Cairo.) The Clives were often there, and Jean Brandon.

Leo Dettrick could not bear Fanny being friends with Andrew Wallace. He could bear anything else, but not that. He had meant to stay in the country all the summer, but when he knew that Fanny was going to be in London he could not resist being there too. He was by way of writing another book, but he was doing little. When asked to go anywhere, he explained that he never went out. He ended by going anywhere if he knew for certain that Fanny would be there too.

It was in July. Michael had been given a box at Drury Lane for the Russian opera. Chaliapine was singing in *Ivan the Terrible.*

Michael had invited an Italian lady they had met in Egypt, Madame (Contessa) San Gervasio, Leo Dettrick, and a young Russian who had come over for the horse show at Olympia, Dimitri Toll, who was in the *Chevaliers Gardes.*

In a box opposite there was a party of Russians, and among them a young Countess Zhikov.

Michael was struck with the beauty of this lady.

"Who is she?" he asked his Russian friend during the *entr'acte.* His friend explained, and added, "Would you like to know her?"

"I should indeed," said Michael.

"Then I will take you round and introduce you."

Some friends came to see Fanny, and Michael and Toll made room for them.

While this conversation was going on, the people in the box opposite, who consisted (besides the Russian lady and a Russian man called Kranitzky) of Guy Cunninghame, George Ayton, and Lady Jarvis, the hostess, were discussing the party in Michael's box.

"Who is that Misha Toll is with?" asked Countess Zhikov. "Is she foreign?"

Guy Cunninghame explained.

"I find she is very beautiful," said Countess Zhikov, meaning Fanny.

Guy Cunninghame looked across the house critically and then delivered his verdict.

"Yes," he said, "she *is* beautiful this year. She has improved out of all knowledge."

"But she is so young," said Countess Zhikov; "surely she must always have been well."

"Well," said Guy, "she was a pretty girl. Then she married, and I think she was ill, but there is no doubt that she lost her looks for a time – and that she has got them back; she is prettier now than she has ever been."

"You have so many beauties in England," said Countess Zhikov, "it is discouraging; but I find her the most interesting I have seen."

"Do you see any colours round her?" asked Lady Jarvis.

Countess Zhikov said that sometimes, willy-nilly, she saw *auras* round people, or saw them *as* colour.

"Yes," she said, "clouds like smoke – with a flame in it. All silver and, how you say? *feuilles mortes.*"

"And round him?"

"Oh, red and white-hot *comme un fer rougi* – incandescent?"

"And round Mr Dettrick?"

"He is the author of those books – yes? I read one in the Tauchnitz, but I found it a bore. He is blue, like the blue of the sea in Greece and Sicily, a transparent green-blue. And in the blue there are spots of turquoise and round all the blue there is a white *nimbe*."

"Do you see all that like a halo, or are those just the colours you think represent the people, as in the game of analogies?"

"I don't know. I can't explain it. Sometimes I think it is one or sometimes the other. It is a flash, and it goes – or sometimes it stays."

Toll and Michael, who had been detained on the way, came in, and he was introduced to the foreigners. George Ayton and Guy Cunninghame went to talk to Fanny.

When Michael was introduced to Kranitzky, the latter said to him, "I think I know a great friend of yours. Canning."

"Oh yes, Jack. How is he? He never writes. Did you see him in South Africa?"

"Yes, I travelled out with him the last time he went. About a year ago. He is coming to England soon; I shall miss him."

Michael then talked to Countess Zhikov, and before the end of the *entr'acte* he had invited Lady Jarvis and all her party to supper in his house.

"I suppose there will be something to eat?" he said to Fanny when he told her this piece of news.

"Yes," said Fanny, laughing, "because as I knew *we* were going to have supper, and as I knew that you would be likely to ask half the theatre to supper, I took my precautions. There will be plenty to eat and plenty to drink – in fact, we might ask some more people. There's Andrew Wallace, I see, downstairs in the stalls."

"Need you ask him?" said Dettrick.

Fanny took no notice. "And there's Jean Brandon, we might ask her. And there's Raphael Luc, and Solway, the pianist; let's ask both of them and have a night of music."

"Yes, let's," said Michael; "Russian songs. I'll do it in the next *entr'acte.*"

"Andrew Wallace is sure to come here now he has seen us."

"Yes, trust him to do that," said Dettrick.

Fanny laughed, and then she added, "There's Margaret and Dick Clive and the Wisters. Let's ask them all!"

The curtain went up. During the next *entr'acte* the invitations were made and most of them were accepted. Fanny's dining-room was quite full – mostly of young people. Then they had music upstairs: serious music at first, growing less serious as time went on. Raphael Luc sang songs from Offenbach and Gilbert and Sullivan, and Toll, who had raised a guitar, played and sang *Tzigane* duets with Countess Zhikov. It was a breathless July night. People sat anywhere and everywhere, some of the guests on the floor. The window on the park was wide open.

Solway played all the valses he knew – valses of every epoch, from Johann to Oskar Strauss. Raphael Luc and Toll relieved him. The tunes ranged from "The Blue Danube," via "*Trop Jolie*" and "The Chocolate Soldier," to tangos and foxtrots.

The furniture was flung away at the first note of the first dance, and the dancers danced in tune.

There were some striking silhouettes among the dancers. Countess Zhikov, a Bacchante with dancing eyes; Madame San Gervasio, glowing like a Titian; Jean Brandon, pale as ivory with eyes like sloes; Margaret Clive, as fresh as a primrose; and Fanny, rhythmical and silvery.

When they were tired they had more supper and more music. The older people went away, but the young stayed on. The music became sentimental.

Raphael Luc sang plaintive songs by Fauré and Hahn. The Russians sang *Ochi Chernie*, and *Nochi Bezumnia*, and *Utro Prokladnoe*, and others.

Most of the young people were sitting on the floor, as the furniture had been moved for the dancing. Fanny found herself sitting on the balcony talking to Kranitzky, who was not a dancer.

Raphael Luc was singing a sad song about the frailty of mortal things, the pain of separation, and the sharpness of death. The young people listened in an ecstasy.

"They like those *sad* songs," said Fanny.

"Yes, they are young enough. I am always thinking of Shakespeare's *Twelfth Night* when I see young people enjoying melancholy songs – the fool – is it the fool? – singing 'Come away, Death,' and all the young people listening."

"Yes," said Fanny, "the young enjoy *idle* tears."

"But you are young enough for that kind of enjoyment too? I, alas! am not."

"I'm afraid I'm not either," said Fanny. "It's frightening how fast time goes…" She changed the subject.

"You knew Jean Brandon before?"

"Yes, I met her several years ago, and in France at a watering-place last year."

They were talking about Fanny's friend, the dark girl with the white complexion – she was still unmarried. Fanny knew that Jack Canning had been in love with her for years and still wanted to marry her.

"She's very pretty, isn't she?"

"I have seen her look very interesting."

"You don't think she does now?"

"I used to admire her very much, and although I had not seen her for a year till tonight I admired her still in my memory. But I no longer admire her, because I have seen something of the same kind that puts her out for me, annihilates her. I have seen *you*. I am not making banal compliments – I am saying the truth. You are what she might look like if only *the lamp were lit in her.*"

"You knew her well?"

"I asked her to marry me, but I do not know whether I have known her well."

Fanny was genuinely astonished. She had never known of Kranitzky's existence.

"Shall I relate you the story?" he asked.

"Do."

"It is so easy to talk to strangers about intimate matters – so impossible to one's friends."

"The odd thing," said Fanny, "is that I don't feel you are a stranger – but do tell me the story."

"Well, I will relate it; if you find it a bore you will stop me. I must begin by telling you that although Russian I am a Catholic – my mother was Italian, and I was brought up in her religion. I always have been *croyant* and was at one time *pratiquant*, and always wished to be. Then, when I was about twenty-six, I fell in love with someone. She was married and had children, and she was Russian and Orthodox. It lasted a long time – seven years. She meant everything in the world to me, I thought of nothing else, and had to arrange my life accordingly. At last I could bear it no longer, and I asked her to divorce and leave her husband and marry me. She would not. Then I left Russia, and I thought all was over. I went to Haréville to take the waters and there I met Miss Brandon – I had met her once more. She was staying there with her aunt. We got to know each other well, very well this time. I asked her to marry me, and she said she would. All of a sudden Canning came from Africa. He sees the situation, and goes away. There was a friend of Miss Brandon's there, called Mrs Sommer."

"I know her," said Fanny.

"Well, we told no one of the engagement, and I thought all was happy, and then the day after this happened I had a letter from my friend in Russia who said she *would* divorce and *would* marry me. What was I to do? It was a puzzle – I was dreadfully bothered. I felt it was my duty to marry Miss Brandon and not to *renouer* that old affair; and yet I felt an undying obligation to my old friend. I knew now, directly I read her letter, that I could not marry Miss Brandon. I saw that it had been a dream, a mirage, the mirage of rebuilding a new existence. But I saw this was a momentary thing, and that I belonged to the past, for better for worse. But still I did not know what to do, or how to do anything. I consulted Mrs Sommer. By the way, is she alive?"

"Yes, she is. She is in London."

"She was Miss Brandon's great friend, and she agreed with me it was a mirage – a mistake. She said that Canning would always be Miss Brandon's true and year-long mainstay, and that she would marry him."

"So what did you do?"

"I did nothing. There were no explanations. Mrs Sommer cut the knot for me. I went away. Miss Brandon understood."

"But you see she hasn't married Jack Canning."

"She will this year or next – or some time."

"And do you think she didn't mind?"

"It was also to her a mirage. She never thought of it as real in broad daylight, if you know what I mean. It was a day's romance, a dream – she woke up – "

"I wonder if you are right. After all, there was nothing to prevent her marrying Jack Canning. If he left because of you, he must have known, when you left her too, that there was a mistake."

"Perhaps he wanted to give her time, not to hurry things. And he knew *he* would never change. He is that kind."

"Like you?"

"Oh, not like me! I am not that kind. I am capable of great fickleness, of any *coup de tête*; but I always must go back to my first magnet. I could never break away."

"But you *did* break away."

"Ah, I couldn't let her divorce because of me! For her own sake and for the children's sake, and also through personal scruples – and a distaste for it. Hence Africa."

174

"And that was the end?"

"No, it was not the end. When I had been in Africa a year I could bear it no longer, and I cabled to my friend that I would do anything; that I would follow her to the end of the world."

There was a pause.

"And then," he went on, "she cabled back that it was too late. She could not. And now I go to Russia tomorrow. I shall try to see her once more, if only for a day, and if this is not possible I shall go back to Africa. Perhaps she will not change her mind. I missed the opportunity when she wrote the first time; such an opportunity never comes twice."

"I wonder whether Jean will marry Jack Canning?"

"Oh, you may be sure of that."

"I wonder… Her version of the story might be different."

"Mrs Sommer agreed with me; but I agree, one never knows. I only know that Canning will always be faithful, and she in the long run will say 'Yes.' But I have talked enough about my own affairs. It is your turn."

"I have nothing to tell."

"If you won't talk about yourself, let me talk about you. Shall I tell you what I am thinking? May I?"

"You can say what you like," said Fanny.

"Well, I am thinking this. That there are three people who are…what shall I say?…intrigued about you. First of all, that *homme de lettres.*"

"Who? Leo Dettrick?"

"Yes; and secondly, the other one."

"Which other one?"

"The other novelist you introduced me to."

"Oh, Andrew Wallace."

"Yes; and *ils se détestent.* But that is not the interesting thing. The interesting thing is your husband. He is learning how to be jealous."

"Of Leo Dettrick and Andrew Wallace? Oh dear, no," she laughed sincerely. "Leo Dettrick practically lives with us, and Michael has never given a thought to either of them."

"Oh no, he is not jealous of them; he never will be."

"Then who is it?"

Solway was playing the valse from the *Rosenkavalier*. One or two couples were dancing.

"Who knows?" said Kranitzky. "There is a possible rival."

At that moment Guy Cunninghame came up to Fanny and asked her to dance.

"The next one," said Fanny, looking at Kranitzky. Cunninghame nodded and quickly found another partner.

"Did you mean him?" asked Fanny slyly.

"No, I meant Lord Ayton."

"He has *had* his romance," said Fanny. "It's too long to tell you now, but he has never recovered."

"He *will* recover," said Kranitzky. "He is not a *grand amoureux*. I am not sure he has not recovered already. *You* have cured him."

Fanny blushed.

"Oh no, that would be too – you know his heart was broken?"

"You have mended it."

"You think nothing lasts?…"

"Not with most men…sometimes there is a Jack Canning…"

"And with women?"

"Women are different. How should I know? But certainly longer with women than with men…women care more *when* they care…"

"I have never given George Ayton a thought in that way."

"No? It is he that gives the thought – you are the *Étincelle*."

"You think I am?"

"Coquette?…no, worse…you are like…you are like…something apart…something aloof and classic… Artemis – only with mischief. People watch you from afar and grow mad; but you

176

go your way, not noticing, not caring…you make no effort. You never compete nor strive. You do not care. You think that all is indifferent to you. You take life as it comes, and enjoy the opera and dancing and music, and the sky, the fields, and the trees…you feel safe, serene and secure…that nothing can touch you…people may worship, that is their affair. You enjoy it. It makes you comfortable and happy…that kind of happiness; but if one day…well, if one day there should be a careless Brangäne who should leave a *philtre* lying about, and you were to mistake it for wine and drink it… Ah, then…ah then… I say all this to you because I have never seen you before and shall probably never see you again. As I told you, I leave tomorrow, so what does it matter?"

"What would happen then?"

"Then you would be mad…but you would love like a tigress and like a *grisette, comme une…* well – *bêtement*; but it will be, I feel, not someone like any of these people, not like Mr Dettrick or Lord Ayton – someone unexpected – and then – oh, your poor husband! He already suffers now, when it is not real – what will he not suffer then?"

Another dance had begun. Guy Cunninghame came up to Fanny to claim his dance.

She smiled at Kranitzky, got up and danced with Guy. Michael was standing with George Ayton and Leo Dettrick at the other end of the room. They all three of them were watching Fanny and her partner in silence. Michael danced seldom, George clumsily, and Dettrick never. Kranitzky stood near the window, watching too.

There was at first only one other couple dancing, and as soon as Fanny and Guy started, they stopped. The field was left to Fanny and her partner by tacit consent. They danced so beautifully together. Guy Cunninghame not only had an unerring sense of time, but you felt he was enjoying himself with every fibre of his being. It was like seeing a good skater on the ice. As for Fanny, it was a revelation to see her dance. She seemed to come to life, or to live more intensely in swift motion. She was dressed in clinging silver tissues. Dancing showed the beauty of her line: the curves, the rippling texture of her neck and shoulders, her arm which was as if chiselled by a nameless sculptor in the springtime of Greek art. Dancing animated her serenity. It revealed the essence, almost all the possibilities of her beauty, half of which belonged to the fourth dimension; and dancing was perhaps a right, a necessary condition for its almost complete expression – almost, because for its complete expression another factor would be necessary: love given and reciprocated.

"Die schlanke Wasserlilie," murmured Kranitzky to himself, as he looked at Fanny. He sat down next to Jean Brandon, and they talked once more comfortably like old friends. Fanny noticed this as she danced past and wondered. "Does everything," she thought, "always come to an end? Michael and Hyacinth. He has forgotten now, forgotten her."

It was true. Michael stood watching Fanny with more than admiration, with amazement. This often happened now. She had become a new person to him. He gave no thought to Hyacinth, not even an afterthought. The image of Hyacinth had faded from his mind. It had been driven away by the more vivid and ever-present image of Fanny.

It was the last dance. The sky had turned from a deep blue to a cold grey. The trees in the park looked ghostly.

Fanny proposed eggs and bacon downstairs.

They had a final meal at a round table, and then everyone went away.

Michael and Fanny were left alone.

"I think they enjoyed it, don't you?" said Fanny.

"Yes, but all the same – damn! damn! damn!"

"Why?"

"Because I can't dance."

"You dance quite well. Didn't you dance tonight?"

"But I mean properly, like Cunninghame – "

"Oh! Guy – yes, he is exceptionally good."

"Yes, good at everything I can't do."

Fanny laughed.

"I believe you're in love with him."

Fanny laughed again, a rippling laugh.

"Well, at any rate he's in love with *you.*"

"My dear Michael – "

Michael walked to the door and lit a bedroom candle: "And, by the way, there's a rumour, George is going to be given something in the Cabinet. It's a secret. *Splendid*, isn't it?" he said, with slightly hoarse emphasis.

"Yes, *splendid*!" said Fanny, and she thought to herself, " It was all nonsense what Kranitzky said about George, but he *is* right about Michael"; and she marvelled at the Russian's intuition.

As they were walking upstairs the door knocker was violently rapped. Michael went down and opened the door. On the doorstep stood Countess Zhikov, in a wonderful pink *sortie de bal*, with a floating cloud of tulle round her neck, looking like a creature of the woods.

She was arguing with a recalcitrant taxi-driver. "He will not go on! He has come back," she said, wringing her hands. "I pay him twice, but he says he is *weak!*" She meant that one of the driver's tyres was down, and that she had, in vain, offered him double his fare. Michael found her another taxi.

CHAPTER XV

Jack Canning came back from Africa in July, and Michael wanted to take him to Scotland.

He was discussing the matter with Fanny at breakfast in London.

"Of course you would come, and the children," he said.

"Would the house be big enough?"

They had taken a small shooting lodge, where there was a little rough shooting, and excellent fishing.

"Oh yes; big enough for all of you, and more. We would ask some more people."

They had always asked George Ayton before, and Fanny wondered whether Michael was *not* going to suggest him. He seemed embarrassed.

"We ought to ask someone for Jack," he went on. "Why not Jean Brandon?" He knew the story.

"That would be fatal," said Fanny.

"But I thought he was devoted to her."

"That's why; one must not force these things."

"And then there's George…" Michael said tentatively.

"Yes, there's George." Fanny's voice was toneless, non-committal.

"We ought to ask someone for him."

"I think," said Fanny, "that perhaps I and the children had better go to Devonshire and stay with mother, and you had better have a man's party. It will be simpler in the long run."

"If you don't come, I shan't go at all... We'll ask George and we'll ask Leo?"

"He's going abroad for the whole of the autumn."

"Well, you must think of someone for George and Jack."

Michael rushed out of the room and went to his office. Fanny was left pensive. There was no doubt, she thought, that Michael was jealous of George. If he only knew how unnecessary it was. It was finally settled that Jack, George, Dick and Margaret Clive were to be asked. They accepted. Fanny would not ask Jean Brandon, for she felt certain that Jean had seen Jack since his return, and was not yet inclined, or had certainly not yet decided, to marry him. That being so, the less they saw of each other just at this moment, the better for Jack Canning's chances.

They were settled in Scotland by the end of July. The house that Michael had been lent was a square white house in a glen close to the river, on the west coast of the Highlands. Fanny had asked Lady Jarvis at the last moment. She felt she needed the presence of an older woman. She liked Lady Jarvis, and she was a great friend of George Ayton's.

The summer holidays started well. The men were happy fishing and sometimes shooting; the children enjoyed every moment of the long days; the three women were happy together. Fanny and Margaret fished themselves; sometimes they would go for expeditions, or take the children for picnics. The weather was fine and hot.

Michael seemed happy. Everything went off so simply and naturally that Fanny began to think she need not worry. Michael's anxiety, his causeless jealousy, had been a momentary phase; it had been dissipated by reality, by the facts of everyday life...all was well. And so the summer holidays came to an end. At the end of August they were all going south.

Michael and Fanny had to go to Hockley; George Ayton had engagements; Dick Clive had to go back to his work, and Lady Jarvis was going abroad.

On the last evening but one before they went south they had been asked to dinner by some Americans who had taken a neighbouring lodge, and whom they had made friends with.

Fanny's little girl, Hester, was not well. She had a slight temperature, so Fanny thought she would stay at home; she had sent for the doctor. George Ayton had gone out fishing late in the afternoon. When the time came for starting for the dinner, he had not come back.

"I suppose," said Michael, "he has forgotten all about it; it's just like him!"

It had been his habit lately to stay out late, and he often did not come home till nine in the evening. They waited some time – till the last possible moment. Then Michael suddenly became impatient, and said to Fanny:

"We can't wait any longer; we shall be late as it is. You must tell him if he comes that he has behaved very badly, and give him some cold grouse."

Then Michael bustled them into his motor, which he was driving himself.

Fanny had a little food. There was no sign of George. In the meantime the doctor arrived and had reassured her. Hester was asleep. The doctor said it was best not to wake her. He would come again in the morning. It would, he thought, be nothing.

About nine o'clock George strolled into the house. He had caught a salmon, a large one. He had played it for nearly an hour. He could not, of course, he said, leave it. He had not forgotten the dinner, but he thought Michael would have guessed, and that they would all understand.

"You will find some dinner in the dining-room," said Fanny, ringing the bell.

After exchanging a few more words, and telling him the news of Hester, Fanny went out into the garden. It was a quiet evening. It was still broad daylight. There was not a cloud, and a faint golden-pink tinge spread all over the west made the sky warm and soft. It was not a large garden; there were a few beds by the side of the river, but the flowers grew wonderfully well. The last tenant had been an enthusiastic gardener. There were night-flowering stocks, tiger-lilies, white phlox, and marigolds. The flowers looked strangely distinct and white in the evening light that had no hint of darkness in it. There was a delicious smell of flowers in the air. Fanny walked down to the river and watched the still, brown water; every now and then a fish would rise.

"It has been a successful holiday for Michael," she thought; "on the whole, I think he has enjoyed it…and all that nonsense is over, which is a comfort. The children, too, enjoyed it, and so did Lady Jarvis and the Clives. Poor Jack was rather sad. Jean, I feel sure, has refused him again; what a goose she is! If she is not careful she will get left… She is getting on. She must be thirty now, or nearly thirty. How foolish people are! I don't believe she loved that Russian. I believe she loves Jack, but what is it that stops her accepting him? …a sense of duty to that tiresome aunt? or is she waiting for a fairy prince? But she has had her one, her only romance; she won't have another… however, I do not despair. One could do a lovely sketch here. Leo would have enjoyed this place. I wish he was here, but he seems happy at Amalfi; the new book is evidently getting on, otherwise he would write longer letters. His letters are getting shorter and shorter."

Such was the tenor of Fanny's thoughts. She walked up and down, and then she sat down on a seat. While she was dreaming in this way, George Ayton strolled out of the house and walked up towards her, smoking a cigarette. He did not appear to see Fanny at first…then he caught sight of her, walked up to her, and sat down on the seat.

"It's delightful out here," he said.

"Yes, isn't it."

"I like these long evenings. It's rather sad to think it's the last evening but one."

"You must come here next year."

"I will – if you ask me."

There was a pause.

"How is Hester?"

"She is asleep. The doctor thought it best not to wake her. She must still be asleep, as I told Nanny to tell me at once if she woke. The doctor thinks it will be nothing. He's coming tomorrow morning."

"That's all right. I hope they won't think it rude of me not to have gone."

"Oh no, they will understand; they fish themselves."

"I can't believe that tomorrow will be our last day."

"It has passed quickly. We must look forward to next year. Michael said he was going to come here next year if he could get the place, and I'm sure he will; they always let it."

"Next year; that's a long time ahead. Who knows where we shall all be next year?"

"I wonder… I often play that game of wondering where I shall be next year. So far it has nearly always happened that I have been in exactly the same place, either at Hockley or in Scotland. Of course, one never knows, but still, touching wood, and D.V., and all that…"

"I didn't mean 'all that'… "the words came out slowly and painfully… "I mean I shall never come here again."

"Why not?" asked Fanny, quite naturally.

"Well, I suppose you know all my private affairs. Everybody always does…know everybody else's private affairs…"

In a second, Fanny veered from a cheerful, almost flippant, indifference to sympathy. She knew George's history, the story of his romantic attachment to the beautiful Mrs Housman, whose husband had died in the nick of time, but who, instead of taking advantage of the fact, had become a nun; but she only knew it as "everybody always does." She had even carefully refrained from asking Lady Jarvis, who she knew had been intimate both with Mrs Housman and with George, for a grain of information. Fanny had a horror of second-hand gossip. Above all, she loathed the talk and the back-chat of those who live outside the world, but nibble at the fringe of it; who consider themselves apart, aloof, and above society, and who, while assuming this superior attitude and taking up a position of critical indignation and severe judgment, feed on gossip as caterpillars on leaves, spread gossip and ensue it, increase the untruth of it, swell the chorus of lying tongues, broaden the slander and spread the poison. She knew Mrs Housman had become a nun a year ago, but she had an idea that the step was not yet final or irrevocable, or that the final act had not yet been made.

"Now," she thought to herself, "it has been reached, and George has just heard of it."

Fanny looked at him with a searchlight of sympathy in her eyes.

"I am so sorry," she said gently; "I *don't* know your affairs more than, as you say, ' everybody knows about everyone else's,' and that is so often wrong, but whatever has happened, if anything has happened to make you unhappy, I am really sorry for you."

"I am unhappy because you have been so beastly to me," he said, in a low voice, looking on the ground.

Fanny was bewildered.

"I'm sorry," she said again, "so, so sorry. It's true; I have been *quite* beastly."

Fanny remembered that all through George's visit (it was Kranitzky's fault, and the silly idea he had suggested to her) she had ignored the possibility of there being anything serious in his mind and heart. She had never spoken to him except in a matter-of-fact or flippant manner; she had never sent him one slight unexpressed signal of sympathy or understanding which, after all, cost nothing, and was immensely valued.

"I didn't know," she stammered. "You see, I know really nothing… I never asked."

"Oh, you don't understand! You were beastly because you made *me* beastly…disloyal *both ways.*"

"I really don't understand, George. You know I never listen to gossip about other people, least of all my friends' private affairs. Of course, one can't help hearing something, but that, as we know, is generally wrong. I leave it at that. I really don't understand."

But as she said the words and saw George look at her, she did understand fully, instantly and retrospectively, only it was too late.

"I won't leave it at that, and you understand perfectly well," he said. His voice was low, but shaking. He seized hold of her. She did not scream or cry, and there in that quiet garden in the evening daylight, aromatic with white nightstocks and other staring plants and flowers, a slow, silent contest took place. George was strong, but Fanny had wrists of steel, and she managed to bend back his hand and then his fingers, till she made him leave go. They neither of them had said a word. She stood up, and her eyes were flashing in the half-light, as bright as black diamonds. She looked like an angry, outraged priestess, defending a sacred shrine, ready to do and dare anything; but deadly calm. She was in complete control of herself; boiling with rage within, but outwardly calm as ice.

She saw there were only two courses: a scene, or to ignore it; to talk *through* the situation, as if nothing had happened; (a third possible course, to treat it as a joke and have a laugh over it, she was inwardly too upset to think of – not because of what George had done, but because she, by the peculiar situation, had brought it about). She chose the second course.

"The river's very low;…if we don't have some rain soon there will be no more fishing."

Nothing could have been more quiet, but nothing could have been more decisive or final. The sentence was like the falling blade of a guillotine. George stammered something. Fanny sat down on the seat, and she went on talking about plans for the next day and the future.

George suddenly interrupted her:

"I suppose I ought to say I'm sorry. Don't be frightened; I've got my senses back. I *am* sorry, and I'm not – not a bit…"

"It's over," said Fanny.

"Don't talk about it, please."

"I must say one thing," said George, very slowly and sadly. "It was partly your fault."

"My fault?" She looked at him so honestly with her quiet, serious eyes that he crumpled up.

"Sorry," he said. "I'm not all there."

"You said I was beastly – not beastly enough, apparently."

"That *is* just it."

"Supposing I had been less beastly – or more?"

"It would have been the same. It's no good blinking the fact, Fanny – I love you. I can't help it. I have loved you for a long time; I know it's idiotic, and I know I'm to blame – but not for what you think – not because of Michael. It's no good pretending you love old Michael. I *know* you don't – you *like* him. My crime is different – worse. I've been disloyal to someone and something else…like being disloyal to the dead – I've betrayed – but it was your doing. It's not your fault, in a way – you couldn't help it. I knew it was hopeless. I knew you could never love me."

"Oh!…please, please stop. I can't bear it. I'm going in. Forget all about it. I'm going to Hester. I'm sorry if anything was *my* fault. I thought, you see, you – well, I thought wrong."

"You were right…till you changed me. You made me forget."

"Don't; that's enough. Let's forget and be friends," she said, with infinite weariness.

"Friends! Good God!"

Fanny got up.

"I must go."

She went into the house. Hester was asleep. She stayed a little time in the nursery, talking to Hester's Nanny. Then she went to her bedroom and looked at herself in the glass. Her hair was a little dishevelled; her cheeks white, with burning spots; her eyes abnormally bright. She lay down on her bed and cried. She felt utterly miserable – alone and friendless. George's outburst and confession was the most cruel, inopportune thing that could have happened. She foresaw that Michael would – no, had guessed right, and how complicated this would make it. She felt like Hamlet when he said, "That it should come to this! But two months dead!… Frailty, thy name is woman!" Yes, as much as you like, but man, too; man and woman – mortal.

> "How weary, stale, flat, and unprofitable
> Seem to me all the uses of this world."

Fanny did not think of the actual lines at this moment, but they expressed exactly what she felt, and the motive that caused the thought was in a way the same.

Another thought which stung her to the quick was this. She felt in a way an unwilling fellow-conspirator, that she had been partly to blame – unconsciously, but nevertheless partly responsible. She felt that she had helped to betray Mrs Housman, that she had been made to do it. The thought of Mrs Housman at present in a nun's cell, perhaps debating whether she was to take final vows or leave the convent for ever, tore her heart.

Fanny lay on the bed in a storm of tears. And then she thought of Hyacinth, and how Michael had now forgotten her; and of Michael's attitude towards herself; and of the whole chain, the whole lamentable chain of misunderstanding and error; the tangle, the false positions, the right thing happening at the wrong moment, the cross-purposes, and the counter-currents; and the constant, permanent irony. She thought of how desperately she had loved Michael, and then of her shattering disillusion. But although this passed through her mind, it was not that which was making her miserable, not that which was making her cry.

It was the bitter disillusion. The sense of dust and ashes, and the vanity of everything; "the frailty of all things here."

She thought of that beautiful Mrs Housman, whom she had seen once at a party, whom she had heard sing in a way which she would never forget as long as she lived. And that woman, she knew, had turned her life upside-down, through George, if not because of him. At any rate, she had loved him with all her being. That Fanny knew, and she must have gone through, on his account, a terrible crisis, when she might have married him and didn't, and became a nun instead. Fanny did not know the whole facts, but she knew the rough outline of the story. She guessed that for Mrs Housman it must have been a great, a tremendous thing; and now, when only a little more than a year had passed, here was George, who was supposed to have been broken and shattered, his life devastated – here he was, forgetting all about it, and making love to someone else – his friend's wife.

She did not blame him particularly; he was, after all, only a man, like any other. Perhaps, for a man, he had been unusually faithful and restrained; but oh, how bitter was the thought that it should be so! And the crowning irony was now happening: Michael was falling in love with her, and was not only falling in love, but jealous – jealous of a man to whom she had never given a thought, while she could no more love Michael now than fly. She longed to be able to. She would have given worlds to love Michael, but she couldn't. Whatever it was that had made her love him once was now irrevocably dead, and could never be brought to life again, except by a miracle.

"And now," she thought, "Michael will be more jealous than ever because, with the instincts of the jealous, he will guess what has happened. He will see it on George's face, if not on mine."

At that moment she heard a motor-horn blow.

"There they are, coming back," she thought. She jumped up from her bed and washed her face with rosewater, tidied herself, taking as long about it as possible. "George will say I am upstairs with Hester." She looked at herself in the glass. She would pass muster at a pinch, for a man, but a woman would see at a glance that something had happened. Lady Jarvis would see. That did not matter; she did not mind what Lady Jarvis saw. She would not mind what she knew. Presently she heard Michael rushing upstairs. She opened the door and said:

"Sh! Sh! Hester's asleep."

She detained Michael as long as she could in the dim bedroom, and told him in a whisper what had happened: that the doctor had been, that he was satisfied, that Hester had slept ever since half-past seven.

"Now let's go down," said Michael.

They went down.

George was explaining in a halting way, which made him look guilty, why he had been so late and why he had not gone to the dinner, and all about the salmon – in deep detail.

"We explained," said Lady Jarvis. "They quite understood."

Michael said nothing, but looked on grimly.

"It's a beautiful fish," said Fanny. "Have you seen it?"

"No," said Michael. "You are a lucky dog," he said savagely to George. "I've never caught a fish like that since we've been here."

"I must go up and have a last look at Hester," said Fanny.

She said goodnight; and when she said goodnight to Lady Jarvis she saw that Lady Jarvis had seen that she had been crying.

CHAPTER XVI

Fanny had been right. Michael's instincts told him something had happened, and he saw that Fanny had been more upset than Hester's illness warranted. Hester was quite well the next day, and they all went south.

They spent a day in London, and then they went back to Hockley. Lady Weston came to stay with them; Fanny had plenty to do. Michael had speeches to make.

Their life went on as usual till Christmas. Fanny saw the Lyleys; made music with Cuthbert and Mr Rowley, the Rector; corresponded with Leo Dettrick; did her duties as a Member's wife, was a great deal with her children – in fact, she had a busy, occupied life. She was well, she looked well. On the surface, and to the outside observer, Fanny and Michael seemed to be an ideally happy couple. Fanny was admired now in the country, as well as in London, and the neighbours copied her clothes and tried to imitate her manner, not without making reservations while they did so.

It seemed as if they had everything that could make them happy. They were praised on all sides. No one, except Cuthbert Lyley, and perhaps Mrs Saxby, the doctor's wife, had a suspicion that there was anything amiss.

Leo Dettrick guessed what Fanny was feeling, but he had no idea what was going on in Michael's mind. Fanny was partially in the dark herself. George had gone abroad. This did not make Michael any the less jealous. His absence was as bad for him as his presence. Fanny would allude to him from time to time naturally. But Michael could no longer mention his name without there being a strain in his voice, and without his face contracting as with pain. He hated him, and hated himself for hating him. Fanny knew he had been jealous, but she thought that it was now over; she did not realise what he was going through; she was conscious of something – she had an inkling – but she did not know the whole truth.

At Christmas, Leo Dettrick came back from Italy. He had finished his book. He came straight to Hockley. Michael was pleased to see him. He was never jealous of Leo. He liked talking to him. Leo thought that both Fanny and Michael had altered since he had been away. Michael seemed absent-minded; Fanny more aloof than ever, almost as if she were living in another world, or looking at people with detachment, as through the wrong end of a telescope. She was more beautiful than ever, and gay, and apparently happy.

Michael and Fanny were going to London for the opening of Parliament, and Leo Dettrick had taken a flat in London for six months. Just before they left Hockley, Cuthbert Lyley asked if he might come over to luncheon and spend the afternoon, and bring his sister and his cousin. When Cuthbert Lyley and Mrs Tracy arrived, to Fanny and Michael's surprise the cousin was Basil Wake. Michael had not seen him since Hyacinth's death. After luncheon a walk was suggested. Leo Dettrick had a cold, and said he would stay at home. Mrs Tracy said she would stay with him. Cuthbert asked Fanny to show him the garden; he wished to seize the unique opportunity of doing this without his sister being present. She hesitated, but Michael backed Cuthbert up, and insisted. Thus Basil Wake and Michael were left together. Michael had expected to feel awkward, and Fanny had expected the same thing for him in a still higher degree, but she was wrong. He did not feel awkward.

Basil suggested a walk in the woods.

"Yes," said Michael, "by all means." Michael fetched his retriever, Sally, and they started off for a walk. They happened to take the same road and to go the same way as Michael had been with Jack Canning at his last bachelor party. The country looked different now – none the less beautiful, but to Michael there was something morally as well as physically wintry about everything, and especially about the bright mocking sunshine…

The ground was hard, but it was not freezing. There was no trace of snow, no wind. The bare boughs, gemmed with shining drops, made Chinese-like patterns against the serene sky. It was what is called seasonable weather. Michael enjoyed that kind of day above all things as a rule, but today the exhilaration had seemed to have left the brisk atmosphere – for him.

Basil and Michael walked along the broad woodland, on one side of which there was a mere, and on the other some fields, and every now and then a clump of firs. They walked in silence for a little time. Michael did not feel uncomfortable with Basil Wake; on the contrary, he found his company, and even his silences, soothing.

"I wanted to come over," Basil Wake said, after a time. "I wanted to see you. In fact, I was just going to write to you." He coughed. "The other day," he went on, "I was turning out some old drawers in a writing-table, and I came across in a small writing-desk that Hyacinth once bought at a sale, a drawer inside a drawer – a ' secret' drawer, I suppose, except that there was no secret about it – but I had never noticed it. I had opened the desk before, and taken out the papers that were in it, among which was Hyacinth's private will; but in this little 'secret' drawer there were two more letters – one addressed to me, and one small envelope marked 'A medal for Michael, if I die,' with a date on it. It was, as you see, just before her operation. Here it is," he said, and he took from his pocket an envelope the size of a visiting card, which had inside it a hard object.

Michael opened it. Inside the envelope was a penny medal of Saint Anthony. Michael did not recognise the subject, as he knew nothing of such things. There was nothing else, no writing.

"Thank you," said Michael, taking it.

"I am glad to have found it, and glad you should have it. She was fond of you always, you know, right up till the end. Hyacinth was a person who didn't change." Michael felt there was nothing to be said. "When she died I wanted to see you, but I couldn't see anyone for a long time," Basil went on; "I couldn't…then, after a time, I would have liked to have seen you, but…well, I just let things be. I thought we might perhaps meet…but we didn't…the other day I found this, so when Cuthbert asked me to stay here, I was glad, as I thought I should have the opportunity of seeing you. I never see anyone who knew her… I mean who knew her really. I know lots of people who think they knew her, and didn't… There's Edith Tracy; but she didn't really know her at all… Cuthbert might have, but didn't…it's nearly five years ago now since she died, but I feel just the same as when it happened. I don't find that time makes any difference – I mean difference to the sense of loss; I think it makes it worse. Of course, the actual pain of the blow goes – the sharpness of death, you know – but what takes its place, the feeling of gap, *that* is always there, and grows, I think, worse as time goes on. She was glad you had made such a happy marriage. She said she thought your wife was *remarkable*, 'one in a thousand,' and she thought you would be happy. I blame myself often. I think I ought – I think I could – have made her happier than she was. I made life dull for her."

Michael shook his head.

"Yes, I did. I know exactly; don't try and console me. And now I often feel remorse. You see, she was so unselfish that if there was anything she liked, and she thought I didn't, she would give it up, cut it out of her life, however much it meant to her. I never ought to have allowed that to happen. But she did those things quietly, without one's knowing it. Now it's too late. I often think of that, and I'm sorry."

"Whatever she's thinking of now, she's not thinking of that."

"Ah, if one could believe that things went on...if only... I can't, but she could; she felt quite certain...it was wonderful."

"Yes," said Michael. "I know that must have been a great comfort to her."

"Do you know what she used to say about you?...do you mind if I tell you something rather personal?" he asked wistfully.

"Anything you like," Michael stammered.

"Well, she said, talking of your marriage, after she had met you both, that she wondered whether you appreciated your wife. I said, of course you did. She said she knew you did in a way, otherwise you would not have married her; but she said she wondered whether you appreciated her to the full. She said your wife was a *remarkable* woman, with a great deal in her that nobody suspected. Of course, this was, she said, guess-work. She hardly knew her. She only saw her once or twice, I think, but then her guesses were nearly always right; they were better than other people's certainties. She said she thought your wife needed understanding – well, if she sees what is going on now...she ought to be pleased. She was pleased when your son was born. That's all. I beg your pardon if you think I have been tactless or indiscreet; I didn't mean to be, but I felt I ought – I felt I *had* – to tell you this, and I thought you would understand."

"Yes, thank you; I...do...understand," Michael said slowly. He felt bewildered and ashamed of himself, ashamed of himself for a thousand reasons, and perhaps mostly because he realised how completely the image of Hyacinth had faded from his mind. All Basil's talk seemed to him about ghostland, and yet it affected him with a bitter remorse.

"Life, and especially mine," he thought, "is in a tangle. I have made a mess of things. I have done everything wrong I could have, made every possible mistake. I have only myself to blame – and the worst thing of all is what I have done to Fanny. What is it Othello says about the base Indian throwing away a pearl richer than…all his tribe?…and I dare to be jealous! and here is this man…whom I…" and he compared himself with Basil Wake… He felt sure that there was no deception about the situation: that Basil Wake had known and knew everything, saw all round it, understood whatever there was to understand, forgave what there was to forgive; it was nothing to him compared with his immense, infinite love for his wife, which had been, and still was…and Michael thought of the past and of the present, and was ashamed.

"At any rate," he thought, "there is one thing I can do – that is to stop being idiotically jealous of George…and at least try to make Fanny happier."

He made the resolution in all sincerity. But he was haunted by the fear that it was now too late. He would never win Fanny's love now. He had destroyed the possibility. His marriage had been a crime. He knew it at the time. He had hinted as much to his aunt and to Mrs Branksome. They, of course, had had no patience with such ideas. It was a crime to marry a woman like Fanny because it was convenient…no doubt marriages of convenience were often successful, sometimes the best; no doubt marriage was a lottery, and love matches were often a failure and ended in disaster; but none the less it had been a crime for him to marry Fanny, and he was being punished for it. The worst of it was that his punishment made her suffer…he would try his best – he would win her love. After all, he might, it was possible; he loved her, and she had loved him. Why should she not love him again? But at the back of and through all these thoughts echoed the words "too late."

During the rest of the walk they talked of other things.

While this was going on, Fanny was showing Cuthbert Lyley the garden, and they talked about what would be best for the coming spring, and of the future of the garden. The main arrangements had already been made in the autumn, but there was plenty to talk about. Intermingled with their talk on gardening, they discussed other matters. Fanny could say anything to Cuthbert; she knew him intimately now, and had given up wearing a mask with him. It was no use.

"Leo Dettrick is looking well," he said.

"Yes, isn't he? he enjoyed his stay abroad."

"I have never seen him look better. He has changed since he came to live here."

"Has he? I didn't know him before…at least, I only saw him once."

"He is very much changed. You have changed him completely."

"I?"

"Yes," Cuthbert smiled gently. "You, of course…surely you know it?"

"He seems to me exactly the same."

"The same as he has been since you have known him, but different from what he used to be before you knew him."

"Is he?"

"Yes; you see I have known him for years. I knew him when he was devoted to Daphne Adeane. I never saw anyone so devoted except one other – that was his friend, Francis Greene."

"Francis Greene, the doctor?"

"Yes."

"Was he devoted to her, too?"

"Oh yes; madly devoted to her."

"And which did she love best?"

"I don't know – both, perhaps neither; nobody ever knew. I didn't know her well."

"But you *do* guess that sort of thing."

"I had and have no idea. She was a strange woman, unlike anyone I have ever met."

"She must have had great charm."

"It was not what most people call charm…at least there was little vivacity, although every now and then there were exquisite ripples of amusement; but she affected one like old-fashioned music, and the more you saw her, the more you wanted to see her. Seeing other people after seeing her was like hearing a pianoforte when one is used to older instruments; harpsichords, spinets. It is intolerable. Everyone felt like that, and yet she said little and did nothing. But Leo Dettrick thought of nothing else; he lived for her; she was his whole life, and now he has forgotten her; you have made him forget her."

"Oh, don't say that; *please, please* don't say that," said Fanny, thinking of George and Mrs Housman, and the old bitterness came back.

"It's true. He is no longer unhappy; he is happy; he no longer lives in the past, but in the present. You see, my dear child, the dead have no chance when they compete with the living…the living win; and it is right that this should be so. Let the dead bury their dead. It is only fair. Don't blame yourself; you have done no harm. You have made him work, you have made him want to live again. You have brought him back to life."

"You know he has never made up to me, never said a word of…"

"I know; but all the same he is a changed man. Of course he isn't conscious of this himself, and if he was told that he had forgotten Daphne Adeane, he would not admit it for a moment; but she had done her task, and even her death has made him renew his life, because he would never have loved you…if it hadn't been for Daphne. You know you are a little like her – not in the least really; she was darker, and her eyes were a different colour, and she looked more Southern – but there is something; sometimes it hits one. It is like hearing a tune that is like

198

another and yet different – not an imitation, but something kindred. I expect people have told you this before."

"Yes, they have," said Fanny. "Colonel Branksome thought so."

"It is the most elusive likeness in the world, but I'm sure it has struck everyone who ever saw Daphne Adeane, and who knows you. Without any flattery or compliment making, she had not a tithe of your beauty – she was never thought to be a beauty; but she had a grace and a fascination of her own that nobody has been able to define, let alone to draw or to paint. It was wonderful to see her kneel in the chapel at Seyton."

"She was a Catholic, too?"

"Too?"

Fanny had been thinking of Hyacinth and of Kranitzky, and that it was odd that two dead people who had played a part in the life of those who were near to her were both of them Catholics.

"I mean that she was a Catholic, although her husband wasn't?"

"Yes; he isn't."

"And has he forgotten her?"

"Adeane?"

"Yes."

"No. I don't think he ever will."

"Did you like him?"

"An excellent fellow. Ordinary, solid, sensible, rather dull, but good through and through – as good as gold."

"Some men are faithful." She was thinking of Basil Wake. One glance at him had been enough for Fanny to decide that he, at any rate, had not forgotten Hyacinth.

"You think that most men are fickle?"

"Indescribably fickle."

"Isn't it sometimes the woman's fault?"

"In what way?"

"I think that sometimes a man is made fickle because he thinks the woman – his wife, let us say – does not care, has stopped caring, or cares for someone else. First of all he becomes jealous, and then – well, then, anything happens."

Fanny laughed.

"You mean that for me?"

Cuthbert smiled.

"You think I may drive Michael to a state of fickleness?"

"Possibly."

"He has always been *fickle* – that is to say he has never cared for *me* really."

"I am certain he does now."

"That proves it. He cares for me at this moment, and for the moment, because he is piqued."

"I think you are playing with fire."

"Where is the fire? What fire? Not Leo?"

"Oh no; but you say Michael is piqued. That must be your fault. I am sure Michael is unhappy."

"And it's my fault?"

Cuthbert said nothing.

"What am I to do?"

"If you can't make him happy, don't make him unhappy."

"What makes him unhappy?"

"Other people – all you do *outside* his life."

"Leo?"

"Oh no, not Leo; he doesn't mind Leo. He likes Leo; but he isn't the only man you see. You're surrounded now, and admired, and talked about, and I suppose it is galling for Michael to have no part in it; he's proud of you, but you don't let him share it."

"Cuthbert, you don't understand that I do what I can, but I can't give what I haven't got; one side of me is dead. I am fond of Michael; I would do anything for him; I respect him. I try to be, I believe I am, a tolerably 'good wife.' I would never do him a wrong or an injury. I have no friends that are not his. I keep nothing from him. I live in public. It is he who asks Leo; he who asks…well, anyone. But I can't bring to life what is dead in me, and give what I once had and have no longer got; it's not there."

"Things often seem dead, when they are only dormant; like Mount Vesuvius, they break out again unexpectedly in eruptions."

"It is not dormant; that particular thing in me, that side of me, is dead, killed; but I'm quite happy all the same; the rest of myself is alive, but I can't tell you how indifferent I feel. Sometimes, in one sense, I seem to care for nothing and nobody, like the Miller of Dee."

"That is just what I say, and just where I think you are so mistaken, or rather, short-sighted. You say you keep nothing from Michael – you keep your soul from him; everything. Do you remember Shakespeare's sonnet:

'They that have power to hurt and will do none,
That do not do the thing they most do show,
Who, moving others, are themselves as stone,
Unmoved, cold, and to temptation slow'?

You think you are like that. You are living up to that. I know you are indifferent, detached from the world; that you have your home, your children, your husband, your duties; you do it all conscientiously, beautifully. You are surrounded with friends. It's all perfect…but… I may be wrong – I don't think you are really like the sonnet, and I am sure Michael doesn't think so, only you are behaving like that to him."

"I usen't to be like that to him."

"It's very impertinent and officious my saying all this, but I am, after all, old enough to be your father – almost your grandfather – and I am so fond of you both. I think, if you could make everything a little different for Michael, all would be all right; if you don't, I think it might lead to something dangerous."

"In what way?"

"Well, I think something might come along, and then there might be an eruption of Mount Vesuvius, which would lead to unhappiness all round."

"I haven't seen anyone I have given a thought to in that sort of way, not since I have been married. But I believe you are right in one way. I think I am making Michael's life dull. It's not that he doesn't see his friends. I am always asking people to amuse him here and in London, the people he likes, or not asking them when he doesn't want me to. It's not that…our public life…you are quite right, is perfect…it's our private life…our inside life that is bad. I am shutting him out of my inner mind. I will try and do better. I will try to pretend to open, even if I really can't open, what I ought to throw open. I have been selfish, and stupid, and unimaginative. I will try and turn over a new leaf. I will try and make Michael happier. There, I promise, Cuthbert."

Then they talked of gardening again.

While this conversation was going on, Mrs Tracy and Leo Dettrick were sitting in the panelled hall, by the fire, and they, too, were discussing Michael and Fanny.

"She has come on tremendously," said Mrs Tracy. "When she first married she was pretty, and then afterwards she looked peaky and thin; but since she went abroad last year, she has become a different being. I admire her enormously, so does Cuthbert. He thinks she is curiously like Daphne Adeane."

"I see what he means; Francis Greene thought so, too."

"Cuthbert thinks so, too, but he thinks Fanny is more beautiful than dear Daphne was. She has the same intangible charm, but much greater beauty of line and features as well."

Leo didn't contradict her.

"That settles it. He's in love with her," thought Mrs Tracy, and she was glad, because she liked romance. "I think they are happy, but Michael seems to me a little bit down in the dumps this winter."

"He doesn't appreciate Fanny," said Leo. "He appreciates her in a way; looks after her, does anything for her; is attentive and generous – what is called 'an admirable husband,' but he has no idea of all that there is in her. I consider Fanny Choyce to be one of the most remarkable women I have ever seen. Michael has no idea of that. You see, Michael is the best fellow in the world, but he has no imagination."

"No one is a prophet to their own husband, I suppose."

"No, but it is a pity. I think she is lonely."

"Lonely? There are always dozens of people at Hockley."

"Yes, that's just it. You see, Michael…"

The conversation was then interrupted. They were joined by the others.

CHAPTER XVII

When Fanny and Michael went up to London for the opening of Parliament, they had each of them resolved to turn over a new leaf.

"This ever-diverse pair" thought that by turning over a new leaf the diversity would cease, the unexpressed discords would be resolved, and that union would be reached.

Michael made up his mind that he would never be jealous again, and he urged Fanny to ask George to the house. Fanny understood his motive and professed to comply – that is to say, she did not refuse to do this, but she left it undone as much as possible. It was George who did the refusing.

Fanny's methods towards Michael were much the same as his towards her.

She was always asking to the house the people – the women, that is to say – she thought he liked, even when she disliked them. She did not see that he wanted the society and the presence of no one save herself.

Everything went on till Easter smoothly and uneventfully. Nothing of interest happened.

They spent the Easter recess at Langbourne with the Branksomes. Both Margaret and Alice were there with their husbands.

After Easter they were back again in London.

Leo Dettrick was in the middle of a book, and he had undertaken to finish it before the end of the summer.

He suddenly felt that it would be impossible to work in London. He sub-let the flat he had taken for three months, and he left London for France. He took a small house on the Seine, not far from Rouen.

There he found peace and leisure. This change of plan of his was as unexpected to himself as it was to Fanny. He had met her at a small dinner one night, and she had asked him to come and see her the following day. Instead of his coming, she received a telegram, which said that he was going abroad. The next she heard of him was two weeks later. He wrote as follows:

"I am now settled down. The house is small, white, and clean. There are polished *parquet* floors, grey and white *boiseries*. A nice, empty garden; a kind, large, old woman called Marianne who cooks divinely, and appears to be seldom without a *marmite* in her hand. It takes her over three-quarters of an hour to make coffee; possibly a little longer. She roasts it in one of those round roasters you see in old pictures, 'Cries of Paris,' in which you see people doing it at the corner of a street.

"Apart from watching the coffee being made, my day is like this:

"I am called early, at half-past seven; I drink *café au lait* and eat a crisp *croissant*. Then I get up, and I work till the coffee-roasting has begun, at about a quarter to twelve. At half-past twelve I have *déjeuner* and drink the coffee. Then I have a slight siesta. It is hot here, hotter than in England. Then I go out and go on the river in a boat; if it is hot enough I bathe at the island. I take books with me. I come back between five and six, work till dinner, have dinner at eight, stroll in the garden, talk to Marianne, read, smoke, go to bed. The same routine every day. I have seen no friends, no neighbours.

"You know the reason I have left London? To write my book? Yes; but why can't I write my book in London? Because of Mrs Choyce – Fanny Choyce. She is distracting. That is the solemn truth. The book is going on quite nicely, thank you. Write, please, from time to time, if you have time, which you won't have."

Fanny answered a few days later as follows:

> 145A QUEEN ANNE'S GATE,
> *May* 1914.

"DEAR LEO, – Thank you for writing. I have been rather rushed lately, and haven't had a minute to write. Michael spoke in the House last night: really very well, and I think he was pleased. We are going to mother's for Whitsuntide – to Devonshire; Madame de Luce and Madame San Gervasio are both coming to London after Easter. I have asked both of them to Hockley for Michael. He is in good spirits, and is rather taken by Mrs Otis, a beautiful American, and I really think he is happy about himself. He sends you his love. I am glad your book is going on well, but I think you could have done it just as well in London! It is not as if one sees much of you in London!

"Must stop. – Yours, etc.

> F.C."

A little later Leo wrote as follows:

"Your letters grow shorter and shorter. You must be having what the Americans call a hectic time. It is difficult to realise it here. I have been here now for three weeks, and I feel as if I had lived here all my life. By writing a little every day, I have almost finished my book. As Baudelaire said: *'L'inspiration c'est de travailler tous les jours.'* He was right. I shouldn't have done that in London, whatever you say. I have not exchanged a word with a soul, except the people in the shops and with Marianne, since I have been here. French people have the artistic sense in everything, which is equivalent to realising that there is a wrong and a right way of doing everything, and that there is a place where one should stop – a definite line which must not be crossed. Marianne, while she was cooking a cutlet for me yesterday, described to me that she had watched her niece Adèle roasting a goose, and towards the end of the proceeding Adèle had sprinkled half a spoonful of – a slight ingredient, I forget what – onto the goose as it was being roasted, and she, Marianne, told me, when she observed this she had said to herself, '*Tiens, Adèle a du goût.*' That's it; that is the root of all art: *Adèle a du goût* – or she hasn't, as the case may be. I'm afraid the new book will make you say that Adèle has been lamentably deficient in *goût*! However, it can't be helped. It will be finished by the end of June, I hope. I shall come back to London as soon as it is finished – for a little time; but I mean to take this house *on* if possible, and to come here again in August. You and Michael must come and stay with me. There is plenty of room. – Yours,

L.D."

After Whitsuntide the correspondence dropped and died. Fanny was too busy in her crowded life and Leo was too absorbed in his solitude to write letters. Fanny's life had all of a sudden become feverishly full. Leo's work had all of a sudden taken the bit into its teeth – taken charge, so to speak – and run away with him.

Fanny sat down once or twice during May and June to write to Leo, but as soon as she began to try and formulate a retrospect in her mind, she realised that she had forgotten what she had done. The immediate past was a pleasant-coloured blur. She and Michael saw a number of people. There were always friends coming in and out of the house at Queen Anne's

Gate, and Michael invited friends to stay at Hockley every Friday, generally the same people.

Michael was busy in his political life.

Politicians were absorbed by many burning questions – the Irish Conference; the Suffragette question. Ulster was said to be arming; but the horizon of foreign politics was said to be clear. Michael said to Fanny one day:

"Our relations with Germany are better than they have been for a long time, and our relations with France and Russia are good, too, of course."

One morning, at the beginning of June, Stephen Lacy strolled into the dining-room at Queen Anne's Gate while Michael and Fanny were having breakfast.

"I've got some news for you," he said. "My brother has married Rose Mary Troumestre."

He was alluding to Walter Troumestre's widow.

"Oh, really?" said Michael cheerfully.

"Really," said Fanny, with a simulated cheerful interest. "When were they married?"

"Yesterday," said Stephen. "Quietly. It's in *The Times* today. They have gone to France. Someone has lent them a house. It was only settled about a fortnight ago."

Stephen didn't appear to be greatly pleased, nor did Michael. He hardly knew Stephen's brother, and Walter Troumestre had been one of his greatest friends. As for Fanny, the news gave her a stab. It was another reminder of the frailty of mortal affairs. She felt she realised this frailty all too well already, without these daily reminders. She felt that both Stephen and Michael minded this having happened – Stephen because he had been fond of Bernard's first wife, and Michael because he had been fond of Rose Mary's first husband. Life, she thought, is a curious game.

After he had delivered this piece of news Stephen went to the City and Michael to his office.

Fanny was right both about Stephen and Michael. Michael minded. It saddened him. It confirmed the idea that came to him when he talked to Walter during his last bachelor party. So, after all, it was true. Walter's marriage had not been a happy one...perhaps Windlestone had loved Rose Mary the whole time. Were there such things as happy marriages? He was sure that everybody thought that Fanny and he were what is called "happily married." So they were, in a way. That is to say, their life was smooth. On the surface it seemed perfect. But, but...he felt lonely, isolated, never more so than now when Fanny, as he saw, was making every effort to fill his life, and to amuse him.

"She thinks," he thought, "I enjoy having people like Madame San Gervasio and Madame de Luce or Mrs Otis to stay with me, and I have to play up to it... She little knows that I wouldn't care if they were all stricken dead...agreeable, nice people, to be sure...nice-looking, charming; but what do they matter to me? I would give anything for her to say once she would rather be alone with me." And as he walked through the bright noisy street to his office he felt cold. "Why can't she love me?" he asked himself. "The reason why is, I suppose, because I played her false originally."

Fanny was feeling equally lonely and comfortless. She felt as if she had heard a warning note, a knell in the middle of a feast. She longed to discuss the matter of Rose Mary Troumestre's marriage with someone. She rang up Lady Jarvis, and asked her to come to luncheon if she was doing nothing else. Lady Jarvis came to luncheon, and they went out together afterwards, driving in a motor, shopping.

Fanny told her this piece of news.

"Walter Troumestre," she said, "was a great friend of Michael's – perhaps his greatest friend. He minded his death enormously. I had always thought his wife was supposed to be devoted to him."

"Yes?" said Lady Jarvis. "I hardly knew them."

"And did you know Lady Windlestone?"

"Only by sight. She didn't go out much in the last years. She was delicate. I admired her immensely. She had distinction."

"Do you think," said Fanny, "that people – that men – well, men and women if you like – always forget? It seems to me so extraordinary that a man like Stephen's brother – if he was as devoted to his wife as people say he was, and if she was as charming and beautiful as people say *she* was – can marry again so soon – and that Walter's wife can have done the same – don't you think so? if she was fond of him – and everybody says she was fond of him?"

"Lord Windlestone was said to be in love with her before – I don't know. I didn't know them – but I don't think it is odd. These things happen: 'elective affinities,' you know. You remember that funny little story by Rudyard Kipling called 'A Wayside Comedy'? I think that is typical of so many dramas in life. I have certainly seen some astonishing things of that kind. I've seen people change I thought would never change."

Fanny was uncomfortable. At the same time she wanted to hear what Lady Jarvis was going to say.

"Who?" she asked, suspecting what the answer would be. She foresaw the possible answer – one she feared, but felt that Lady Jarvis could not possibly know enough to make it.

"Well, Leo Dettrick," said Lady Jarvis.

Fanny was relieved. She was afraid Lady Jarvis might say George Ayton.

"You mean he has forgotten Daphne Adeane?"

"Yes – well, if not forgotten, he has got over it; that's the same thing, isn't it?"

"I don't think he *has* forgotten her," said Fanny, "I don't think, in a way, he *will* ever get over it."

"Ah! if you had known him before. It's you, Fanny, darling. You have made him get over it, and a good thing too – after all."

"His relation to me is most peculiar," said Fanny. "He never makes up to me; he never has. We made friends on the footing

– on the positive understanding – that he belonged to the past once and for all, and that nothing would ever change that."

"Something has changed it, all the same. Men, of course, think they won't change; but they do – they can't help it. They are changing while they say it. I dare say he still thinks he is just as faithful to Daphne's memory as ever – but I, who knew them at the time, can assure you it isn't so."

"Was she fond of him?"

"My dear, she was crazily in love with him."

"Oh no; really?"

"Crazily in love with him. She couldn't see for love."

"Really! That is very interesting. I was always told that she cared for no one. Possibly for her husband, but that no one knew."

"A man must have told you that, my dear."

"It was a man, but an acute and sensitive man, a man with intuition, and someone who knew her. It was Cuthbert Lyley."

"He didn't really know her, or…well, perhaps he did, perhaps he knew her well enough, well enough to *know*; perhaps he said that to you out of loyalty to *her*. He would respect his knowledge – her secret, that is to say – if he knew. Yes, Fanny, I believe you are right. Of course you are right! Of course he knew! He couldn't *not* have known, but he would never tell, not any woman, not even you, still less a man. But I can promise you that she was in love with him; far more in love with him than he was with her. He loved her, yes…in a way he loved her *infinitely*…and he loved her with plain, ordinary love; but it was she who began it, she who took the initiative, although she seemed to do nothing but smoke cigarettes. She conquered him, annexed him, and made him hers. Of course he was in love, as I say, but there was this vast difference. He was the *only person*, the only *thing*, that Daphne Adeane loved; but Leo loved something else. I am not sure Daphne had the first place – in fact, I am quite sure she hadn't – no, not the first place in his life. It's all nonsense, of course, saying he could only love one person; he could love a dozen, and all at the same time – any artist can, and they usually do."

"But who had the first place?"

"It wasn't a person, and it never will be. It was no one. It was and it is his work and his books. He is a real artist in that way, as in others. No one, no woman, will ever have complete hold of him. He will always elude them, always escape. Because, you see, his real mistress, his first mistress, his *only* mistress, is his art, his work, his *métier*, which he may *hate* at times; but which he will love *and* hate if he hates it, and that is the fiercest of all love. But the man who was crazily in love with her was the other man."

They were driving through Regent's Park. Fanny noticed some people rowing in a boat on the lake and some children playing on the grass, and that vignette was destined to remain in her mind, that trivial sight was imprinted in indelible colours, and destined to come back again often and often in after years, when so much else was forgotten.

"Who was the other man?" she asked. She knew what the answer would be.

"Francis Greene."

"The doctor?"

"Yes. Do you know him?"

"Only professionally. I have only seen him twice, but I have heard a lot about him from Leo Dettrick. He is his greatest friend."

"Yes, and they both loved Daphne: and the odd thing is, this created no jealousy between them, because I think that each of them thought that Daphne loved neither of them; that she was apart, aloof, out of reach. They little knew, poor fools! I am almost certain that if Leo Dettrick had asked Daphne to go to the end of the world with him, she would have done it, almost certain, not quite."

"Really?"

"Well, I know she would have had a dreadful struggle not to do it. Possibly the idea of the children might have prevented her. No, I don't think even her children would have prevented it at one moment. She was *crazily* in love with him, at one moment."

"And he didn't know it?"

"No, he never knew how much she loved him, never knew to what extent she loved him; and she tried her best to hide it from him and succeeded – only it killed her."

"She died of it?"

"Yes, she died of it."

"Wasn't she a devout Catholic? Wouldn't that have had an effect?"

"Yes – she was, I think, a believing Catholic; but I don't myself believe religion ever affects conduct much. Of course there are cases – Clare Housman's life, for instance, I think was affected by her religion; but then that was different."

"I didn't know her," said Fanny, rather uncomfortably. "I only saw her once at a party."

"There is a case," said Lady Jarvis, "of the opposite."

"The opposite of what?"

"The opposite of what we were talking about – of people, of men, getting over things and forgetting."

"How?"

"Well, George Ayton. He was madly in love with Clare Housman, and when she went into the convent he really was broken. Well, he is, I think, as miserable as ever – more miserable than ever, perhaps."

"Yes, I'm sure he is," said Fanny, immensely relieved, "just as miserable as ever."

"I thought for a moment in Scotland this year that he was rather attracted by you."

"Oh!" said Fanny. "I always had the feeling that he was mentally comparing me with some *original* in his mind, and finding me wanting; just as if one had been a piece of spurious

213

china or imitation furniture – a fake. He made me feel like a fake."

"Nonsense, nobody would ever take you for anything but an original. My only wonder is you haven't made more havoc than you have, but perhaps," she laughed, "you have. Perhaps you are taking me in. I never trust still waters, and, you know, you are not unlike Daphne Adeane. People must have told you that?"

"Yes, they have."

"Not to look at, exactly – you are very different. She had not your looks – but there is something – and the effect you have on people is the same *kind* of effect."

"The effect I have? Do I have an effect?"

"On everybody – Leo, Michael, Cuthbert, George Ayton even."

"I never seem to have any effect at all."

"That's because you don't care – but the day you care – "

"What will happen?" Fanny blushed and laughed uneasily.

"Oh! I don't know – eruption, catastrophe, earthquake, a sort of Pompeii. Everybody says, you know, dear, that you and Michael are ideally happy; perhaps you are, in a way; only, only…"

"It's my fault, I'm a bad wife – or, at least, I have been a bad wife – stupid, selfish; but I have been trying to be better lately."

"Michael is tremendously fond of you – in love with you, in love *now*, I mean."

"Do you really think so?"

"Yes, I am sure of it."

They had reached Lady Jarvis' house. Fanny dropped her, refused to go in and have tea, and drove home. On the way back she pondered over what Lady Jarvis had said to her. "She doesn't know about George," she thought. "That is just as well, but she sees exactly how Michael and I stand. Why can't I do better?"

When she got home she went up to her bedroom and had a cry. Once more she felt desolate and isolated. She washed her face and scolded herself, like Alice in Wonderland, and went down to have tea. Some people dropped in; and they thought she was in excellent looks and spirits. She telephoned to the Ritz and asked one of Michael's American friends to dinner on the following Monday...

During the whole of the month of June, Fanny was so fully occupied that time went by with a rush. Michael, too, was absorbed in his work, and the domestic political situation. Leo Dettrick had stopped writing. Then, at the beginning of July, Fanny suddenly got a letter from him saying that he was coming back at once. He arrived in London twenty-four hours after the news had come of the assassination of the Austrian Archduke. He came straight to see Michael in Queen Anne's Gate. He had landed at Southampton.

That night he dined with Michael and Fanny. They discussed the political situation, but only among other things, and more the domestic than the foreign situation. That was, they thought, the usual "trouble in the Balkans." Leo Dettrick had finished his book. They made many plans for the future (he was going back to France), and Michael and Fanny promised to spend the month of August in France with him.

"I think," he said, "it will be lovely there in August, and we will be able to have a real lazy time, just bathing and rowing and doing nothing."

"That will be just what I should like," said Michael. "We're not going to Scotland till September, and I should like a good loaf first."

CHAPTER XVIII

The answer of the Serbs to the Austrians' note had, so Michael had told Fanny, been so reasonably, if not meekly "couched," that it would be difficult for the Austrians to go to war without consenting to the calling of a conference first. And, of course, there would be offers of mediation. But the contrary happened, and Lady Weston, Fanny, Michael, Leo Dettrick, and George Ayton found themselves on a Sunday, in July, discussing what they would do, now that war between Austria and Serbia was a certainty.

Michael wanted to go to the war. He was sick of Parliament, sick of London, sick of his life. He would throw up his seat without a qualm. He hardly dared to think of the possibility of a war, so much did it crown his undared-of hopes.

They were sitting in the garden. It was a hot Sunday afternoon.

"I think that would be a mistake," said George.

"I can't see it," said Michael.

"Now *I*, of course, not only could throw up my job, but *should*," said George.

"I think it's far more difficult for you."

"I don't see that at all."

"After all, you're an Under-Secretary in the Government."

"Yes, but I'm in the House of Lords. That doesn't really count. Now, Michael is what's called a 'coming man'…"

"Oh, don't," said Michael, "people have been telling me I'm a 'coming man' for the last fifteen years, ever since I got into Parliament."

"But you can neither of you want to go either to Serbia or to Austria," said Lady Weston. "It would be silly."

Fanny said nothing, war clouds of any kind made her pensive. Cuthbert Lyley and Mrs Tracy came over during the afternoon. Mrs Tracy was in a state of energetic effervescence. She wanted to organise a caravan ambulance and to go to Serbia and to look after the wounded. She wanted Fanny and Michael to go with her. Michael favoured the idea. "I should like to go," he said.

"But what about your seat in Parliament? what about Fanny and the children?" asked Lady Weston.

"I should go too," said Fanny. "There's nothing I like better than nursing."

"My dear child!" said Lady Weston. "One has to be trained. Amateur nurses are more a hindrance than a help."

"Well, let's do that," said Mrs Tracy. "Cuthbert shall come with us, he's so sympathetic with the sick."

Cuthbert smiled benignly.

"My dear children, what nonsense!" said Lady Weston. She appealed to George. "Isn't it nonsense, George?"

"Well," said George, "I really don't know. I do think, perhaps…"

"For all we know," added Lady Weston, "the whole thing may blow over."

"I suppose we might be drawn into it," said Cuthbert.

"Not as things are at present," said George, "we should never go to war for Serbia. The country would never stand it."

"Yes," said Cuthbert. "But if Russia, Germany, and France…?"

"I don't think it would be a certainty, even then," interrupted George. "I mean, I'm not sure it would be to France's interest for us to come in at once…later, perhaps. But I don't think it will come to that."

"I had a letter from Kranitzky, that Russian who came to supper with us, this morning," said Fanny. "He's on his way home…to Russia. He says he wants to be in time for the European war."

"Then he thinks there will be a European war?" said Cuthbert.

"Apparently," said Michael.

"He thought so last year," said Fanny.

"I think it's nonsense," said Lady Weston. "All that is put about by the Tories and *The National Review.*"

Fanny said nothing. She felt something like the approach of a thundercloud, but she did not visualise it in the form of a European war.

"What would you do if there was a European war, George?" asked Michael.

"I should go to it, somehow, of course."

"So should I."

"I suppose everybody would," said Michael.

"Everybody would try," said Fanny. "But it may not be possible for everyone."

"Some people would have duties at home," said Lady Weston.

"Not the young men," said Fanny. "At least, I hope not."

Lady Weston sadly reflected that it was absurd to call Michael a young man; he was middle-aged, and so was George, as to that. But she made no comment.

"I don't think that people with responsibilities will be able to rush off to the war," she said.

"We don't know that there is going to be a war," said Michael.

"There is a war already," said Fanny.

218

"We shall not go to war for Serbia," repeated George. "The country wouldn't stand it. Your constituents would never stand it, would they, Michael?"

"No, of course not."

"Well, if there's a war," said Leo, "I should like to go to one of the Eastern countries. I should like to go with you and Michael," he said to Fanny.

"What, to Turkey?" said Lady Weston.

"Oh, I don't suppose Turkey will be in it, although in the Balkans, of course, anything is possible," said Leo. "Everything is so much easier in the East for amateurs. Will you take me with you?"

"Of course," said Michael.

"I mean to go to Serbia, seriously," said Mrs Tracy. "I have a great many doctor friends, and I'm going up to London tomorrow morning to see Hanson – the surgeon, you know – and get the best advice from him as to whom to take."

"We'll go too, won't we, Michael?" said Fanny. She knew that Michael wanted to go, she was not going to be an obstacle, especially in a matter of this kind.

"Oh yes, of course," said Michael eagerly. He really felt it would be best for Fanny not to come unless…unless everything by some miracle could be different.

By the end of the afternoon it was settled that Mrs Tracy would go to Serbia with an ambulance and that Michael and Fanny and Leo would go with her. Lady Weston disapproved, but thought the plan too fantastic and unreal to discuss; she was certain it would come to nothing.

The following day, a Monday, Michael and Fanny went up to London. Michael called by Leo's advice on Dr Greene, but he was not back from Australia, although he was expected that week. He then called on Mrs Tracy's friend, who gave him a letter of introduction to another doctor – one who could speak several languages. They wanted a doctor who would go with them. The doctor to whom Michael was given a letter of introduction was called Goldsmith, and he was working in a hospital at Westminster.

Michael called on him and exposed the plan, an ambulance financed by him and Mrs Tracy, for the Serbian wounded: and the need of a doctor.

"I will go on the Austrian side," said the doctor with a guttural accent.

"But we can't go on the Austrian side," said Michael. "We may be at war against the Austrians in a week's time, because the Austrians are the allies of Germany, and we may be at war with Germany."

"It will only depend on Russia if Germany is involved. If anyone else is drawn in, it will be the fault of Russia," said the doctor, pronouncing the word Russia more gutturally than ever.

Michael looked at the doctor's black hair, rather thick aquiline nose and pince-nez, and again said:

"But Austria is Germany's ally, and we have certain obligations to France. There is, after all, the *entente*; if there is a war between Germany and France we shall have to back up our ally."

"England is not the ally of France," said the doctor. "There is only a so-called *entente.*"

"But there are obligations; we shall not be able to let France be attacked... It's not a question of sentiment or honour, or even if it is, it is much more than that. It is a question of life or death, of our very existence."

"It will all depend on Russia. I will go out with you on the Austrian side."

There they were back again at the beginning of the argument. Michael gave it up as a bad job. "The man," he thought, "evidently *is* an Austrian or German Jew."

"Very well," he said, and got up.

"I would not go on the side of that *rabble,*" said the doctor.

"What rabble?" asked Michael.

"All those treacherous Slavs… It will all depend if Russia backs them up, but I do not think she will; she only bluffs, Russia. She has bluffed before."

"Very well, then; there is nothing more to be said. Good afternoon," said Michael.

The doctor bowed stiffly from the waist.

That night Michael and Fanny went to a dance they had been asked to at the Thames Hotel.

The evening newspapers said that the excitement in Berlin was great, and that the crowd was favourably disposed towards England.

Michael felt uneasy. He thought that if the Germans made war on France, we should be in honour bound to come in, whether we liked it or not…and yet he did not feel it was inevitable, not as inevitable as he wished it to be. He reviewed rapidly in his mind those in the Cabinet who would be for or against war. He knew there was an anti-war current in the Cabinet.

At the dance the atmosphere seemed to him graver than it had been during the last few days. He talked to some of the foreign diplomats and to a clever Frenchman. They all took a grave view of the situation, especially the Frenchman. He talked to several friends, and he watched the dancing.

There was supper at little tables. Michael had a feeling as of the Day of Judgment about this entertainment. Many of the people he knew best were there, and some men of importance in politics and diplomacy, both English and foreign.

Perhaps in a week's time, perhaps sooner, these elements which now constituted a polished and ornamental social whole, would be scattered to the ends of the earth… He thought of Versailles on the eve of the Revolution, of Brussels before Waterloo… He passed a table where Jean Brandon, Jack Canning, Dick Clive, and Dick's sister-in-law Alice, were having supper. They beckoned to him to join them, which he did.

Jean's appearance startled him. She was looking beautiful, her eyes were shining like stars, her expression was radiant. Jack too seemed unusually happy.

"Well, what do you think of things? Do you think we shall be dragged in?" Michael asked.

"I hope to God we shan't back out," said Canning, "but I'm not sure. I wouldn't trust the Government a yard."

"Not Grey?" asked Michael. "What rubbish!"

"Oh! well, *he* may be all right, but he may get talked down; there are traitors in the Cabinet."

"Oh rot, Jack!"

"At any rate…they are so weak – and so shifty – and we always *do* climb down."

"Well, then, that would be everybody's fault. Yours – mine – public opinion."

"If Germany attacks France and we don't come in, I shall join the French army as a private – and so will a great many others."

"But," said Jean, "something may still happen to prevent the fire spreading. The evening newspapers say that they shouted *'Hoch England!'* opposite the British Embassy at Berlin today."

"That's because they think we shall be neutral," said Canning. "And they may not be far wrong, worse luck. Damn them!"

"I think they are *quite* wrong," said Michael; "I think they will have a rude awakening." He said this loudly and aggressively, as he noticed that at the next table, within earshot, there was one of the secretaries of the German Embassy whom he knew by sight but not by name. "They will be bitterly disillusioned," he repeated, still more aggressively – "if there is a war – "

The German secretary heard what he said, and made a mental note that living in England was likely to be disagreeable in the immediate future.

Michael's aggressive tone was really the fruit of fear, just as one scolds children most when they have frightened one by getting into danger. Michael was afraid, especially after the conversation he had had with the Frenchman, that it was not at all certain that England would come into the war… "And if we don't come in at once," he thought, "it will be too late, and we shall be ruined, as well as dishonoured. People don't understand." He thought of his stolid constituents hearing England was to go to war because of Serbia. Michael became restless. He could no longer endure the sight of people dancing. He said goodnight to Jean and Jack, left the supper-table, and went in search of Fanny.

Fanny had been dancing, and she was now sitting out with a Russian diplomat called Agoura on a sofa in a room next to the ballroom.

"So you think we shall all be in it?" she was saying.

"Yes, I do think so," said the Russian; "you will have to come in sooner or later to save your own skins, so you had much better come in at once."

"I can't imagine it," said Fanny.

Michael came up to them. Another dance began, and Agoura took leave of Fanny.

"Do you want to stay?" asked Michael.

" No," she said truthfully, "I would rather go home."

" Have you had supper?"

"Oh yes, long ago" – this was not true – "let's go."

As they went home, driving in a taxi, Fanny said: "Jack Canning and Jean Brandon are engaged at last."

"Did they tell you?"

"No, I saw it by his face."

"Then you don't know for certain?"

"I'm morally certain. I would bet anything."

"Well, that's funny. I asked Jack to Hockley for Sunday, but he wasn't sure if he could come."

"That proves it," said Fanny; "we must ask them both."

"Who was that George was having supper with?" she asked a moment or two later.

"Lady Windlestone. Poor old Walter's wife. Poor old Walter."

"Oh, really. She's very pretty and young looking."

"She *is* young…he – Stephen's brother, I mean – is much older than she is."

When they got home, they went into the dining-room.

"I'm hungry," said Fanny.

"I thought you'd had supper."

"Well, I did and I didn't… I should like a biscuit."

Michael fetched some cold tongue and some lager beer. They sat down and both of them had some food.

"Do you really think there is going to be a war?…a European war, with us in it, I mean?" she asked.

"I think there will be a big war; whether we shall come in or not I don't know, but I hope so with all my heart."

"Hope so?"

"Yes, of course… If we don't, we shall be ruined, besides not ever being able to look anyone in the face again."

"*Perfide Albion*?"

"With a vengeance. Imagine what the French will say, and rightly."

"But you think we *shall* come in?"

"How can one tell? – these things are like a Greek tragedy. Everything is on the knees of the gods."

"As everything else."

"Yes, I suppose so."

"But if there's a war, and we are in it…will you go?"

"Of course."

"But how?"

"I don't know, I haven't thought – somehow."

"So shall I."

"Hospital?"

"Yes; I don't suppose Edith Tracy will want to go to Serbia now?"

"Not unless things change very much tomorrow…"

"She is sure to want to do something."

"Yes, she is so efficient."

"After all, it's no worse than what has often happened before, is it? – Agadir? and what was the other time?"

"I think it is a little worse."

"Well, bedtime," Fanny said.

They said goodnight, and Fanny thought this ought to have been the supreme moment of their lives. Alas! it was not. Michael felt the same thing, and the taste of life was at that moment bitterer to him than he had ever known it.

"Goodnight, Fanny," he said. "I'm going to fetch a book." He fetched from a bookcase – it was from force of habit – *Happy Thoughts*, by Burnand. As he looked at the title he laughed.

During all that week Michael was almost demented. He thought towards the end of the week that England was not coming in, that nothing was going to be done, that if we did come in, it would be too late. He felt it all the more keenly because he was a Liberal and on the Government side, and he could not endure Jack Canning's taunts. Jack Canning was a Tory, and had been a professional soldier. Leo Dettrick was as violent as Jack. Fanny remained calm. She felt the matter was already decided one way or the other. On Friday, Michael had given up hope. They went to Hockley on Friday afternoon.

Michael had telephoned to Jack Canning the day after the dance. Fanny had been a true prophet… Jack announced his engagement to Jean Brandon. They were both asked to Hockley, and they accepted.

Lady Weston was in Devonshire. George Ayton had been by way of coming, but the march of events and the increasing gravity of the situation made this impossible. He had to stay in London. There were Cabinet meetings on Sunday. The question of peace and war was hanging in the balance.

Fanny and Michael spent the most feverish and restless Sunday they had ever experienced at Hockley. The engaged couple disappeared, happy in spite of everything, perhaps because of everything. George telephoned to Michael once during the day, after luncheon, but he knew nothing.

On Monday morning they went back to London. Fanny went to the House of Commons to hear Sir Edward Grey's speech.

When Michael came in after the debate, he found Fanny in the drawing-room.

"It's all over now," he said; "it will be all right now, whatever happens."

"It means we shall come in?"

"I think so, but not necessarily at once."

They dined alone that night. All the next day – Tuesday – Michael was busy. Mr Asquith spoke in the House in the afternoon, and Fanny again went to the House of Commons. Late at night, as Fanny and Michael were walking home – they had dined and spent the evening with George Ayton – they met Dick Clive on his way back from the Foreign Office.

"War has begun," he said. "Goodnight."

"We are at war," said Michael, with a sigh of relief. Fanny sighed too, but was hers relief or sorrow?

The next day was one of dream-like reaction for them. At breakfast Michael said to Fanny: "I am going to give up my seat."

"How will you get out?"

"I have settled it," said Michael. "I am going to learn to fly. I am going down to the War Office to see about it today."

"To fly?…"

"By the time he has learnt perhaps the war will be over," she thought…but flying was dangerous, war or no war.

Fanny felt as if she were looking on at herself as at a person in a play…not really taking part in the events. "Well," she said, "if you go, I shall go too… I shall be a hospital nurse."

"And the children?"

"Mother will look after them. Do you think it will be a long war?" she said, as if war were a daily occurrence.

"I don't know… I hope not…"

Michael went to the War Office and arranged matters. He was to go to Netheravon and learn to fly at once. But as he had many matters to arrange, he would not leave London before the following Sunday.

They dined alone again. Later in the evening they heard from their open windows the noise of a crowd.

"The people are going to Buckingham Palace," Fanny said. "Let's go and see."

They took a taxi and drove to Buckingham Palace. They got out and stood in the crowd. The King was cheered. Fanny cried silently. They walked back, and instead of going home they walked up Whitehall towards Trafalgar Square. The crowd there was less impressive. A man…in wine…on the top of a taxi was waving a flag and making a speech. They passed two women who exchanged words in German; they were in floods of tears. They heard the words: "Grässlich!" – "Entsetzlich!"

During the next days came rumours of battles fought in Alsace and of Germans mowed down in the frontal attacks on Liège. There was uneasy feeling that the news was less good than it seemed.

On Sunday night Michael and Fanny had their last dinner at Queen Anne's Gate. Michael was going to leave for Netheravon after dinner. Lady Weston had come to London, and she dined with them. Leo Dettrick was there too. He was going out with the Red Cross. His friend, Francis Greene, who had come back from Australia, was arranging this for him.

Mrs Tracy dined with them as well. She had come up to London. She was organising a private hospital which she decided to start somewhere on the French coast. She had asked Fanny to go out with her, and Fanny had promised to do this as soon as she passed her V.A.D. examination. They dined early.

They talked of the situation, of the news, the rumours, the future possibilities. Were the Germans mad? Or had they some new invention?

After dinner Michael said goodbye to his guests. He went downstairs alone with Fanny, and he said, "Goodbye, Fanny dearest. We shall meet before we go to France. I shall be able to come up and see you before you go or before I go. We'll have a race to see who is ready first. I believe Leo will be out before any of us."

"Goodbye, darling Michael," whispered Fanny. He was happy. He felt that the problem of his life was about to be solved. As he kissed Fanny, tears rained down her cheeks. On the stage the picture would have seemed perfect. She was more than moved by the situation…overwhelmed, broken, but she felt bitterly, in spite of what she was feeling, what an immense gulf, what an essential difference…a difference in *kind*, not in degree, and of an infinite kind…there would have been if only she could have felt just a little more, only a grain more. The grain of love which would have moved mountains was not there.

"Am I a bad woman?" she wondered. "Have I turned into a stone?"

She saw Michael off and watched the motor-car start, and then she went into Michael's sitting-room downstairs, and she felt so cold that in spite of the warmth of the night she shivered. She stayed there by herself for a moment.

Everything looked just the same, and yet the whole world from now henceforward would be, she felt, a different, a changed place. She suddenly felt uneasy about the children, and she ran upstairs to the nursery. They were both of them fast asleep.

She went back to her guests in the drawing-room.

CHAPTER XIX

Fanny was not able to go out to France till the end of September. She experienced a sequence of minor disasters. First of all her boy, Peter, was ill, and as soon as he got well she was immobilised by a sprained ankle which came to her through slipping on a piece of orange peel in the Strand.

Michael wrote her cheerful, gay letters from Netheravon. He was getting on splendidly, and felt as if he were at Cambridge again.

Fanny settled to start for France at the end of September, and Michael came up to London to see her off, and to say goodbye. He hoped to be going to France soon himself – he would, perhaps, not have the chance of saying goodbye to her again.

The children were with Lady Weston in Devonshire.

Fanny met him at the station. He looked ten years younger in khaki, in a "maternity" jacket. He had got his wings. They had luncheon together at the Carlton Restaurant, and talked of nothing but the war. The armies were still at the Aisne, and the rush for the coast had not yet begun. In the afternoon – it was Saturday – they went to a *matinée*, and in the evening they went to the "Palace" rather late, after dinner.

When they got home, Michael said he was hungry; they had dined early; and Fanny fetched some cold meat and some lager beer.

"It's just like that night before the war began – over again," said Fanny. "What years ago that seems now!"

"Yes," said Michael, "as if that time belonged to another life." They sat in silence for a little.

"I wonder whether we shall meet in France?" said Michael.

"When do you think you will get out?"

"Not till next year."

He discussed the possibilities in detail, and went into technical matters which he explained.

"Our show is only just beginning – it will grow."

There was a long silence, and then Michael said:

"Do you think we will ever meet again, Fanny?"

"Yes," she said, "I am sure we will."

"I wish…" he said, and then stopped.

"What?" she asked.

"I wished you loved me, Fanny. Loved me really…"

"I do love you, Michael – "

"Yes, you do love me – in a way, but you know what I mean. I mean – love me as I love you."

"Then you do love me?"

"Surely you know that by now."

"Yes, I think I do. I wish, too, Michael – that everything had been different…that I had been different… I feel such a beast…it was all my fault, I feel sometimes like a monster… I am frightened at myself…but there it is, I have tried; you see, it was…it is too late. I would give anything to change…to be changed, to be different…but I can't… I can't give what I haven't got. I can't be better than I am. What I haven't got *now*… I think I started wrong – I have been selfish. I ought to have made you happy. I didn't – I have been vile – unworthy of you. It's like a fairy tale, when the Princess is given every advantage and does everything wrong and throws everything away."

"But that's just what I feel I have done."

"You did nothing wrong – it was *my* fault, and now it's too late."

"Is it too late?"

"Well, I feel I may never see you again. The fact of war is already half like death, isn't it? I feel that whatever happens, nothing will ever be the same again."

"No, I don't suppose it will – but something perhaps will come out of it for you and for me. I am so, so sorry."

"You mustn't talk like that, Michael darling. When you talk like that you make me feel so wretched. If you only knew what I feel about myself."

"But how can you blame yourself?"

"Well, I do blame myself. I was young and foolish when we were married – and oh! so sure! And there were all sorts of things I didn't understand. I thought I understood everything. I understand *now*, Michael. I understand everything. You see, when we were engaged I was so absurdly young – and so arrogantly happy."

"What made you change?"

"Hyacinth."

"You knew?"

"Yes."

"Who told you?"

"No one. At first I knew nothing. I knew she was a friend of yours. You see, I had lived so little in England, and I was naïve too. I knew, and I didn't know, about things. In some ways I knew a great deal more than most girls – than most English girls. For instance, I felt years older than Margaret and Alice Branksome, but in other ways I was like a child – like a baby. It was when we first went to London, to the house in Grosvenor Place, that I felt there was something. I didn't know what it was, but I felt as if there was a ghost coming between you and me. Nothing could have been nicer than you were then – you were angelic – attentive – unselfish in little things…too unselfish. But there was something – wrong, and I knew it. I didn't want to know more. I was afraid. I was like someone in a story who is outside a forbidden cupboard…and then came that party at the Wisters – when Raphael Luc sang – do you remember? I shall never forget the moment when you were listening to the music and Teresa Wister came and asked you to play bridge. I didn't look at you. I was looking at the wall opposite at a picture by Brabazon – Venice on a Rainy Day – and I remember saying to myself, 'Venice on a rainy day is my idea of hell,' and I repeated the word hell and spelt it to myself, H E L L, like that, quite slowly – so it seemed, and yet that only took a few seconds because you said, 'Of course I will,' and your voice told me…well, told me all that I didn't want to know – all that I was afraid of…but even then I, in a way, hoped against hope. I clung to my ignorance. I prayed not to know more, I wanted to let things be…and then Raphael Luc sang – a sentimental French song, and I looked at Hyacinth…she was quite white. I hated her at that moment, really hated her. It was the first time in my life that I understood what *hate* meant – and that made me understand a lot of things…but in spite of that even – I still clung to my tattered rags of ignorance. I still tried to be like an ostrich. And a few days later the truth dawned on me suddenly – finally – the door of the cupboard was burst open. You can't think what I felt like then, Michael…and it's that that made me vile. But don't think I blamed you – I didn't."

"I was to blame – I behaved like a beast."

"No, you didn't – it was nobody's fault – it was life. But how I hated Hyacinth then… I felt I could never forgive her…quite unreasonably, of course, if anything it was for *her* never to forgive me – only I see now what I didn't see then, that she must have been a wonderful woman. I couldn't do her justice then, but I can now. She must have been wonderful."

"Yes, she was – "

"Noble – I couldn't have done what she did. I got the better of my jealousy of Hyacinth more or less; at least, when she died I was sorry for you. I was sorry, *so, so* sorry. I longed to tell you. But I couldn't. I was as sorry as I would have been for someone who had nothing to do with me – just a friend. That it was you and Hyacinth, that Hyacinth was Hyacinth, made no difference. I mean it didn't make me less sorry.

"Life is curious. For years I thought I should never get over Hyacinth's existence, of your having loved her. You see my jealousy was all *retrospect*. I couldn't forgive you and her the past…and then when later I realised that you had forgotten her – all my past jealousy was nothing compared with the new heartache that that gave me. It sounds insane, doesn't it? Don't try and understand. I can't explain. But it was then that I felt life to be really bitter."

"But that's all done with. That all belongs to the past," said Michael. "Can't we forget it? Can't we turn over a new leaf? Can't you give me another chance?"

"It's I who can't give myself another chance. It's I who can't turn over a new leaf. I can't tell you how much I long to – I would give anything in the world to. But one can't turn on one's feelings like a tap. I was very young when I married you, and very foolish, but my love for you was like a china vase or a glass bowl, and instead of guarding it like a treasure, I broke it and nothing could mend it."

"It was I who broke it – but I don't see why it shouldn't be mended. I believe if one doesn't try to mend things they sometimes mend themselves. I agree about the tap. One can't force things, but I believe if one lets things alone, they may come right. I think if *we* only leave things alone they still may come right. You see, I love you so much, Fanny. I understand what a fool I was, what an idiot."

"My poor darling Michael, it wasn't your fault – you are *not* to blame – I promise – I swear. You see, I was foolish, *I* ought to have known better – I ought to have known that I was doing something foolish, but I was young and I was in love – I was sure of myself. No, it was no one's fault except mine."

"But don't you think there is a chance of things coming right – if we don't commit new follies?"

"Perhaps. Miracles do happen."

"You don't love anyone else, do you, Fanny?"

"Oh, no!"

"Not Leo?"

"Oh dear no!" She laughed gently.

"Not George?"

"George Ayton?"

"Yes."

"No, no, no!"

"I'm so glad – I thought at one moment you did."

"No, I promise you – I think he was inclined to be silly about me for a moment – but it's all over now. What is he doing?"

"He wants to join his Yeomanry, but he's still in the Government. Well, I have made a hash of things, but I haven't given up hope yet. I feel the war will make a difference…if we get through it…don't you think there's a chance of that?"

"Yes, perhaps; but I am afraid, Michael, that one part of me is dead. I sometimes think I have been turned to stone as a punishment."

"I don't understand. You are to me *all* alive – every bit of you is alive – and I feel it isn't for me. Only what I do say is that extraordinary things happen in life, and that things do change. They are always changing."

"I wish I was better," she said. "You can't think how horrible I feel. I wish I had made you happy, really happy. I would have given anything to do that… But it's no good pretending to be what one isn't, is it? I couldn't play the part – I couldn't take you in. We must make the best of things as they are. I will try to do better."

"And then, perhaps, when we least expect it, we may meet."

"Like the people in the poem?"

"What poem?"

" 'Go thou to East, I West,' by Coventry Patmore.

" 'Making full circle of our banishment,
Amazèd meet!' "

"I remember. But they were both fond of each other, both equally fond of each other."

"Or they had been."

"To us the right things have always happened at the wrong time."

"It's an annoying, perplexing, contrary world, isn't it?"

"Perfectly damnable!"

"Poor Michael, I'm so sorry. I wish I had been different."

"Don't say that: it was my fault, all my fault from the very beginning. You see, if one breaks the rules one has to take the consequences; if you make a certain mistake in a game of cards you can't win the odd trick. I made a mistake of that kind right at the beginning of the game. I threw away the odd trick. Only sometimes, owing to what other people do, the wrong may come right at the end of the game. That is what I hope may still happen to you and me. But don't let's worry about the past any more."

"The worst of it is I feel everything is too late now."

"I don't believe anything is ever too late," Michael said, with decision.

"We may neither of us come back from the war."

"That would solve the situation."

"I shouldn't mind for myself," said Fanny, "but for the children – what *would* happen to them?"

"Yes, what would happen to them? I have often felt that the children would somehow or other make things right for us some day."

The children were at Lady Weston's in Devonshire, and Michael and Fanny had met there a fortnight earlier. Fanny reflected that the children had not made things right then. But then they were still so small. Peter was only six and Hester only four, and already Peter seemed to look at the world with inquiring eyes, and Fanny sometimes felt that he instinctively suspected the absence of something.

"They are very happy," said Michael. "I went over there once more after we were there."

"Mother likes having them."

At that moment there was the hoot of a motor-horn in the street and a ring at the front door bell, and two of Michael's Flying Corps friends arrived in a taxi. They had come up to London on leave for the night, and they had not been able to find accommodation.

"Can you put us up, old bean?" they shouted.

"Yes, of course," said Michael. "Come in!"

Fanny made the necessary arrangements. They were then given supper, and Michael opened a bottle of champagne for them, and they all launched into an interminable flood of flying shop. One of them was a pilot in a new squadron that was in the process of being formed, and the other was an observer.

Fanny stayed with them for a little. Then she said goodnight and went to bed, leaving them to talk, which they did till the small hours of the morning.

Fanny went to bed, but she did not go to sleep. She lived again through the conversation she had just had with Michael, and she lived through a great deal of her past life. She felt more than she had said to him. It was impossible to tell him the whole truth. What she had said was true, but it was not the whole truth. The real truth was she felt everything was too late. She felt she could never love Michael again as she had loved him when she was engaged, however much he loved her. Never. His love for her could not work the miracle. It was too late. What he had said had been strangely true. Just those things which she had denied, as he said them. She saw now how true they were. It had been a question of initial mistakes. They had both made a mistake. And now the situation was reversed.

Fanny thought of the future and wondered. There were the children. Would they make a difference as they grew up? Fanny was passionately fond of Peter, the boy who was, she felt, like herself. She liked Hester, the girl, less, and Hester was the image of Michael. Michael liked them both. He was fond of children.

What would happen? she wondered. What could happen? And then there was the war – life seemed to be shrouded in a blanket of nightmare. You couldn't get rid of it. You remembered it every morning as you woke up. Not at first. You woke up for a moment, everything was all right, and then you remembered there was something, and then you realised what it was. The war. Then the day began once more, and day followed day as those of convicts serving a term of penal servitude, so Fanny thought, at least. And it was all so long and so slow. One got through it – one had to, but the vista ahead was appalling.

Fanny was glad to be going to France, but she felt so numb that whether life was to be in one place or another seemed almost a matter of indifference.

"What would happen to Michael?" she wondered. He was at any rate happy for the moment, engrossed in the present, thinking of nothing but his job, his new life, his work, his new friends. He would go to France, or somewhere else perhaps? Everything seemed unreal to Fanny. He might be killed, wounded or crippled in an accident – it happened every day. That word *crash*, which came now so glibly and so naturally to his lips. Michael crippled, helpless! He might disappear, she might never hear of him again. Missing. That word was becoming familiar too. And the worst of it was she felt she knew that if this did happen, she would not be able to respond as she should, she would not be able to feel what she ought to feel.

They might both be killed. She might die – of a cold. Death? What did it mean? Fanny then lived through conversations she had had with Leo Dettrick, with Mr Rowley, the clergyman at Hockley, with Lady Jarvis, and her discussions by letter with Kranitzky. Her friends, with the exception of Mr Rowley and Kranitzky, were agnostics. Mr Rowley had the faith of a child. He believed in a future life simply and frankly. Leo did not want to, but she sometimes thought he had misgivings.

"Ah! but the apparition, the dumb sign!" That was a line of verse he had quoted to her one day, and she had never forgotten the tone of voice as he spoke it.

Kranitzky believed in a future life, but then Kranitzky was a Catholic, and he accepted that among other startling propositions on the authority of his Church.

Lady Jarvis thought that all religion was man-made, and that people had invented religions because they wanted to believe in religion. But she sympathised with those who had faith.

"Perhaps that's what I need, what I am without," thought Fanny. "Faith – faith in something, even if only in oneself, and that, I imagine, presupposes a faith in something beyond and outside oneself – outside the world. The grain of mustard seed. I haven't got it. I have no grain of faith and no grain of love, except for Peter. It was taken away from me. How can I get it back? And supposing I had faith? What then? What should I do? Go to Mr Rowley's church in a different state of mind? Become a Catholic? Catholics? They have faith. Hyacinth probably had faith. Perhaps that was the secret of her life. Perhaps she went through a great deal. Poor Hyacinth! Fancy if she knew now what had happened! Fancy if she could look down into the world and have a glimpse of Michael! What would she think? She would understand." And then there were those two other women she had never known – they were Catholics – Mrs Housman whom George had loved. Fancy if she knew – well, she would not mind, probably…it would confirm her in what she had done. She was still in the convent, and Lady Jarvis said she was happy. And there was Daphne Adeane, who had loved Leo, so Lady Jarvis said. Leo had forgotten her, so Lady Jarvis said, and she knew him as well as anyone. Lady Jarvis said it was her fault, Fanny's, but that was not true. Lady Jarvis said that Daphne had loved Leo crazily. Fanny wondered whether that was true. Somehow or other she could not imagine someone being crazily in love with Leo Dettrick. "But perhaps I am wrong. I am judging by myself. Much as I like him I could never be in love with him."

She had heard from him that morning. He was somewhere near Dunkirk with the Red Cross, happy and busy. Everyone who was busy seemed to be happy. "Perhaps I shall be happy when I am busy," she thought. Leo wrote to her almost daily.

She went to sleep, and she dreamt of Daphne Adeane. She dreamt she was at Seyton. But the house was not as it was when she had last seen it – not dismantled in any way, and there were no covers on the furniture. It was inhabited. It was summer, Fanny realised, and the drone of a mowing-machine came from outside, and she waited a little time in the square ante-room downstairs, which looked the same as usual, except that the books on the table were hers, Fanny's, and not the books that belonged to the house, and the panelling belonged to Hockley and not to Seyton, and yet Fanny knew it was Seyton. And then suddenly Daphne Adeane walked into the room. She was dressed in old-fashioned clothes, but of a fashion that was not startlingly unlike those of 1913 and 1914.

"She is like the Empress Joséphine," thought Fanny, "but not nearly so pretty."

She took Fanny into the drawing-room and asked her if she would like some tea, and Fanny said, "Yes; tea and muffins." And then they talked about the war and when Michael was going; and whether Leo Dettrick was enjoying it, and how he was getting on. And then Fanny suddenly said to her:

"There is one thing I should very much like to know, Mrs Adeane. Were you in love with Leo Dettrick?"

Daphne laughed, and then grew pensive, and Fanny said to herself, "That picture by Henriquez *is* very like her," and yet at the same time she knew as she said this, in her dream, that the face she was looking at was in reality different from that of Henriquez's picture.

"No," said Daphne; "I was never in love with Leo – never, never for a moment – but I was in love. Ah! so in love, with the other one."

"Who was the other one?" asked Fanny.

"Oh!" she said. "*L'autre.* Now I will show you the house."

"May I see the rooms you keep locked up?" asked Fanny.

"Of course." As Fanny dreamt this, she realised that the rooms had not been locked up till after Daphne died, and although she realised this fully, it seemed natural and right. They walked along a dark passage which Fanny did not remember, into a rather dimly lit bedroom which had a large four-posted bed with Morris curtains. Over the pillows hung a large crucifix.

"This is the room I keep shut," said Daphne.

"Yes," said Fanny; "and I forget why."

"Oh, because of the ghosts and the cats," said Daphne, "and because I died here."

Then Fanny felt a great desire to get away, and all at once she was horribly frightened; she had the sense of being shut in and that no escape was possible. She turned round and faced Daphne, and said: "Why have you shut me in?"

"Because," said Daphne, "you have taken away *both* my lovers." And Daphne walked towards her in a menacing way, and Fanny suddenly thought of the description of Vashti in *Villette*: the evil-ravaged, Eastern, sorrow-stricken "stage-empress" – she tried to scream, and awoke. It was early dawn.

CHAPTER XX

Mrs Tracy's hospital was on the coast not far from Boulogne. Among the VAD's there were several of Fanny's friends: Margaret Clive and her sister, Alice Lynne, and others. Dick Clive had joined the Naval Division. Jack Canning was with his regiment; he was in the cavalry.

Just as Michael with the RFC, so Fanny at the hospital felt that she had begun life again as a new person, in a new world. She thought little of the past. Leo Dettrick, who was somewhere near Dunkirk, wrote to her every day, but she had only seen him once so far.

Michael wrote short, happy letters from England. At Christmas, Fanny went home, and both she and Michael had leave. They spent it at Hockley with the children. Fanny stayed six weeks in England. Michael had only a fortnight.

The next event of importance in the lives of Michael and Fanny was Michael's departure for Egypt to join a squadron there in August. Fanny went to London to say goodbye to him, and she stayed a month with the children and her mother in Devonshire.

She was back in France by September. Dick Clive had died of fever on his way to the East. Jack Canning had been wounded and invalided home. George Ayton had given up his Under Secretaryship and was "somewhere in France"; so was

Stephen Lacy. All round her there were gaps. It was a day or two after she came back, at the beginning of September, that a doctor from one of the larger Red Cross hospitals at Boulogne visited Mrs Tracy's private hospital and was introduced to Fanny by Mrs Tracy as Dr Greene. He was in khaki.

"We are old friends," said Fanny, when she saw him. He stayed to luncheon, and at luncheon he sat next to Fanny. They talked of Leo Dettrick, whom he had only seen once since the beginning of the war, and of Dr Greene's experiences before and during the war. He was settled for good, so he thought, at his hospital at Boulogne. He was looking after cases of shell-shock and nerves.

Fanny was glad to see him. It was like a whiff of her pre-war world. It brought back Leo Dettrick to her and many other sights, persons, and episodes. She thought the war had aged him. But for the first time she noticed his looks. "What a curiously arresting face," she said to herself.

The last time she had seen him had been immediately after her accident, when she was not herself. She had then thought of him as a doctor only, and not as a human being. Now she felt herself looking at him as a human being.

Was he good-looking? Not like Michael or George Ayton. He was tall; his forehead was high and thoughtful; his features were well-cut; his hair was dark and thin; he stooped a little, but his eyes were bright and serene; he looked older than his age; his face was white as ivory; and, as it were, carefully carved by experience; and when he was not talking his eyes seemed to be looking beyond you into another world or plane.

But when he spoke, they beamed on you like the searchlight of a friendly harbour, with a flash of embracing understanding. There was something comprehensive and penetrating in his expression which lit his face, and you forgot his pale face, his ivory skin, and tired stoop; you were electrified as by a sudden illumination. Fanny noticed his hands. They were large, over large, and cool, and yet she felt certain that they were capable of delicate dexterity and subtle manipulations. His voice, too, was attractive; it fitted well with his other characteristics, or rather with his main characteristic, which was serenity; it was quiet, but resonant – a singer's, a sailor's voice. This serenity, Fanny felt, was that of a volcano.

She felt, too, that he was detached. As detached as Cuthbert Lyley…she understood why Leo had liked him so much. He asked after Michael.

"He is very happy," said Fanny; "but he hopes to get to France later – next year perhaps."

"And your children?"

"They are enjoying the war – they are staying at the moment with my mother in Devonshire. We told Peter nothing about the war; he's six you know, and mother found him playing with soldiers in front of her bedroom door, and asked him what he was doing, and, pointing to the soldiers, he said, ' Those are *dead* Germans!' "

"Yes, it's no good bowdlerising to children; they put one to shame if one does."

"My little girl, who can hardly talk, pointed to a speck in the sky, and said to her Nanny, 'Aeoplane!' It's a comfort not to have grown-up children now."

"Yes, indeed!"

Fanny wondered whether Greene was married. He was not married when she had first known him. Leo had told her that, and then she remembered the romance about Daphne Adeane. She felt uncomfortable; she felt he was reading her thoughts. She felt this still more strongly when he said:

"Up till now I always thought it was a mistake and a loss not to be married, but now I am thankful."

"I wonder – " Fanny blushed. She felt she was giving herself away.

"I think," she said, "that it is terrible for the – "

She broke off abruptly. She had been on the point of saying, "terrible for the young wives whose husbands have been killed," thinking of Margaret, and she checked herself. She might so easily be in the same situation – and she knew that if she were to be in the same situation, it would not be the same thing for her as it was for Margaret now. "Terrible for the women with young grown-up sons," she said.

"Yes, worst of all for them."

She felt he was not taken in.

"I used," Fanny went on, glad of this new train of thought, "when I was quite young, to enjoy reading the Greek stories, and any stories about those who died young, and everything the poets and the story-tellers said about them. I enjoyed that more than anything – and the plays and the operas. Hotspur – "the very straightest plant," and Henry V – "all furnished, all in arms"; "young Harry with his beaver on"; and Siegfried, and the sadness of Achilles when he foresaw – and now I can't bear to think of all that. War is all very well in history and poetry and plays and operas – in the distance, in fact, but when one is face to face with it…"

"It's as bad as peace."

"Yes, I suppose that's true. What *you* have seen in peace is not worse than what all of us are seeing in war."

"I think there were too many people in the world and too much prosperity, and too much *base* prosperity – and a great surgical operation is being carried out."

"You believe there is some purpose in it?"

"I believe in the laws of nature."

"But who made the laws of nature?"

"Well, it can't last for ever."

"It can last a very long time."

They then discussed the news of the day: the hopes, the fears, the rumours that were current in their circle. When Dr Greene went away, and he was slow in going, he said to Fanny:

"When I am off duty, could I come over on one of your off-days, and we might go for a walk to Boulogne or somewhere?"

"Yes, certainly," said Fanny, "and we might try and get hold of Leo Dettrick. He knows I am here, but it is difficult for him to get transport."

"Very well," said Francis Greene, and he jumped into his car. He came again the next week, and Fanny and he went to Boulogne, and had lunch at a restaurant. In the afternoon they walked on the windy cliffs and had tea at a little châlet. It promised to be a habit, and happened again.

The third time they had met was towards the end of September. They had had luncheon at Boulogne, but as it was drizzling, they thought they would do some shopping in the town, and Fanny wanted to buy some fish at the fish-market. They bought what they wanted, and as they walked back along the dripping quay up the hill – it was warm and muggy, Greene in his Burberry and Fanny in her mackintosh hardly noticed the rain – Francis said to Fanny:

"You know, it is rather odd, but you remind me in some ways of someone I used to know very well."

Fanny knew what he was going to say.

"Mrs Adeane?"

"Yes, although you are not really like her. Did you know her?"

"No, but I once saw her picture, and the house where she used to live is not far from us, and Colonel Branksome, Margaret Clive's father, used to say I was like her."

"Oh yes, I remember now Leo telling me he went to Seyton with you."

"You know it too?"

"I used to stay there sometimes – not often. It was a place that had charm – romantic – I thought."

"It was through Leo I knew it."

"He used often to go there."

"He knew them very well?"

"Very well."

"She must have been charming."

"She was delicate, too delicate for England and the English climate. She ought never to have been allowed to live there."

"Was it necessary?"

"She insisted on it. She did it for her husband's sake. She thought he disliked being abroad. Perhaps he did. I don't know, I'm not sure he did. He went abroad when she died. But she thought that, and she was strong-willed. She had a will of steel in a frail body, and I think the effort of her will killed her. She was meant for the sun and the South."

"Poor thing! Mr Adeane is still alive, isn't he?"

"I believe so."

"I suppose he was miserable without her?"

"He never got over it."

"And the children?"

"They are still at school. I think the eldest boy is about sixteen. If the war goes on for another two years, they may still be swallowed up."

"Pray Heaven it won't! Are they nice children?"

"I haven't seen them for some time; they are being brought up at the Oratory, the Catholic school at Birmingham. I believe they are doing quite well. Their mother worshipped them."

"Is their father fond of them?"

"I imagine that everything that reminds him of his wife gives him pain. He is one of those reserved, shy men who feel things deeply."

"Poor children! How dreadfully lonely they must be!"

"I sometimes wonder, since it is the destiny of almost every – well, I think of every human being to be lonely – whether it is not a good thing to get used to it as soon as possible?"

"But children have mothers and fathers to love them, as a rule?"

"Or to hate them!" He said this bitterly, and Fanny wondered what his youth had been.

"I was brought up in Australia," he said. "My father was not a born Australian, but an emigrant. We lived on a ranch."

"That must have been fun – for a boy?"

"It was – only – well, the country was beautiful. We lived in one of the most beautiful spots in the world. Not that children notice landscape – they accept it – at least I did; the appreciation of landscape came later with youth – to me; then I was sent to school, and the master beat me savagely. My mother died. She was delicate and cultivated. Everything went to pieces. Home became a hell. My father took to drink. I ran away – went to sea. I was fifteen. My first and last voyage was to Liverpool in a windjammer round the Cape. I got through it, but I had no real vocation for the sea. Then a romance happened – one of the things that only happened, I thought, in books. The day after I landed at Liverpool I saw a notice in a newspaper saying, 'If Francis Greene will communicate with Joseph Greene, Edinburgh, he will hear something to his advantage?' and it gave the address. Joseph Greene was my uncle; I had heard my father talk of him often. I think they had been friends in youth, and then had quarrelled. I went to Edinburgh. I had my pay. I found my uncle a dignified, quiet man with greyish hair – a surgeon, and, as I found out afterwards, a distinguished surgeon. He told me my father was dead, that his wife had died recently, that he had no children of his own, and that he felt badly about his behaviour to my father. He said it had been owing to his own behaviour that my father had emigrated to Australia. He wanted to make amends now. He was willing to adopt me, to treat me as his son, and to help me in every way he could to the life and career towards which I felt inclined. Did I want to be a sailor? He knew of my adventure. Would I like to go into the Mercantile Marine? I told him I had no vocation for the sea, that I was addicted and had been addicted from my earliest years to books and study; that I was fond of natural history, insects, bugs – all that; interested in biology, physiology, psychology – that, most of all; in fact, that what I yearned towards was science, knowledge, research.

"He was delighted. He sent me to school – the Aberdeen Grammar School – he taught me himself – and his mind was a rich one – and then, later, I became a medical student at the Aberdeen University. I was a medical student for five years, then I took my degrees; I went to Germany, studied in Vienna for a year; practised in Edinburgh for five years, and a few years later George Thompson, whom I had got to know, and who had read some papers I read to various societies, took me as his underling, and later as a sort of partner; and since then I have devoted all my time to what has been my principal interest in life: nerves – the most important factor in the world and the fact we know least about."

"Is your uncle still alive?"

"No, he died a long time ago. He was a remarkable man."

"To have one's hobby as one's profession must be ideal."

"I have never looked upon science as a hobby, any more than a soldier looks upon fighting or war as a hobby. That's his job. That's my job. I've had hobbies too."

"What are they?"

"One used to be singing. I once thought I might be an opera singer, or at least a concert singer. Don't laugh. It was not so out of the question as you would think. As a boy I had a wonderful voice, till it cracked; and as a youth I had the makings of a fine baritone. I think that sea voyage did for it. I used to sing to the sailors and I strained it; but even at Aberdeen, when I was still a medical student, I met a man called Solway, a student at the College of Music, who, just from hearing me hum a tune, said I was a musician. He made me sing to him, and I did. He said with a few years' training of the right kind – instruction rather than training – I could become a first-class *lieder* singer, a real concert singer. Well, in my spare time at Aberdeen I used to have lessons. My uncle encouraged it with a slightly knowing smile – he knew it would come to nothing – and I became good enough, so they said, to be a professional. I went up to London, to be vetted by Solway, who, although quite young, was looked upon as a swell in the musical world, and I sang to him."

"What did you sing?"

"Schubert. He was delighted. I stayed with him in London, and he sat up nearly all night begging me to give up medicine and research, and to become a singer. Well, he almost persuaded me to become a musician. I said I would think it over till the next morning. He said, 'Longer than that; that is really not enough!' It is true that it was then past four in the morning. Well, I said I would think about it till the next evening. I was going back to Aberdeen by the night train. I did. I went through one of those curious wrestling dramas – Jacob and the Angel – that happen, I suppose to every human being at least once in his life, when not what you *want* to do is in conflict with what you *ought* to do, but when you think one duty seems to be in conflict with another. There were so many arguments on both sides. I was passionately fond of music; on the other hand, I was passionately fond of science – a bad artist, or rather an artist who just missed it – I knew I wasn't 'bad' – was a terrible thing to be; on the other hand, a man whose aim is research – and who fails! It was not as if I wished to be a general practitioner all my life – it would have been so much easier to settle to be that – but even then I had already made up my mind that I would not do that. Well, I went to bed. I slept a little. I was up and dressed by half-past seven and I went out for a walk by myself. Solway lived in Kensington. I walked to Kensington Gardens. It was a lovely summer morning at the end of May. I walked in Kensington Gardens, and I stayed there a long time – hours. I had some coffee at a kiosk, and I stayed there so long that I remember people arriving on *bicycles* – not many (bicycling had just started being the fashion that year); but I remember two couples arriving and sitting down in a kind of enclosure and ordering breakfast and strawberries – and they seemed so light-hearted and gay. Then I put it to myself – which of the two things did I know in my heart of hearts I would be best at? And I knew it was science. It might have been the other, but it wasn't; for if it had been the other, I felt I should not even be having the discussion with myself. Science is an inexorable master – but art is an unreasonable mistress, whom no one can withstand. If I could withstand her as much as I had already, then I knew I was not really an artist. Just as I was thinking this out, a girl came and sat next to me on the seat where I was sitting. She was reading some typescript – quarto sheets bound in brown paper. She was neatly but rather shabbily dressed. She had waves of the most lovely fair hair I ever remember seeing, and large china-blue eyes; she was exaggerated, rather like what children draw when you ask them to draw a beauty, or like those illustrations in cheap pink newspapers. She looked at me and smiled, and then pointing to her typescript she said, 'My part. I'm understudying Gabriel Thornton.' I had never heard of Gabriel Thornton. She was, I learnt afterwards, a star at the Frivolity. We fell into conversation. She told me the story of her life. She had a slightly Cockney accent and her articulation was too precise, but I, as a musician, noticed the quality of her voice, and thought a lot could be done with it. She had lived a life bordering on starvation, from the moment she had left her home – a village – to go on the stage. She had worked and starved, and now, after five years, she had arrived at the possibility of being the understudy of the star. She was radiantly happy. I asked her if, in exchange for assured, permanent security and comfort – assured to the end of her life – she would, if she were given the chance, give up the stage. She looked at me with pity, as if I was one of those people who are to be pitied because *they can't understand.* 'Give up the stage?' she said. 'No fear!' and there were tears in her eyes as she laughed.

"Well, that settled it for me. If someone had said to me, 'Will you give up the idea of being a singer?' I shouldn't say, 'No fear!' On the other hand, if they said, give up science, give up

250

medicine, I'm not at all sure I should not have said, 'No fear!' I said, 'Thank you very much! Let me know when you are playing,' and she promised she would. I gave her a card, and she told me her name – 'Elsie Phillips. Frivolity Theatre finds me,' she added. 'I'm in the chorus.'

"I went back to Solway and told him. He saw it was hopeless, and he argued no more. He had already said all he had got to say the night before. That is how I settled my career."

"Did you ever regret it?"

"No, never, really – and now I am thankful. I know I should not have been good enough. My voice wouldn't have stood it. It has almost gone – and I have loved the other."

Fanny thought he said this rather sadly all the same. They were nearing the top of the hill. The rain had stopped. In the east there was a rainbow. The sun was setting in a riot of watery gold. The houses and steeples and domes of the towns beneath stood out distinct, quiet and tidy and peaceful. A hospital orderly passed them whistling "Gilbert the Filbert." The Angelus rang. They were passing the doors of a small church.

"Let's go in," said Fanny.

The church was crowded with French women, some French soldiers, and a great many English soldiers and orderlies. The Rosary was being said. Fanny and Francis stood near the door and listened to the rhythmical drone and beat of the priest's petition and the braying response of the crowd. They were saying the five Glorious Mysteries. Fanny and Francis Greene both knew that they were on the eve of what was called "a big push," the new French offensive, of which great results were expected.

After the Rosary there was Benediction. The Litany of Loretto was said in the vernacular. Fanny found herself joining in to the monotonous responses, *"Priez pour nous,"* mechanically, and the words, *"Refuge de pécheurs,"* *"Consolatrice des affligés," "Secour des Chrétiens,"* stabbed her. After Benediction there was a French hymn. They stayed till the end.

When they came out it was dark. Francis Greene took Fanny home to the hospital in his car.

"Do you think this offensive will be a triumph?" she asked.

"Not yet, somehow," said Francis. They said little else on the way home.

CHAPTER XXI

The next time that Fanny and Francis Greene met was after the battle of Loos. Fanny wanted to go to Bergues to see Jean Canning, who was working in a private hospital there, and Francis Greene had to go to Dunkirk, and was able to give her a lift there and back. Fanny had luncheon with Jean and her fellow VAD's. Jack, so Jean told her, was well again and was back at the front. She had had news from him quite lately.

As they were driving home Francis Greene told Fanny that he had come across Leo Dettrick for a moment. He had been passing through Dunkirk on his way to Boulogne. He was going on leave.

"I wonder where he'll go, and whether he has any friends in England now," said Fanny.

"He's going to stay with Lady Jarvis."

"In the country, at Rosedale?"

"Yes."

"He likes her, doesn't he? It was through her I came to know Leo Dettrick, but I have always rather wondered at their being friends – not their being friends, because I would think it an odd thing if they weren't – but I have often wondered how it came about, how such a shy and retiring person as Leo Dettrick came to be friends – great friends – with such a *public* person as Lady Jarvis..."

253

"It was through Daphne Adeane."

"Did he get to know Daphne Adeane through Lady Jarvis?"

"I introduced him to Daphne Adeane first, but Lady Jarvis was a friend of the Adeanes, and if it hadn't been for Lady Jarvis Leo would never have seen much of her. Daphne Adeane and her husband used to stay with Lady Jarvis. Lady Jarvis was fond of her and liked him, and so Leo went there too. When Daphne Adeane was there he was nearly always there too."

"Wasn't Mr Adeane jealous?"

"Oh dear no! – you see he understood. He was a man who said little, but he understood his wife."

"You mean he knew that she only cared for him?"

"He knew that she only liked Leo as a friend; as she liked everyone else."

"But I thought she was in love with Leo, crazily in love with him?" said Fanny, quoting Lady Jarvis' words, and she saw Regent's Park, the children playing, the people rowing in the boats, as she said this.

"Oh no," said Francis, in a tone of quiet certitude and authority that carried conviction.

As he said this, Fanny felt a stab and a pang. She felt a sudden change in the kaleidoscope of her soul. She could not have defined the nature of the change, but it was as if she had *heard* the click of the little facets of glass falling into their readjusted new position and shape, and she was dimly aware of a new pattern and a fresh scheme of colour.

What did she feel at this moment? Disappointment? Fear? Hope? Jealousy? Hate? Was it hate? Could it be hate? Yes, it was. It was hate – but hate of whom? Of Daphne Adeane? But why in the world should she hate Daphne Adeane, especially, as she was now told, and told with authority by someone who ought to know, that Daphne Adeane had never loved Leo? And even if she had, what would it matter? It was all the more absurd as she, Fanny, had never loved Leo, nor had Leo loved her – so there was no possible cause for jealousy.

"But Leo was in love with her?" she said.

"Leo worshipped her. He put her on a pedestal. He loved her as he had loved everyone else...that is to say, as an artist. Leo's like that. He would be the first to admit it himself. In fact, I have often discussed this with him. He must have beauty. He feeds on it, but he must have *variety* as well. Leo has never loved *one* woman only. One woman is not enough for him. His heart is large enough for hundreds. There always have been, and there always will be more than one – *and at the same time*. That's the point."

"But Daphne Adeane came first?"

"Yes, till he used her up."

"How do you mean 'used her up'?"

"Used her up as 'stuff,' what the Germans call 'stoff'... subject-matter for his books."

"Do you mean he put her in his books?"

"Oh no. Only in the sense that a flower left in a book may leave a fragrant stain, or perhaps only the poor clinging ghost of a scent on all the pages. Leo's books are saturated with Daphne Adeane, although among all the characters he created there is not one who is in the least like her. He is fully conscious of this."

"But he enjoyed her society more than that of anyone else?"

"Yes, infinitely; although, as companions and friends, Leo only likes people who are interested in what interests him, and there is only one thing that interests him – his work...work – art, if you like. I don't mean the professionals, the people of his own trade; he has always avoided them – shop bores him. I mean any ordinary people – the laity; he only really cares to be with those, and *certainly* only opens out fully to those who are interested in what interests him, and who belong to the freemasonry of artists – not people who talk about art, but who talk of everything from the angle of the artist. *Musicians* often don't want to see other musicians, but they can only talk about music with people who look upon music from the angle of what they call being *musical*. Now I feel, when I am with Leo, that I am falling short, that I am being insufficient, not up to the mark."

"But wasn't Daphne Adeane extremely refined and cultivated?"

"Oh yes, refined – as refined as possible, as delicate, as soft, as lace – as for the rest, neither Leo nor anyone else bothered about it. It would have been madness to ask oneself whether Daphne Adeane was clever or cultivated. That didn't matter. That wasn't the point. She was far more than all that. Even beauty with her didn't matter. One didn't say, 'Is she beautiful?' One accepted the overwhelming fact of what she was – like the sound of a tune or the scent of a flower. As a matter of fact, she wasn't in the least what you generally mean by 'cultivated,' or what you expect Leo to like – what, in fact, he does like, and needs and asks for. Daphne Adeane hardly ever read anything except a few French novels. She was inarticulate, Southern, and really what people call 'uneducated,' but to know her was more than any education – "

"But wasn't she musical?"

"She accompanied herself gracefully, just as she painted charming little water-colours. She played on old-fashioned instruments – the harpsichord or the spinet, and she sang snatches of Spanish songs. I used sometimes to long to know Spanish."

" 'I must learn Spanish one of these days.' "

"What?"

"Nothing, only a quotation that came into my mind."

"Well, she had little voice and little musical education, but Leo worshipped her music and he worshipped her. To him she was the most beautiful woman who had ever lived. They used to say she wasn't a beauty. I don't know, but I know she was *more* than a beauty – her features, they said, were irregular – well, yes – irregular as a flower is irregular – she was nearly always pale, and she often looked tired, ill, and pulled down. I used to give her tonics…but…but…but…wasn't there a French actress about whom someone asked, 'Est-elle jolie?' and the answer was – 'Non, elle est pire.' Daphne Adeane was like that – she was worse. Her beauty was of the kind that steals upon you unawares and grows upon you, and seems to pervade everything, and makes all other people seem ordinary, flat, and commonplace; and her eyes made me understand what the word glamour meant. They were like magic pools."

Again Fanny felt a stab.

"She must have been charming."

"Charming seems such a silly, inadequate word for what she was…she was unique, totally different from anyone else, not in degree but in *kind.*"

"I suppose," said Fanny wistfully, "she was *sympathetic.*"

"Yes, made of sympathy. She understood everything that she couldn't express – she understood what anyone was feeling and dreaded pain for others."

There was a slight pause. Fanny wondered which was the right version of the story. Leo's, Lady Jarvis', or Francis Greene's. "Men are nearly always wrong," she thought, "and I don't know how well Lady Jarvis knew her. I shall never know."

They talked about other things till they arrived at Boulogne. When Francis Greene said goodbye to her, they made an appointment for the following week.

They met again the following week, and went for a walk, and again made an appointment for the next week; but when the next week came, Fanny had her day off, there was no Francis Greene. He sent a message to say he would not be able to come. He was too busy. Fanny felt strangely disappointed. She went for a walk by herself and thought over things.

The blank she felt was so great that she felt a little bit alarmed. She was surprised at herself. "After all," she said to herself, "Francis Greene means nothing to me. I am being absurd." And yet throughout the whole of that lonely walk along the cliffs, on a cold and rather windy October afternoon, she kept on seeing the image of Francis Greene, hearing the words he had spoken, reconstructing the talks they had had. "I can't," she thought, "be falling in love with him. It would be too silly, too impossible."

She looked forward to the next week. So far the weeks had seemed to go by quickly, but this week seemed to her interminable, and when the day came round once more, there was a message from Francis Greene to say that he was detained by his work. The message was brought her by Father Rendall, a Catholic priest, who often came to see the Catholic soldiers in the hospital. Fanny knew him well, liked him, and often consulted him on practical matters. Francis Greene had met him in Australia, and they were great friends. He was a nephew of the well-known preacher,[2] and had spent his life among the most hard-working of the poor – miners, bushmen. He was middle-aged and looked older than he was. There was something square and solid about him, and not, one felt, one shred of nonsense. But you felt he would never blame but always sympathise.

When he delivered Francis Greene's message, Fanny's disappointment was so acute that she could not disguise it. It surprised, bruised, and overwhelmed her. Then she felt ashamed of herself and thought: "I am losing my head. I am crazy."

She asked Father Rendall whether he was busy, and whether he wouldn't care to go for a walk on the cliffs before going back. Father Rendall noticed her agitation, if he did not account for it, and he assented.

They went for the same walk she had last taken with Francis Greene. They talked about the hospital, the men in the hospital. Hospital shop, in fact, for some time. They could do this without ending, as they had a great deal of experience and subject-matter in common. Fanny asked Father Rendall about

[2] *Cat's Cradle,*

Australia. They talked a little about Francis Greene, and Fanny found she was able to do this naturally.

"Francis Greene is a remarkable man," said Father Rendall. "It is a pity he has not a little more ambition – the right kind of ambition, I mean."

"He is absorbed in his work, isn't he?"

"Yes, absolutely. But I mean he deserves to be better known and to have a wider field for his remarkable gifts; and the reason that he has not, as yet, had full scope, is that he has always refused to put himself forward, even when it was not only legitimate, but may have been said to be his duty."

"I suppose that's what makes him nice?" Fanny said absent-mindedly.

"He is a single-minded man," said Father Rendall, "and they are rare; but he goes too far in self-effacement."

"I expect that what he is doing now will have an effect," said Fanny.

"I hope so, but I am afraid he will not stay here long."

"What do you mean?"

"It has been suggested that he should go to England to take on some rather less interesting work. It is not yet settled, so he told me, but he thought he would very likely go."

Fanny felt she was turning cold.

"But," she said, "he will, I suppose, have the choice. He's not being just sent?"

"He will have the choice, but I think he is certain to choose the course that will be personally less agreeable or advantageous to himself."

"Yes, yes."

"He said to me at the beginning of the war, when I asked him what he would like to be, what job he would like to get best, that it was a matter of complete indifference to him, and that if he was told to clean stables he would be contented. I disputed this. Not that I doubted his feelings, but I told him that I disagreed with his point of view. I think that in a war like this you want to get the best out of everyone, and it would be simply waste, and ultimately a hindrance to everyone, for a man like Francis Greene to clean out stables, and not to do what he could do better than other people. Of course, I knew at the time he was only exaggerating, but it does throw a light on his frame of mind."

"Have you known him for a long time?"

"No; I never met him before we met in Australia. You see, I have been away for some time."

"But you haven't always lived in Australia?"

"No. I used to live in London."

"I have known many Catholics, but none intimately," said Fanny. "The only one I knew at all well, really, was a Russian, and I only got to know him by letters. He is a Russian, and is now, I think, at the front."

"Russian Catholics are rare."

"So he told me. His mother was an Italian. Apart from that, there was no one." But Fanny was thinking of Hyacinth and of Daphne Adeane. Was it thought transference? for at that moment Father Rendall said:

"It is an odd thing, the only Russians I have ever known I met at the house of a Catholic friend of mine – Mrs Wake."

"Was that Hyacinth Wake, the wife of Basil Wake, the barrister?"

"Yes," said Father Rendall.

"Did you know them well?"

"I knew her well – Wake less well; he is not, as perhaps you know, a Catholic."

"I know. I saw him not very long ago. He is a cousin of some neighbours of ours in the country. I liked him so much. Was Hyacinth Wake always a Catholic, or did she become one?"

"She was not born a Catholic. Her mother was converted after her husband's death. The child was then brought up as a Catholic."

"I knew her very little," said Fanny, "because I lived entirely abroad till I married, but I admired her, and I think she must have been a remarkable woman."

"She was."

"Full of character?"

"Yes; full of character."

"And I should say very unselfish?"

"She was very good to all our people – I mean the poor."

"She died suddenly, didn't she?"

"Yes. I saw her just before she had the operation. She was making light of it."

"Poor Basil Wake! I don't think he ever got over it, or ever will."

"What is he doing now?"

"I believe he is in the Red Cross – out here somewhere, I should think. Soon everybody we know will be here."

"But I have no doubt he will do well, and I dare say he will prefer his new life to the Bar."

"Doesn't he like the Bar?"

"Not much, I think."

"You still see him?"

"Occasionally. He always comes to Mass to my church on the anniversary of his wife's death."

"But he's not a Catholic."

"No; he is an agnostic, but he has no feelings against us."

"They never had any children, did they?"

"Never. It was a great grief to him."

"And I suppose to her?"

Father Rendall said nothing, as if the statement or question called for no comment or answer. After a while Fanny said:

"There is one thing I would like to ask you, unless it is indiscreet, in which case you would say so."

"I would," he smiled.

"Well, it's this – what I should like to know is this. Well, to begin with, you say Hyacinth Wake took her operation lightly.

We all do that – all women, I mean. We all pretend to, especially if we have got husbands, but we often feel quite dreadfully badly about it. But I suppose – I take it for granted that although she took it lightly or appeared to do so, she knew quite well it was serious. She knew she *might* die."

"She took the operation lightly, thinking it was not a serious one. She did not take the possibility of death seriously."

"Well, that's just what I mean. What I want to get at is this. If she realised it might be serious – say it had been a far more serious operation – although what happened proved that there is no 'more or less serious' in these matters – but say she had thought so – would the fact of her being a Catholic, and, as I presume she was, a practising Catholic, have made a difference to her? That's what I want to know, because I have so often heard people say that religion makes no difference to conduct – I know that Catholics are often not better than other people – often worse – but what I want to get at is this: does the fact of being a practising Catholic make a difference to someone like Hyacinth when she is faced with a critical situation – say an operation – a serious operation? Would she face it more calmly – would it honestly be a help to her?"

"Yes, provided she had Faith, even although that Faith was purely the consent that arises from reason and had nothing emotional about it."

"But surely Hyacinth Wake was not a woman who was made up simply of dry, unmitigated reason?"

"Oh no. She had the Faith that is founded on reason and which is confirmed by the experience of the *heart*. The heart has its reasons. The quotation is a little musty?"

"But she was quite calm."

"Perfectly calm."

"But then she thought that the operation was a trifling one?"

"No. She treated the fact of *any* operation as being *relatively* a trifling matter. She did not think this particular operation would be necessarily dangerous; but she knew that apart from operations she might die any day at any minute; she had faced the fact. She never expected to live long. If once that fact is really faced and realised, an operation is a mere detail. If it is not today it will be tomorrow, as Hamlet says."

"Yes, yes, yes…but that's what I've always felt. The special Providence in the fall of a sparrow, but if one feels *that*, as I do feel it, and as strongly as I do feel it, and have always felt it all my life, how can one believe in free will? How can one have what *you* call Faith?"

"Faith is a gift. I suppose one cannot explain it to those who have not got it, any more than one can explain colour to the blind or tone to the deaf, but when it is there it makes the problem no less difficult, but acceptable in spite of being insoluble and incomprehensible. Faith enables you to accept the mysteries as mysteries. The mysteries of Faith are not more easy to understand than the mysteries of science or mathematics. They proceed from the same Author. Mathematicians recognise the existence of their mysteries – the contradictions; what in their science is at the same time *possible* and *impossible*. Our intelligence is limited, we can get to a certain point, and no farther; we can get as far as recognising the existence of the mystery and in believing in it. We cannot with our finite intelligence hope to understand it."

"Yes, but my whole point is this: was Hyacinth, because she was a Catholic, able to accept the mystery – did she accept it? Did she think, ' this makes it all right,' or did she say to herself, 'after all, this is a patent medicine like any other. It can't do any harm, it may do good'?"

"You mean to say, was her religion a help, a reality?"

"Yes, in supreme moments – before an operation, for instance?" (But what Fanny really wanted to hear was whether her religion had ever influenced her conduct.)

"If you had seen her you would not have asked the question."

"Well, then, I think that's wonderful, I could never feel like that... Only perhaps situations, operations, war, may cause certain frames of mind."

"But," said Father Rendall, "Hyacinth Wake had the advantage and benefit and assistance of the Faith all her life long, and not only at the time of her death."

"And you think it always made a difference to her?"

"The whole difference."

As he said this Fanny felt instinctively that Hyacinth had made a great renunciation in her life, and that in making it, her religion had perhaps played a part, and that if Father Rendall had known about it, he would certainly have encouraged her, he perhaps *did* encourage her to do so. She felt, too, that he guessed that she, Fanny, was more interested than she liked to admit in Francis Greene, and that he would disapprove. She changed the subject; she did not wish to think of it, or to talk of anything which might possibly fringe on those subjects any more. They talked of other things till they reached the hospital.

CHAPTER XXII

After this walk and that night, when Fanny went to bed she still would not admit that she felt anything more for Francis Greene than an extremely friendly interest.

Before she went to bed she glanced at a little volume of Shakespeare's Sonnets which Leo Dettrick had given her, and her eye fell on the sonnet that begins:

> "How like a winter hath my absence been
> From thee, the pleasure of the fleeting year!
> What freezings have I felt, what dark days seen!
> What old December's bareness every where!
> And yet this time remov'd was summer's time;
> The teeming autumn, big with rich increase…"

It was no longer "summer's time," and the "teeming autumn" was drawing to its close.

She read the sonnet that followed next in the book:

> "From you have I been absent in the spring,
> When proud-pied April, dress'd in all his trim,
> Hath put a spirit of youth in everything,
> That heavy Saturn laugh'd and leap'd with him.
> Yet not the lays of birds, nor the sweet smell

Of different flowers in odour and in hue,
Could make me any summer's story tell,
Or from their proud lap pluck them where they grew;
Nor did I wonder at the lily's white,
Nor praise the deep vermilion in the rose;
They were but sweet, but figures of delight,
Drawn after you, – you pattern of all those.
    Yet seemed it winter still, and, you away,
    As with your shadow I with these did play."

Nothing could have been less appropriate to the actual season. It was cold and windy, it rained often. It was often damp and foggy. The season seemed to suit the dismal situation, and yet she said, "This sonnet even more than the first one expresses exactly what I feel.

"I used in old days to love the autumn, the changing tints, the berries, the falling leaves, the ripeness, the harmony, the rich increase, the pageant of the dying woods, the ragged trees in their flaming robes, crimson flaunting yellow and gold and pale green, but now –

"As with your shadow I with these did play."

and winter seems to have come before its hour.

"But Shakespeare's sonnets," she said to herself reassuringly, "are after all an expression of *friendship*, not of passion, not of love. I am friends with Francis Greene – friends, nothing more – just as I am friends with Cuthbert Lyley. It is right, simple, and natural. There is nothing wrong about it. There is nothing odd or even unusual about it. But I do feel something like what is expressed in these sonnets – and how different that is from love."

The next day when she was having luncheon some one at the table happened to mention the name of Francis Greene.

"Oh!" said Margaret Clive, "I heard Dr Elwes say this morning that Dr Greene has gone to England for good. He's going to work at a hospital at Greenwich."

Fanny felt her heart stop, and the whole room seemed to swim round her.

"It can't be true," she thought; "he can't have gone away without saying goodbye."

And then she knew without any possibility of disguise that she loved him, him and no one else, and nothing else and that in comparison with this love nothing in her life counted – not her husband, not her children, not her mother; she knew she would give anything in the world to see him for only one second. "If he has gone without saying goodbye," she thought, "I shall not get over it – I shall die!"

But the next day she heard from him. He was going to England, but not yet. He was going in December, before Christmas. He hoped to see her before then. The following week he came, but Fanny was not able to go out that day. She had had to shift her day out because Margaret Clive was suddenly laid up with excruciating neuralgia. There was nothing to be done. She saw Francis for a moment, and they had a few moments' conversation, which was soon interrupted; but in those few moments Fanny managed to tell him that she too was going home for Christmas, and she hoped to see him in England.

As it turned out, they met on the leave boat. Fanny was so overjoyed at seeing him unexpectedly that she felt like one intoxicated or demented. She felt a radiant joy flooding her whole being. She knew that she had never felt like this before. Francis Greene looked after her. They walked up and down the deck and had a talk, which lasted long, and yet seemed to have gone by in the flash of a minute.

The conversation, as usual, went back to Leo Dettrick, and as usual Daphne Adeane was mentioned and discussed, and Fanny asked several questions about her.

When the subject seemed to have been almost exhausted, Fanny said to Francis Greene: "Did you love her?" She felt she could not have put this question at any other time.

"Yes," he said quietly, "I loved her more than all the world."

"And you always will love her?"

Francis said nothing, but Fanny thought that his silence meant consent, and she hated Daphne Adeane with all her mind and with all her strength.

She went to her cabin and she cried.

The next day Francis Greene travelled up with her to London, and drove her to her house. She was staying the night in London, and meant to go to Hockley the next day to meet her mother and the children, who were there.

Francis Greene said he would be busy all day, and was dining with his old chief – but his chief liked to go to bed early. "May I come round after dinner," he asked, "and say goodbye?"

"Of course," said Fanny. She hoped he would say this, but she had not dared to express the hope to herself.

She was alone at Queen Anne's Gate; there was only a caretaker there. She boiled herself some eggs early. The house was shut up, all except the dining-room, which she used as a sitting-room. Francis Greene came at about half-past nine, and Fanny let him in herself, and took him into the dining-room. It was a cold night. She had lit a good fire. They sat near the fire and talked.

Francis told her of his future plans. He was not going back to France.

"I shall miss you," said Fanny, and indeed the prospect of being at Boulogne without Francis' weekly visits seemed to her intolerable, unthinkable. Francis said nothing.

"I suppose," she went on after a moment, "I shall never see you again?"

"Not *never*, I hope. What are your plans?"

"It all depends on Michael. He expects to come home after Christmas – at least that is what he said when he last wrote – I

268

don't know what he will do then. He is sure to try to go to France. If he goes to France, I shall go back. If he doesn't, I think I shall leave Mrs Tracy's hospital and try and find some work here. There is, after all, plenty to do here, and plenty of work for me at home."

"Yes," said Francis; "I should think there was, if anything, more for you to do here than abroad – you have been abroad long enough."

"I have indeed. You won't go back to France?"

"Not for some months, at any rate."

He explained to her how matters stood with him – his life and his work.

"It has made a great difference to me knowing you," said Fanny, "and now it is over, I don't know what I shall do. I want you to know that I have…well…what I have felt about it. I am grateful. I couldn't bear you to think that I was ungrateful."

"I know," said Francis, looking down. Fanny was staring into the fire. The firelight played on her face and burnished her hair. She looked as white and lovely as a ghost, and her eyes were serious and sad like those of a reproachful, suffering, dumb animal.

Francis looked at her and looked down again. There was something, he thought, almost sacred about her; and he looked at the darting flames of the fire, and he thought of Brunhilda, and the fire music came into his head, and the yearning passion of the Wolsungs, with its unbearable weight of sadness, catastrophe, and doom. He seemed to live through all that epic tragedy in a few seconds.

Fanny looked at him. He, too, looked sad and infinitely tired. If somebody were to paint him now, she thought, one could call the picture "War." It would be the best of all comments.

His eyes were larger and sadder than usual. "I wonder," she thought, "what he is thinking about. He has no idea, no idea at all, what I am feeling. He is probably thinking of Daphne

Adeane. It isn't fair for the dead to interfere with the living in this way!"

"You see," Fanny went on, after a pause, and not looking at Francis, "I may seem silly to you and absurd – and I expect I am silly and absurd – but this has been new and strange and unique to me. I have felt about our friendship…what I couldn't feel, or could no longer feel. It has brought me back to life in a way, or made a new life for me. I felt quite dead before; I felt my life was over, and that all that was left for me was to live for others. It has been to me like suddenly seeing someone one thought was dead, like the resurrection of the flesh."

"But that's exactly what I've felt."

Fanny's heart gave a wild bound.

"Do you mean," she said slowly and seriously, "it meant something to you?"

"Don't you know?" His voice had altered. It was quivering. Fanny's heart leapt again, a wild hope sprang up in her and flooded her soul. Her spirit soared like a balloon that is cut adrift, and leaves the world for the empty sky. The world was far away, apart, and no longer counted.

She had up to now, all these last days, been thinking of what she had felt and was feeling for and about him. She had never dared to dwell on the possibility of his feeling something. She thought him too aloof, too detached, and like one who lived in the past. She thought his heart was in the shades with Daphne Adeane, beyond the Styx, in a paradise of shadows.

She thought of Francis as of one nothing now could touch or reach. She loved him for being like that, but she longed to enter the region where his soul dwelt and to share its life. But she felt this was impossible, more than impossible – *forbidden*. There was now a world of adoration in his eyes. There was something that nothing could hide or disguise.

"I have thought –" he said, and as he said the words his voice shook – to Fanny it was like the music of the spheres to hear the words; they brought balm to her wounded spirit and solace and a flood of superhuman joy. "I have thought of nothing but you...nothing but you ever since we went for that first walk...more than that, I loved you before; I don't mean when I first saw you at the time of the taxi accident...but long before that – for always and ever – without knowing it... Didn't you know?"

Fanny felt the world reeling. She hardly could heed the sense of his words, so intoxicating was the sound to her.

"Do you mean" – the words came out with difficulty – "you really care for me a little?" She didn't dare to look at him.

"Care for you a little?" His voice trembled and broke, and his eyes filled with tears. "Oh, Fanny, I love you so...more than life – more than I knew I could love."

Fanny looked at him, and they said nothing more. She was in his arms, and his first kiss seemed to last for ever. And for her and for him the world stood still. They were far away in another world, beyond the stars, above the skies, under the seas, east of the sun and west of the moon... Fanny felt that she was dying of happiness, that she had died, not one but many deaths, and had been born again, and that she was living and soaring through aeons of bliss, exploring new circles of Paradise, that seemed to open and unfold like the petals of a rose of fire.

She knew she was cut adrift from what had so far been her life, and as far away from it, as the sun is from the earth; that she was ready to sacrifice everything: husband, children, mother, friends, duty, home, reputation...she cared for nothing but Francis...all this was but a flash in her mind; she was almost unconscious from happiness, which was so sharp and so extreme as to be terrible...

The minutes, the hours went by; they heard Big Ben strike midnight...it was only then that they were recalled to existence and came back to earth.

"It's late," said Fanny. "You must go."

"I suppose I must..."

"Tomorrow," Fanny said, and the word now sounded to them sweet, for they knew they would see each other again, even if it should be for the last time.

"Tomorrow," he repeated, "we will meet, won't we?"

"Yes," said Fanny, and she looked at him, and once more happiness flooded her being and carried her away as on a wave...

"Goodnight, my darling," she said.

At last they broke away from each other – and they said a real last goodnight. On the doorstep they arranged their plans for the next day.

They had little time, for Fanny was obliged to go to Hockley, and Francis had a great deal to do. But they would be able to have luncheon together.

They arranged to meet at Prince's Grill-Room.

Fanny watched Francis till he was out of sight; then she went back to the dining-room and sat in front of the fire for some time. At last she went to bed, and she lay awake for some time almost unconscious from happiness, and at last she fell asleep, and she dreamt a curious dream.

She dreamt that she was walking with Francis on the cliffs near Boulogne. It was grey and windy, and the sun was setting just as she had often seen it set.

They were happy talking and laughing, and Fanny knew that they belonged to each other, but all at once she was aware of somebody walking behind them – a presence she felt, but could not hear. There was no noise of footsteps.

She wanted to turn round, but she could not. It was, she thought, nothing ugly nor terrifying, but a soft, invisible, obstinate presence. They were talking about music and the operas they liked best – as they often did – and Francis was saying, "I like Schubert's operas best, only they are never given," and Fanny wondered to herself whether there were any operas by Schubert...but she said, "Oh yes, of course; so do I. The one I like best is the *Götterdämmerung*," and that sounded quite natural... "you know when the world comes to an end, and drifts away like a dead leaf..." And as she said this, she felt that the presence behind them was suffering, and she felt a sharp sense of pain herself...she cried out in pain... And Francis said, "Fanny, Fanny, what *is* the matter?" She said, "Francis, don't you see, don't you know, don't you feel it? We are hurting *her*. We can't – we can't do this any more." And Francis said, "Hurting whom?" And Fanny thought to herself, "His grammar is always correct." "Hurting what?"

"Why, Daphne Adeane, of course!"

"Daphne Adeane! Who is Daphne Adeane?"

And then Fanny thought there was a noise like a scream. She woke up sobbing bitterly.

"I believe," she said to herself, "that the ghost of that dead woman is coming between us, and will be between us for ever."

She could not go to sleep again, and she got up as soon as it was daylight, and went for a walk. She walked as far as Westminster Cathedral and went inside. Mass was being said in many of the side chapels, and in St Patrick's Chapel there was a drummer boy kneeling by himself in his uniform, stiff and straight in front of the altar in a rigid ecstasy of prayer.

"I wonder what he is praying for," thought Fanny. She walked up to the Lady Chapel. Mass was being said there, and there were a few worshippers. She saw a woman put up a candle, light it, and put twopence in the box. She did the same thing, and she knelt down and said this prayer:

"If all this, dear God, means anything, teach me to understand it, and bless Francis, and let him never stop loving me, whatever may happen. If it's wrong, forgive us – and explain it to Daphne Adeane, and tell her to leave us alone."

At one o'clock, she went to Prince's Restaurant, and found Francis waiting for her. When they sat down at their table, they noticed at another table in the farther corner of the room, a man in khaki, with greyish hair, and with several medal ribbons, who seemed to be waiting for someone with impatience.

Fanny knew him by sight, but could not recall at first who it was. Then she remembered. It was Stephen Lacy's eldest brother, Lord Windlestone. Fanny and Francis both noticed him, and they both noticed his impatience. Presently he was joined by an elegant figure in furs.

Francis Greene asked Fanny if she knew who it was.

"It's Mrs Bucknell," she said; "I only know her by sight."

After luncheon they had only a short time left to them. Francis Greene drove Fanny to Liverpool Street Station, and they made a plan to meet the following week. It seemed, oh, so far off to both of them – unbearably far off.

"I must be at home for Christmas," said Fanny, "but I will be able to come up directly after, even if it is only for a day."

Lady Weston was surprised at Fanny's appearance when she arrived at Hockley. She seemed in radiant looks, quite different. "The war is doing you good," she said.

"Boulogne," said Fanny, "is a healthy place. The climate suits me there; we are so busy that one has to be well – I am well – very well – " and she laughed out of the fullness of her heart.

CHAPTER XXIII

A new life began for Fanny. It was not she felt a *real* life, and it was a blend of anguish and infinite happiness. She seldom saw Francis, but she heard from him every day. She went up to London when she could. They met at odd moments and in strange places for scraps of time. She had heard from Michael. He was due back in England in January. He did not know what he would do next, or what would be his fate. Fanny prolonged her stay in England to the utmost limit. But towards the end of January it was necessary for her to go back to France. She saw Francis in London the day before she left. But only for a short time. All his time was taken. Never had he been so hard worked. It was difficult for him to see Fanny even for half an hour. They did manage to snatch more than that…an hour. They met at an A.B.C. shop in the Strand, and they drank, or pretended to drink, coffee. Fanny was anxious.

"I feel it's coming to an end," and yet her looks belied this statement. Happiness radiated from her eyes.

"I don't think so, Fanny," Francis said, and as he looked at her and seemed to enfold her with and bear her upon the great waves of his love, she felt assured, calm and confident like a swimmer borne upon buoyant waves.

"But what is to happen, what shall I do when Michael comes back?"

"Don't let's think of the future now."

"I can't help it…you know I hate lies. I hate pretence. I have never pretended to Michael. Even by not doing so I have caused him pain. I think I have been wrong, but I can't help it. I am built like that."

Francis nodded. He agreed she was like that. Daphne Adeane had been the opposite. She would tell any lie, play any part, pretend anything, to avoid giving pain. She was compact of tenderness and compassion, qualities which Fanny lacked, and the irony of the situation was that Francis now admired Fanny for being without those very qualities which he had once regarded when he met them in Daphne as the supremest and the most necessary.

"Yes," he said proudly, "you can't lie, you don't know how to. You are above all that, but we won't think of that now. It is no good facing imaginary situations…it is no good facing any situation till it arises."

"Do you really think so? Don't you think that is simply drifting?"

"No, not at all. You can't face a situation till you know what the situation is, and we don't know."

"Don't we?"

"No, not yet…"

"Well," said Fanny, "whatever happens, whatever Fate may have in store for us, I shall regret nothing…nothing, and I shouldn't mind saying this to all the world, and I shall say the same at the Day of Judgment. I thank God for every moment of our love; nothing can take it away."

"I think the same."

The moment of separation came all too soon. Fanny felt that it was unbearable…

That afternoon Fanny left for France, Francis went to Greenwich. She had not been back in France a week before she heard from Michael. He was in England, and was coming out to France at once. Fanny made a plan of campaign in her head.

She would, she thought, tell him the truth. But one side of herself at once objected. "Have you the right to do that? Won't it make him very unhappy?" "Yes," said the other side, "it will. But I respect him and like him too much to deceive him, to cheat him, and then I am a bad actress. I can't act. I can't pretend." "Wait, wait," said another voice. "Don't do anything rash." She wondered what she would do when the critical moment arrived.

Michael flew over to France with his squadron, and he sent her a card telling her that he would be able to drive over and see her soon. He would do so on the first possible opportunity. Then he wrote again – this was in the early days of February – making a definite appointment for the following Saturday. He would come in a light tender which was going to Boulogne to get food for the mess.

Fanny was in an agony of mental agitation. She did not know what to do. Could she leave Michael? There were the children. She couldn't leave Peter…and yet deep down in her heart she knew she could, and would, if it came to the point…she loved Francis better than anything. She was obsessed. She had drunk the fatal potion, and she could think of nothing else. It was beyond reason. She knew she could never give him up.

Michael was enjoying himself. He was in a single-seater squadron, and was now a Flight Commander. He had been out on reconnaissance, had been "archied," and had seen "Huns" in the air. He was, he said, in the best of all squadrons. He was longing to tell her all about it. Never had he been so happy.

So he said in a letter that Fanny received on the Thursday before she expected him. She said to herself, "I needn't after all do anything in a hurry." But then another part of herself said, "Surely he will see, he will read what has happened to you on your face. How will you be able to hide it?" and the other self answered: "You know that Michael will see nothing, and that you will be able to hide anything easily."

On Friday, the day before she expected Michael, Fanny went into Boulogne, and that morning, as indeed every morning, she had received a long letter from Francis. She did some shopping, she bought some cigarettes and other things at the canteen for the men. She met Father Rendall in the street; he stopped and talked to her for a moment.

He mentioned Francis Greene, and said he had only heard from him once since he, Greene, had left, but he was, of course, too busy to write.

"Oh, far too busy to write," said Fanny, thinking of the eight closely written pages she had received that day, and she felt she was blushing.

She changed the conversation. Father Rendall asked after one or two people at the hospital, and then he said goodbye. When she got back to the hospital, Margaret Clive said to her, as she came in: "There's a telegram for you."

"I wonder who it's from," she thought. "It can't be from Michael, and Francis doesn't telegraph, at least not to France." She took off her things and then asked for the telegram.

"I expect it's from Mother," she said to herself. "I hope the children aren't ill?"

She opened the telegram. The letters were printed in black on strips of blue paper. It was easy to read. It told her in the official phrases that her husband, Captain Choyce, had not returned from a reconnaissance. He was "missing."

She ran up to her room. She had been alone when she received this telegram. She wanted to avoid Margaret's sympathy. She would have to go through with it...but not at once, not this minute. It was nearly tea-time. She would only have a few moments to herself. It was a knock on the door of fate with a vengeance.

Fanny was stunned. She seemed to lose all power of thought or reason or feeling. She had not felt like this since the great disillusion she had suffered after her marriage...once more life seemed to fall about her like a pack of cards...but this was

something different and greater…she was full of a desolating
devastating sorrow. She was sorry not for herself, but for
Michael. She felt that a dark, permanent cloud had descended
on her life. She had brought about this retribution, but it was
not that that she minded. She felt no remorse for what she had
done, but she minded for Michael, she minded his death for
him…she was sad – completely sad – she tasted the sharpness
of death. She wished it could have been otherwise…and at the
same time in spite of this heavy thundercloud of gloom, in spite
of this eclipse, which she thought would be lasting, deep, deep
down in her heart, there was the seed of a wild hope. She knew
it was there, although she tried not to think of it, tried not to
acknowledge it; but it was there, unmistakable, obstinate,
persistent, a still voice not to be denied, not to be silenced.
Perhaps, who knows?…it might mean that one day…some far-
off day in the dim future…everything would turn out for the
best. Perhaps she might be able to marry Francis. Perhaps this
was her destiny. She tried to put away the thought. She tried
not to think of it.

"Well," she said to herself, "I must face it."

She washed her face and walked downstairs, and she found
Margaret.

"Michael," she said, "is missing."

Margaret, who had been through the same thing the year
before, was all sympathy, and said all the things one does say
on such occasions: that there was every chance of his being a
prisoner; that he must have made a forced landing; that this
happened every day; that the Flying prisoners were well looked
after in Germany – all the usual things – that, of course, she
must at once write to So-and-so, and So-and-so, neutrals, that
she would be sure to get news.

Two days later, she received a letter from Michael's
Squadron Commander. He did not tell her anything fresh or
further. Michael had gone out on a reconnaissance, and he had
not returned. The Germans had not reported having brought an

English machine down that day, so he had perhaps made a forced landing somewhere. He added some complimentary remarks about Michael. But time went on, and no news came of Michael. In a month's time she heard from neutral sources that the Germans knew nothing of Captain Choyce, nor of his machine.

"He may have had a forced landing in France," people said to Fanny, "and he may now be lying hidden somewhere on the other side of the line. This has happened, and people have hidden for months like this. He may turn up any day. At any rate, if he had been killed, it is most likely the Germans would know it."

Fanny felt she could not endure being in France any longer, and at Easter she left the hospital for good, on the plea that she had been away too long from the children. She went back to England, first to Hockley, and then to London. She begged Francis to find her some work. He arranged for her to work at the canteen at Victoria Station.

She saw Francis at least once a week. She lived for these days. Nothing was changed. Nothing, thought Fanny, will ever make a difference. It is above and beyond everything else, and nothing can efface it, because it has a life of its own. It is out of reach of everything else. Lady Weston took the line that Fanny was being unbelievably brave. She was herself puzzled and perplexed. She thought Fanny seemed really better and looked better than she had ever done in her life, and at the same time she felt that Fanny had become intangible, that she could no longer reach her, and she wondered what could have happened, and what was going on inside her. She knew nothing about Francis Greene. Fanny had managed easily to keep her and everyone else in ignorance.

Time went on, the summer passed, and still there was no news of Michael. Every source of inquiry was tapped without success. Letters were written to important people all over Europe, but without result. The German authorities said they had no knowledge either of Michael or of his machine. He had flown away into space and disappeared.

Fanny stayed in London for the rest of the year till Christmas, which she spent with her mother in Devonshire. Francis Greene was still at Greenwich. After Christmas she came back to London, and brought the children with her, and went on with her canteen work.

Leo Dettrick had left France and gone to Italy. Fanny had seen him for a moment on his way through London. Stephen Lacy had been killed, and George Ayton had been badly gassed and sent home. Leo Dettrick still wrote to her every day. He thought a great deal about Fanny, and he was nursing within his heart a hope that he hardly dared to formulate; if it turned out that Michael was really killed, perhaps some day, when the war was over, and wounds were healed, Fanny might marry him. But he put aside the thought as being too wonderful to be true. "At any rate," he said to himself, "she won't marry anybody else."

When he saw her, as he passed through London on his way to Italy, he felt there was something different about her, that something had happened to her, but Michael's disappearance was, he thought, a sufficient explanation. It has been a great shock to her, he thought. He knew she had got to know Francis Greene. Francis had told him himself, but Leo had been pleased – pleased that she appreciated his friend, and he never dreamt that they were intimate. Leo had been so absorbed in his own life, being as he was sensitive to new impressions, that he had not had the time to diagnose the experiences of his friends; he had just taken for granted that things were as he was told they were, as they seemed on the surface. Francis and Fanny had made friends because they had met once or twice at Boulogne, and because they both knew him. What could be more natural? Of course they seldom saw one another now, because Francis was at Greenwich and Fanny was in London.

But Leo was struck by Fanny's appearance. Never in her life, he thought, had she looked so well. She was well. She had the health and the looks that come from great happiness and from being loved. Francis' love for her was as great as it had been on the first day, and it wrapped her round with a warm flame, which made her impervious to everything else.

So was her love for him. She seemed to tread on air. She could not believe that such happiness was possible. Nothing seemed to matter, not the war, nor anything to do with it. Her love was like a rainbow to her which was firmly set in the darkest clouds, and however dark the clouds might be, that rainbow was there – tinging the universe with joy and hope.

And so matters went on till the end of the war. Fanny was in London the whole time, with the exception of short visits to Hockley and to her mother's house in Devonshire. When the air raids began, Fanny thought that Hockley was more exposed to Zeppelins (which it was) than other places, and she sent the children, Hester and Peter, to her mother's in Devonshire in the summer and autumn; but she had Hester with her in London in the winter. Peter was at school at Brighton.

Leo Dettrick went to Italy and afterwards to Salonika. Francis Greene stayed at Greenwich, and the bond between him and Fanny not only remained the same, but became more and more binding, more and more important to them every month. They could only see each other rarely, and for a brief space of time when they did meet, but this made their love and their happiness more intense and acute.

> "Therefore are feasts so solemn and so rare,
> Since, seldom coming, in the long year set,
> Like stones of worth they thinly placèd are,
> Or captain jewels in the carcanet."

That is what they each of them thought, and their feasts when they met surpassed all Fanny had ever dreamt of. She

was so happy that she felt something dreadful must happen –
Francis would be sent abroad, would die of typhoid, or be
killed in an air raid.

But none of these things happened. The war came to an end,
and Francis and Fanny were both of them alive. The children
were alive. Nothing tragic had happened. Providence seemed
to have looked on smiling at their fate, and to have connived at
their happiness.

The war was over, and there was still no news of Michael.
Fanny felt certain now, and everyone told her, that he must
have been killed. His machine must have crashed. It happened
sometimes that there were no traces of a crashed machine.
Perhaps he had fallen into the sea and been drowned. Francis,
after the Armistice, had given up his work in Greenwich and
had gone back to London. He now saw Fanny every day, and
they discussed the question of marriage. They had settled to
marry. Nobody knew of it. Fanny had told no one except her
mother. Lady Weston had been stunned with surprise, but she
was philosophical. Fanny introduced Francis to her, and she
liked him; but she could not help saying that she thought this
post-war rage for marrying was hysterical, and she advised
Fanny to "wait."

Leo Dettrick was coming home from abroad. He had cabled
directly after the Armistice to Fanny from Cairo that he hoped
to be in London soon after Christmas.

He knew nothing as yet about her affair with Francis
Greene, and Fanny wondered how he would take it. "After all,
he is not in love with me," she thought, "and it is no good his
pretending he is; but men, and especially men like Leo Dettrick,
are odd about such things, and one never knows how they will
take them." One day when they were sitting in her drawing-
room at Queen Anne's Gate she said to Francis: "Do you think
Leo will mind our being married?"

"Why should he mind?"

"Well, because I don't think he likes his friends marrying; he thinks they belong to him in a way."

"Do you mean he wants to marry you himself?"

"Oh no."

"But he was very fond of you; he has been devoted to you all these years – I mean he was certainly in love with you, wasn't he?"

"I don't think so," said Fanny. She thought of Daphne Adeane, and she reflected that the image of Daphne Adeane had perhaps successfully come between her and Leo, if unsuccessfully between her and Francis. Francis, she thought, has forgotten Daphne Adeane, and I don't believe Leo did, whatever they may say. He may have at one moment, but he went back to the image of her. "I don't think so," she repeated, "but he could be jealous all the same. By this time he probably loves someone new."

"I don't think so," said Francis, and he thought of the past and of Daphne Adeane. It was odd, he reflected, how Fanny had obliterated the image of Daphne in his mind. It was, he thought, because Fanny's was the stronger personality. It was as if Daphne had been the sketch, and Fanny the finished portrait. It was odd that they should have been physically so strangely, undefinably alike, and so different in character. Daphne was to Fanny what moonlight is to sunlight, what water is to wine. Once you had lived in Fanny's presence, the idea of Daphne could but become faint. She was a ghost compared to a living spirit, and this was one not only because she was dead. Even if she were still alive, it would have been the same, and Francis thought that Leo was probably conscious of this, had always been conscious of this, ever since he had known Fanny.

"I am sure," said Fanny, "that when Leo does come back from the war he is certain to find a new love."

"I wonder," said Francis; "in his case, you know, the new love never kills the old; they go on together."

"I believe you're right," she said, and she laughed, happily and gaily. "I hope he won't mind, all the same, because I am fond of him, and I should hate to hurt him. I think I had better write and tell him. It will be easier than telling him face to face."

Fanny had been officially informed that all hope of finding any trace of Michael had been definitely given up, so she now considered herself free.

Leo came back to England sooner and quicker than Fanny had expected, and he drove straight from the station to her house. It was just after Christmas. Fanny had spent it in London. Leo was bubbling with suppressed news. He was leaving for America, as it was imperative that he should go to New York to arrange about an edition of his books which was coming out there. During the whole war he had, of course, not been able to write anything, but what was more important, he had not been able to pay any attention to his literary affairs, to the business side of his books.

They talked of one subject and another, and every moment Fanny said to herself, "Now in three minutes I will tell him," but the three minutes went by, and she found she had told him nothing.

"They have quite given up all hope of ever finding any trace of Michael," she said.

Leo said he was sorry. "One never knows," he added.

"I think I must have heard something by now," she said. There was a long pause.

"I think some day I shall marry again," said Fanny, with a slight nervous laugh.

Leo's heart gave a bound. He said nothing.

"For the sake of the children," she added; "it is a great drawback for them to have no father."

It never crossed Leo's mind, even at this moment, that she was thinking of someone in particular. "What sort of person do you think you will marry?"

"I should like to marry someone who would be kind to Peter, and who understood children. Stepfathers are, as a rule, kind – kinder than stepmothers. I should like to marry a sensible man – a kind of man like…"

"Who?"

"I don't know, like, perhaps, what I imagine Mr Adeane…"

Leo laughed.

"Why are you laughing?"

"I can't imagine you married to Ralph Adeane – you don't know what he is like…"

"I might have met him easily in the war; he was in the Red Cross, and he is still working at Geneva. It was from him, oddly enough, I had a letter telling me that I must give up all hope of ever finding Michael."

"But you have never seen him?"

"Never."

"If you saw him, I don't think you would say he was the kind of man you wanted to marry. Now I must go," said Leo.

"Stop one minute."

"What is it? Do you want to tell me something?"

"How long will you be away?"

"Only a week or two. I shall come back as soon as I can. Goodbye, Fanny."

Fanny got up and walked to the front door with him. He opened the door, and they stood together talking on the doorstep.

"No," she said to herself, "I can't tell him; ridiculous as I know this is, I can't."

Leo divined that a hesitation was flickering in her mind, and said, "Fanny, what is it?"

"Nothing, nothing."

Leo felt there was something. He looked at Fanny.

"Well," he said, "goodbye."

"When do you sail?"

"Tomorrow."

"I will write to you." Leo could not tell why, but he thought this was ominous.

"Yes, do, but write at once or I shan't get it. I am coming back as soon as I can."

"Very well. Goodbye."

"Goodbye, Fanny."

Leo looked at her sadly. He felt there was something final about this goodbye, more final than he had ever felt about any other. Then he left the hall and shut the front door gently.

That night Francis talked of putting a paragraph in the newspaper announcing their marriage, but Fanny said she could not do this before writing to Leo.

"But he would get the letter before he could see the paragraph."

"One never knows," said Fanny; "odd things happen to letters. Let me write."

That night she wrote as follows: "Leo, I am going to marry Francis Greene. It is still a secret."

The letter reached Leo two days after he arrived at New York.

He read it, and thought his eyes must have read the words wrong. Then he felt his heart stop. The world suddenly became a grey place. At this moment, in his mind the images of Fanny and of Daphne Adeane became merged into one – a tragic symbol of baffled desire, mocking happiness, and permanent regret.

CHAPTER XXIV

A week later Fanny and Francis were actually engaged, early one morning just after breakfast, in drafting the paragraph they intended to send to the press about their marriage when the parlour-maid brought in a telegram. It was a foreign telegram, and the place of issue was unintelligible to Fanny, besides being illegible, but it seemed to her Flemish, the kind of name familiar to anyone who had lived in Flanders. It ran as follows:

"Nuns St Joseph's Convent Hoogebeke Belgium reported January 1 harbouring British officer suffering complete loss memory since 1916. On checking records suspected possibility officer being Captain Choyce. Proceeded Hoogebeke with colleague and doctor. Found officer in question was Captain Choyce. Memory apparently completely gone when questioned by doctor but on seeing me suddenly and apparently completely restored. Doctor says recovery will be permanent. Very well physically perfectly normal fit to travel. No need for you come over. Propose proceeding London immediately unless hear contrary. We can arrive tomorrow evening. Please wire Hotel d'Angleterre Calais. BASIL WAKE."

Fanny handed the telegram to Francis. For a time they said nothing. Fanny was the first to break the silence.

288

"We must face the situation now, at once," she said. "How shall I tell him?"

"You mean to…"

"Anything else would be impossible…out of the question… I think…unless you have changed…"

"No, I haven't changed…but you realise all that it will mean…apart from everything else, it would mean giving up Peter."

"Not entirely. Michael will let me have him sometimes – in the holidays." Peter had already been at a private school for the last three years. "After all, the same kind of thing happens every day now. I couldn't go back to Michael *now*, however much I might want to; it wouldn't be honest, would it?"

"I can't judge it from your side. I'm too prejudiced."

"Unless," said Fanny, going on with her train of thought as if Francis had said nothing, "you are tired of me, and you would like to give me up. Would you? Tell me."

She looked at him with a grave expression.

"No, I couldn't give you up of my own accord – you know I couldn't."

"Yes, I *know* you couldn't," and they sat hand in hand like two frightened children who have been threatened that a bad fairy will come and separate them. They both felt desperate, and ready to do anything desperate, and they were both afraid that, in spite of all they might or could do, Fate would still be too strong for them…

"How shall I tell him? how *shall* I tell him?"

"What an extraordinary thing to have happened!" said Francis. "I mean extraordinary that nobody found him before. It's true he has only just recovered his memory."

"I expect it was the sight of Basil Wake that brought that back."

"Nothing could be more probable. It must have been someone or something connected with his pre-war life that brought it back. I suppose he knew Wake well?"

"Yes, before we married; very well. Don't you remember? – I told you all about it…"

"Of course. But it's extraordinary, the nuns saying nothing about it."

"They are very unpractical, and I suppose they didn't dare till the war was over. I expect they did communicate afterwards. They probably did it wrong. I wonder if he is well. Supposing he wanted looking after?"

"The telegram says the doctor is satisfied."

"He would be sure to say that."

"Recoveries of this kind are for the greater part sudden, complete and permanent…it is not as if he had suffered from shell-shock or had been subject for a long time to the racket of trench warfare."

"I shall leave a letter for him," said Fanny, "and go to Mother, I think that will be best."

"Couldn't you get Lady Jarvis to tell him?"

"I know she would – only I think he would mind that more."

"Fanny, are you sure?"

"I can't give you up…and what's the use, even if I did? Isn't all that has happened quite irrevocable? We can't put back the clock now, can we? I mean, supposing Michael knew, he wouldn't want to take me back…and I have never lied to him in my life, and would you like me to go and act a daily living lie? I couldn't do it."

"Well," said Francis, looking at his watch, "I must go to work. You will tell me later what you decide on."

"I will," said Fanny. "Come back as soon as you can this evening. I shall have to send for Mother and tell her. I shall have a terrible time with her, I know. She won't see reason."

Francis left the house, and Fanny felt a need of and longing for human advice. She wanted to talk the matter over with someone – with someone she didn't know well preferably. Her mother was in Devonshire with Hester. She thought of Lady Jarvis; she thought of Mrs Tracy; she thought of Cuthbert Lyley;

she thought of Mr Rowley, the Rector of Hockley. She rang up Lady Jarvis. Her ladyship had just left for Cornwall. She would be away three weeks. Cuthbert Lyley and the others were out of reach. She wanted to discuss the matter at once. She put on her hat and jacket and went out into St James's Park. She walked right across the park up St James's Street, through Berkeley Square, Hill Street, South Audley Street, and South Street into Hyde Park, up along the broad walk as far as the Marble Arch, and there, near the gate, she sat down on a chair. She was no clearer in her mind than before. That is to say, her decision was just as firm as ever, but she had not settled what immediate step to take. She had decided on what she meant to do, but she had not yet decided how to do it. She sat on the seat for about half an hour. It was unusually warm for the time of year. There were signs of spring in the earth as well as in the sky.

Everything was being born again. Life was beginning again after the war, a new world was being born, a new life was beginning for her. At the beginning of the war she had never dared hope that this would happen – that life would begin again. Then she thought of her children. Would it mean she must lose Peter for ever? She thought not. He was, after all, at school, and that was the greatest loss of all. It would never be the same as it was before. Would he reproach her when he grew up? She thought not; she thought he would understand, and she knew, she realised perfectly well, that even if it meant giving up Peter for ever, she would do it rather than give up Francis. Hester? Would she reproach her? Perhaps; but she was too young to mind. Nothing in the world would make her give up Francis – nothing, nothing, nothing. Just as she was thinking this, a familiar form passed her – a man; he looked back, hesitated, then she recognised him and called to him:

"Father Rendall."

She got up from her seat and she said, "You are the very person I want to see, although, to be honest, I was not thinking of you."

"Oddly enough," said Father Rendall, "I passed someone about five minutes ago and I said to myself, 'That is Mrs Choyce,' and it wasn't you after all, and here almost directly afterwards I meet you."

"Are you in a hurry? Where are you going?" asked Fanny.

"I am going home. I am staying near Notting Hill, but I am in no hurry. I will go where you like and do what you like."

"If we walk through the park up Bayswater way, will that do?"

"That will do beautifully."

They crossed the main road and walked along a path opposite Bayswater, inside the park.

"I want to ask your advice about something, or rather to hear your views. I want you to say to me what you would say – exactly what you would say – to a Catholic who came and told you what I am going to tell you, under the seal of the confessional. The reason I am doing this is that I know you will have a definite opinion, and an opinion that is not *only* your own, but that of your Church; you have the authority of the Church behind you. Well, I want the authoritative view on this matter, not that of the Scribes. I can go to a thousand Scribes. I have lived all my life among the Scribes. At the same time, I don't want you to think for a moment that I will accept the authoritative view or take your advice. I am not in your fold, and I don't think I ever shall be. But I want to hear what the authoritative view is; it will help me, not to make up my mind – that is already made up – but it will help me all the same."

Father Rendall nodded. "I will do my best," he said.

"Well, the matter is briefly this. I married when I was quite young – twenty. I was madly in love. My husband was thirteen years older than I. I was passionately in love with him, and I thought that he loved me. For me it was love at first sight, and

I thought it had been the same for him. It wasn't. He had loved another woman for years. I didn't know this, and only found it out later. He didn't tell me. I don't blame him for not telling me. On the contrary, I think he was quite right not to. He never saw her after he married, and I am sure he tried to forget her, but he couldn't; she behaved nobly and died soon after – died of that very possibly. He couldn't forget her, he couldn't help comparing me with her, and finding me wanting; we drifted apart. I had three children, one died. I lost my looks; I lived by myself; I gave up; then I made friends with Leo Dettrick, the writer. We became friends – nothing more. I came to life again. I went abroad; I thought I was making Michael's life dull. I turned over a new leaf. I recovered my health and my looks, and Michael fell in love with me; but for me it was too late. I could give him nothing. Then came the war, and I met Francis Greene in 1916, and I fell in love with him in a way I had never been in love before, and he fell in love with me. I gave myself to him once for all. Almost immediately after this came the news that Michael was missing. Later I was told that there was no hope of his being alive, and then quite finally, after the Armistice, Francis and I settled to marry, and we were about to send the news to the press today, when I got a telegram to say that my husband is alive, that he has been found in a convent, where he was looked after by some nuns, and that he had completely lost his memory, but has now recovered it. That he is quite well and normal and that the recovery will be permanent. He is coming home at once; he will be here tomorrow afternoon. Now I have quite settled to marry Francis Greene, provided he still wants to marry me. I know he does. He says he does, and I know he is telling the truth. I suppose Michael would allow Peter, my son, to come to me for half of every holidays; but even if he didn't, even if it meant never seeing Peter again, I should still not go back to Michael – I should still marry Francis. This is not only because I love Francis more than all the world, although I do; not only because he loves me more than all the world, and he does, and I couldn't leave him – not only because of all that, but also because I couldn't behave so dishonestly to Michael. I have never lied to Michael in my life; how could I then go back to him now and pretend that this thing has not happened? I have been living with Francis for three years. I am his wife. Do you expect me to go back as if this had not happened, and to take up life where I left off with him? So put the question of marriage out of court. I shall marry Francis, and so far I intend to tell Michael the whole truth, and I suppose he will then divorce me. But I would like to know what you would say to a Catholic woman if a Catholic woman came to you with this story. You needn't think that what you say might affect one way or the other the possibility of my becoming a Catholic, because as you know, as I have often told you, I am a Pagan – not the "roses and raptures" Pagan. I believe in, not what people foolishly imagine to be Pagan, but in Fate and Law, with small hope for the future. I don't believe in a future life. I don't believe in a personal God. I don't believe in a revealed religion, and I think that all the creeds for which men have fought and died, and which have caused such oceans of blood to flow, are *man-made*, made by men because they wanted to believe these things, wanted to have a creed, idols, churches, altars; and each race and country gets the creed it deserves. But I believe in Destiny. So you mustn't think, 'If I advise her in this sense it will be very awkward for her should one day she were to wish to become a Catholic,' or ' This will put her off the Church.' All that will not affect me. I have no faith – not a grain. I wish with all my heart I had." And here Fanny nearly broke down. "But tell me what you would say to one of your own people. Only put the question of marriage out of court. *That* is settled."

"Well," said Father Rendall, "if one of my people, one of my Catholic penitents, were to come to me with this story, I should say: 'I can't put the question of marriage out of court. I can do nothing to facilitate a life of adultery.' You and your husband were properly married I assume?…"

"Yes, there is no way out there."

"Well, I should go on, ' I cannot advise you to ask your husband to provide grounds for divorce by himself committing or faking adultery, for it would be a sin of another kind did he do so. Nor can I advise you to break his heart; he loves you now, and he is coming back from the horrors of war and all he has been through with hopes of a happy life…wonderful hopes…nor can I advise you to put a horrible memory about their mother into the minds of your children who, I hope, trust you.'"

"Then you would advise me to return to my husband?"

"Most decidedly."

"But if I did, I should have to tell him the truth. As I have already told you, I have never lied to him in my life. He believes in me and knows I am truthful. How could I lie about this, the greatest of all things? how could I go back and be a lie and act a lie every minute of the day? Other people may be able to do that – it may be right for them – but I couldn't do it, so it's no good asking me to."

"I should then say to my penitent," Father Rendall went on calmly, " ' If you return to your husband, I should certainly not advise you to tell him.'"

"But I should feel dishonourable."

"I should answer, 'You will have to put up with feeling dishonourable. That is a position you have created for yourself. It is rather like a young man who wonders whether he ought to tell his fiancée what he has done before his marriage. He ought NOT. You yourself say your husband was right *not* to tell you about his affair.'"

"But I should feel such a hypocrite."

" 'It can't be helped,' I should say to my penitent, and I say the same to you, that it is a part of your punishment, if you like to accept it as such. But if you do not return to your husband, you are in a fix. I cannot recommend your telling him what would give him grounds for divorcing you, nor that you should force him to give you grounds for divorcing him. In short, there is only one path open to you – that is, heroic self-sacrifice. It is constantly so. By any other road you will only reach and create unhappiness. There is no other way out of it."

"But all that Michael, my husband, feels for me is based upon the fact that I have always been truthful to him, that I have never morally lied to him. I don't mean, of course, never *told lies* – that I have done every day...but I have been fundamentally truthful to him, and he knows that, he feels it unconsciously. Now if I begin to act a part, he would feel *that* unconsciously."

"Well, you would have to face that – that too would be part of the punishment."

"You may be right, but I feel I can't do it. If I belonged to your Church, you could say to me, 'It doesn't matter what you think – this and this only is what the Church tells you is your duty.' But I don't. I am without a guide. You see I am a Pagan, as I have often told you, Father Rendall."

"Very well, granted you are a Pagan. From my point of view that is so much to the good: because I know from what you have told me before, that you understand what Pagan means: and the Church has retained and contains all that you admire – all that is noble and fine in Pagan thought – for Catholic Truth contains all truths. Now, nobody, as you know, believed more firmly than the Pagans did in the certainty of retribution. You got the retribution whether the sin you committed was deliberate or accidental. Œdipus, through no fault of his own, suffered a terrible chastisement. They believed in expiation. What they were without is the mystery of Forgiveness. We believe that sin must be expiated, but we also believe that sin is forgiven and the wrong is put right. But if any great and virtuous Pagan were alive today, judging your case according to his lights, I do not think that he would hesitate to tell you that if you did what you say you intend to do, you would be preparing for yourself and for all those connected with you – your husband, your lover, your children – a Nemesis. A purgatory on this earth. Do you think you will make Francis Greene happy if you marry him in these circumstances?"

"But if we are ready to face and share the unhappiness?"

"You think that, judging the situation as it is *now*; but you must remember it will change and be different after the event."

"We shall never change; we would be like Paolo and Francesca in the whirlwind of fire...

'Together on the never-resting air,'

and never complain."

"I believe that; I believe that is what you both feel. But what about the others? Would you be able to forget that they are alive and unhappy? Let alone the children; I am not insisting on that because I know it is not necessary. You have faced that sacrifice, and I guess what it must mean. But think of Francis Greene. It is *he* who will be the unhappy one."

"Oh, I shan't be like Anna Karenina. I always detested her all my life, and I see now how right I was. She made such a hash of things."

"We all make our own hashes."

"I dare say; but the long and short of it is that I can't. And you know, Father Rendall, I don't want to be cynical, but it's all very well to talk of retribution and Nemesis and tragedy and Purgatory, but you must remember that the same thing is happening every day to people I know, and it often appears to me perfectly successful; the Nemesis may happen in the next world, but as far as this world is concerned, I know many people who have divorced and married again, and who are perfectly happy; and some of these with children who are friends with both parents...and it all works wonderfully well."

"You can only judge from the outside, and no one can judge even the outside of such a thing before the drama is played out to the end. But I can only say this: I think that no philosopher of any time has ever maintained that you can break the law with impunity. You can't put yourself above the law."

"Love is above the law."

"No, the law *is* Love. It is precisely the Love of God against which you are sinning."

"I can't, I can't, I can't, Father Rendall." She sat down on one of the park seats and burst into tears. Then she controlled herself, got up, and went on walking. "It is so easy for you. It is all mapped out for you, but I don't believe in the maps – that is to say, in the authority of the maps, frankly; and if I don't believe in the maps, why should I be bound by their measurements?"

"And yet you do, to the extent of asking me what course I advise. You ask me what my map says."

"Yes, yes, yes; because I want to get things clear in my own mind. I am willing to admit that you may be right. I may be wrong, but I, being what I am, cannot believe in the map of my own accord, and I am too independent, too wilful, too rebellious, if you like, to take it on trust. Besides which, it doesn't convince me. I am a born Protestant, only without faith – no, a born Pagan."

"You, who like Pagan sentiments, do you remember what Antigone said to Creon, when she performed the funeral rites for her brother after Creon had forbidden it? – 'Nor did I think that thou, a mortal man, couldst by a breath cancel the immutable unwritten laws of God. They are not of today nor of yesterday.'"

"But that is just it. I say *I am* obeying the unwritten law. Antigone was accused of breaking the formal law of man. It is laws of man I am breaking – the conventions of the world – of society."

"On the contrary, the laws of man will allow you to divorce as much and as often as you please. It is the law of God you are breaking. The law that Antigone broke was the man-made law – a fortuitous, cruel, and unjust law – made for a special spiteful purpose; and she said expressly that the law she broke was not ordained of Zeus nor enacted by Justice. The law she kept was the Law of God. The law you wish to break is the Law of God: ' Thou shalt not commit adultery.' "

"But I have broken that already...so surely it doesn't matter what I do now. It's too late."

"According to our belief, it is never too late; and according to our belief, it matters immensely."

"That's the vicious circle again. According to your creed."

"You must make up your mind whether you are appealing to Caesar or to God, and you mustn't confuse your tributes."

They were already further than Victoria Gate.

"I must go back," said Fanny, "I will think it over. Thank you for all you have done and said. You have been most kind. Even if I don't take your advice – and it is most probable, it would indeed be a miracle, I think, if I did take it – you have helped me; you have been very kind, and ' I am sorry,' as they say at the exchanges, 'to have troubled you.' "

"May I ask you one last question?" said Father Rendall.

"Yes, of course."

"You say you are a Pagan. What is, in your opinion, the fundamental idea of Paganism? What is the essence of Greek tragedy?"

"Sacrifice," said Fanny, without hesitation.

"There!" said Father Rendall; "Now believe me that in every act of sacrifice we make there is a *balm*, and in every act of *self* that we make there is an aftertaste of fire, smoke, dust, and ash. Goodbye." And he looked at her with steady compassion.

"Goodbye," she said, "and pray for me."

Then Fanny walked back as far as the Marble Arch, and there she took a taxi and drove home. She had so little time.

She wanted to get things clear in her head before she saw Francis again. He would probably come between six and seven if he could get away...at any rate, they would dine together. When she got home she found on the hall table a telegram from Michael confirming what Wake had said, and saying they were starting and would arrive "tomorrow." There was also a letter from Peter, from his school. It ran thus:

"*Sunday.*

MY DARLING MUMMIE, – Please write to me. There is a Gymnastic examination next Wednesday. It is a lovely day today. We are going to have a paper-chase. Please come and see me soon. Please send 2 pounds of shot and the elastic. Mind you have *the elastic* THIN ENOUGH. Goodbye. – Your *very loving*

PETER.

"P.S. – When you come please bring 20 of those little fluff monkeys. PLEASE do. Do you know where it is possible to get sneezing powder?"

CHAPTER XXV

Fanny had luncheon by herself. After luncheon, she wrote Michael a long letter. It took her till half-past five o'clock. It was a confession, not an *apologia*, and she told him as honestly as she could all she had felt ever since her marriage, and the reasons why she had now determined to leave him. As soon as the letter was written she felt the deed had been done. She felt the action to be irrevocable, and she at once began to wonder whether it was right. She sat for an hour and a half brooding over the fire. She was expecting Francis. He was late. He was probably busy. At half-past six the front door bell rang.

"That's Francis," she said to herself.

But the parlour-maid brought a card on which was printed:

MR RALPH ADEANE,
ELM PARK HOUSE,
KENSINGTON.

"Show him up," said Fanny. She felt alarmed. Just as the parlour-maid went downstairs the telephone bell rang. It was Francis. It would be impossible for him to come to dinner. Somebody wanted to see him on an *urgent* matter, and could only come then. He would try and look in before dinner. If not, early the next morning for certain.

"Very well; goodnight," said Fanny, and at that moment Mr Adeane was shown in.

He was a short, baldish, tidy man with a trim grey beard and quiet, shrewd eyes. He seemed shy. Fanny begged him to sit down.

"You didn't get our telegram?" he said, with hesitation.

"The telegram from Michael?" said Fanny. "Yes; I got it this morning."

"Oh, then there must have been a delay. It was sent off from Hoogebeke the day before yesterday."

"Then 'tomorrow' in the telegram meant today," said Fanny feverishly. "Has Michael arrived? Is he here?" She got up.

"No, no, Mrs Choyce," said Ralph Adeane, with obvious embarrassment. "I have come by myself. That is exactly what I have come to explain. I must begin by the end of my story. The telegram was sent off early on Sunday morning from Hoogebeke in Belgium. I confess I did not send it myself. I should have done so. I didn't. We went by road in a motor-car to Calais, and we spent the night at the hotel, at Calais. We were to have started this morning – Mr Choyce, Wake, and myself – and to have arrived in London this afternoon. At the last moment, when we were almost on board the boat, Mr Choyce" – he coughed – "well, Mr Choyce probably had a return, a semi-relapse of…his weakness." He coughed again. "He has been suffering from loss of memory ever since he was reported missing, and had, as you know, been laid up." He paused. "Well, Mr Choyce was seized by a sudden and unaccountable reluctance to travel – to start. He took us apart and said he could not travel. We expostulated. We explained to him that you were awaiting him, that we had telegraphed. The cruel disappointment it would be for you…and…" – he coughed again slightly – "for your children – for all concerned. Then he begged us to walk back to the hotel. There was not time enough, but we walked as far as the *buffet*, and we engaged a table and we ordered some coffee. There was very little time before the boat was sailing – ten minutes at the most – no, no, I am wrong, six minutes. We had engaged a cabin, all our luggage was on board. Your husband had no luggage – only a small suitcase which he had bought in the town that morning. Well, we tried to take the matter lightly…and we said, 'Come, come, the boat is starting; we shall miss it if we don't start at once. The sea is smooth; it will be an easy voyage' – we had engaged a cabin – 'and a comfortable journey.' Then Mr Choyce – your husband – buried his face in his hands and was, well, overcome…the journey and the – the fatigue, no doubt, and the motor-cars drive dangerously fast in France, although we warned the driver that we were taking, not an invalid exactly, but someone who had been an invalid, but they do not seem to understand… Well, Mr Choyce, your husband, buried his face in his hands and said he could not go home…and we asked him why – quite gently, of course. He then said – of course you know it is all due to what he has been through, and the doctors say it is most usual and happens almost every day – in fact, that those who have had a shock, or concussion, may suffer from strange fancies. Well, he said, 'I can't go back because my wife' (he hesitated) 'because Fanny' (he coughed) 'doesn't want me to come back.' And then he seemed to think, he argued, in fact, that his wife, that Mrs Choyce, that you, Mrs Choyce, had – had, well, that you no longer wished to see him – in fact, he said, 'She doesn't love me,' and the kindest thing, so he said" – Mr Adeane coughed again – "would be to stay away. We argued, we expostulated, but there was so little time – the boat was starting – Wake and I had to take a quick decision, and we decided that it would be best if Wake were to remain with Mr Choyce – I mean Captain Choyce – and that I should take the boat so as not to disappoint you, and so as to inform you as to what had occurred."

"Of course," said Fanny, "I was not expecting you till tomorrow."

"No, of course not. It was the servant from the Belgian convent who dispatched the telegram, or rather who was told to take it to the telegraph office, and no doubt she made a mistake. They always do – nuns, I mean. But I feel sure it is only due to momentary over-fatigue. Your husband after all these months has perhaps done too much all of a sudden – and he is already probably perfectly well and normal and fit to travel. Wake found an excellent doctor, and he is in excellent hands. I think you may expect him tomorrow or the next day. Wake is certain to telegraph. But Wake and myself both think it essential that you should lose no time in sending him an encouraging message. We are both convinced that that is the only thing which will remove the obsession he is suffering from. We think it would be advisable for you to cable at once."

"When did you first hear of him? – When you first saw him, did you think he was quite well?"

"I will now go back to the beginning of the story. It was like this. We first heard of Captain Choyce from the Belgian nuns who had hidden him in their convent. They had no idea what his name was, but they said they had an officer in hiding who had completely lost his memory. They said that as soon as the Armistice had been signed they had communicated with the British Red Cross at Geneva. They said they had written more than once, but I have no doubt that they directed their letters inaccurately if they wrote at all, which I am not sure of, as, in a good cause nuns are so untruthful, and they were very fond of your husband. However that may be, their communications must have gone astray except the last one, which reached us some time after the Armistice, about three weeks ago. In this letter they gave details about this British officer. He had said he was a Flying officer, and that he had set fire to his machine – he was very proud of that – and repeated it to them in French over and over again. Apart from that, he could tell them nothing; he had come to them out of space; he had nothing on him to identify him – no disc, medals, or papers. He said he had burnt everything; he could remember nothing. They could not give him up before the Armistice because he was in the Belgian territory that was occupied by the Germans. They were fond of him, they called him *'Ce très cher Monsieur'* and *'Notre Anglais,'* and they hid him till the end of the war with ease. We received this communication – Mr Basil Wake and myself, who have been working at this...this...well, this 'job' all through the war...and when we received it we thought at first there might be a mistake, but on looking up the records, we came to the conclusion the officer in question might possibly be Captain Choyce. We did not communicate with you immediately in case we were mistaken, and so as not to raise false hopes...and we decided, Wake and myself, to go at once to Belgium, and investigate the matter for ourselves, as Wake knew your husband.

"We drove to Hoogebeke from Boulogne – a long drive – and we took with us a doctor who had dealt with cases of concussion and nerves...and we arrived at Hoogebeke on a Saturday afternoon. When we found the convent, we interviewed the Mother Superior. She confirmed what she had written to us and suggested that we should interview the officer. We saw him in the parlour. The doctor and I saw him first. Wake was engaged – he was checking the records that the Mother Superior had kept. The doctor and myself saw at once that he was an officer and a gentleman, although he was dressed in a blouse as a French gardener, and had been working in the garden." Mr Adeane coughed again. "But we could get nothing out of him, – absolutely nothing. We gave it up as hopeless, and then towards the end of my interview Wake came in, brought by the Mother Superior, and as soon as he saw Wake – well, it was miraculous. I could hardly believe my senses. He said, 'Hullo, Basil!' and everything seemed slowly to come back to him. The doctor afterwards told us this was not an unusual occurrence. He said he had gone out on a reconnaissance. He had 'crashed'; he had burnt his machine and all his papers, he felt confident of that; and that was all he could remember. Of course he did not know me. How should he? I had never seen him before, but he seemed to be in the best of spirits, and the nuns said that he had been fairly well but *'souffrant'* every now and then, and that he had shown no wish to go away, or to do anything. He was listless, like a man in a trance; and he tried to remember sometimes, and that hurt him. The nuns were childishly delighted, and said that it was all owing to the *Novena* that a certain sister had organised for the recovery of your husband's memory, which apparently had come to an end, that very day. They are, of course, super-stitious. We at once arranged that we should send you a telegram and get to England as soon as it might be possible. There were, of course, a few formalities that would be necessary, but we knew we should be able to manage all that. Your husband, Captain Choyce, that is to say, seemed to be delighted at the prospect, and then and there we arranged to start for Calais. Wake sent you a telegram and your husband wrote another, and he gave them to someone connected with the convent – I do not know who it was, a boy or a girl, but I expect they were equally incompetent – to take to the telegraph office in the village. Wake and myself had to motor to Boulogne first and then back to Calais, and we arrived at Calais late Saturday night. We spent the night at the hotel at Calais, and we made arrangements to arrive in London Monday evening. I tried to telephone to you on Sunday, but we could not get on. There was, they said at the exchange, 'No answer.'

"We started this morning to cross by the earliest boat, and I have told you the rest. I am certain that all will be well, but I think the new shock" – he coughed – "the shock of recovery, was perhaps trying for your husband, and that he will need time to get over it; but all will be well without doubt once he is reassured, only I think the matter now lies in your hands and in that of doctors. I think, Mrs Choyce, if I may say so without impertinence or without" – he coughed – "seeming in any way

to interfere, that it is for you to take some immediate, some –
er – decisive step to prove to your husband, or rather to
convince him that he is suffering from a baseless delusion – I
think it will only need a word. I think it will be sufficient for you
to send him a telegram, or if a telegram should be too abrupt, a
letter to say that you are anxiously expecting him and all will
be well. Here is the address of the hotel where they are
staying." He handed her a slip. "I feel convinced of it. I have
made an appointment tonight for dinner with one of the few
sensible doctors I have ever met in my life, and who happens to
be an expert in these matters, and I mean to ask his advice. He
is an authority in this very branch of medicine – nerves,
concussion, shock – but he is sensible, in spite of being an
expert, and he is a judge of human nature – and a sound fellow
– a decent man – and I mean to ask his advice…"

"What doctor is that?" Fanny asked faintly.

"Greene – Francis Greene."

"Oh."

"Do you know him?"

"Oh yes; very well. Will you be able to see him this evening
so late?"

"Yes, yes; I cabled to him I want him to dine with me. I am
sure he will come. I told him the matter was urgent. I will
communicate with you after I have seen him. Among many
other things, he has a profound knowledge of human nature,
and he has studied nerves all his life."

"Thank you so much…" said Fanny still more faintly. She felt
sick and bewildered.

"Well," said Mr Adeane, "I must be off. Dear me, I had no
idea how late it was," he said as he looked at his watch – a gold
repeater. "I hope, I know – I feel convinced that all will be well
– and if I can be of any use – of the slightest use – I will let you,
I mean I pray you will let me know at once."

"I will," said Fanny as she led him to the door. "Do you –
would you like them to call you a taxi?"

"No, no, thank you. I will find one round the corner."

Fanny said "Goodbye," and "Thank you so much. I cannot tell you how grateful I am."

"I am sure," said Adeane, "that all will be well – all will be splendid."

"Splendid," said Fanny. She rang the bell.

Mr Adeane thought at that moment that it was Fanny rather than Michael who needed a doctor's visit. He walked downstairs, the parlour-maid showed him out. On the doorstep he met Francis Greene, who was just getting out of a taxi.

"Ah!" said Adeane. "Just the very man I wanted to see. You received my cable?"

"Yes – I shall be delighted to come to dinner. What time?"

"Seven-thirty or eight, if you don't mind. Are you going to see Mrs Choyce?"

"Yes – I was just looking in."

"Well, I would be much obliged if you would put off seeing her till I have had a talk with you. It is desirable that I should see you before you see her. I look upon it as providential to have met you here, in this way – but the fact is I am, as you know, in the Red Cross, investigating the missing. Well, we have found Mr Choyce – Captain Choyce, I should say – in a Belgian convent, looked after by Belgian nuns, ever since he came down in the German line. He is all right, normal – more or less all right. He had lost his memory, and he seemed to have regained it completely; but just as we were starting for London he seemed, he seemed, well – I must tell you the whole story, but it is important that you should see me and hear all the details from me before you see her. It is now past seven. I ordered dinner at half-past seven. You may just as well drive back with me. By the time we get home dinner will be ready."

"Very well," said Greene, and they got into a taxi and drove to Kensington.

During the drive Mr Adeane told Greene the full details of the story, and when he had reached the end of the story he said:

"It is imperative for you to see Captain Choyce as soon as possible, and to deliver him from this curious obsession and delusion, and it is equally imperative, in my opinion, for you to see Mrs Choyce and to get her in the right frame of mind for receiving her husband. A great deal, I think, may depend on that. She seems to me to be in a nervous state – an almost abnormal state of mind herself."

They drove to Kensington. Mr Adeane's house was a large, low two-storied house that stood by itself in a garden. They went through the hall into Adeane's study, which was on the ground floor. It was sparely furnished, but he had a large collection of pipes, the *Encyclopædia Britannica,* and a few pieces of old English china, which he collected and which were kept in a small cupboard with glass doors. The room reeked of tobacco smoke. There was over the chimney-piece a large engraving of the Heidelberger Schloss.

Dinner was announced shortly after they arrived.

The dining-room was long and low. Francis Greene remembered it well. It was unaltered since the days of Daphne. He had never been in the house since her death. It was a dark panelled room. There was a picture over the chimney-piece of a lady in fancy dress, painted by an eighteenth-century painter, and on the other side of the room some coloured prints representing Viennese life at the end of the eighteenth century – and some exquisite glass on the sideboard.

Adeane and Greene talked little during the meal. For both of them it was a reunion which evoked ghosts. Greene could hardly believe he was alive.

When dinner was over, Adeane gave Greene a cigar. He himself smoked a long rosewood pipe. He had acquired the habit in his early youth in Germany.

"But you think he will get all right?" said Greene, resuming the earlier conversation and going back to Michael.

"Yes, without any doubt whatever; but I think it will need a man like yourself to look after him for a considerable while –

to look after *both* of them. For either of them – given the circumstances – might make a mess of things, and bring about a catastrophe. I am convinced that he only needs a little care and he will be right – quite right…"

"Yes, I see…"

"Mrs Choyce seems a sensible woman. I have never seen her before. She is good-looking, too. Oddly enough, I thought – you will think me fantastic perhaps – but I thought tonight she has…well, she reminds me – she reminded me in a curious fashion," he coughed, "of Daphne – although they are not in the least alike really. She has not Daphne's beauty, of course – nor her charm – nor her intelligence – but she is in a way, to my mind, like a ghost, a poor understudy, of Daphne." And his voice broke.

Francis said nothing, and went on smoking.

"I have got her picture here now," said Adeane. "It has been varnished. When you have finished your port I will show it you. I think it looks well. I think it looks better here than at Seyton. It was never meant for Seyton, and I could not leave it there. I could not live without it."

"No."

"It's a good picture, although of course nobody could paint her. She was unpaintable."

"Yes, unpaintable."

"Let's go upstairs."

They left the dining-room, and Mr Adeane led the way upstairs into the drawing-room on the first floor, to which Francis Greene remembered coming so often in the old days. It was an old-fashioned room. There was a faded yellow silk on the walls and faded curtains, a few pieces of Georgian furniture, and a little early Victorian pianoforte, one of the first to be made.

There were two large armchairs in the corner of the room by the round mahogany table, on which there always used to be a bowl of flowers. There was a wood fire in the fireplace – it was lit tonight – that is where they used to have tea in the evening after dinner. There was a long low table with the newspapers on it – the newspapers were there. Adeane turned on another light. "The picture," he said, "is in the little room next door."

Next to the drawing-room there was a small, high, round room which Daphne Adeane used to call her sitting-room, although she seldom sat there. It was a small room, panelled and painted a pale green, with one low Georgian sofa and a satinwood table, and some beautiful stiff chairs, an exquisitely carved marble fireplace, a bust of a child in the corner of the room, and on the wall over the chimney-piece was Henriquez's picture of Daphne Adeane. In the dim light – for the room, in spite of one electric lamp, was dim – the picture was more living and speaking than ever.

Adeane led Francis Greene into the room, and then he left him abruptly. Francis Greene heard him blowing his nose, and he felt he was crying; as for him, he was at first a little bewildered, then he looked at the picture, and the sight was a shock to him and a revelation.

The picture seemed to be alive. Daphne seemed to be there, looking at him and speaking to him, and looking at him with so gentle a reproach... "You have not forgotten me," the picture seemed to say, "not your old, old friend?"

Those eyes – that hand – that look – what in the world had there ever been to compare with that? what in the world could ever compare with that? "You are not going to leave me? you are not going to forget me? you are not going to play me false?" said the picture – and the past came back to Francis Greene with a thousand scents and sights and sounds, echoes, words, tunes, accents, phrases, jokes – and he knew that his heart was there, and that never, never, never could he feel once more what he had felt then. He felt like a man who has been asleep or drugged, and who has had a sudden awakening. "It has been a dream," he said to himself, and suddenly the story of Siegfried came into his head: how Siegfried after pledging his troth to

311

Brunhilda, had drunk of a potion and forgotten her, and then had married Gudrune; and how the effect of the potion had worn off (suddenly in the opera, slowly in the Icelandic version), and how Siegfried had remembered when it was too late, and how Brunhilda had been the instrument of his doom. He had drunk of a potion, he had forgotten; and he remembered once more, now, when it was too late – and, oddly enough, this did not make him forget Fanny or love her any the less – he loved Fanny as much as ever – only he knew that from henceforth the ghost of Daphne Adeane would for ever be between them. It would no longer be – it could no longer be – as it had been before.

"No, Daphne," he said, "I shall not forget you any more. I am sorry – sorry I forgot you for a while. I am sorry I played you false."

He went back into the drawing-room. Adeane was sitting in one of the armchairs reading *The Spectator* and smoking his long pipe.

"It's a good picture," he said, "and it looks better now that it has been varnished, doesn't it?" His voice was still husky. "During the war I was so anxious lest it might be damaged or destroyed in the air raids that I kept it in the cellar; and then I was afraid that it might have been damaged by the damp. That is why I have had it varnished. But to go back to what we were talking about. I think, Greene, it is essential that you should see Mrs Choyce tomorrow – tomorrow morning early. I expect to hear from Wake, and I will let you know what he says."

"Yes," said Francis Greene, "please do."

Then they talked of other things, and Adeane told Francis Greene some of his youthful adventures at Heidelberg. Francis Greene knew the tales, but he was not sorry to hear them once more.

CHAPTER XXVI

The moment Mr Adeane left her house, Fanny felt that she must at once and without a moment's delay grapple with the greatest crisis she had ever been faced with in her life. She knew that the issue was not only a foregone conclusion, but that it had been decided. She sat down at the writing-table and she wrote two telegrams, one to Michael and one to Wake.

The purport of both of them was, "Expect you arrive at five o'clock at Victoria tomorrow. Will be at station." In the telegram to Michael she had begged him to come without delay. She had telegraphed to the headmaster of Peter's school, asking that he might be sent up for the night if possible, and also to her mother, who was in Devonshire with Hester. Then she rang the bell and had the telegrams sent off.

"I ought," she thought, "to get the answer tomorrow morning." She burnt the letter she had written to Michael.

She sat down and thought over the situation. The tremendous, the unexpected, the inevitable had happened. She could hardly realise it yet. She was still stunned by the blow. The inevitable – the end had come – what she had feared – what they had both feared – had happened. Fate or Providence had stepped in as surely and suddenly, as irrevocably, as in a Greek tragedy, and had separated her and Francis once and for all, and for ever. She knew now not only that she could not desert Michael – that it was out of the question…but that she could not go on seeing Francis. All she wanted was for Francis to understand this. She felt he would not understand, or rather he would understand, and in spite of this he would want her not to give him up – men were so illogical. She felt distracted.

She felt sure that Francis would understand and approve of her telegrams. She knew he would tell her it was her duty to behave like that, but she felt at the same time that, unless Francis suddenly ceased to love her that evening, he would want things to go on as usual, and think it natural. He would find reasons – no casuistry is so great, she thought, as that of a man in love – if he is still in love with me, and I think he is…he was this evening, at any rate. How shall I explain it to him? What shall I say to him? because men are so unreasonable that if I tell him the truth he will at once suspect that something *else* is true…he will think that I no longer love him – he is capable of suspecting me of loving someone else…men are like that…they are blindly selfish when they love…it is no good telling them the truth. It was, she thought, perplexing; it would have been, had not the whole situation been so agonising. For the third time in her life Fanny felt that she had been through an earthquake, and that the whole fabric of life and of her soul had come down with a crash…the first time it had been the fabric of hope and youthful illusion that had fallen in ruins about her, the second time it was the fabric of life as she had rebuilt it which was shattered when she received the news that Michael was missing, and this time it was the fabric of joy, of passion, of happiness…of the mature joy of her whole being… "Well, those things are, I suppose, short-lived," she thought, "and it is silly to wish it otherwise." At the same time, as she sat down in the armchair near the fire, she felt a desolation, an estrangement, a blank, and an agony that was beyond all words…she was too sad for tears. Her grief was hopeless. She saw nothing ahead of her – no glimmer in the future…infinite pain, infinite sadness, infinite desire, infinite despair. She would have to play a part, and how could she? Would not this be the worst of all, to be found out by Michael? and after all he was not a fool, he was full of intuition. Merciful God, she thought, what is to happen? It is hopeless, hopeless, hopeless, from whatever angle one looks at it. She could not even cry. She felt as if her soul had been seared with a hot iron that had shrivelled it up, and as if there were nothing left but a burnt cinder. She rang for some tea, which she hardly touched when it came, and then she thought she would go to bed. Before going upstairs, she went into the room which had been Michael's sitting-room downstairs, the room where they had said goodbye to each other at the outbreak of the war. There was in it a large bookcase, full of miscellaneous books, with glass doors.

Fanny looked at the books, and they made her wonder. She had hardly ever looked at them carefully before. How she had misunderstood Michael! Here were Browning's poems, a Globe Shakespeare, Bernard Shaw's plays, Alexandre Dumas, Kipling, Maupassant's stories – nearly all of them – *Vanity Fair*, *Great Expectations*, *The Shropshire Lad*, Heine, Keats, Chesterton's poems, Wells' novels, *War and Peace*, the *Irish R. M.*, *Happy Thoughts*, *Les Misérables*, Harriet Wilson's *Memoirs*, *The Diary of a Nobody*, *The Life of Stonewall Jackson*, the works of Pitcher, Herrick's poems, several of Henry James' novels, Arnold Bennett's *Buried Alive*, *Border Ballads*, Swinburne's *Atalanta*. All that was Michael's mind. She had never entered into all that, never approached it. She noticed a black book with an elastic band round it. It was lettered *Roman Missal*. She took it from the shelf. It was the *Roman Missal* with an English translation. On the fly-leaf was written:

'HYACINTH BURNHAM. 1886.'

She took it upstairs with her, and she went to bed. She also took a novel, a new novel that had recently come out by a writer of promise, but she found she could not read it. She

315

suspected that it was clever and well written, but the words did not hold her attention; she was suddenly aware, after reading for ten minutes, that she had reached page twenty and had no idea what she had been reading.

She put down the novel. She was not in the least sleepy. She took up the *Missal,* and began reading in it here and there.

She read the Order and the Canon of the Mass.

She read the *Hebdomada Major*…the rites and ritual of Holy Week – Palm Sunday, Maundy Thursday, Good Friday, The Mass of the Pre-sanctified, Holy Saturday, Easter Sunday…and then, as she laid down the book – and it was past midnight – she said to herself, "But surely all this is the incarnation of the Greek idea…this *is* sacrifice…this *is* the very thing…what I have been groping for all my life…here it is. But then, if that is so, then I…then I…must I one day be a… Catholic?"…and her premises seemed to have led her to a conclusion so tremendous, so vast, so glorious, and so overwhelming that she could scarcely bear to face it – as if all of a sudden she had been brought face to face with the sun rising out of a starless night over a snowy mountain and flooding the world with glory…

She shut her eyes, and she lay motionless for a long time, and she felt the sense of balm of which Father Rendall had spoken…then she fell asleep.

The next morning when she woke up her first sensation was that something terrible had happened, and then as she became more wide awake she said to herself, "No, not so terrible." She got up and she felt calm.

She dressed and had breakfast, and at ten Francis Greene arrived. He was looking ill, Fanny thought. He came into the dining-room.

"I couldn't come last night, because…"

"I know," said Fanny. "I saw Mr Adeane; he told me you would dine with him."

"Oh."

"You know what happened?"

Francis Greene nodded.

"He told you everything?"

"Yes, he told me. What have you done?"

"I have sent Michael a cable."

"Yes…of course."

Fanny felt by the way he looked and spoke as he said these words that something new had happened to Francis, something beyond the news of Michael's condition, something beyond the new development in the events of their joint drama.

"You dined alone with Mr Adeane, I suppose?"

"Yes."

"And he told you everything?"

"Everything."

"They will be here this evening. I cabled to Mr Wake too, answer paid, to know if they start…"

"Yes."

Then Fanny knew what had happened. "Daphne Adeane has taken him away from me," she thought; "she has taken him back, and small blame to her…" And this conviction, which Fanny felt was infallible, made things at the same time more easy and more bitter. It made them more easy in the sense that she felt she would no longer have to fight Francis about the future. At the same time, that he should no longer care as much as he had cared yesterday, that he should care one fraction of the millionth part of an inch less, was the crowning bitterness of her whole life: the last drop of the chalice. "And yet," thought Fanny, "it is right that it should be so; I have deserved it." And then she suddenly felt sick with grief – as if she could enjoy being stoned to death. She felt like the star-crossed king who said:

"On that very day
When in the tempest of my soul I craved
Death, even Death by stoning, none appeared,

To further that wild longing…"

Nobody was there to further her wild longing for death; but just as Francis was a little different from what he had been yesterday, so did Fanny know that she was different, a little different, and perhaps – who knows? – the difference might turn out to be vast…a difference in kind… At the back of all the misery and all the despair there was a tiny glimmer of light…a voice that said, "All this does not matter…all is ordered for the best."

But on the surface her sadness was infinite…only there was this difference, that the bitterness seemed to have gone out of it. She was like a patient who has been mortally sick, who is in the last stage of weakness, but whom the fever has left.

"When I am strong enough," she thought, "I shall perhaps recover in time…in time…if only I am given time…and Francis, he too is sick," she thought, "but he will recover more quickly."

They sat till half-past ten, saying desultory things to each other. At half-past ten Francis said, as he had said every day, only today he had stayed longer than usual, "I must go…" He had put off the moment for saying that sentence as long as he could.

"Yes," said Fanny.

They got up.

"This is the end, Francis," said Fanny. "It's all over, but well, you know…" She was pale, and seemed like the image of grief.

"The end," said Francis. "Must it really be the end?"

Fanny said nothing, but she nodded. Her nod was like a decree of Fate.

"Well, I shall not forget. I suppose we have brought it all on ourselves, but I wouldn't have it different…not any of it."

"Don't, don't," said Fanny. "I can't endure it."

He took her in his arms, and they whispered goodbye to each other in one last kiss, and then Fanny heard the front-door bell ring.

"That's the front-door bell," she said. "I'm sure it's a telegram."

It was the front-door bell. Fanny opened the door, and Francis met the parlour-maid in the hall.

It was a telegraph boy. He brought two telegrams. Francis left. Fanny opened the telegrams.

One was from Michael saying: "We arrive five-thirty. Quite well; all love; hope see Peter and Hester."

The other was from Basil Wake: "We arrive this evening; all well. – BASIL WAKE."

Later, another telegram came from the headmaster of Peter's school, saying the boy might have leave. Peter would arrive in London at 3.35; he would be expected back on the following day.

Fanny was busy. First of all she went to the station to meet her mother, who had settled to come up directly she had heard from Fanny, and who had brought Hester.

Lady Weston was delighted at the turn events had taken. She had known all about Fanny's project, but she was wise enough to say nothing... Fanny gave her to understand that it was over, and Lady Weston accepted it as an example of war nerves, strain, and hysteria that was so prevalent, and as an incident without significance. One ought to thank Providence, she thought, that it had been no worse.

She was most sympathetic, and ready to help in every way she could. Fanny, who had slightly dreaded seeing her, was delighted to be with her. She needed the presence of a human being, of someone who loved her; she was so sore and so raw – raw in every nerve; it was as if her soul had been laid bare, her heart flayed alive. Lady Weston arrived before luncheon. They went together to meet Peter at the station after luncheon.

He looked the picture of health and the image of his father. He was full of his school doings. He was high up in the third division, and he was thought likely to win the hurdle race in the athletic sports. He was going to play the treble in a trio at the school concert – the trio consisting of three boys at one piano.

When they had driven home, Fanny felt so dreadfully tired physically that she felt she must have half an hour's rest. Peter was happy with Fanny's maid, who loved him, and he taught her the Greek declensions.

Fanny went up to her room. Lady Weston went home, and promised to call in later after dinner.

"No," said Fanny; "come and dine with us. Basil Wake will be there too. It will make us four…do please, Mummie darling."

"Very well, if you wish it," said Lady Weston.

Fanny fell into a deep sleep, and she was called in time to go to the station. The train was due at half-past five, but it was an hour late. Fanny had an agonising wait, during which she went through everything all over again – only in shadowland, as it were – the drama was done – what she went through now was the memory, the reflection of the drama… She had settled what to do, what course to take… It was over… She no longer said to herself, "Is it honest? Is it honourable?"… She knew it was a part of her sacrifice, and she was ready to accept the sacrifice…the whole sacrifice…to carry it out to the very end.

"All I have to do now," she thought, "is to live for others, for Michael and the children, and try and make them happy. God give me strength to do it!"

At last the train arrived. There was a crowd – the usual crowd of people… At last Fanny saw Basil Wake, who looked bent and considerably older – and then Michael!… Michael, in odd ready-made clothes…a *complet* bought off the peg at Calais, and trousers that were too short for him… Yes, he looked much…not older, but…thinner – so thin…and as if he had been through a great deal… And he was lame – he limped…but his eyes were not unhappy… but meek…there was something piteous about him… He looked like a child who has been too long at school without a holiday, and starved – starved, physically and mentally, not only of food, but of love…

Fanny felt a great rush of pity when she saw him, and when he ran to her and took her in his thin arms and kissed her over and over again – she felt that she could now love him and protect him as a mother protects her son.

"Peter, old chap, how you've grown!" he said. "I should never have recognised him."

It was arranged that Basil should dine with them. They drove home, and Michael told them the extraordinary story all over again…how kind the nuns had been…yet all that period was a blur to him…how kind Basil Wake had been…and Ralph Adeane… "such a good fellow… Has he arrived? Did you see him? So hard-working. The work he has done out there for the 'Missing' is quite extraordinary… You know he is the husband of that Mrs Adeane who lived in that queer house near us – Seyton. Do you remember? And he was a great friend of Leo Dettrick's. By the way, where is old Leo?"

"He went to America, but he is by way of coming back soon."

"We must send him a cable tonight."

"Yes. We will indeed."

"Daddy, what happened to your machine when it crashed? Why didn't they find it?"

"I set fire to it; that is all I remember…and nobody knows what happened to the remains, and whether anybody found it or not. If they did find it, they wouldn't have thought it very extraordinary. There is such a lot of wreckage about everywhere."

"But you don't know where you landed?"

"No, old boy…nor how; and I must have walked some way."

"But weren't you insensible?"

"Well, I had concussion. I didn't know what I was doing. But I could walk about and talk all right, and I went, I suppose, straight to those nuns, who looked after me like angels."

When they got home, and Michael went into the familiar rooms, he said, "It is extraordinary to be back once more; it's like beginning a new life. It is a new life we are beginning,

321

Fanny, isn't it? I'm afraid I made rather a hash of it before. I am awfully sorry, Fanny – but I hope to do better this time."

"It was I made a hash, if anybody did," said Fanny.

"Well, we won't think about it any more; we won't think of the past, only of the future."

"Only of the future," said Fanny, smiling bravely. The words went through her like a sword...but she knew that, come what might, and whatever she might feel – she would go through with it. Michael would never know, and she would make him happy, even if the effort were to kill her...and she knew, thanks to the pity she felt for him, that she could make him happy now. She could never have done this before, in the old days. The pity wasn't there. It was there now in abundance... She pitied him with her whole heart.

Basil Wake and Lady Weston came to dinner. Lady Weston was perfect. She made everything easier, and Michael enjoyed telling her all his experiences before his accident, which he remembered clearly.

"It's an odd thing," he said at one moment, "to die and to come back to life again. I remember people saying in old days before the war that it would be a mistake to do that – that if people came back from the dead they would find they were not wanted, however much they had been loved during life. But that's not true about us, Fanny, is it?" he said, laughing.

"No, it's not true about us...certainly not," said Fanny, laughing; and she thought to herself, "I used to think I couldn't act and couldn't pretend. But I think, on the contrary, I am a consummate actress..."

"We must get hold of Ralph Adeane," said Michael. "You know, I believe his wife was a beautiful woman and a fine character. They say he has never got over her death. Someone once told me she was rather like you, Fanny, but far less good-looking, of course. By the way, what splendid looks you are in, Fanny! Isn't she, Maria?" – he called Lady Weston "Maria"; it was a nickname which had originated no one knew how. "I

322

don't think I have ever seen you look so well...not since we were engaged. I thought you looked rather tired at the station; but now you are in blooming looks. Now we must all drink Fanny's health." He poured out champagne for Lady Weston, Wake, and himself.

"Here's your very good health, Fanny." The wine had slightly gone to his head; he was unused to it. "I am sure you have got Daphne Adeane or anybody else beat, as far as looks are – anybody in the whole world. There's no one to touch Fanny. She's one in a thousand. Here's Fanny's good health. No heelers, Basil – Fanny!"

"Fanny!" Lady Weston echoed.

"Mrs Choyce!" Basil said shyly.

"No, not Mrs Choyce – Fanny!" Michael interrupted.

Basil flushed.

Basil and Michael drained their glasses. Lady Weston sipped Fanny's good health. Fanny, who was slightly flushed from fatigue and strain, smiled at them; and never, Michael thought, had she looked more beautiful... Basil, too, thought she looked beautiful...but sad... "It's the excitement," he thought.

Soon after this toast had been drunk the parlour-maid brought in a telegram for Fanny. It was a cable from New York, from Leo Dettrick.

Fanny read it, and said:

"It's a cable from Leo Dettrick." She tore it up absent-mindedly as she spoke. "He is sailing today. He has seen the news."

She threw the torn-up telegram into the fire.

MAURICE BARING

C

Baring's homage to a decadent and carefree Edwardian age depicts a society as yet untainted by the traumas and complexities of twentieth-century living. With wit and subtlety a happy picture is drawn of family life, house parties in the country and a leisured existence clouded only by the rumblings of the Boer War. Against this spectacle Caryl Bramsley (the *C* of the title) is presented – a young man of terrific promise but scant achievement, whose tragic-comic tale offsets the privileged milieu.

CAT'S CRADLE

This sophisticated and intricate novel, based on true events, takes place in the late nineteenth century and begins with Henry Clifford, a man of taste and worldly philosophy, whose simple determination to do as he likes and live as he wishes is threatened when his daughter falls in love with an unsuitable man. With subtle twists and turns in a fascinating portrait of society, Maurice Baring conveys the moral that love is too strong to be overcome by mere mortals.

Maurice Baring

The Coat Without Seam

The story of a miraculous relic, believed to be a piece of the seamless coat won by a soldier on Mount Golgotha after Jesus of Nazareth's crucifixion, captivates young Christopher Trevenen after his sister dies tragically and motivates the very core of his existence from then on, culminating in a profound and tragic realization.

In My End Is My Beginning

This historical novel tells the tragic story of Mary Queen of Scots, from her childhood until the beginning of her end, whose unwise marital and political actions provoked rebellion among Scottish nobles and forced her to flee to England, where she was beheaded as a Roman Catholic threat to the throne. The clash of opinion over whether Mary was a martyr or a murderess is perfectly represented by four eye-witnesses (The Four Maries – her ladies-in-waiting) who narrate this captivating story with distinctive conclusions.

MAURICE BARING

TINKER'S LEAVE

Reserved and unworldly, young Miles Consterdine and his epiphanic trip to Paris is Maurice Baring's first bead on this thread of a story based on impressions received by the author in Russia and Manchuria during wartime. From here Baring allows us to peek through windows opening onto tragic and comic episodes in the lives of noteworthy people in remarkable circumstances.

THE PUPPET SHOW OF MEMORY

It was into the famous and powerful Baring family of merchant bankers that Maurice Baring was born in 1874, the seventh of eight children. A man of immense subtlety and style, Baring absorbed every drop of culture that his fortunate background showered upon him; in combination with his many natural talents and prolific writing this assured him a place in literary history.

In this classic autobiography, spanning a remarkable period of history, Maurice Baring shares the details of an inspirational childhood in nineteenth-century England and a varied adulthood all over the world, collecting new friends and remarkable experiences. It has been said that Baring's greatest talent was for discovering the best in people, that he had a genius for friendship, and in this superb book his erudition and perception are abundantly clear.

'A classic autobiography' *Dictionary of National Biography*

OTHER TITLES BY MAURICE BARING AVAILABLE DIRECT
FROM HOUSE OF STRATUS

Quantity	£	$(US)	$(CAN)	€
☐ C	8.99	16.50	24.95	16.50
☐ CAT'S CRADLE	8.99	16.50	24.95	16.50
☐ THE COAT WITHOUT SEAM	8.99	16.50	24.95	16.50
☐ IN MY END IS MY BEGINNING	8.99	16.50	24.95	16.50
☐ THE PUPPET SHOW OF MEMORY	8.99	16.50	24.95	16.50
☐ TINKER'S LEAVE	8.99	16.50	24.95	16.50

ALL HOUSE OF STRATUS BOOKS ARE AVAILABLE FROM GOOD BOOKSHOPS
OR DIRECT FROM THE PUBLISHER:

Internet: **www.houseofstratus.com** including author interviews, reviews, features.

Email: **sales@houseofstratus.com** please quote author, title, and credit card details.

Hotline: UK ONLY: **0800 169 1780**, please quote author, title and credit card details.
INTERNATIONAL: **+44 (0) 20 7494 6400**, please quote author, title and credit card details.

Send to: **House of Stratus Sales Department**
24c Old Burlington Street
London
W1X 1RL
UK

Please allow for postage costs charged per order plus an amount per book as set out in the tables below:

	£(Sterling)	$(US)	$(CAN)	€(Euros)
Cost per order				
UK	2.00	3.00	4.50	3.30
Europe	3.00	4.50	6.75	5.00
North America	3.00	4.50	6.75	5.00
Rest of World	3.00	4.50	6.75	5.00
Additional cost per book				
UK	0.50	0.75	1.15	0.85
Europe	1.00	1.50	2.30	1.70
North America	2.00	3.00	4.60	3.40
Rest of World	2.50	3.75	5.75	4.25

PLEASE SEND CHEQUE, POSTAL ORDER (STERLING ONLY), EUROCHEQUE, OR INTERNATIONAL MONEY ORDER (PLEASE CIRCLE METHOD OF PAYMENT YOU WISH TO USE)
MAKE PAYABLE TO: STRATUS HOLDINGS plc

Cost of book(s): —————————— Example: 3 x books at £6.99 each: £20.97

Cost of order: —————————— Example: £2.00 (Delivery to UK address)

Additional cost per book: ————— Example: 3 x £0.50: £1.50

Order total including postage: ——— Example: £24.47

Please tick currency you wish to use and add total amount of order:

☐ £ (Sterling)   ☐ $ (US)   ☐ $ (CAN)   ☐ € (EUROS)

VISA, MASTERCARD, SWITCH, AMEX, SOLO, JCB:

☐☐☐☐☐☐☐☐☐☐☐☐☐☐☐☐☐☐☐

Issue number (Switch only):

☐☐☐

Start Date: **Expiry Date:**

☐☐/☐☐   ☐☐/☐☐

Signature: _____

NAME: _____

ADDRESS: _____

_____

POSTCODE: _____

Please allow 28 days for delivery.

Prices subject to change without notice.
Please tick box if you do not wish to receive any additional information. ☐

House of Stratus publishes many other titles in this genre; please check our website (**www.houseofstratus.com**) for more details.